TIME

The death of an unfaithful wife [...] Blarney with twin daughters to raise and a farm to run on his own. Desperate and angry, he challenges Destiny to bring him a new helpmate—and is rewarded with a breath-taking gift from across the seas of time.

TIMESWEPT BRIDE

When Priscilla Pemberton found a century-old message in a bottle on Galveston beach, she never dreamed a magical wave would carry her back to the author of the heartfelt mis-sive. Now she is caught up in an inescapable past—and determined *not* to end up the un-pampered wife of a struggling dairy farmer. But Jake's passion will not be denied. For the proud, handsome Irishman knows the resist-ing lady is the answer to his prayers—and that neither time nor tide can diminish a remark-able love that Fate itself has decreed.

"HURRAH FOR THE TALENTED MS. RILEY!"
Romantic Times

If You've Enjoyed This Book,
Be Sure to Read These Other
AVON ROMANTIC TREASURES

EUGENIA RILEY

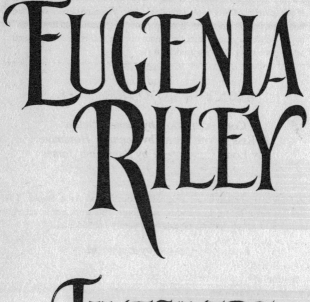

TIMESWEPT BRIDE

An Avon Romantic Treasure

AVON BOOKS ◆ NEW YORK

TIMESWEPT BRIDE is an original publication of Avon Books. This work has never before appeared in book form. This work is a novel. Any similarity to actual persons or events is purely coincidental.

AVON BOOKS
A division of
The Hearst Corporation
1350 Avenue of the Americas
New York, New York 10019

Copyright © 1995 by Eugenia Riley Essenmacher
Published by arrangement with the author
Library of Congress Catalog Card Number: 94-96863
ISBN: 0-380-77157-8

First Avon Books Printing: August 1995

AVON TRADEMARK REG. U.S. PAT. OFF. AND IN OTHER COUNTRIES, MARCA REGISTRADA, HECHO EN U.S.A.

Printed in the U.S.A.

RA 10 9 8 7 6 5 4 3 2 1

To my darling niece, Jennifer,
and her wonderful husband, Jeff,
in honor of their marriage
December 3, 1994

Congratulations, Jen and Jeff!

Prologue

Galveston, Texas
The present

*I*n *my next life, I'm going to be beautiful*, Priscilla Pemberton thought.

On the beach on the west end of Galveston Island, Priscilla sat alone, dressed in a jade silk caftan and matching satin slippers. She was guzzling Dom Perignon straight from the bottle, and feeling sorry for herself. Behind her rose her mother's beach house, its lights winking, its walls vacant. Priscilla had the cottage to herself for the night, since her mother was staying with friends on the mainland.

For early October, it was a cool, blustery evening. The wind was howling as if to warn of Judgment Day, high waves pounded the beach, and laughing gulls swooped about in panic, cawing raucously. Salty spray battered Priscilla's face and body, and the brisk breeze tugged at the delicate silk of her caftan. Yet she felt heedless.

She may as well fling herself to the tide, she thought dismally. For she'd been dumped—or nearly so. Dumped mere weeks before her scheduled wedding, by the only man she had ever wanted to marry. Dumped by the biggest catch on Galveston Island— J. Ackerly Frost V. She and Ackerly were to have had a dazzling fall wedding at Trinity Church, then go island-hopping through the Caribbean.

Until this. With trembling fingers, Priscilla pulled

Ackerly's stylish monogrammed note from her pocket and reread it for the hundredth time by the wan light of the full moon:

> *Dear Priscilla,*
>
> *With regret, I must inform you that I'm having second thoughts about our relationship, and I must take time to think things through. It may be best that we postpone our wedding. I'll be in touch when I return from my London business trip. Please take care with Mother's ring, since I may have to request its return.*
>
> *Regards,*
> *Ackerly*

Priscilla savagely crumpled the note in her hand, but couldn't quite gather the nerve to throw it into the Gulf. Oh, the cad! Just like that, he'd set aside the two years between them, and had jeopardized all their future plans. He hadn't even given her a reason!

But Priscilla had inadvertently guessed the reason today when she had called the bank to demand an explanation from Ackerly. The receptionist had awkwardly informed her that "Mr. Frost has already left the country on business," and when the flabbergasted Priscilla had demanded to speak with Ackerly's secretary, the embarrassed woman had reluctantly admitted that the secretary was missing, as well: "Ms. Sweet has accompanied Mr. Frost to London."

That was why Priscilla was now sitting forlornly on the beach, drowning her sorrows. It hadn't taken a Rhodes scholar to figure out why Ackerly had taken his "Sweet" confection with him to London, nor why he had hired the busty blonde in the first place three months ago, over Priscilla's staunch objections! The woman's credentials had been unimpressive, her skills marginal at best.

Now all that remained was to wait for the proverbial other shoe to drop, Priscilla thought bitterly. And how dare Ackerly ask her to take good care of his mother's ring—even if it was a cherished family heirloom—when he no doubt intended to snatch it off her finger the minute he returned, and present it to his bimbo!

Priscilla felt deeply shocked and hurt by Ackerly's sudden and seemingly rash actions. It was not like the meticulous Ackerly to so abruptly postpone their wedding, or to go off impetuously on a fling. Not *the* J. Ackerly Frost V, president of the Frost National Bank of Galveston, to whom pedigree and prestige were everything. Ackerly was sophisticated, intelligent, calculating, and so cold in conducting his business affairs that most of the island community privately referred to him as "Jack Frost."

Yet his "frostiness" hadn't bothered Priscilla Pemberton in the least—to the contrary, she had found his aloofness an asset. Ackerly and Priscilla had met two years ago on the mainland, at a lecture on the mating habits of blue-footed boobies. They had dated, and had found they shared the same passions—art, the symphony, historical preservation, and bird watching. Theirs had been a match made in heaven.

Priscilla had liked the idea of being in a marriage in which her future station was secure while her emotions could remain inviolable. She had been raised by an overly critical, verbally abusive father who had disgraced and deserted his wife and child, leaving his family destitute; in Ackerly, Priscilla had thought she'd found both the security and the social status she had lacked all her life. Now, Ackerly's forsaking her seemed all the more cruel and difficult to bear when juxtaposed against memories of those earlier wounds and betrayals by her father.

"It's not fair!" she shouted, and got up and began pacing the beach.

It wasn't fair. Becoming J. Ackerly's fiancée had ensured Priscilla both a prosperous future and a place in the Galveston social register. Until today, Priscilla's sole goal in life had been to become Galveston's newest social butterfly. She had spent much of recent months planning her Caribbean honeymoon, writing her married name—Priscilla Pemberton Frost—and designing her monogram. Now this! How would she ever live with the disgrace, or hold up her head in the Galveston community?

The louse! The selfish, arrogant womanizer! She took another gulp of champagne and thought, *I have no class. I drink Dom Perignon without a glass.*

She giggled. Ah, she was waxing poetic tonight, getting all sloppy and sentimental. And tipsy, no doubt. Priscilla did not normally drink, a habit of her father's that she avoided. Now the champagne was rapidly going to her head. What would her freshman composition students at the university think if they could see their staid, sober "Miss Pemberton" now?

"Ackerly, how could you do this to me!" she cried to the wind.

There, she'd done it again! Hopelessly waxing poetic!

In her heart, she knew why he'd done this to her. Ackerly was having second thoughts because she wasn't beautiful. Oh, Priscilla was attractive in her way—a freckle-faced, girl-next-door type, her best feature being her shoulder-length, curly, red-gold hair. A twenty-six-year-old semivirgin who looked much younger. *A farm girl who wanted to be queen.*

She took another gulp. Perhaps she should call Ackerly in London and give him a piece of her mind. He always stayed at the Connaught, didn't he?

Heavens, she *was* getting drunk. She would make a fool of herself.

More likely, she would beg him to take her back!

But wasn't it possible that Ackerly's trip was pure business, after all? she asked herself with forlorn hope. Wasn't it conceivable he would come to regret cruelly leaving her hanging this way? Should she give him another chance?

Like hell she would!

In any event, she definitely needed to tell him off, she decided tipsily. But first, she would throw his cruel note—and his diamond ring—into the tide!

On her now wobbly legs, Priscilla went weaving toward the water, battling the fierce wind. She was about to pull off the ring and cast it into the surf when she was distracted by the sight of an ancient-looking bottle washing ashore, abandoned on the beach by the retreating waves. She blinked, at first sure her eyes were deceiving her. But no, the bottle was definitely there. Curious, she staggered over and picked it up, heedless of the surf crashing nearby and the spray battering her. The bottle indeed looked very old, with a long neck. The glass was murky and yellowed, as if the small vessel had floated about in the Gulf for aeons.

And there was some sort of message inside!

Greatly intrigued, Priscilla stepped back slightly, set down her champagne, pulled the cork from the bottle, and shook it, until finally the piece of paper became lodged in its neck. She retrieved the scrap with a fingertip ...

She unfolded the slip and stared at the faded note written in strong, decidedly male script on yellowed parchment:

> *Accursed tide*
> *Bring me a bride*

Priscilla gazed, mystified, at the odd message. So her mysterious correspondent was waxing poetic, as well! But what a perfectly horrid message, written in dreadful iambic dimeter. The accent was off, as well, unless one put it on *ed*.

She read it aloud. "Accurs*ed* tide, bring me a bride."

What did the message mean? Why was the tide being both blasphemed and beseeched to furnish a bride? It made no sense at all, and was insulting, to boot. Here she had already received a "Dear Jane" letter on the worst day of her life, and when she did receive another missive, it was of the dumbest variety.

"Accursed tide, bring me a bride," she repeated for the third time.

Still trying to grasp the logic of it, she picked up her champagne and took another gulp—

A split second later, a strange roaring roused Priscilla from her swigging. She lowered the champagne bottle and jerked her head toward the Gulf, only to gape in horror as she watched the biggest wave she had ever seen in her life come surging toward the shoreline. *Merciful heavens, where had it come from?* The swell couldn't be more than fifty yards away from her, a gigantic wall of water rising like a vengeful demon and heading straight toward her!

"Oh, my God!" she cried. A feeling of sick premonition staggered her already wobbly knees. Somehow, she just knew this particular wave had "Priscilla Pemberton" written all over it. Had her morbid musings about throwing herself into the tide caused *this?*

For an instant, sheer panic almost rooted Priscilla to the spot. At last, with adrenaline pumping fiercely, she turned and ran for her life, trying to outdistance the pending catastrophe, knowing all the while it was useless. An explosion of water lanced her ears. The tidal wave came crashing, howling over her, then everything went black . . .

Chapter 1

Galveston, Texas
The past

It was night. Priscilla was tugged to consciousness by the sound of a man's voice, deep, distant, and resonant, singing "Poor Wandering One." At first she was both lulled and mesmerized by the poignant Gilbert and Sullivan tune, sung in a rich tenor:

> *"Poor wandering one*
> *Though thou hast surely strayed,*
> *Take heart of grace,*
> *Thy steps retrace,*
> *Be not afraid.*
> *Poor wandering one,*
> *If such poor love as mine*
> *Can help thee find*
> *True peace of mind,*
> *Why, take it, it is thine."*

Priscilla shook her wet head and shivered. She lay on the beach with cold waves sluicing over her. She was sopping wet, chilled, and miserable. Staggering to her feet, she realized she had lost her slippers, for she could feel cool water and sand sliding between her toes. She felt disoriented, slightly dizzy, and very much like a "poor wandering one." Glancing about her in bewilderment, she could at first see only ocean and night. She flinched as she spotted the distant

7

crescent moon ... Hadn't it been a harvest moon before? She could still hear the song drifting toward her, the strength of the male voice somehow prevailing over the wailing wind and loud waves.

And then she heard something else ... The sound of babies crying! How odd!

She looked down at herself, feeling amazed that she had managed to survive the tidal wave that had just crashed over her. Her drenched caftan clung to her, and she still held the Dom Perignon in one hand, the note from the bottle, now damp and crumpled, in the other. Feeling a distinct need for fortification, she took a gulp of champagne, only to spit it out as she tasted seawater. Damn, she thought, tossing the bottle aside in disgust, she'd just ruined a hundred dollars worth of champagne—or what remained of it.

At least she hadn't drowned. But where in God's name was she? Again she gazed at her strange surroundings. She must have washed up somewhere far away from her mother's beach house, for nothing in the vicinity looked familiar. The rows of cottages that had risen behind her were absent now; she stood on a deserted expanse of shoreline, with only a small house in the distance, its windows winking with wan light—

Yes, that was where the singing and the crying were coming from!

She heard a horse neigh and glanced to the left of the bungalow. Good heavens! Was that a corral? And beyond it, could she spot the murky outlines of a chicken coop, a barn, and a long shed that could be a stable or dairy? Mercy, she seemed to be on a small farm, but that made no sense at all! Priscilla knew practically every inch of Galveston Island, and she had never seen this particular area before.

Oh, well, at least there were people around. Priscilla's home was on the mainland, but she had a friend in Galveston, Janet Eckland, who she was sure would be happy to come fetch her and help her find her way back to her mother's beach house.

Starting toward the odd cottage, she watched the moonlight glint off the diamond ring on her left hand. Hell, the tide hadn't even washed away Ackerly's accursed ring! Perhaps it was for the best. Perhaps Ackerly was simply experiencing a case of prenuptial jitters, resulting in a last-minute fling. Maybe he'd soon come home, contrite, his tail tucked between his legs, begging for her forgiveness, eager to reconfirm their wedding plans—

Maybe she was having delusions!

Moving closer to the house, she gasped. Good Lord, the structure appeared to be as old as the famous Williams cottage back in Galveston proper! The home was clearly "Texas primitive," a raised white frame cottage, with steep front steps, shuttered windows, a sprawling wraparound veranda with porch swing, and a high-pitched tin roof. The cottage and its environs appeared so ancient, in fact, that Priscilla felt as if she had stepped into a "living farm" exhibit such as she had once seen in the Texas Hill Country, when she and a group of professors had gone to central Texas on a university-sponsored trip. But there was no living farm on Galveston Island—at least, none Priscilla knew about!

Stifling a shiver, she climbed the creaky steps to the cottage, aware that the wailing and singing had stopped. Crossing the darkened porch, she rapped on the door.

A moment later, a tall, dark-haired man, wearing a flowing white shirt and black trousers, flung open the panel. He stared at her in mystification. Priscilla gazed back at him in equal awe, for he was clearly the most handsome man she had ever laid eyes on. Appearing to be in his late twenties and looming at least six feet tall, he possessed a muscular, broad-shouldered frame and a striking face graced by high cheekbones, strong jaw, beautifully sculpted male nose, sensually full lips, and piercingly bright, deep-set blue eyes, shaded by long black eyelashes and topped by nicely curved brows. A shock of thick

dark brown hair outlined his head and curled about
his collar, while a nest of matching ringlets peeked
out from the vee of his shirt.

Priscilla felt totally taken aback by the appearance
of this stranger who seemed to ooze raw masculinity.
In his old-fashioned attire, he looked as if he had just
stepped out of a Gilbert and Sullivan operetta. He
had to have been the one who was singing, she realized dazedly. A voice with such heavenly depth
could only come from this godlike body.

Priscilla's supposition was evidently correct. When
the man spoke, his voice was incredibly deep and
sexy, with a heavy Irish brogue . . .

"My heavens, lassie!" he exclaimed, looking her
over. "What are you doing out and about on a night
the likes of this, you so scandalously dressed, and
sopping wet? Why, you'll catch your death of a chill."

Bemused by the man's eccentric manner of speech,
Priscilla glanced past him at a large, old-timey room.
The expanse was furnished with several antique
chairs and a rocker near the hearth, a country-style
dining table with chairs in one corner, and a modest
bed with pine frame and quilted coverlet in another.
Dimity curtains, a braided rug, and a blazing fire in
the flagstone grate completed a feeling of homeyness.
The room was lit by what appeared to be antique
hurricane lamps, and a crude ladder staircase near
one wall led to what Priscilla presumed was a sleeping loft. Even standing in the doorway, she could
smell the quaint scents of burning cedar, pomander
balls, and must.

At the far side of the room, she spotted two
cradles—and standing in each was a pink-cheeked
baby! The tots, who appeared little over a year old,
were obviously twins with their matching cherub
faces, button mouths, and curly black hair. Both wore
identical lacy white nightgowns, and were staring at
Priscilla in fascination. Near the cradles was an old-
fashioned daybed stacked with diapers and baby
clothes.

Priscilla could not have been more mystified. "Where am I?" she managed to ask the man.

"Why, on Galveston Island, lass," he answered, staring at her as if she had lost her mind.

"Thank goodness," she replied.

He gently touched her wrist, his fingers hot and firm on her clammy, shivering flesh. "Now, get inside, lassie, before you expire right here on me stoop."

Taken aback by his aggressiveness, Priscilla cringed from him and hurled him a frosty look. "Are you kidding? Why, I'm not about to enter the home of a stranger—not in this day and age!"

He chuckled. "I commend your caution, lass, but do you really have a choice under the circumstances?"

Priscilla glanced behind her at the beach, at the darkness that seemed to stretch in all directions for as far as she could see. The man had a point, she had to concede. She had no idea where she was, or how to get back to her mother's beach cottage.

"Well, maybe just for a minute," she muttered.

Before Priscilla could entertain second thoughts, her host again caught her wrist and firmly pulled her inside the warm room toward the fire. One of the dark-haired babies giggled and cooed, and Priscilla had half a mind to go pick up the adorable moppet. Had the man been singing to the babies to soothe them? she wondered. If so, he surely couldn't be too dangerous.

But where was the children's mother?

"My heavens, lass, you look a scandal," he said.

Priscilla turned and caught the man staring at her with an odd intensity. She glanced down, saw the way her drenched, near-transparent caftan clung to her chilled flesh, and blushed vividly. With its tight bodice, spaghetti straps, and the slit up one leg, the wet garment left nothing to the imagination!

"Oh, my," she gasped, embarrassed.

"Here, lassie." The man grabbed an afghan from

the rocking chair and hastily draped it about her shoulders.

"Thank you," Priscilla said stiffly. "I seem to be lost."

"Aye."

"May I use your phone?"

"Phone?" He appeared flabbergasted. "What is this contraption you speak of?"

"Your *telephone*," Priscilla clarified.

"Telephone?" The Irishman threw back his head and laughed. "You think I have a telephone? Who do you think I am, lass, Colonel A. H. Belo himself, publisher of the *News*?"

Priscilla was unprepared for this odd response. "I don't really care who you are, sir," she replied irritably. "I am simply lost and in need of a telephone so I may get out of here and go back to the mainland!"

"Back to the mainland?" he cried, aghast. "Are you planning to swim, lass? There'll be no more trains running to Virginia Point this late at night."

By now, Priscilla was sure she was conversing with a lunatic. "Look, just tell me where the nearest phone is, and I'll call my friend Janet, or a cab—"

"A cab? Lass, there are no hansoms running to this end of the island—"

"Hansoms?" Priscilla repeated, dumbfounded.

"And the mules have all been tucked away at the barn, I'll wager—"

"Mules?" she exclaimed. "Why mules?"

"For the trolley, lass."

"A mule-drawn trolley?" Priscilla inquired shrilly. "Are you insane?"

He flashed her a stern look. " 'Tis you, lass, who is sounding demented—ranting about telephones and trips to the mainland. What has happened to you this night, anyway?"

Priscilla groaned, brushing a wisp of soggy hair from her brow. "I'm not sure."

"You must have some idea how you ended up on my stoop."

Priscilla figured she may as well try to explain. "Well, actually, a little while ago, I was sitting outside my mother's beach cottage, when I watched this ancient-looking bottle wash ashore, with a note inside. I read the note, and the next thing I knew, this wave came crashing over me ...."

"Aha!" the man cried, clapping his hands.

Priscilla glanced at her host, who looked as if he had just gotten religion. "What do you mean,'Aha'?"

"Why, that explains everything, lass!"

"I wish it explained everything to me."

"You're the one, then," he announced proudly.

"What do you mean, I'm the one?"

He was grinning from ear to ear, displaying dazzling white teeth. "You see, I'm the bloke who put the note in the bottle—"

"*You* sent the note?"

"Aye." He spoke with great animation. "And tossed it into the tide, I did. Now, praise Saint Brigit, here you are!"

Priscilla was developing a splitting headache. "What do you mean, here I am?"

He touched her arm in reassurance. "I can see you're baffled, lassie, so I'll explain."

"Please do."

A scowl gripped his handsome visage. "You see, a year ago, me wife up and left me for a traveling tonic salesman. Deserted me back when me darling twins were but wee babes, not even weaned."

Glancing at the adorable babies, Priscilla shook her head. "I'm really sorry. What a rotten thing for your wife to do."

"Aye. But that's not the worst of it, lass. The two fools tried to navigate over to the mainland in a skiff, and were drowned that very night off San Luis Pass."

"No!" Priscilla cried.

"Aye. 'Twas a year ago today."

"You mean you got dumped on this very night a year ago?" she asked, stunned.

His frown deepened. "Dumped, lassie?"

"Deserted."

"Aye. I blamed the tide for taking me bride, and for depriving me twins, wee Sallie and wee Nellie—" he paused to jerk his head toward the cradles—"of a mother."

Priscilla again gazed at the babies, one of whom was sucking her thumb while the other bounced and giggled. Her heart twisted with compassion at the thought of these precious mites being motherless.

"Go on," she encouraged her strange host.

"So I decided the accursed tide that took away me wife owed me a new bride. Thus I penned a poetic note and placed it in a bottle, throwing it into the ocean." He paused to rub his hands together and grin at her. "Now, a year later, the luck of the Irish is definitely with me—for here you be, lass."

Priscilla's mouth fell open. "*Me?*"

He winked at her lecherously. "Aye, lass. You're the one I sent for."

Priscilla shrank away from him. "Now, wait just a minute, mister! I do have oceans of sympathy for you, losing your wife and all, but you cannot possibly mean to presume that *I'm* the bride you summoned! Why, that is preposterous!"

He clucked compassionately. "Now, now. I know you've suffered a shock, lassie, being spit up by the ocean and all, but you'll adjust to your destiny in due course." He looked her over again, with a thoroughness that quickened her heartbeat. "Not a bad one, you are, either. Not quite beautiful, but plenty pretty enough for a dairy farmer's bride. And strong, by the looks of you. Nice wide hips for childbearing, too."

Priscilla blushed to the roots of her hair. "I beg your pardon, sir!"

Leaning toward her confidentially, he cupped a hand around his mouth. "Not to seem indelicate, lass, but we'll be needing a passel of strong lads to help with running the dairy. And the sooner the better."

Priscilla was literally trembling with shock, outrage, and indignity. "You, sir, are stark raving crazy!"

But he had already turned away and was striding toward the cradles. A moment later he returned, grinning, with a plump baby perched in the crook of each strong arm. "Here, lass, hold wee Sallie and wee Nellie for me," he instructed, transferring the hefty babies to her arms over her stammered protests. "I'll just go hitch up the buggy and then we'll be off."

Priscilla was staggering beneath his words, as well as struggling to contain the stout, squirming babies. "Off to where?"

He regarded her as if she had lost her mind. "Why, to rouse Father O'Dooley from his bed, of course. You cannot stay the night here, lassie, unless we are first wed. Otherwise, 'twill cause a scandal."

Priscilla was appalled. She stepped forward and carefully but firmly transferred the babies back into her host's arms. "Hold it, mister! I have no intention of going with you anywhere, let alone marrying you. Now, if you will *please* kindly direct me to the nearest phone—"

"I told you, lass, 'tis in town."

"Then where is your closest neighbor?" she burst out in exasperation.

He was frowning while trying to balance a baby in each arm. "There's no one else around on this end of the island." He moved closer. "Look, lass, the hour is late—if you'll just take these babies—"

She held up a hand. "You stay away from me! I am not going anywhere with you, sir, or spending one more instant with a madman such as yourself."

"A madman?" He laughed heartily and leaned over to kiss the cheek of each baby. "Do you hear that, wee Sallie and wee Nellie? Calling your pappy a madman. Why, I'm as steady in my mind as I am sure that 'tis the year of our Lord 1880."

"The year *what?*" Priscilla gasped, her hand over her heart.

"Eighteen eighty, lass."

Priscilla Pemberton fainted dead away to the floor.

Chapter 2

A feather tickled Priscilla Pemberton's nose. She awakened to find herself in a strange bed, lying on what felt like a down mattress, her face pressed against an embroidered linen pillowcase from which the offending feather protruded. Sneezing and jerking away, she caught a lungful of the scent of the bedcovers—a combination of mustiness and the distinct, not unpleasant, smell of *man*. Wrinkling her nose as her vision began to clear, she turned her head and spotted the Irishman sitting on the bed beside her.

"God bless you, lass," he said solemnly.

Her heart hammering, Priscilla struggled not to flinch, though not from revulsion. Looming so close to her, her host looked even more handsome and rakish than before, his bright blue eyes focused on her intently, the smell of bay rum wafting over her. His white shirt tugged at the sculpted perfection of broad shoulders and muscled arms, and with two top buttons left undone, she could again see sexy, coarse brown hair in the vee of his chest. She even dared a glance lower, gulping as she observed the way his dark trousers hugged his powerful thighs. His skin was tanned and glowed with good health, his hands were beautifully shaped and huge. All in all, he appeared to be a man who performed his labors outdoors and thoroughly enjoyed doing so. Never before had Priscilla laid eyes on a man with such raw physical beauty and obvious strength. Ackerly, with

17

his white skin and slim, ascetic body, definitely paled by comparison.

Beyond them across the room, Priscilla spotted the two babies, asleep in their cradles. She almost smiled at the endearing sight. She could feel the warmth of the fire, hear the snap of the flames, and smell their cedary scent. It occurred to her that it was not at all unpleasant being here.

Then she glanced back at the Irishman and remembered what he had just said, what had precipitated her collapse—that it was the year 1880! Heavens, the man was a lunatic, and the sooner she escaped his clutches, the better!

"I'm glad you're awake, lass," he murmured.

"Not I," she replied ruefully. "I was really hoping this was a nightmare and I might awaken. But no such luck."

He chuckled, reaching out to brush a tendril of damp hair from her brow, and Priscilla felt oddly comforted. His touch felt rough, yet warm and assured. Despite her fear, she could not quite summon the strength to pull away.

He gazed at her with compassion. "I'm sorry you swooned, lass. I didn't take into account how things must have seemed to you, being dragged here by the tide and all. Tell me, did you come here from far away?"

"You have no idea," Priscilla replied drolly.

He scratched his strong jaw, which, Priscilla noted, was lined by a sexy five-o'clock shadow. "You said something about being from the mainland?"

"Yes. That's where I live. But I was here on Galveston at my mother's beach cottage when I found the note."

"*My* note, lass."

"Whatever. Then a huge wave swept me away."

He shook his head in wonder. "I'll be dashed. So the magic really worked."

"Magic? It seemed a lot more like madness to me."

He nodded. "I suppose it must have been quite an

ordeal for you—being summoned by the muses, so to speak. And when you got here, so confused and bedraggled, I should not have burst out with my story that way. Considering the wording of my note ..." He flashed her a charming grin. "You must have thought it all quite bizarre."

"To say the least," came her prim response. Indeed, as far as bizarre stories were concerned, Priscilla had a feeling she could match this outrageous Irishman tit for tat.

"The fact is, lass," he went on solemnly, "when the wife up and deserted me, then drowned, I did blame the sea. 'Twas the ocean's fault, you see, for luring me Lucinda away and leaving me babes motherless. And I knew 'twas up to the sea to set matters right. That's why I tossed in the bottle, asking the tide to bring you to me." He patted her hand. "And here you are, just like a gift from the saints."

"And that's the craziest story I've ever heard," Priscilla said in disgust.

He winked at her. "If 'tis, then why are you here, lassie?"

Why, indeed? Priscilla thought, feeling slightly awe-struck at the possibilities. She sat up, fighting a lingering wave of dizziness.

"Hell, I don't know," she muttered, combing her fingers through her disheveled hair. "But I do have to figure a way to get out of here."

He touched her arm. "But, lass, you cannot go a-traipsing off in the dead of night."

Annoyed, she jerked away from his touch. "Watch me."

"But there is nowhere for you to go!" he burst out.

"Not true. My mother's beach house has to be around here somewhere."

He shook his head and made a clucking sound. "No, lass. There's no one living this far west on the island but me, the babes, our cows and chickens. Mayhap your ride through the surf made you lose your bearings, confused you."

She snorted with contempt. "And it's the year of our Lord 1880, right?"

"So 'tis," he agreed amiably.

"You, mister, are nuts!"

"Lass, I realize you've had a shock," he continued with forbearance. "But again, there's naught to be done but to hitch up the buggy, head out for town, rouse Father O'Dooley, and have him perform the wedding mass posthaste."

Pulling the afghan around her shoulders, Priscilla heaved herself to her feet. "Listen carefully. I have no intention of marrying you—whoever you are!"

The man also stood, and for a moment he stared at her in perplexity. Then he snapped his fingers. "That's right, lass, we have not yet been formally introduced." He bowed from the waist. "Jake Blarney at your service, miss."

Priscilla rolled her eyes. "Priscilla Pemberton—not at yours."

Undaunted, he eagerly looked her over. "Priscilla. You know, your name has a very nice ring—and 'Priscilla Blarney' sounds even better."

"Hah!" she scoffed. "Priscilla Blarney sounds like someone's cleaning woman."

"Mayhap you will soon become someone's cleaning lady," he teased back.

"Over your dead body."

He chuckled. "Ah, lass, you're so amusing and full of spit. You are making a funny, are you not?"

Priscilla balled her hands on her hips. "Look, Mr. Blarney, I've tried to be patient with your demented ramblings, but enough is enough. It's been a distinct pleasure meeting you—but now I must leave."

He appeared flabbergasted. "Leave? Haven't you been listening to me at all, lass? There's nowhere for you to go, so late at night, with no conveyance!"

Priscilla was rapidly tiring of this outlandish conversation. "No conveyance, my foot! What are you, some kind of throwback to the Stone Age?"

Heedless of him following her, Priscilla stormed to

the door and flung it open. The cool wind battered her as she stepped out onto the porch. She shivered and glanced about, once again bewildered. She glanced to the east and the west—and, just as Jake Blarney had predicted, she could see nothing but deserted beach and sand dunes for miles and miles around!

Priscilla began to shudder in earnest, and suddenly she knew to her soul that something was terribly wrong. What had happened to her? She realized she felt as she once had as a four-year-old child, when she had gotten lost from her mother in a department store. Priscilla had become fascinated with the store's escalator, and had foolishly decided the device was a toy. She had gotten on, not realizing she would be deposited on another floor. When she had gotten off, everything had been the same, yet nothing had been familiar. Her mother was nowhere in sight. She had been terrified, lost—

She was lost now! Where *was* her mother's cottage, and the other homes that had been there less than an hour ago? Where *was* she? She had that same sick feeling she'd had as a child—of being torn away from all that mattered to her, of having arrived on another plane, perhaps even in another dimension—

She jumped as a warm hand was laid on her shoulder, and jerked about to view the sympathetic face of her host.

"Lass, come back in before you catch your death," said Jake Blarney gently. "Whether you decide to brave this wretched night alone or not, we must get you out of those wet, scandalous clothes. I've still a gown or two of the wife's stashed away that might suffice for you."

Numbly Priscilla followed Jake Blarney back inside. He was right that she should not venture forth anywhere sopping wet, and minus her slippers. She watched him go to a weathered sea chest, flip open the lid and dig inside, then remove a long, old-fashioned calico dress, some odd and equally ancient-looking undergarments and a pearl-plated hairbrush. Returning to her side, he shoved the items into her hands. "These should do."

Wide-eyed, Priscilla studied the quaint garments, which included lace-trimmed pantaloons and a camisole. "You've got to be kidding!"

He sighed. "I realize the frock is not the latest fashion—"

"That's the understatement of the century!"

"But 'tis all I have available for you, lass." He pointed toward an old-timey dressing screen with a yellow gingham cover, which stood in a corner near the bed. "You can change there."

Priscilla remained stupefied. "Are you certain you have nothing else I might wear?"

He shrugged apologetically.

Shaking her head, Priscilla ducked behind the screen, skinned off her wet caftan and panties, and donned the odd garments—the camisole and bloomers, a petticoat, and the high-necked, floor-length gown, a print of yellow and nutmeg brown. Gazing down at herself, she decided she looked like a refugee from a Conestoga wagon. She tugged the antique mother-of-pearl hairbrush through her hair and wondered why Jake Blarney had kept these items of his deceased wife's—and why *she* had worn such ridiculous garments in the first place! Were these people members of some odd religious sect or something?

At last, Priscilla emerged awkwardly . . .

Jake Blarney grinned as he studied her. "Ah, lass, you do look a picture." He held up some outlandish button-top black shoes, a pair of gray silk stockings, and garters. "Now don these. You can sit by the fire."

Muttering under her breath, Priscilla took the items and went to sit on a ladder-back chair by the hearth, while her host parked his large frame in a rocking chair nearby. Raising her skirts to put on the stockings, she spied Jake Blarney craning his neck to watch, and she at once shot him a chastening look. He coughed and glanced away, and she was left having to quash a traitorous smile. She slid on the stockings and the garters, then struggled with the absurd shoes and their many buttons. Before she finished with her task, she caught Jake stealing several more greedy glances, and was appalled to find herself again feeling secretly thrilled.

At last she clumsily stood, fighting for balance in the cumbersome shoes. "Well, Mr. Blarney—"

He clapped his hands. "So you're all set now. If you'll just watch the wee babes while I hitch up the buggy—"

Priscilla, who never lost her temper, stamped her foot, and almost toppled over in the process. Watching her host reach out to seize her arm, she grabbed the top rung of the chair to steady herself, and held up her free hand to keep Jake Blarney at bay.

With as much dignity as she could muster, she retorted, "For the last time, sir, I'm *not* going anywhere with you—much less marrying you!"

He appeared bewildered. "Then what will you do, lass?"

"I don't know," she admitted irritably. "If only you had a phone. It seems ridiculous that you don't."

"Not to me, lass," he replied indignantly. "As I already told you, I'm not A. H. Belo, nor John Pierpont Morgan. And right now, Colonel Belo has the only telephone on Galveston Island."

"Oh, for heaven's sake!" she declared.

He regarded her in bemusement, then sighed. "Very well, lass. Stay here the night. We'll settle this on the morrow."

Gulping, she began to back away. "Stay here—with you?"

"Careful, lass, you'll singe your skirts," he warned.

"Oh!" she gasped, jerking away from the fire, even as sparks flew from her skirt.

The Irishman grabbed a handful of Priscilla's skirts and soundly shook the folds. Then, evidently satisfied that she hadn't ignited, he straightened, studying her with amusement dancing in his eyes. "Why so skittish, girl? Do you think I'll be attempting to ravish you—with my wee ones sleeping within earshot?"

Feeling acutely embarrassed as well as very clumsy, Priscilla glanced again at the angelic babies. "Well . . . er . . . no. Still, it wouldn't be right to . . . I mean, to impose . . ."

"But what else will you do?" he demanded with a passionate gesture. "Set out for the city proper on foot, in this blustery weather?"

Priscilla rubbed her temples; her head was throbbing unmercifully. "Very well, you have a point. It appears I have no choice but to accept your hospitality, Mr. Blarney." She stiffened her spine. "But I must have your promise that you'll keep your hands to yourself—"

"Keep me hands to meself?" he asked with that unholy mischief in his eyes. "Haven't I so far, lassie? And mind you, shaking the sparks off your skirts don't count."

She had to smile. "I suppose you have been a gentleman—for the most part."

He stepped closer, and tweaked her under the chin. "I won't be having to seduce you, lass. 'Twill cause enough of a stir, you staying under my roof—a maiden lady and all."

"A maiden lady? A stir?" she scoffed. "What kind of retrograde moron are you, anyway, Mr. Jake Blarney? Haven't you ever heard of the sexual revolution?"

He glared ferociously. "The sexual what, lassie? Why, shame on you for mouthing such filth under me roof, in the presence of me wee babes, no less." His gaze narrowed on her. "Don't tell me you're one of those bloody suffragettes?"

"Suffragettes?" Priscilla waved her hands. "Will you kindly quit pretending we're living in the nineteenth century?"

"But we are, lass," he cried in exasperation.

"You, mister, are a crackpot!" she half shouted back.

"What pot did I crack?" he asked confusedly.

She made a sound of supreme frustration. "I don't know if you're pulling my leg—"

"I'd never pull your leg, lass," he put in solemnly. " 'Twould not be seemly."

"—or if you were just born with half a deck. I strongly suspect the latter. At any rate, if you'll just leave me in peace so I can get a little rest, in the morning I'll get out of your hair forever."

"But that is impossible, lass!" Jake retorted with an incredulous laugh. "You'll have to wed me after spending the night under me roof."

"I'll *have* to do nothing of the sort!" she raved. "Furthermore, I can't marry you! I'm already engaged!" She thrust her left hand toward him. "There! Look at this ring."

He stepped forward and scowled at the large, square-cut diamond surrounded by numerous smaller stones. "What manner of ring is that, lassie?"

"It's called an engagement ring."

He frowned darkly. "But you cannot be engaged to marry another if you're going to wed me—"

"Precisely. That's because I'm *not* going to wed you! Haven't you gotten anything through your thick skull? I'm engaged to marry Mr. J. Ackerly Frost."

Abruptly the Irishman threw back his head and laughed, totally baffling Priscilla. With tears of mirth in his eyes, he scoffed, "You're affianced to J. Ackerly Frost himself, you say? Lassie, you're deluded!"

"Deluded? And why, pray tell, is that?"

"Because that pantywaist is a confirmed bachelor."

Priscilla ground her teeth in fury. "He is nothing of the sort. Our engagement was announced in the *News* months ago. Your claim is preposterous. Besides, you can't possibly be talking about *the* J. Ackerly Frost the Fifth."

He appeared stunned. "But I'm not, lassie. I'm

talking about the *only* J. Ackerly Frost, who last year established the Frost National Bank of Galveston."

"What do you mean, last year?" she asked, her voice cracking.

"Just what I said, lass. J. Ackerly established his bank in the summer of seventy-nine. Caused quite a stir, here and on the mainland. Especially to the Moodys, the Sealys, and the Kempners, who would like to think they own every bank between here and Halifax."

Priscilla flung a hand outward in frustration. "What you are saying is absurd. The Frost National Bank is practically the oldest bank on the island—"

"Nay, lass, 'tis the newest." Suddenly he snapped his fingers. "Here, I'll prove it to you."

As Priscilla watched, mystified, the Irishman charged across the room to a dresser, and returned momentarily with a newspaper, holding the front page up before Priscilla's astonished eyes. She found herself gaping at an apparently fresh copy of the *Galveston News* dated October 4, 1880. The headline read, "J. Ackerly Frost honored by Galveston Chamber of Commerce."

Priscilla began to tremble. Beneath the headline was a picture of a man who looked very much like her own J. Ackerly, but with longish hair and sideburns, and a goatee. He was dressed in a long black frock coat, dark trousers, and a top hat, and was surrounded by several other gentlemen who were similarly attired.

"There, lass! Now do you believe me?" Jake Blarney asked triumphantly.

There was no reply, only the tinniest, most desperate sigh. For the second time that evening, Priscilla Pemberton crumpled to the floor in a faint, while her flabbergasted host still stood holding the newspaper.

Chapter 3

◦───◦◦───◦

Jake Blarney stared at his gift from the tide as she slept. At last he could examine her features more closely. She was even prettier than he had first thought. She possessed a rounded face and wide mouth, a dainty, upturned nose with a sprinkling of freckles across the bridge, delicately arched brown brows, and long eyelashes resting against fair cheeks. What color had her eyes been? A vibrant green, if he recalled correctly. Envisioning the color in his mind, and studying the rosy glow highlighting her cheeks, the mass of long, curly, red-gold hair spilling about her face like a gilded corona, he wondered if she hadn't a bit of the Irish in her ...

He'd like to *put* a bit of the Irish in her! he added wickedly to himself.

She was a fetching lass indeed, but also an odd one, inclined toward the vapors, if her behavior so far was any indication. Would she have the stamina necessary to become a dairy farmer's bride? He examined the rest of her with a scowl. Sturdily built, she seemed—not much of a bosom, but a nice slender waist and curvaceous hips. Her ankles and calves were handsome, too, from the greedy glimpses he'd stolen a moment ago, while removing her shoes and stockings.

As for her behavior and the swoons ... God knew, the lass had been through a shock, riding the waves to arrive on his stoop tonight. Where had she come from? Although it wasn't strictly within Jake's nature

27

to question a gift from providence, the woman's bizarre manner and peculiar speech had him thoroughly intrigued. Her voice was cultured, and she appeared an educated lass, but she spoke so oddly, using outrageous terms. By the looks of it, she might well be one of those emasculating suffragettes.

Well, he'd gentle such foolish notions out of her pretty head in no time!

For there was no doubt in Jake Blarney's mind that he was looking at his destiny, the lady who was meant to become his second bride and stepmother to his poor wee babes. Although Priscilla Pemberton's appearance at his door tonight might seem odd to some, it made sense to Jake, who was a firm believer in the myths and superstitions of his beloved Ireland. When he had lost his first wife and could find no solution for his woes in the ancient folklore of the Emerald Isle, he had created his own magic by sending a supplication to the Fates, an entreaty that had been answered tonight. Priscilla Pemberton was his vindication, his retribution, his compensation from the Almighty for Lucinda's heartless betrayal and desertion. This last year, raising the babes alone had been a trial, despite the delight he took in them. Were it not for the help of his good Christian housekeeper, Bula Braunhurst, he would have been doomed. But now his heavenly salvation had arrived at last ...

Though 'twould take a bit of persuading, Priscilla Pemberton was definitely the one to share his bed and help him run his dairy. Why she insisted she was affianced to Ackerly Frost, he had no idea. Although she might not acknowledge it yet—her fair head being filled with outlandish notions for whatever reason—she would have no choice but to marry him on the morrow, else face disgrace. She had sealed her fate by remaining under his roof tonight. His Sleeping Beauty would soon become his, if he played his cards right.

Then, as if he had summoned her with his

thoughts, he watched her eyelids flutter open, and she stared up at him and gasped.

"You're having a rough time of it tonight, aren't you, lassie?" he teased gently. "Two fits of vapors in very short order. Why, I was just thinking I might awaken you with a kiss."

She jerked upright and gaped at him.

"Don't worry, there will be plenty of time for getting acquainted later," he added.

"Not if I have anything to say about it," came her stout response.

Jake grinned. "My, my, you're a feisty soul, aren't you, Miss Pemberton?" He turned to pick up a half-filled snifter of brandy from the bedside table. Extending the glass toward her, he urged, "Here, lass, have a bit of this to fortify yourself."

Taking the snifter, she raised an eyebrow at him. "Are you trying to ply me with drink, Mr. Blarney?"

He chuckled. "I'm trying to cure your vapors, lass, before you do yourself permanent harm during one of your toppling episodes."

She actually smiled, and the sight of it gladdened Jake's heart. He solemnly watched her take several sips.

"Thank you, Mr. Blarney," she murmured, handing back the snifter.

Jake downed the rest of the liquor, taking perverse delight as he caught her wide-eyed expression. He set the snifter aside. "Now, Miss Pemberton, why don't you just relax and get some rest? There's all of the morrow to sort this out."

"I suppose there is," she muttered. She glanced about the room again, and a moan of misery escaped her. "But how can I rest when I've landed in some mind-boggling netherworld?"

"Well, at least you haven't been cast back to the days of the fairies and the Druids," he rejoined solemnly.

She rolled her eyes. "At least not so far."

"Will you be wanting to dress for bed, then?" he

inquired awkwardly. "I've taken the liberty of removing your shoes."

Priscilla looked down and wiggled her bare toes. "And my stockings."

"Aye," he admitted with a guilty grin.

She shot him a suspicious glance. "I think I'd feel safer remaining in my dress, thank you."

He reached for a quilt at the foot of the bed. "Whatever you say, lass."

She tensed as he draped the quilt over her. "Where will you sleep?"

"In the loft," he replied, inclining his head toward the ladder against the far wall. " 'Twill take only a few winks for me, since I'm up with the cows each morn."

"Whatever," Priscilla mumbled. She sank back into the bed and clutched the quilt to her neck. "I suppose it would be good to get some rest."

He coughed. "If you're needing to ... er ... see to your needs before retiring, the necessary is out back."

"Necessary?" she repeated in mystification. "Necessary for what?"

He laughed heartily. "My, those waves must have jostled your brains." In a conspiratorial whisper, he informed her, "The outhouse, lassie."

Priscilla groaned. "Oh, brother. I think I can wait until morning."

He stood, but lingered, staring down at her.

"Is there something else, Mr. Blarney?"

Jake spoke passionately. "Aye. I thought it could wait till the morrow, but now I find I cannot contain myself."

Priscilla was appalled. "You mean *you* must visit the necessary?"

He howled with mirth. "Nay, lass. That's hardly the urge I cannot contain—"

"Then what?"

In answer, Jake fell to his knees beside the bed, curled an arm around Priscilla's neck, leaned over, and captured her lips with his own—

Priscilla was astonished by the unexpected, ardent kiss. Her attempted protest became drowned beneath Jake's hot, firm lips. Excitement stormed her nerve endings at the audacious assault. Jake's kiss was a torrid stamp of ownership, as raw, brash, and irresistibly sexy as the man himself. He tasted of brandy, salt, and man. Never had Priscilla felt her lips being possessed quite so masterfully. She felt treacherously aroused, shockingly tempted to open her mouth to the rough, tormenting tongue that teased so insistently between her lips.

Then, as abruptly as it had begun, the kiss ended, and Jake Blarney pulled back to stare at her, both of them regarding each other breathlessly.

"What was that for?" she cried.

He smiled tenderly. "To wish you good night, lass—and because you looked so lost." He reached out to grip her chin. "Just remember, angel, you are lost no longer. You're Jake Blarney's woman now."

With her heartbeat pounding in her ears, Priscilla felt too shaken to respond.

He roved his index finger over her lips in a caress she found shocking. "Our first kiss, lassie. Mark the occasion well. There will be many, many more."

As he stood and strode confidently away to snuff out the lamps, Priscilla found herself half believing him. Her lips still throbbed where Jake had kissed her, and when she licked them, she tasted him again and found new tremors of longing coursing over her.

Mercy, she was losing her mind, letting herself be kissed by a madman—and enjoying it! Shivering, Priscilla sank beneath the covers. This had to be a nightmare. Tomorrow she would awaken safely back in her own bed in Clear Lake City. There would be no note in the bottle, no ancient dairy farm, no demented Irishman overloading her circuits with a single, brash kiss. What's more, Ackerly would have come to his senses . . .

Yes, if only she could last until tomorrow, all would be well . . .

* * *

Jake Blarney lay on a pallet in the sleeping loft upstairs, staring out at the moon, at the waves that had brought his bride to him tonight. He realized he had risked everything just now by so impetuously kissing Priscilla Pemberton good night. But the gamble had proven worth it. The lass had looked so fetching, so forlornly irresistible in his bed, as if she were desperate for a man to hold, cherish, and protect her.

Jake was determined to become that man, to satisfy all of Priscilla's needs. He knew she had responded to his kiss, and ah, it had been so sweet! The lass had felt as if she belonged in his arms, and the taste of her lips, so honeyed and warm, had been heavenly.

She might be a strange one, confused and vulnerable. But his poor lost nymph from the sea had found her salvation in Jake Blarney. Never would he let her go!

Chapter 4

Priscilla dreamed that she was bobbing about on a cloud. She awakened to the sound of cooing, followed by the daunting realization that a person or persons were in bed with her—

Surely he hadn't! This was her first mortified thought as she jerked open her eyes to observe the room flooded with sunshine. Relief inundated her as she spotted two curly-haired moppets bouncing about on all fours beside her.

The babies! Distantly Priscilla remembered hearing both girls whimpering, shortly before dawn. Jake had been absent, and Priscilla had stumbled from bed, exhausted, to grab both babies and bring them back to bed with her. She supposed her reaction had been pure instinct, a throwback to the summer during her college years when she had stayed with her married cousin, helping Evelyn care for two small children. Occasionally during the wee hours when Evelyn's tiny son and daughter had started crying, Priscilla had simply taken the children to bed with her.

Now she smiled at the adorable little girls who had evidently dozed beside her for some time now. The twins were obviously Jake Blarney's daughters, with their blue eyes, curly dark hair, and exquisite rose coloring. As the babies caught Priscilla staring at them, one chortled at her and rocked on all fours, while the other fell back on her bottom and began sucking her thumb. Both tots needed a fresh diaper, she noted from the wetness that had seeped into the covers beside her.

"Good morning, darlings," Priscilla murmured, tweaking the soft toes of the baby sitting closest to her. "Which one of you is Sallie and which is Nellie?"

"That's Sal giggling, and Nell with her thumb in her mouth," answered a deep male voice.

Priscilla gasped and turned to watch Jake Blarney stride through the front door bearing a wicker tray, bringing with him the crisp scent of the sea breeze. So she hadn't imagined him—or any of the bizarre events that had transpired last night. She had either landed in the clutches of a madman, or she'd been thrust back in time over a hundred years!

Not at all comforted by the thought, she observed her host coming toward her with the tray, his tall body outlined in the dappled sunshine drifting through the front curtains. Watching hard muscles ripple against shirt linen and snug trousers, she steeled herself against his incredibly sexy image, and tried to speak calmly over the pounding of her heart. "Where have you been?"

"Why, milking the cows, lass, and slaving away out back in the kitchen, preparing breakfast for you and the wee babes." He placed the tray on her lap, then handed each baby an old-fashioned nursing flask filled with milk. As the children sucked greedily, he sat down near the foot of the bed and grinned at Priscilla. "Have some breakfast, lass."

"Thank you." Musing that he was really quite thoughtful to bring her food, Priscilla glanced down at a steaming pottery cup and a bowl filled with a lumpy white mixture. "What is it?"

"Why, grits and coffee."

"Oh, I see." She took a sip of the strong, hot brew. "Did you sleep well, lass?"

"I slept like the dead," she admitted ruefully, setting down her cup. "Indeed, I was really hoping I would awaken safely back in my own bed—but it appears I'm out of luck there." She glanced about the large room. "I'm still quite lost."

"Why, you're not lost at all, lass," he protested indignantly. "Not now that me and the babes have found you. And the luck of the shamrock was most assuredly with you last night. You're exactly where you're meant to be, my dear Miss Pemberton."

Priscilla's attempt to glower at her host disintegrated into a spontaneous smile as she watched little Sal blow milk bubbles at her. Watching the child toss her bottle onto the quilt, Priscilla lost the battle with her motherly instincts. Setting aside her tray, she pulled the baby onto her lap. She sighed at the incredible softness of Sal's rounded little body. She retrieved the bottle and gently offered her the nipple. At once the child snuggled in her arms and resumed nursing. Priscilla was truly floating on a cloud, entranced by the darling child who rested her head so contentedly against Priscilla's shoulder and gazed up at her with precious, dark, trusting eyes.

"Ah, lass, she looks like a vision in your arms."

Priscilla glanced up at Jake and felt her face burning at the unspeakably tender look in his bright blue eyes. A powerful, poignant emotion flared between them, and Priscilla knew they both felt the magic. Feeling embarrassed and acutely vulnerable, she smiled down at the baby. "Your children are delightful. But they both need fresh diapers, you know."

Jake chuckled and picked up Nell, kissing her cheek, settling her against his arm, and feeding her the bottle. "Aye, they keep me poor housekeeper dancing a jig boiling their little britches. We'll see to their changing directly." Jake slanted Priscilla a chiding glance. " 'Twas good of you to bring the babes to bed with you, lass, as I'm delighted you're becoming better acquainted with me twins. But in the future, have a care for the fire."

"Oh," Priscilla muttered, glancing across the room, where embers still glowed in the open grate. "Your fireplace needs a screen, Mr. Blarney."

He raised an eyebrow wickedly. "Aye. Otherwise, I might end up searing the skirts off a certain befuddled lassie—eh, Miss Pemberton?"

Ignoring his naughty remark, she continued with bravado, "Beyond that, you and I have no future."

He only chuckled devilishly and wagged a finger at her. "Ah, but we do, lass. Sealed it with a kiss last night, we did."

She groaned. "Look, Mr. Blarney, it is hardly my fault that you are still harboring delusions regarding my appearance here. As soon as I finish this meal, I must get out of here ..." She paused, entranced as she watched him with Nell.

Jake had hoisted the plump baby over his head, and Nell was gurgling at him in glee and kicking her precious little feet. "Aye, 'tis off to town for the lot of us, to find Father O'Dooley and make an honest woman out of you. Isn't that right, wee Nell?"

Priscilla was about to protest when she was distracted by the sound of footsteps and muffled voices out on the porch. A moment later, a man called out in a heavy Irish brogue, "Did someone mention me name?"

Both Jake and Priscilla flinched, craning their necks toward the doorway to watch a portly, balding man in a cassock enter, followed by an equally plump middle-aged woman in a black dress and feathered hat. Both newcomers gaped in horror at the astonishing domestic scene on the bed—the disheveled Priscilla with Sal in her lap, and Jake nearby holding Nell aloft.

Wild-eyed, Jake set down the baby and stood. "Father O'Dooley! Bless me soul, what are you doing here, man? Or did me words summon you, dear friend?"

The flustered priest cleared his throat. "Well, it does appear you're in need of some ... er ... salvation, my son." He nodded toward the red-faced woman. "But actually, I'm here because the axle on Bula's conveyance broke. I offered your housekeeper a ride—knowing how you depend on her for the wee babes."

" 'Twas thoughtful of you, Father O'Dooley," murmured Jake.

"And it appears we haven't arrived a moment too soon," the priest added, staring pointedly at Priscilla.

Jake clapped his hands and grinned. "Ah, yes, I'm forgetting meself." He inclined a hand toward Priscilla. "Father O'Dooley, Mrs. Braunhurst, may I present me ... er ... guest, Miss Priscilla Pemberton. The tide washed her in just last night, you see."

"The tide washed her in?" repeated a clearly flabbergasted Father O'Dooley.

"By Saint Gall!" exclaimed the woman in a pronounced German accent.

"Aye, washed her up on me beach just like a pretty conch shell," Jake continued proudly. He winked at Priscilla. "Miss Pemberton, may I introduce me friend and priest, Father Jamie O'Dooley, and me housekeeper, Mrs. Bula Braunhurst?"

"How do you do?" Priscilla inquired awkwardly.

The two nodded back stiffly.

The priest slanted an admonishing glance at Jake. "May I have a word with you outside, my son?"

"Of course, Father." He nodded to the housekeeper. "Mrs. Braunhurst, if you'll kindly see to the dressing of the babes—"

"*Ja*, sir," she replied with a bob of her feathered hat.

The two men stepped out the door, and the housekeeper lumbered over to the bed. "I take care of the babies now," she said firmly, holding out her arms.

Priscilla handed Sal to the woman. "They both need a diaper change, you know."

"*Natürlich*—I take care of that, as well," came the cold reply as the woman hoisted Nell with her other arm.

Priscilla watched the sturdy woman cross the room with the babies and set them down on the daybed near the cradles. She stood and smoothed down her skirts. "Look, Mrs. Braunhurst, this situation is not at all what it appears—"

The woman merely rolled her eyes as she reached for fresh diapers. Priscilla considered offering to help the housekeeper, then thought better of the instinct. She quickly found her stockings and shoes, donned them, then brushed some order into her hair. She realized she badly needed to go to the necessary, but the cottage evidently had only one door at the front, and she hated the thought of parading past the men. She had doubtless created enough of a sideshow already. She could hear the men's muffled laughter out on the stoop, and wondered what they were talking about—*her*, no doubt.

Her curiosity was satisfied a moment later when Jake and Father O'Dooley stepped back inside. Both appeared eminently pleased—which Priscilla did not interpret as a propitious sign, under the circumstances.

"Well, then, lass, it's all settled," declared Jake Blarney with a cocky grin.

"What's all settled?" she asked suspiciously.

Jake stepped toward her. "We cannot marry today, lassie, since I'd forgotten the necessity of a marriage license. But Father O'Dooley assures me that one of our parishioners, a proper spinster, will provide you with lodging until the license is secured."

Priscilla fumed at his effrontery. "There'll be no securing of any license, Mr. Blarney." She turned decisively to the priest. "However, Father O'Dooley, I would certainly appreciate your giving me a lift back to Galveston."

The man glanced helplessly from the glowering Jake to the determined Priscilla. "Why, I'd be happy to assist you, young lady. But surely you realize you must marry Mr. Blarney. Do you not know you are ruined, having spent the night under his roof? Why, a proper Catholic marriage, posthaste, is the only possible solution—"

"Don't be ridiculous," scoffed Priscilla. "You're beginning to sound more full of blarney than our host."

The priest scowled at her words. "But you'll have no future if you don't marry. Think of the scandal, my dear—"

"Aye, lass," added Jake with triumph and amusement. "Think of the stir 'twill cause."

" 'Twill cause not the slightest stir unless one of you three"—Priscilla jerked her head toward each adult in turn—"spreads gossip. If you do, I swear I'll sue the lot of you for character assassination."

For a moment, there was only stunned silence in the room. Jake and Father O'Dooley exchanged mystified glances. Even the housekeeper paused as she tugged a long linen dress over one of the babies.

Then Jake chuckled, a deep, rumbling sound. "She's a feisty one, is she not?" he asked Father O'Dooley.

"Aye, full of the Devil's own mischief," he concurred solemnly.

Jake regarded Priscilla with pride. " 'Twas the ride on the ocean that made the colleen so contrary, I'm thinking."

"Aye, it must have been some ride," said the priest. "Where do you hail from, lass?"

"From the mainland," she snapped, about to lose all patience with the annoying conversation.

The priest whistled. "And you swam all the way here?"

"Look, I've already been over this, under this, and through this with Mr. Blarney," Priscilla replied. "Will you take me back to town or not, Father O'Dooley?"

The priest appeared suitably chastened. "Why, certainly, miss."

"May we go now?"

"If you so desire."

"I so desire."

Jake strode up to Priscilla and regarded her severely. "Lassie, I'll be coming in to town to see you. This is far from settled between us."

"Hah!" she retorted. "Although your hospitality has been exemplary, Mr. Blarney, my fondest hope is never again to lay eyes on you."

He appeared stricken. "Lassie, how can you be so heartless? Deserting me, and me poor orphaned babes."

Fighting the assault on her conscience, Priscilla attempted to glare at him, then wilted as she heard one of the babies crowing. She glanced across the room to see both girls sitting on Mrs. Braunhurst's lap, looking irresistible in fresh lacy white dresses. Nell was again sucking her thumb, while Sal waved her plump arms at Priscilla. She felt like a traitor.

"Well, lass?" nudged Jake.

Priscilla gathered her courage. "You just take good care of those darling girls," she scolded him. Impulsively she crossed the room, leaned over, and kissed each baby's cheek. She almost lost her resolve as she absorbed the tots' softness and sweet scent. "Bye-bye, angels." Bucking up her spine, she turned to the priest. "Shall we go, Father O'Dooley?"

He cast Jake a pleading look, and the latter nodded resignedly. "Aye, miss."

Priscilla charged out the door, only to stop in her tracks as she viewed a quaint black buggy awaiting her on the beach. With its folding top and huge wheels, the small carriage was clearly straight out of the nineteenth century. Harnessed to the conveyance was a large nutmeg-colored horse that neighed at Priscilla and swung its tail at a swooping barn swallow.

This was hardly the type of "lift" Priscilla had anticipated! Her desperate hope that she was still in the twentieth century was being severely undermined, and the resulting deluge of unreality left her trembling.

To her credit, she did not faint this time, although

she was grateful for the steadying hand Jake Blarney applied to her quivering forearm.

"I think I need the necessary," Priscilla Pemberton said.

Chapter 5

Within moments, Priscilla was in the buggy, jouncing down a long expanse of deserted beach with Father O'Dooley at her side. The jovial priest hummed "In The Gloaming" under his breath as he worked the reins. The morning was cool and blustery, scented with the fishy odor of the Gulf, which stretched to their right. Laughing gulls swarmed about the whitecaps, and on the marshes Priscilla spotted marbled godwits and long-billed dowitchers digging for worms and crabs. At least the birds and the smells were familiar, Priscilla thought ruefully.

The nutmeg-colored horse that pulled the rattletrap conveyance was kicking up sand with his hooves, causing Priscilla to wipe the grit from her eyes and skin. Before she had left the Blarney cottage, Mrs. Braunhurst had handed her a bonnet—a huge calico affair with slats. Priscilla had found the archaic headgear ridiculous—but now she could see the wisdom behind the design with its huge protruding brim.

She couldn't believe what was happening to her! As long as she had been at the Blarney cottage, she could cling to the illusion that Jake was merely some lone lunatic, that he was harboring delusions about living in the nineteenth century, and she would soon find her way back to the place where she belonged. But now that she had met the equally quaint Father O'Dooley and Mrs. Braunhurst—now that she was being conveyed down the beach in a rattletrap buggy—the case was rapidly building that she had landed somewhere far away from her prior, sane existence.

Was she truly living in the nineteenth century, or was she merely lost among a colony of oddballs? Despite the claims of these bizarre people, Priscilla was beginning to suspect that she was not on Galveston Island at all. Ahead of them stretched nothing but beach, with only a forlorn palm tree or two waving in the distance. Where were the other beach cottages, the state park, the stores and fast-food restaurants that lined the West End of Galveston Island? Could she have washed up in a different locale—say, Bolivar Peninsula—where there were still some uninhabited expanses? But if this were true, how could she explain these strange people, their ancient attire, their insistence that she was indeed on Galveston Island— not to mention the newspaper Jake Blarney had thrust into her face last night, with its date of October 4, 1880, and its picture of *the* J. Ackerly Frost?

Even the priest sitting beside her seemed an astounding anachronism, dressed in his old-fashioned belted cassock, with a heavy gold crucifix on a long chain hanging from his chubby neck and the liturgical cap on top of his balding head. He didn't look like a madman, with his round, fleshy cheeks, bulbous nose, and placid expression. Why was he, like Jake Blarney and his cleaning lady, pretending to be living in the year 1880? Priscilla had heard of historical reenactment festivals being staged, but never one that went *this* far! Even during such an event, wouldn't there be some clues to give away the actual time period, like power lines or a plane flying over? So far, she hadn't spotted anything modern!

Suddenly Priscilla tensed in her seat as she watched three rare Eskimo curlews sail over the buggy toward the Gulf. She gaped after the birds in disbelief. Three Eskimo curlews! As far as Priscilla knew, the bird was all but extinct, and was almost never spotted! To observe three of the species at the same time was unheard-of!

Oh, heavens! Where *was* she?

Amazed, she turned to the priest. "Did you see those birds?"

At her query, he ceased his humming. "Ah, yes. Do you mean the little brown things with the long beaks? They're forever digging for bugs on the church lawn."

"Not on any church lawn *I've* ever seen," insisted the astounded Priscilla.

The priest regarded her quizzically. "Where did you say you hail from, miss?"

She managed to flash him a stiff smile. "From the mainland. I live near NASA."

"NASA?" he repeated in bewilderment. "What is that?"

"I live in Clear Lake City."

"Clear Lake City?" he repeated. "Why, I've never heard of that, either."

"No, I suppose you wouldn't have," she muttered. She craned her neck to look ahead. "Just where did you say you're taking me?"

"To the home of one of my parishioners at Saint Patrick's, Rose Gatling. Rose is a good Catholic woman, a widow lady for five years now, and she lets out rooms in her home on Broadway."

"Broadway," Priscilla repeated, frowning at the priest's mention of this famous elegant thoroughfare in Galveston proper. She decided she was tiring of this game. "Look, Father, why don't you just stop pulling my leg?"

"Your limb?" he asked confusedly.

"Yes." She gestured expansively. "We can't possibly be on Galveston Island unless everything on the West End has been swept away by a hurricane more powerful than the Great Storm of 1900—"

He stared at her as if she had lost her mind. "The Great Storm of 1900? Why, the year 1900 is still twenty years away, young woman!"

"Twenty years away, my foot!" scoffed Priscilla. "And if you've never heard of the storm, it's simply because we're not on Galveston Island!"

He laughed in disbelief. "We're not? Then where are we, pray tell?"

"I'm not sure," she admitted, "but this is definitely not Galveston, because there are no homes and businesses." Impatiently she pointed ahead of them. "Furthermore, I can see well into the distance. There's no evidence of the grade raising, for heaven's sake!"

"Grade raising?" he repeated, perplexed.

"Yes. Following the Great Storm, the entire East End of Galveston was elevated seventeen feet."

"Why, I've never heard of anything so outlandish!" protested the priest. "You cannot possibly be in your right mind there. Raising up an entire island, indeed!"

Priscilla stifled a groan. "Please just drive," she said in disgust. "I don't know what is going on, but I'm beginning to suspect that you're every bit as demented as your parishioner, Jake Blarney."

The priest made a sound of outrage. "Jake demented? Why, by Saint Brendan, Jake Blarney is one of the finest men I know! Jake and I immigrated to the United States on the same steamer ten years ago. He's a good Catholic and a faithful member of the Order of the Hibernians, I'll have you know. I'd advise you to consider yourself lucky that he's offered to wed you—under these very compromising circumstances."

"Oh, you would?" she countered indignantly. "I'm supposed to leap at the chance to marry a dairy farmer simply because I spent the night under his roof! Of all the chauvinistic claptrap! Besides, if Jake's such a catch, why did his wife leave him?"

The priest shook his head and clucked under his breath. "Lucinda was a selfish, sinful woman—who is no doubt burning in hell at this very moment." He glowered at her righteously. "And I might add, miss, that you may find yourself in similar straits if you don't mend your ways."

She harrumphed. "I seem to find myself in similar straits now." She crossed her arms over her bosom and glared ahead, effectively curtailing their conversation.

They proceeded in grim silence filled only by the plodding of the horse, the rattling of the buggy, the rushing sound of the waves, and the squawking of gulls. It was a full twenty minutes later when Priscilla tensed in her seat as she viewed the beginnings of a city—and such a city it was!

They had moved slightly inland. First Priscilla spotted what appeared to be the end of trolley tracks extending down to the beach, and beyond them, some scattered old-fashioned cottages, palm trees, and oleanders. At the nearest cottage, she spotted a plump woman in a dress similar to hers coming out on the porch and beating a rag rug against a railing.

"Good morning, Mrs. O'Herlihy," Father O'Dooley called out to the woman as they clattered past.

"Good morning, Father," she called back in a thick Irish brogue.

The hair on the back of Priscilla's neck began to stand on end. As they continued on, the houses grew denser—mostly narrow one- and two-story bungalows of Greek Revival or Victorian design, many painted in quaint color schemes such as white accented by yellow and oyster blue, or brick red embellished by buff and teal green. The homes were actually quite charming with their bright shutters, jaunty porch railings, and elaborate roof structures that included bracketed cornices, dormers decorated with finials and turrets, and gables sporting recessed windows and bargeboards. In picturesque little side gardens she spotted elaborate dovecotes, heavily carved garden seats, and cherub statuary.

Priscilla could only shake her head. She had traveled extensively throughout the South, yet she didn't recall seeing such a conglomeration of Victorian splendor!

Streets lined with crushed shell began to jut off to their right and left. Priscilla felt really nervous when she still spotted no power lines, no cars. Her anxiety surged into panic as they were passed by another buggy containing a man and woman, both in elegant nineteenth-century attire. Both waved to Father O'Dooley, who bellowed back a friendly greeting. In the next block, a wagon stacked with bales of cotton creaked past, a black man in a straw hat and tattered clothing driving the two shaggy work horses.

"Oh, my God!" Priscilla muttered, gaping at a mule-drawn trolley clacking across the side street ahead of them, its bell clanging loudly.

"Are you all right, miss?" the priest asked from her side.

"Hardly." Indeed, Priscilla feared she had lost her mind. Either that, or she truly had been swept back in time to the year 1880! The possibility was unnerving, frightening!

As they turned onto a busier street, people began to appear on the walkways—men in sedate frock coats, long trousers, and top hats, women in long, colorful, bustled dresses, carrying fringed parasols and wearing gaily feathered bonnets. Some of the ladies tugged along small children—little girls in lacy, ribboned frocks, pantaloons, and flower-bedecked hats; boys in sailor suits. A young couple pushing a huge, ornate black baby carriage called out a greeting to the priest.

"Bless you, my children!" Father O'Dooley exclaimed, then turned to smile at Priscilla. "That's the McIlvesters. Just had their first—little Timmy. I christened him Sunday last."

"How nice," muttered Priscilla, fighting to control the trembling of her hands.

They eventually wended their way onto a street that resembled Broadway, where Priscilla at once recognized several raised, green-shuttered Victorian cottages she was certain had been present in the Galveston she remembered. Yet across the street from the cottages loomed a pillared, white Greek Revival mansion she had never seen before. She was even more confounded when they passed the famous Episcopal Cemetery—yet it was devoid of all but the most ancient tombstones and monuments!

Priscilla felt close to a panic attack. How could the street look so familiar, yet be so different from the Broadway she remembered? The esplanade—lined with towering palms back in the twentieth century—was all but bare here, except for trolley tracks where the palms should have been. The myriad traffic lights, the cars, and the familiar statue to the heroes of the Texas Revolution were all missing, as well.

Then, as they entered a new block, Priscilla caught sight of another well-known landmark. "Ashton Villa!" she cried.

The priest glanced at her askance. "You're referring to the J. M. Brown residence?"

"Y-Yes," she replied haltingly.

Priscilla stared mystified at the three-story, red-brick, Italian Renaissance home, which appeared, with its black iron lace grillwork, hauntingly similar to the grand homes she'd once seen in the Garden District of New Orleans. But, like the street itself, the estate was both highly recognizable and equally strange. The house itself appeared little altered, but the manicured lawn, and the sign welcoming visitors, were absent. Instead, she viewed an unfamiliar wrought-iron and brick fence, and a bevy of fruit trees she'd never seen before! Increasing Priscilla's confusion was the illogic of the house's mere presence, since she'd still seen no evidence of the grade raising that elevated the East End of Galveston Island from the West End. And if there was no grade raising, how could this be Galveston at all?

Unless she truly had been swept away to the year 1880, decades before the grade raising had been completed! This was beginning to sound like the only explanation that made any sense at all! Oh, mercy, had she died or what?

Priscilla felt light-headed!

"Oh, look, there's Miss Rebecca pruning her roses," said Father O'Dooley, pointing toward the lawn.

Priscilla craned her neck to view a middle-aged woman in dimity dress, muslin apron, and slat bonnet, industriously clipping away in the midst of a lush rose garden. "Ah, yes, I see her," Priscilla mumbled. "Who is she?"

"Why, she's Mrs. J. M. Brown, mistress of the household," came his indignant response.

"You mean the house is no longer open to tours?"

"Tours?" the priest scoffed. "Why, it's been the Brown family residence for over twenty years. Fine people, I must say, even if they are Episcopalians. That Miss Bettie is a scandal, though—smoking cigarettes and studying art off in Vienna. Disgraceful conduct for a maiden lady—don't you agree?"

Priscilla felt too befuddled to attempt a reply, especially as she spotted the familiar steeple of Trinity Episcopal slightly to the north of them—more proof that she was in Galveston, yet *wasn't* in Galveston.

She heard Father O'Dooley heave a great sigh. "Look, Miss Pemberton, before we arrive at Miss Gatling's boardinghouse, we'll be needing to come up with a story for you."

Priscilla frowned. "A story?"

"I'm not a man to lie," he continued soberly, "but I think sometimes the Almighty knows the truth will do more harm than good."

Priscilla was perplexed. "What are you babbling about?"

He raised an eyebrow at her. "How will we explain your presence in Galveston to Rose Gatling?"

"Oh, I hadn't thought."

"Well, you had best think, miss, since I know Rose well, and she will never let out a room to a woman of questionable virtue."

"Questionable virtue! I beg your pardon!"

"Now, miss, don't get on your high horse," Father O'Dooley soothed. "The true is, we cannot tell Rose that you spent the night under Jake Blarney's roof, and that you fell off a boat or whatever out in the Gulf."

Priscilla paled, realizing the good father had raised a valid point. "Yes, I suppose you are right."

"Indeed. And I have a suggestion. I've a sister in Oxford, Mississippi. Why don't we say you're a daughter of one of Margaret's good friends, newly arrived here to seek a post as ..." He looked her over and scowled.

"A schoolteacher?" Priscilla suggested.

He brightened. "Aye, a schoolmarm. And we'll say your trunk got stolen at the docks."

Priscilla nodded. The story made as much sense as any, she supposed. "Very well. We'll say that."

"Good. Well, here we are at last," said Father O'Dooley, pulling the buggy to a halt before a three-story Gothic Revival mansion.

Priscilla could only gape at the magnificent white frame home, a masterpiece of the "carpenter Gothic" technique. All three stories seemed swathed in white lace, with curlicues and bric-a-brac swirling about graceful verandas that beckoned loungers to while away the autumn hours on white wicker rockers. Delicate porch railings sprouted carved pillars that stretched upward, supporting archways framed by curved trellis panels. Windows gleamed with stained or faceted glass, and vibrant ferns spilled from baskets high in the eaves.

"This is Rose Gatling's house?" Priscilla asked.

"Aye." Father O'Dooley lumbered out of the conveyance and offered Priscilla his hand.

"Why, it's charming," she said, accepting his assistance.

They proceeded through a wrought-iron gate and into the tree-lined yard.

"Aye, a number of the island's young single ladies

reside here, or over in the Silk Stocking District," the priest explained. "Rose keeps the second floor for the young ladies, and the third for the gents. She's had a nice room vacant ever since her daughter, Betsy, married and moved out last month. I'm thinking she will be glad to have you, miss."

"I'm glad to have a place to stay," Priscilla muttered.

He slanted her a stern look. "Now mind you, Rose runs a tight ship. Her dear departed George was a sea captain, and Rose is not one to tolerate unseemly behavior. But you'll do well here in Galveston, dear, if you mind your p's and q's and avoid the harbor and Smokey Row."

"I shall certainly try my best," replied Priscilla drolly.

They climbed the steps to the freshly painted gray porch. The father rapped on the stylish wooden door while Priscilla marveled at its exquisite oval glass panel, the faceted glass sidelights, and the jewel-like stained-glass inset filling the transom.

A moment later, a middle-age woman opened the door. She was of medium height and slender, dressed in a bustled gown of black taffeta. Her long, sharp face with pointed chin was made more severe by a mound of red hair piled high on top of her head. She peered at the newcomers through a lorgnette, scrutinizing Priscilla and her modest outfit in a piercing manner that made the latter uneasy.

She greeted them in a flat, emotionless voice. "Why, Father O'Dooley, this is a surprise." Her gaze flicked suspiciously to Priscilla. "And who have we here?"

"Mrs. Gatling, I'd like to introduce Miss Priscilla Pemberton, who hopes to become your newest tenant."

"How do you do?" the woman asked, extending her hand.

"Pleased to meet you," Priscilla murmured, return-

ing the handshake, finding their hostess's grip limp
and cold. "You have a lovely home."

"Why, thank you," replied the woman stiffly. "Do
come in, both of you."

Priscilla's gaze widened as they moved into what
could only be called a high Victorian entry hall. She
eagerly took in the soaring ceiling outlined by an in-
tricately carved plaster frieze and accented by a
breathtaking cut crystal chandelier, walls papered in
baroque damask of a deep rose hue, marble-topped
pier tables reposing beneath gold filigree mirrors,
and several exquisitely carved walnut side chairs
with tufted green silk brocade upholstery.

"Won't you both join me in the ladies' parlor?"
Rose asked. "I do believe it's vacant at the moment."

As they proceeded down the hallway, Priscilla
glanced to her right at a large room filled with Victorian furniture. She spotted several men inside, reading newspapers and smoking pipes.

"Just this way," Rose called.

Shaking her head, Priscilla moved on. Were there
separate parlors in this home for the gentlemen and
the ladies? Heavens, she surely *was* back in Victorian
times!

Following Rose and the priest, Priscilla stepped to
her left into a large room. A profusion of delicate
plaster scrollwork decorated the high ceiling, ac-
centing two handsome gas chandeliers suspended
from ornate brass chains. An elegant Oriental rug of
emerald green medallion design covered the floor,
and an opulent gold damask fabric adorned the
walls. At the windows, a sweet breeze wafted
through lace panels that fluttered beneath the more
somber shroud of dark green brocaded portieres.
Around the Italian tile and black marble fireplace
were grouped two Victorian red velvet settees and
three matching side chairs. On the carved mahogany
tea table, an arrangement of yellow roses filled a
crystal bowl, and next to it lay a handsome leather
volume of Hardy's *The Return of the Native*. In a far

corner on a gilded pedestal reposed a black-draped portrait of a severe-looking gentleman in a sea captain's uniform; Priscilla guessed he was the dear departed Captain Gatling.

Rose indicated a chair for Father O'Dooley and a settee for Priscilla. Once all were seated, she asked, "May I ring for tea?"

"No, don't trouble yourself, Rose, I can't stay," answered the priest. "I just want to make sure Miss Pemberton has lodging. I take it Betsy's room is still vacant?"

"It is." The woman turned to frown at Priscilla. "Not to pry, Miss Pemberton, but I make it a policy to know something about the background of my tenants. Whence do you hail?"

Priscilla deferred to Father O'Dooley, who quickly spoke up. "Miss Pemberton is the daughter of me sister Margaret's dear friend in Oxford, Mississippi. She's come here to seek a post as a schoolmarm."

Rose appeared skeptical. "An odd time of year to be seeking such a position."

"But aren't the Ursuline nuns and the Sisters of Incarnate Word at St. Mary's Orphanage always in need of additional lay help?" Father O'Dooley countered. "For that matter, we're often shorthanded at our own parish school."

"Well, if you say so, Father." Appearing skeptical, Rose turned to Priscilla. "It will be seven dollars each week, in advance, for room and board. Since the current week is under way, five dollars should suffice for now."

"Oh," Priscilla muttered, feeling embarrassed. "I'm afraid I don't have any money."

Rose Gatling appeared taken aback. "My, this is most irregular."

Father O'Dooley rose and awkwardly crossed to the matron. Digging into the pocket of his cassock, he handed the woman a five-dollar gold piece. "Here, Rose. Just to get Miss Pemberton started."

As Rose hesitated, Priscilla burst out, "But, Father, I can't allow you to do that!"

"Nonsense." He shoved the coin into Rose's hand. "Is she taken care of, then?"

Rose cast another dubious glance at Priscilla, then smiled at the priest. "Well, yes, Father. I suppose it's our Christian duty to lend a hand to those less fortunate."

While Priscilla bristled, Father O'Dooley muttered, "Aye. 'Tis."

"I'll pay you back, Father O'Dooley," Priscilla added.

"I'm sure you will." He nodded to Rose. "I'll see myself out. Just be sure that Miss Pemberton gets settled in."

"Of course, Father."

After he left, the two women regarded each other awkwardly and warily. "May I see my room?" Priscilla asked.

Rose stood with a rustle of taffeta skirts. "Of course. If you'll tell me where your things are, I can send my man for them."

"I have no things," Priscilla admitted.

"You have no things?"

Priscilla stood and faced down the nosy housekeeper, who was already getting on her frayed nerves. "Please, Mrs. Gatling, I've been through a rather trying experience in getting here. If you don't mind, I'd just like to see my room."

"Whatever you say," came the cold response.

She followed the widow up the curving semispiral staircase to the second story, and down a long corridor. Priscilla noted several open doors—to a cozy bedroom, a bathroom, an upstairs solarium—and decided she would go exploring later on.

Rose opened a door toward the front of the house. "Here you are, miss. You're most fortunate. My Betsy had the best room in the house before she married and moved away to Houston."

"So she did," Priscilla muttered, moving into the lovely large room with its pastel Savonaire rug, carved rococo revival furniture, and full tester bed with gold silk hangings and wispy mosquito netting.

"My Betsy liked the view best," Rose went on, moving to the front of the room and opening the French doors. "You have your own private balcony."

Priscilla moved onto the small veranda with its whimsical latticework archways and railings. She gazed down at a beautiful side garden brilliant with roses and dotted with magnolia trees. She took a deep breath of the heady fragrance. "Yes, this will do nicely."

"Good." Rose moved back inside the room, and Priscilla followed. "Let's see, what else will you need to know? We've all the modern conveniences, of course—gas light and heat, and we're first on the list to receive electricity sometime next year, and also a telephone, whenever the exchange finally opens. There's a bathroom down the hall with hot water piped in from a gas heater. Meals are served in the dining room promptly at eight A.M., twelve noon, and six P.M. No one is served beyond fifteen minutes past the hour. No libations are allowed in the rooms, and no gentleman callers may be received in the ladies' parlor after the hour of eight."

Priscilla smiled wanly. "It sounds as if you do run a tight ship, Mrs. Gatling."

"Well, yes, my dear departed captain would have wanted it just so." Coughing, she added, "By the way, the rent money is due each Saturday."

"You'll have it," said Priscilla.

The woman nodded curtly and left.

Priscilla flung herself down on what turned out to be a very comfortable down-filled bed. Oh, what would she do now? She was not only stranded in the nineteenth century, she was totally without friends, family—or money.

For at least the dozenth time, she wondered what

had happened to her. One minute she had been in the twentieth century, then she had been swept away here. Had her morbid musings about suicide truly caused this calamity? Had she drowned in the present, and miraculously become reincarnated in nineteenth-century Galveston?

Should she tell these people where she truly came from? Grimly she shook her head. Already Jake Blarney and Father O'Dooley had accused her of being peculiar and outlandish. If she told them the truth, that she appeared to have traveled through time, they would assume she was demented. As for what they might do with a crazy woman here . . . Well, she didn't even want to think about it!

Besides, how could she explain something she couldn't begin to understand herself? Like the entire bizarre matter of the note in the bottle that had brought her here . . . Where did it fit into the puzzle? She remembered Jake Blarney's claim that he had summoned her. Was she truly meant to become his bride? But that made no sense at all. Of course, Jake was incredibly sexy, and his daughters were adorable. But he was also the exact opposite of everything she had ever wanted! He was brash and coarse where she was refined and sophisticated. The raw, heady excitement he stirred in her scared her to death, as did his uncanny ability to make her respond emotionally, something Priscilla Pemberton studiously avoided doing. Yet, strangely enough, she found she didn't feel nearly as relieved as she should have at having escaped his clutches.

She rose, went outside onto the veranda, and stared down at Broadway, watching a mule-drawn trolley clank past. In the final analysis, her experience could be a dream, and she might awaken at any moment. In the meantime, she would have to muddle through as best she could. That meant, first of all, acquiring financial resources.

But how? She lifted her hand and stared at J. Ackerly's dazzling diamond ring, with the fabulous three-carat stone. She smiled, suddenly thankful she'd been unable to cast the ring to the tides last night. Perhaps knowing Ackerly may not have been such a disaster, after all.

Chapter 6

❦

Trying to fine-tune a plan of action, Priscilla paced her spacious room, touching the furnishings and accoutrements as if she expected them to disappear at any moment. She ran her fingertips over the fine carved mahogany armoire, examined a hand-painted porcelain hair jar on the dressing table, scrutinized the tall, ornate, birdcage-style cast-iron heater that would obviously supply much warmth on cold winter mornings, and tried sitting on the low, uncomfortable, burgundy-colored ottoman that reminded her of a "fainting couch" she'd once seen in another Galveston home back in the twentieth century.

On a whim, she explored a little more of the upstairs, marveling at the sunny solarium, with its whimsical wicker chairs and rockers piled with beautifully embroidered cushions. She chuckled over the large, ponderously decorated bathroom, where Victorian propriety had been taken to the extreme of housing all the necessities—including the pull-chain toilet—behind handsome Elizabethan-style cabinetry. On the way back to her room, she paused by a large étagère to study gewgaws that ranged from a japanned box to a hand-painted Oriental vase to an ornate cast-iron tobacco cutter.

She slipped back inside her room and drew a heavy breath. So she seemed stuck here in the year 1880. She had Ackerly's ring, the rent due on Saturday—whenever that was—and little else. She was a hundred and fifteen years removed from the mother she loved, from Ackerly, from her colleagues at the university, and from the students who would show up for her next classes to find Ms. Pemberton absent.

Of course, things could be worse, she mused darkly. She might be dead. Nevertheless, if she was to survive here, she would first of all need a grubstake—and that would mean pawning or selling Ackerly's ring. She glanced down at the antique, emerald-cut stone. The large white diamond was nearly flawless, and had been worth a small fortune back in the present—surely the reason Ackerly had requested she guard it carefully. Even here, it should fetch a substantial nest egg.

Her decision made, Priscilla went to the dressing table, where she found a hairbrush and comb—as well as pins in the hair jar. Thankful that Betsy had left these items behind, she removed her bonnet, brushed out her hair—which definitely needed a shampooing after last night's dip in the Gulf!—and arranged her locks in an old-fashioned chignon, pinning down the rebellious curls that kept springing about her forehead. Satisfied with her efforts, she replaced her bonnet and left the room.

Down on Broadway, Priscilla stood mystified for a moment, watching a parade of families in horse-drawn conveyances, women pushing baby carriages, businessmen in mule-drawn trolleys, and even a young man on a high-wheeler hobbyhorse, who waved a leather-gloved hand at her as he glided past, wearing a biking suit complete with jaunty cap and red ascot fluttering in the breeze. She waved back with bravado.

Since she was not entirely sure of her bearings, Priscilla proceeded west to the familiar landmark of Ashton Villa—or rather, the Brown residence, as it was now known. The middle-aged woman Father O'Dooley had identified as "Miss Rebecca" was still out in the yard pruning her roses, but a gentleman had joined her—a tall, distinguished man with gray hair and long side whiskers. Mercy, was that J. M. Brown himself, the preeminent Galveston citizen and entrepreneur who had built Ashton Villa? Although Priscilla hardly considered herself a Galveston historian, she had read several books on the city, and Ackerly had introduced her to several ladies in the East End Historical Society. Through attending various events and tours sponsored by the Society, she had acquired further knowledge—and the man standing in the yard of Ashton Villa definitely resembled several pictures she had seen of J. M. Brown. Mercy!

Priscilla turned the corner and proceeded north on Tremont, at first feeling bemused when she spotted no Rosenberg Library on the property directly behind Ashton Villa. But then that wasn't surprising, either since, if memory served, the library hadn't been built until after Henry Rosenberg died in the 1890s. Any doubts Priscilla might have retained that she had truly landed in the year 1880 were rapidly fading.

She continued toward the center of town, passing old-fashioned feed stores and hotels, warehouses and stables. She glanced covetously at several more passing carriages. Her shoes were cramped and uncomfortable, and her feet were already beginning to hurt. She trudged past several Greek Revival and Victorian homes, catching occasional curious glances from housewives out on their stoops, or children playing in yards. At Postoffice Street, on a whim, she turned to the right and went around the block. Sure enough, Trinity Episcopal Church—the one she had so often attended with Ackerly in the present—was there, complete with its single tower and Gothic Revival architecture, although she spotted several trees that had been absent before. Even more disquieting, off to the left of the church, Eaton Chapel was still under construction, with several stonemasons busy hammering away on blocks for the facade! Shaking her head, Priscilla went back around the corner and continued on toward the center of town. Traipsing past additional businesses and houses, she noted that none of the familiar tall buildings of downtown Galveston loomed in the distance—although she spotted numerous three-story, nineteenth-century structures. By now, she had almost ceased to be shocked.

Near the center of town, at Mechanic Street, she glanced to the east and spotted the famous old Cotton Exchange Building, with its redbrick facade and four stories of arched windows outlined in white. She remembered seeing a picture of the Exchange in one of the books she'd read on Galveston—but she also recalled that it had been razed at least fifty years ago, back in the present!

Priscilla was literally limping by the time she emerged on the Strand by the Thomas Jefferson League Building, which had housed the Wentletrap restaurant back in the twentieth century. Like the building, the rest of the Strand appeared both the same and markedly different from the street she remembered from the present. The thoroughfare was clogged with handsome carriages and drays loaded with cotton bales; the sidewalk teemed with citizens in old-fashioned attire and immigrants in colorful old-world clothing ranging from plumed Bavarian caps to Scottish kilts.

Navigating her way across a side street, Priscilla glimpsed the cluttered docks beyond on Water Street—and no sign of the modern ships and tugboats she would have expected. Instead, she viewed old-fashioned steamers, sailing vessels, and fishing boats. Stevedores were unloading cargo that ranged from barrels, crates, bags, and bales, to cuttings of bananas and kegs of beer. Hearing the sound of a train whistle, she caught the outline of a station house near the docks.

In the next block, she moved into an area of fashionable shops and eateries, and encountered businessmen who tipped their beaver hats as they passed, housewives who flicked their cool gazes at Priscilla before proceeding on with their parcels and bags, sailors who ogled her rudely. She glanced into the storefronts, passing a millinery shop, a haberdashery, an apothecary. At last she spotted a sign that read R. MACDOUGAL, JEWELER, and she ducked inside the small establishment.

Half an hour later, after haggling for some time with the Scottish jeweler, Ross MacDougal, Priscilla emerged minus J. Ackerly's engagement ring and with several hundred dollars tucked away in her frock pocket. At last she had her grubstake, and could even afford the luxury of taking a mule-drawn trolley back to the rooming house.

A sign emblazoned with SARAH O'SHANAHAN, LATEST LADIES' FASHIONS, caught Priscilla's eye next, and she eagerly swept toward the small shop. A bell clanged as she opened the glass-paneled door. Inside, she smelled the crisp scent of fabric sizing and perused several old-fashioned dressmaker's dummies arrayed in bustled, high-necked Victorian frocks. She was relieved to note a number of ready-made dresses hanging from pegs along the walls, as well as several tables stacked with lingerie and other feminine accessories.

"May I help you, miss?" called a lilting, Irish-accented voice.

Priscilla smiled at the plump older woman who came toward her dressed in a frilly, long-sleeved white blouse with a cameo brooch at the throat, and a long, dark skirt. The woman's gray-streaked hair was fashioned in a bun, a pencil was tucked behind one ear, and the edge of a measuring tape protruded from a pocket of her skirt. She looked very friendly with her bright cheeks and twinkling eyes.

"Are you Mrs. O'Shanahan?" Priscilla asked.

"Aye, I'm Miss Sarah O'Shanahan, the proprietress," came the warm reply.

Priscilla peeked at the price tag on one of the most elegant dresses, feeling relieved when she saw that it was only a few dollars. "Well, Miss O'Shanahan, I think you're in luck today. I've just arrived here from Oxford, Mississippi—minus my wardrobe."

"Oh?" The woman raised an eyebrow in pleasant surprise. She looked Priscilla over in her calico gown. "Begging your pardon, miss ... er ..."

"Priscilla Pemberton."

"Miss Pemberton. But you don't look as if you just arrived here from Mississippi."

Priscilla laughed nervously at the reference to her decidedly frontier attire. "Yes. Well, my trunk was stolen at the docks, and I had to beg for a change of clothing from a lady at the rooming house where I'm staying."

The woman uttered a sympathetic sigh. "Your things were stolen? What a shame. But I'm not surprised—there's so much riffraff hanging around the harbor these days. Law and order has gone to hell in a handbasket, if you ask me. What with the labor disputes and wildcat strikes, one never knows what ruckus may ensue at the docks."

Priscilla fought a smile as she wondered what this woman would think of the high-crime 1990s that she had just left. She briskly forged on. "At any rate, I'll be needing everything. And I would like to keep my purchases within a fifty-dollar range."

"Fifty dollars?" The woman's face lit up. "I think we can outfit you quite nicely, miss."

"Good."

Miss O'Shanahan helped Priscilla select items ranging from four stylish dresses with matching bonnets to several sets of corsets, bloomers, camisoles and petticoats, silk stockings, shoes, several reticules, winter and summer nightgowns, a warm wool jacket, and two shawls. Priscilla tried on the frocks in the back room, and Miss O'Shanahan decided some of them needed slight alterations, which she promised to complete by the next day. Charmed by the old-fashioned finery, Priscilla decided to wear home the outfit that fit her best—a striking blue and gold paisley taffeta coatdress, with coordinating blue velvet collar, cuffs, and trim on the skirt. The ensemble was completed by a feathered blue felt hat, a matching reticule, and a fringed gold silk parasol. Twirling in front of the full-length mirror and admiring herself in the old-fashioned finery, Priscilla mused that she truly looked like a nineteenth-century lady now—

And wasn't she one? She almost chuckled aloud at the realization that the accoutrements of Victorian times suited her well. Perhaps this *time period* suited her well ... She smiled at the novel thought.

By the time Priscilla and Miss O'Shanahan had finished gathering up Priscilla's new wardrobe, they were on a first-name basis, and Priscilla had a feeling she had acquired her first friend in Galveston. Priscilla had learned much about the talkative, friendly Sarah, notably that she was a spinster who had raised two children for a sister after the woman and her husband had both died of yellow fever while in their twenties. Sarah also tried to grill Priscilla on her own background, but Priscilla was careful to divulge very few details, other than the story Father O'Dooley had already contrived for her. Priscilla did admit to Sarah that she needed to find employment.

"A body can certainly tell you hail from a genteel background," Sarah commented while handing Priscilla the bill.

Slightly taken aback by the comment, Priscilla stared from the invoice—which totaled less than forty-eight dollars!—to the impressive stack of garments and accessories on the counter. "And why is that?" she asked, handing Sarah an old-fashioned fifty-dollar Federal note.

Sarah laid the bill on the counter and opened a cash box. "Why, your voice is so cultured, child. So many young folk here on the island sound like bumpkins, if you ask me. Our educational system is lamentable. No public schools as yet, though we're hopeful a bond issue may pass next year."

"I see."

Sarah handed Priscilla her change. "My niece Polly made herself a fine match—Mr. Carmichael, who owns the brick yard. They're not quite high society, you know, but prosperous. Polly would like to see her children—twins, a boy and girl, aged nine—associating with the offspring of the Browns, the Moodys, and such. But my poor heart has had no luck in getting her twins invited to the homes of the city's elite, and I'm thinking it's because the children sound like a couple of clay eaters. It's a tightly knit society we have here on the island ..." Abruptly Sarah broke into a smile. "But, you know, maybe if the children talked more like you, they'd have a chance."

Priscilla beamed back. "Why, thank you very much for the compliment."

"What kind of post are you seeking?" Sarah went on.

"I'm not sure—perhaps something in teaching."

"Then you have a university degree?"

From over a hundred years in the future, Priscilla thought ironically. "Er ... yes," she replied.

"As a matter of fact, I'd be happy to offer you employment here at the shop—since you'd be good with my customers, and I could spend more time dressmaking." Sarah winked at Priscilla. "But something tells me you're not the type to be satisfied as a shopgirl, young lady."

"Probably not," Priscilla answered diplomatically, "although I do appreciate the offer, Sarah. May I think about it?"

Sarah nodded. "Certainly." She gestured at the stack of garments on the counter. "What would you like done with these?"

"Well, I'd like to take a nightgown and some undergarments with me now. As for the rest, and the dresses needing alteration, can you have them delivered to Rose Gatling's boardinghouse on Broadway?"

"Or course. I'll have my man deliver everything to you first thing tomorrow morning."

"Wonderful," said Priscilla with a smile.

Sarah packed up the items Priscilla wanted to take with her. A moment later, she emerged from the shop with a small parcel tucked under her arm, only to bump up against a very familiar stranger—

"I beg your pardon, miss," the man said stiffly, stepping back and removing his bowler hat.

Priscilla's mouth dropped open. "Ackerly!" she gasped.

Chapter 7

"Are you all right, miss?"

Priscilla stared mystified at the blond, thirtyish man who had just removed his hat and stood staring at her with a combination of astonishment and concern. As in his picture, J. Ackerly Frost was tall and spare, with a thin, angular face accented by long sideburns and a goatee. He wore an old-fashioned striped brown suit, a tan waistcoat with gold watch fob glittering on the satin fabric, and an elaborate black cravat. He looked very much the dignified and sedate nineteenth-century banker—yet he also highly resembled Priscilla's fiancé back in the present! It was absolutely eerie to be staring at this man she knew yet didn't know!

Suddenly a gust of wind tore off Priscilla's feathered hat. Gasping in dismay, she watched a flash of bright feathers go scuttling away, and saw Ackerly dash after the whirling dervish. He retrieved her headgear, returned to her side, and, in the confusion, almost handed her his felt bowler instead of her own hat. They both laughed over his faux pas as he quickly substituted the correct item.

"Thank you, sir," said Priscilla breathlessly.

"You're welcome, miss." With a polite nod, he started off.

She rushed after him. "Ackerly, don't you recognize me?" she asked.

He turned to regard her with a quizzical frown, taking her in from head to toe, making Priscilla feel

67

grateful she had just changed from the homely calico into such an elegant outfit.

"I can't say I have ever had the pleasure of meeting you, young lady," he answered. "Are you one of our customers at the bank?"

"That's right, you wouldn't remember me," she muttered. "I suppose it was foolish of me to even ask, Ack— that is, Mr. Frost."

He smiled in bemusement. "Well, as president of our establishment, I do make it a policy to become acquainted with all our depositors."

Priscilla shook her head. "Oh, no, you misunderstand me. I'm not one of your depositors."

He raised a pale eyebrow. "Then how do you know my name, young lady?"

Thinking quickly, Priscilla explained, "Why, I saw your picture in yesterday's *News*. Congratulations on being honored by the chamber of commerce."

"Why, thank you." Drawing himself up with pride, he related, "We at Frost National Bank are pleased to be named the premier new Galveston enterprise of 1880. We may be a fledgling institution, but we are gaining more respect—and more new depositors— every day. We're giving the Moodys, Kempners, and Sealys a run for their money, if I may be so bold as to say so."

"I'm sure you are." Remembering the cash in her reticule, Priscilla impulsively added, "And I'd like to become your newest depositor."

His face lit up. "You would? Now, there's a young woman after my heart."

You have no idea, thought Priscilla ironically.

"I'm most pleased to make your acquaintance, miss . . . er . . ."

"Priscilla Pemberton," Priscilla replied, extending her gloved hand.

Ackerly shook her hand. "Good to meet you, Miss Pemberton. As a matter of fact, I'm on my way back to the bank right now. May I escort you there?"

"Why, certainly."

Ackerly offered his arm, and Priscilla smiled and perched her fingers on his sleeve. As they started down the street together, she reflected on how odd it was that here she was, walking down the streets of Galveston with J. Ackerly's great-great-grandfather!

Stealing a glance at him, Priscilla mused again that this J. Ackerly Frost certainly *looked* like the Ackerly she remembered—with his sharply etched nose, thin lips, hazel eyes, and pale complexion. Yet this man was obviously a total stranger who had no recollection of her at all.

What did she know of him? Scouring her mind, she remembered Ackerly in the present bragging to her about one particular legend concerning his great-great-grandfather. Indeed, several times he had pointed out to Priscilla a framed *News* article on his office wall that had given details of the famous incident.

According to the account, the first J. Ackerly had become something of a folk hero in Galveston when he had saved the fortunes of a number of citizens on St. Patrick's Day in 1881. J. Ackerly had ostensibly stopped by the Frost National Bank late that night, just in time to save the institution from being robbed by two desperadoes—who were named Flat Face and the Salado Kid, as Priscilla recalled. Evidently, an elderly, absentminded clerk at the bank had carelessly gone home and left the front door unlocked, the cash drawers full, thereby rendering the institution vulnerable to the thieves. With much of the community involved in St. Patrick's Day celebrations that night, legend held that the bank would surely have been robbed had not J. Ackerly stopped in to intervene when he did. Supposedly Ackerly had appeared just in time to single-handedly rout the villains.

Why, this event would occur only six months from now! Priscilla realized with awe.

She glanced again at the man striding beside her, deciding she would dub him "Ackerly I" to keep him straight from "Ackerly V" in her mind. Funny, this sedate man didn't look much like a hero. She wished she had asked Ackerly V for more details about his great-great-grandfather—such as who Ackerly I had married. According to Jake Blarney, Ackerly was a confirmed bachelor. But surely there was a wife somewhere in his future—else Ackerly V would never exist.

Suddenly Priscilla smiled. If she should marry this man, would she then become Ackerly V's great-great-grandmother? The prospect boggled the mind! Or perhaps there would not even be a J. Ackerly V, as such?

What a refreshing thought!

"Are you new in this community, young lady?"

J. Ackerly's voice cut into Priscilla's musings. "Ah, yes, Mr. Frost. I've just arrived from Oxford, Mississippi, and am looking to settle down in the Galveston community."

"Have you family here?"

"No, but my mother is best friends with a sister of Father Jamie O'Dooley. Do you know him?"

"Ah, yes, the associate rector at Saint Patrick's. You are Catholic?"

"No, actually, I'm Episcopalian."

His eyes lit with pleasant surprise. "Ah—you must join us for services at Trinity Episcopal."

"I'd be honored."

The two navigated their way across the Strand, pausing briefly to let a buggy go by, then continued down a side street, passing several shops.

"I don't mean to pry, Miss Pemberton," Ackerly went on, "but do you have plans now that you've joined our community?"

"I'll need to secure a job," Priscilla replied. "I'm eminently qualified—with a master's degree in English from Vanderbilt."

"My kingdom," he murmured, clearly amazed. "Why, when I was still living in New York, I remember Cornelius Vanderbilt mentioning his endowment to the Nashville institution. However, I wasn't even aware they had graduated any female students."

They graduate quite a few in the 1990s, Priscilla answered to herself, remembering her hard-won scholarship, and how she'd been snubbed by many of her upper-crust classmates. With Ackerly, she forced a nonchalant smile and smoothly prevaricated. "It's true that Vanderbilt has precious few female students. I began my studies when the institution was still Central University, and I was actually the second woman to win an advanced degree."

"Well, I'm very impressed," he declared with a grin. "You'll be seeking a post here in the teaching field?"

"Quite possibly."

"I'm sure the community will welcome a young woman with your high qualifications and obvious excellent breeding," he continued earnestly.

Priscilla could not have been more pleased. "Why, thank you, Mr. Frost."

Ackerly steered Priscilla toward a tall, narrow building that stood alone near a corner. "Here, we are—the Frost National Bank," he announced proudly. "Designed by Nicholas Clayton himself, and completed only six months ago."

Priscilla stared in fascination at the quaint, narrow structure. She remembered the tall edifice from the present, although there, it had been an antiques store, the Frost National Bank having moved to a modern high-rise many years ago.

This building was a delight, from its handsome oaken door with frosted-glass panes to its Grecian-style roof. All three stories were of red brick accented with blocks of white, creating a charming checkerboard effect amid a pleasing Victorian hodgepodge of jaunty colonnettes, rows upon rows of Romanesque windows, and carved classical pediments.

"Why, it's enchanting!" she breathed to J. Ackerly.

"Thank you, miss. We're most pleased with the edifice." He swung open the door and gestured for her to precede him inside.

Sweeping through the portal, Priscilla gazed appreciatively at the elegant burgundy carpeting, mahogany desks, tufted chairs, green ferns, and palms. She spotted a couple of harried-looking male clerks in dark suits scribbling away at the desks, and a teller in his cage behind the massive, marble-topped counter. The teller was counting out money for a depositor—a well dressed elderly man with a flowing white beard. He and Priscilla seemed to be the only customers in the establishment at the moment.

Ackerly led her toward a thin, elderly clerk who sat at the nearest desk. Spotting them, the man stood and smiled to Priscilla.

"Fitzgerald," Ackerly announced, "we have a new depositor—Miss Priscilla Pemberton, who has just joined our community from Oxford, Mississippi. Kindly help her fill out the proper forms."

"Yes, sir."

Ackerly bowed. "Well, Miss Pemberton—I'll leave you in the capable hands of my assistant."

She smiled. "Thank you. Nice meeting you, Mr. Frost."

"My pleasure," he said, walking off to speak with the other customer.

The clerk, who had bland features and a balding pate, gestured toward the chair in front of his desk. "Miss, if you'll take a seat."

The two made small talk as the clerk began filling out an account application for Priscilla. At once she noticed how absentminded the man was; he kept asking her to repeat information, and he made numerous errors. Indeed, when he asked her for the third time the name of the street where she lived, Priscilla wondered if she might be looking at the very forgetful clerk who would, on St. Patrick's Day, leave the bank's front door unlocked and render the cash drawers susceptible to the thieves!

"Oh, dear," he muttered, mopping his brow with a

linen handkerchief and grimacing at the application. "Look what I've done now ... I've misspelled both your first and your last names—and you're not really from Jackson, Mississippi, are you?"

Priscilla quashed a smile. "No, I'm from Oxford. Can't you just delete the errors with correction fluid?"

"Correction fluid?" the man repeated blankly.

Priscilla laughed over her blunder. "Oh, never mind. Why don't we just start over with a new application?"

He scratched his head. "Well, you know what they say ... 'Waste not, want not.' " Ruefully he admitted, "The truth is, I make so many mistakes, sometimes I wonder why Mr. Frost puts up with me ..."

Feeling intense sympathy for the confused man, Priscilla reached across the desk, took the application, wadded it up, placed it in her reticule, then nodded firmly. "There. They also say, 'Out of sight, out of mind,' don't they? Now, why don't I fill out a new application for you?"

He beamed his relief and reached for a fresh application. "If you say so, miss."

Priscilla filled out the new application, then drew out most of her remaining cash nest egg and handed it to the clerk.

"Your money will be very safe here," he assured her, licking his thumb then counting out the cash. "Mr. Frost ordered his vault all the way from Chicago—it's supposed to be impregnable."

Yes, and so is the bank—if one remembers to lock the front door and empty the cash drawers, Priscilla thought with wry humor.

As she and the clerk were finishing up, Ackerly strolled back over, smiling affably. "Is there anything else I can do for you, Miss Pemberton? If you are in need of references for a post, I'd be more than happy to oblige."

"Why, thank you, Mr. Frost," Priscilla said as she rose. "I'll definitely keep your kind offer in mind."

"May I see you out?"

"Certainly." She smiled at the clerk, who had also stood. "Nice to meet you, Mr. Fitzgerald. Thanks for your help."

"My pleasure, miss."

Escorting Priscilla toward the door, Ackerly said, "I do hope Fitzgerald assisted you with everything you needed."

Priscilla stifled a chuckle. "Actually, I had to assist him a bit," she confessed.

Ackerly glanced benignly toward the clerk. "Ah, yes, Fitzgerald is an absentminded soul, isn't he? But what can I say? If we didn't keep him on here, he'd likely have nowhere to go."

"It's very kind of you to overlook his shortcomings," murmured Priscilla.

"I try to assist my fellow man where I can."

She beamed. "What a refreshing attitude."

At the door, Ackerly lingered, regarding Priscilla speculatively. "I was wondering, Miss Pemberton . . ."

"Yes?"

He flashed her a smile. "Well, since you mention you are Episcopalian, I just wanted to say I'd be honored to escort you to services at Trinity on Sunday."

"Why, how kind of you, Mr. Frost," Priscilla responded graciously. "Are you sure it would not be an imposition?"

He grinned as he took and kissed her gloved hand. "Why, Miss Pemberton, escorting a lovely, refined young lady such as yourself would be a pleasure."

Priscilla was thrilled by his compliment. "Mr. Frost, you are a charmer," she teased.

"I thought I was only stating the obvious," he rejoined gallantly. "Besides, I know you'll enjoy Trinity Episcopal. Why, there might even be a post available for you at our church school. It is a small institution, but one never knows. In any event, I'll be happy to introduce you to Reverend Lyon and Miss Yard—and to numerous other prominent citizens who attend Trinity."

"How considerate of you."

"Where may I call for you, then?"

"At Mrs. Rose Gatling's rooming house on Broadway."

The gleam in his eyes bespoke his approval. "Ah, yes. Mrs. Gatling is a fine Christian woman and a true pillar of Saint Patrick's. I'll call for you promptly at ten-thirty, then."

"I'll look forward to it," said Priscilla brightly.

She thanked Ackerly and swept out the door. Walking back toward Broadway, she felt amazed by all that had just transpired. She had been in Galveston for less than a day, and already she had acquired lodging, a bank account, a potential suitor, and perhaps even some leads on a job. She may have lost Ackerly V yesterday, but now it seemed she had a chance to nab his great-great-grandfather, and start a new life—here.

Was this why she had traveled through time? she wondered with awe. Was this her second chance, her opportunity to escape the almost certain disgrace and heartache Ackerly had heaped on her in the present?

Still, she felt skeptical. Was it truly her destiny to have taken this radical detour in her life—and in time? How did she know life here would be any more a bed of roses than her existence had been back in the present? For one thing, Ackerly I might prove to be just as wishy-washy toward her as Ackerly V had been ... although so far he did seem very nice, and his indulgence toward poor Mr. Fitzgerald was commendable. Perhaps she had discovered Ackerly's prototype in a more human and caring time, when men were still governed by codes of honor and chivalry.

And there would be other critical differences here, she quickly realized: In Victorian times, Ackerly I would be held to a much higher moral standard than would his great-great-grandson. Unlike Ackerly V, Ackerly I could never afford to go off on a fling to London with some jezebel, and he would likely have to marry a refined, genteel woman in order to fully succeed in the community. He could never afford the luxury of a divorce, either; here, he would have to remain at least outwardly faithful to his wife for life, or risk devastating scandal.

Of course, like his great-great-grandson, Ackerly I didn't quite set Priscilla's pulse to racing. But even if Ackerly Frost I was less than perfect as a marriage prospect, Priscilla had realized long ago that men such as the Ackerlys offered a plain Jane such as herself the best opportunity for winning the stability and prestige she so craved. Especially when the alternative seemed to be a brash bumpkin such as she had encountered last night!

Again she wondered how Jake Blarney figured into the mystery. She was convinced she hadn't seen the last of the arrogant Irishman—just as she couldn't quite banish memories of his searing kiss and astounding marriage proposal.

Granted, his note in the bottle seemed to have set all these bizarre events into motion. Jake Blarney was now convinced she was meant to become the second Mrs. Blarney, just as Priscilla was equally certain he was wrong for her. Already she found Jake reminded her too strongly of her own father—who had also been handsome, passionate, and impetuous.

Priscilla sighed as painful memories came rushing in. She had been born and raised in a small, conservative Texas town south of San Antonio. Her father, Whitey McCoy, had been a rough-edged, short-tempered truck driver who drank and gambled, a man who had blamed his wife and child for every ill that ever befell him. When he drank, Whitey inevitably became verbally abusive toward Priscilla and her long-suffering mother, Beatrice. Priscilla would never forget Whitey McCoy's drunken tirades, when he had referred to his wife and child as "slimy leeches" or "spineless worms." Sometimes, Whitey had even struck Beatrice, and even now Priscilla shuddered at an image of herself as a small, hysterical child, calling the police. Whitey had been hauled off to jail a couple of times, only to be released when the down-trodden, frightened Beatrice refused to press charges. Still, these instances, along with Whitey's incarceration following several barroom brawls, had been enough to label the family as "trash" in the community, and the resulting ridicule Priscilla had suffered at school had been excruciating. Thanks to Whitey's excesses, both Priscilla and her mother had been forced to live in almost total isolation from the community, without friends or lives of their own.

Although Whitey had never struck Priscilla, the scars she bore from his mental abuse were just as bad. From the time she was little, Priscilla could remember her father tearing her down constantly, killing her confidence with his cruel criticisms, often calling her "stupid" and "ugly." When she began to approach puberty, she remembered him taunting that no man would ever want to marry a dull, homely girl such as herself.

At one time, Priscilla's mother had taken her aside and gently explained that her father's harsh attitude was not her fault, that Whitey was deeply disappointed because he had badly wanted a son, and Priscilla was their only offspring. Yet this revelation, rather than comforting Priscilla, had only increased her insecurities and sense of unworthiness. Priscilla hadn't blamed her mother, who had only sought to console her; but Beatrice's reassurance had backfired terribly, nonetheless.

Then, only months before Priscilla's thirteenth birthday, Whitey and Beatrice had had a huge fight after Whitey gambled away the mortgage money. Whitey walked out on his wife and child, leaving them destitute. All he left behind was his collection of bowling trophies—all of which Priscilla vengefully smashed out on the sidewalk. Priscilla and her mother lost their home, and Beatrice was forced to take a job at the local grocery store to try to make ends meet. The gossip and ostracism the two suffered in the Bible Belt town became worse than ever. And Priscilla vowed that one day she would secure a better life for herself and her mother, that they would both hold their heads up high and command respect in the community.

Beatrice became so embittered over Whitey's desertion that she went to legal aid in the city. Blessedly, a sympathetic young lawyer helped Beatrice get a divorce and change her and Priscilla's surnames back to Beatrice's maiden name of Pemberton. At that point, Priscilla would have been delighted to forget Whitey McCoy had ever existed—but, of course, she couldn't erase the scars he had left.

When Priscilla was fifteen, they received word from the authorities that Whitey had been found dead of an apparent heart attack in some sleazy Alabama motel. Priscilla remembered being astonished when her mother sobbed over the news. With tears of outrage and bewilderment in her own eyes, Priscilla demanded to know why her mother was crying, and why Beatrice had ever married such a monster in the first place. Her mother sadly replied, "You don't understand, honey. At one time, your father really was a sweet and charming man."

A sweet and charming bastard, Priscilla had thought.

A small life insurance policy from Whitey's employer—which, oddly, still bore Beatrice's name as beneficiary—helped the mother and daughter somewhat, until Priscilla's grandmother died several years later, leaving Beatrice a more respectable inheritance.

From that point on, Priscilla made it her life's work to prove Whitey McCoy had been wrong about her. She became valedictorian in high school and excelled on her achievement tests, winning the scholarship to Vanderbilt. She helped her mother become reestablished in Houston. And even though Priscilla was not especially popular with men, she swore she would never stoop to marrying a cruel rounder such as her father. When she met Ackerly, she felt her dreams were at last being realized, that she had found the

man who could give her the material security and
social prestige she felt she must have in order to survive, a man who would never make emotional demands on her and would leave her safe in the armor
she had erected against the world, safe to be the person she had created, not the needy, vulnerable person
she shielded away inside herself. She was even prepared to live a less than completely fulfilling life, in
return for knowing she would never again be threatened by the devastating pain of her youth.

Then Ackerly had dumped her ... Then *she* had
been dumped in time.

She thought again of Jake Blarney. One thing was
for certain: Just because she'd gone around the bend
time-wise did not mean she was about to abandon
her convictions and become a dairy farmer's bride,
no matter how masterfully Jake Blarney might kiss,
or how irresistible his daughters might be. True, Jake
Blarney was no Whitey McCoy, but he showed defi-
nite signs of being equally brash and hot-tempered.
Besides, a man who decided one day that he would
wed a total stranger the tide had dragged in might
just as impetuously set his cap on someone else the
next. Most critical of all, Jake Blarney offered neither
the security, the stature, nor the emotional invulnera-
bility Priscilla was determined to attain. He stirred
up her feelings and brought out the worst in her, the
part that might even be similar to her father. So Jake
hadn't a chance as far as she was concerned.

Priscilla continued back toward the rooming house
until, several blocks from Broadway, a display in the
window of a china shop caught her eye. She paused
to stare at an exquisite Old Paris china soup tureen,
and remembered a similar family heirloom her
mother had owned.

Oh, Lord, her mother! After suffering for so many
years, Beatrice at last had a good life and a nice job
Priscilla had found for her on the service staff at the
university. She and her mother were now good
friends, and already Priscilla missed her terribly.

What would Beatrice think when she returned to her beach house tomorrow—whenever that was—and found Priscilla missing? She would surely assume the worst, that Priscilla had drowned in the Gulf. She would panic, and a search would be called.

And what of Ackerly V, when he, too, found out she had disappeared? Wouldn't he feel at least some regret? Although Priscilla's feelings were terribly mixed regarding him, she had to concede that she had no absolute proof that their engagement was terminated. To be honest, she did regret that she'd never gotten her chance to speak with him one last time, to see if he might have come to his senses. Like his great-great-grandfather, Ackerly V had possessed some good traits—he was active in several charities, and fond of Priscilla's mother. Indeed, Priscilla took some comfort from the knowledge that he would likely try to help Beatrice through this difficult period.

Was there any way she could let him and the others she'd left behind know she was all right? But how, unless she threw herself into the Gulf again and risked drowning? Perhaps that was what had happened to her in the first place, and she was now living an entirely new life. Oh, it was all too confusing!

Priscilla was about to trudge on past the window when her eye was caught by a display of several long-necked bottles identical to the one she'd found in the surf yesterday. On a whim, she swept inside and picked up one of the clear bottles with its cork.

"May I help you, miss?" asked a young female clerk.

"Yes, I'd like to buy this bottle," said Priscilla.

"Of course, miss."

Priscilla followed the clerk to the counter and paid for the bottle, which cost only a few pennies. She lingered a moment, pulling the crumpled bank application from her reticule. She nodded toward the inkwell on the counter. "May I borrow your pen?"

"Certainly."

Priscilla tore off a shred of the application, turned it over, and smoothed out the crumpled scrap. She almost laughed aloud at her own silly impulse to write a note and place it in the bottle, hoping to communicate with another century.

But perhaps she could. The magic had worked for Jake Blarney, hadn't it? Why shouldn't it work for her, as well?

But what should she say? And to whom should she address the missive? Her mother? She shook her head. No, her mother was far too inclined toward panic and would become hysterical to learn Priscilla was dashing off notes from the year 1880.

She would write to Ackerly, then. But again, what? Perhaps simplicity was best, she mused. And if she wanted the "magic" to remain in effect, then she had best wax poetic again, as well ... something easy enough for her.

After concentrating fiercely for a moment, she scribbled:

> *Ackerly*
> *Please rescue me*

Staring at the message, Priscilla giggled at her own melodramatics. At least she'd been succinct—a virtue she'd tried to imbue in her freshman comp students. She replaced the pen in the inkwell, blew on the note, then folded it and stuffed it in the bottle, replacing the cork.

"Planning to send a message in a bottle, miss?" asked the bemused clerk.

"You might say so."

With bottle in hand, Priscilla left the shop and crossed over to Bath Street, where she caught a mule-drawn trolley bound for the beach. The trolley deposited her only feet away from the surf. She strolled out to where the tiny whitecaps tickled her feet, and stared out at the endless green waves—the very same waves that had carried her away yesterday, the very same ocean. *So near, yet so far away.*

"Ackerly, what has happened to me?" she cried.

Only the roar of the waves answered.

She sighed. "Well, here goes nothing."

Priscilla tossed the bottle out into the surf and watched it bob about. Again she laughed at her own absurdity. She waited until the tide sucked the bottle out beyond her line of vision. Finally, hearing the bell of another approaching trolley, she rushed back to catch the car back to town.

Twenty minutes later, when she walked back inside the rooming house, she was met by a frowning Rose Gatling. "You have a gentleman caller in the ladies' parlor, miss," the woman announced coolly.

"Thank you." Perplexed, Priscilla started toward the parlor. Had J. Ackerly I already come to visit her? She wondered why the prospect did not excite her nearly as much as it should have.

She stepped inside the room and saw him standing near the window—dressed in a black suit, his dark hair and muscular physique outlined in the midday light that poured through the window.

He turned and grinned.

"Jake Blarney!" she cried. "What are you doing here?"

Chapter 8

Jake Blarney stepped forward to smile at Priscilla. Didn't she look a fine sight, he thought, bedecked in that elegant taffeta coatdress and feathered hat, with her lovely curls tucked away in a prim little bun? She had certainly acclimated herself to Galveston Island with dispatch and ease—and the image of her there, confronting him with such spirit, such fire in those fine green eyes, filled him with admiration and desire. So proper, she was, and so self-righteous, she made a man ache to unravel her. He had missed her since she had left his cottage this morning—and regrettably, they seemed to have gotten off on the wrong foot.

"What am I doing here?" he teased back, stepping closer. "Why, I've come to collect my bride, of course."

Priscilla glowered at the maddening Irishman who stood across from her, though she had to admit that Jake Blarney cut a masterful figure in his trim black suit, with his thick, curly dark hair combed into place and his clean-shaven face such a devastating portrait of strong, handsome male planes and angles. Again she was struck by the vivid blue of his eyes, eyes so intense, they seemed to be undressing her now. Even his scent enticed her—a pleasing mix of bay rum and shaving soap.

Even though he loomed head and shoulders above her, she bucked up her spine and faced him down. "Mr. Blarney, will you kindly cease your preposter-

83

ous claims that I'm to become your wife? Especially here, where we might be overheard! I thought I had gotten rid of you this morning—"

"Ah, lass, but you won't be getting rid of me—not so easily," he cut in devilishly.

"No, it's obvious you're determined to make a thorough pest of yourself!" she fired back.

He only chuckled. "I was concerned about you, lass. What can I say?"

"Dare I hope you'll say you're leaving?" she inquired caustically.

"Not before we've had a little chat." He looked her over thoroughly. "It appears you've been busy since we parted company. You've acquired a smart new wardrobe, by the looks of it. Where did you get the money, lass?"

"That's none of your damned business!"

He appeared amused over her show of temper. "I could have sworn you arrived on my stoop penniless last night. And actually, I much preferred the scandalous little frock you wore at the time."

"You would," she sneered.

He stared her in the eye in an intent manner that made her heartbeat quicken. "The skimpy little shift made you appear like a waif—and so very desirable."

Priscilla said nothing, although she felt hot color flood her face.

He sauntered off and absently stroked the curling edge of a fern. "You left the frock at the cottage, you know—along with the most scandalous pair of drawers I've ever seen in my life."

"Oh, you are crude!"

Undaunted, he flashed her a decadent grin. "You're welcome to come back and fetch the items, any time."

"No, thank you."

He feigned a wounded air. "You mean you won't be coming back to visit us?"

She ground her jaw. "Mr. Blarney—kindly state your business, then leave."

"A feisty one, aren't you?" he asked mildly.

She glared.

He strode over to the fireplace and rested his elbow on the mantel, turning to regard her solemnly. "First, I must know, have you come to your senses as yet?"

"What do you mean?" she asked cautiously.

"Last night you were rambling of such strange matters—cabs and telephones, and your mother living near us on the beach."

"Oh . . . that."

"Have you found your mum as yet?"

"Er . . . no."

He stroked his jaw and scowled. "I'm figuring maybe that's because you and she both live up on the mainland—and you became confused when the tide swept you off to me."

"Good," replied Priscilla. "I'm glad you've figured everything out." She started toward the door. "Now, if you'll excuse me—"

He rushed after her and caught her arm. "Whoa, lassie! I'm not finished with my . . . er . . . business yet."

She turned to him scathingly. "Unhand me!"

"Only if you'll listen."

"Very well. Proceed."

He dropped his hand and stared soulfully into bright, defiant eyes. "My business is, I miss you, lass. And the babes miss you, too."

Momentarily disarmed by his husky, tender tone and the mention of the girls, Priscilla managed to retort, "The babies miss me? They don't even know me."

"Ah, but they do. They know they want you as their future mum."

Priscilla clenched her fists. "Mr. Blarney, please!"

"I've already been by the courthouse to see about our marriage license. 'Twill take a few days, I'm told, but then we'll be well fixed and can proceed."

Priscilla went wide-eyed. "If you aren't the most arrogant, presumptuous—"

Calmly he forged on. "I didn't want to mention this last night, but actually, we haven't a moment to spare in planning our nuptials. You see, ever since Lucinda deserted me and drowned with the tonic salesman, her sister in Houston, Octavia, has been trying to take the wee ones away from me. The witch has even threatened legal action. Don't you think I'll have a much stronger case with a mother for the babes?"

"Aha!" She regarded him in dawning horror. "So that's why you've been coming on to me like an oversexed teenager! You just want to use me to keep your children!"

He scowled murderously. "You don't think wee Sallie and wee Nellie are deserving of a proper mum?"

"That's not my point at all! You are manipulating me, exploiting me—"

"Not just to get a mum for me babes." Abruptly he pulled her close and raked his gaze over her in an unhurried manner that made her feel hot and flustered. "As it happens, I'm dying to possess your lovely body."

For a moment, Priscilla could only stare at him, overcome by shock, excitement, and traitorous lust. At last she gathered the strength to shove him away, and she stalked off toward the fireplace. A painful memory stabbed her, of her father sneering, *Who would ever want a plain Jane like you? You'll never be good enough* ...

When she spoke, her voice trembled. "I'm not lovely, Mr. Blarney," she declared bitterly. "You'll not earn my esteem by lying."

Unexpectedly her arm was seized and she was pulled around to face his amazed countenance. "But you are, lass." He reached out to stroke her cheek. "You're as fair as they come with that Titian hair and those vibrant green eyes. I'm dying to have you, you know."

"You're a three-horned liar!"

He drew her closer, his countenance forbidding, his blue eyes blazing down at her. "Listen to me, Priscilla. I never lie. Maybe you're not a raving beauty, but you're a bonny lass, and you're mine. The tide brought you to me, and I won't be giving you up. You can fight the Fates—and me—if you choose, but you can't win."

Staring at him, so darkly sexy and determined, Priscilla felt terrified of believing him and yet desperate not to. She knew she had to get him out of her hair, out of her life. He was too dangerous, too tempting, and he threatened the self-possession she clung to as her only barrier to the deep wounds inside her. She knew to her soul that she could never marry him, however handsome and seductive he might be. For Jake Blarney *was* too much like her father—too volatile, too unpredictable. She and Jake came from totally different worlds, and she could never become a dairy farmer's wife.

She gathered her forbearance. "Sir, I have had quite enough of your ranting and raving about how I am meant to become your wife. As far as I'm concerned, your claims that the tide brought me to you are pure blarney—"

"Are they, now?" he mocked. "That seems to be precisely what occurred—and there's no doubt 'tis a bit of the blarney you've ended up with."

She fought a smile at his clever humor. "Whatever. The fact remains that I can never marry you—"

"And why not?" he demanded.

"Because you're a bumpkin, sir! A man just like . . ."

"Yes?"

Realizing how close she had come to blurting out the truth, Priscilla muttered, "Never mind. You're crude and uncouth, and not the kind of man I can ever trust. I want nothing to do with you!"

She watched a series of emotions cross his handsome face—astonishment, followed by anger, and then steely resolve. "So you think you're too good for me, do you?" he demanded.

Put on the defensive, she stammered, "I—I never said that."

"You did, if not in so many words. I suppose you think you'll be happier with some pantywaist like J. Ackerly Frost—"

"Yes!" she cut in. "I'll have you know Mr. Frost is not a pantywaist. Furthermore, he is escorting me to church on Sunday—"

"He is *what?*"

"You heard me!"

"Over my dead body, he will!"

"Then we shall be careful not to trip."

After hurling her a glare, Jake began to pace, scowling ferociously and muttering curses under his breath. "I can't believe that mollycoddle is taking you to worship among his hoity-toity Episcopalian friends—"

"I'll have you know, sir, that *I'm* an Episcopalian!"

He stopped in his tracks, aghast. "Bite your tongue, woman!"

"It's the truth."

He appeared utterly confounded, thrusting his fingers through his hair. "I can't believe the tides would have brought me an *Episcopalian!*"

"Well, that's precisely what the tides did," she declared archly. "And since you, sir, are an Irish Catholic, it appears we have nothing in common."

He appeared both indignant and determined, his heated gaze sliding over her again in a way that made her stomach twist. "Nothing in common, eh? I might have to call your bluff on that account, lassie."

She blushed and turned away.

Jake approached her, laying his hand on her shoulder. She flinched, and he tightened his grip.

" 'Tis not an impediment lassie," he murmured thickly. "You'll convert."

She whirled to face him. "To what?"

"To the Church," he answered with amusement. "And to my way of thinking."

"I'll do nothing of the sort!" she asserted. "And furthermore, I'll associate with whomever I please—including Mr. Frost."

Priscilla was totally unprepared for what happened next. Even as she turned on her heel to leave, Jake Blarney muttered a curse, hauled her against him, and seized her lips with his own. Despite her outrage, the shock of his hot mouth on hers was deeply thrilling. She tried to fight him, squirming to get free and protesting incoherently, but Jake only crushed her closer until all resistance faded. With his muscular chest flattening her breasts, his mouth possessing hers so masterfully, and the male scent of him exhilarating her senses, Priscilla soon went weak and giddy. Never had Ackerly kissed her with such consuming passion! Jake Blarney might be an outrageous boor, but Priscilla had to admit he was also the most intense, sexy man she had ever met in her life.

When his rough tongue plunged inside her mouth, then began to thrust and retreat in the most tantalizing manner, Priscilla could only moan deep in her throat. When his fingers stroked the side of her breast, she came to her senses and shoved him away.

"Why, you—"

With a maddening chuckle, Jake grabbed her wrists and pulled her close again.

Priscilla struggled wildly to get free, trying to duck his descending lips. "No! No!"

"Yes, lass."

He pinned her against him and kissed her again, thoroughly. When she wiggled rebelliously, his menacing pinch on her behind, instead of enraging her, only made her melt. When she stopped fighting, he gentled his kiss, eased the restriction of his arms, and seduced her with gentle flicks of his tongue.

His unexpected tenderness was devastating. Soon Priscilla was traitorously responding, opening her mouth wider to him, teasing his tongue with her own, and wrenching a tortured groan from him. Her senses were so filled with him, her pulse was pounding so madly, she feared she might faint. When at last the kiss ended, she panted for breath.

"We're meant to be, lass," he whispered against her cheek. "You know you felt the magic, just like I did, last night when we first kissed. You'll be Mrs. Blarney by week's end—"

"I'll be nothing of the sort!" she asserted, if weakly.

He pulled back to scowl at her. "Then why did you just kiss me as if you'd welcome me inside you?"

Priscilla gulped. "I—I don't know."

His expression grew murderous. "Have you ever kissed Ackerly Frost that way?"

"That's none of your—"

"Have you?" he roared.

"N-No," she answered, too rattled to prevaricate.

"Good."

Even as he moved in to kiss her again, Priscilla sprang back and held up both hands, eyeing him in panic. "Stay away from me or I shall scream!"

He paused, amused by her defiance. Then a frown drifted in as he stared at her left hand.

Finally he chuckled. "Where's the ring, lass?"

"I beg your pardon?"

Jake's eyes danced with devilment. "If you're making time with J. Ackerly, then why aren't you wearing his ring?"

"Wh-What ring?" she stammered.

He shook a finger at her. "Don't you be lying to me, lassie. I'm talking about the ring you flaunted in my face last night."

"Oh, that ring."

"Aye."

"Well, it's none of your damned business!" she asserted.

"Pawned it to get your fine new duds, didn't you?" he taunted. "So it appears you're not nearly as captivated by J. Ackerly as you're letting on. Or has *himself* already demanded you return his extravagant little bauble?"

Jake's words, more accurate than he ever could have known, chafed badly at Priscilla's pride. "You, sir, are a contemptible boor! Now, get out of here before I have the landlady call the police!"

"Oh, I'll be taking my leave, lassie, and giving you a chance to cool off. But I'll be back." He winked at her. "You see, your fiery kisses have left me hungry for more."

"Go to the Devil!"

"I'll go, lass, but I'm leaving a warning." He leveled a stern glance at her. "Go to church with J. Ackerly Frost on Sunday, and you'll be ruing the consequences."

"I'll be ruing nothing of the sort!"

Ignoring her outburst, he added obdurately, "Kiss him like you just kissed me, and I'll spank you."

"Oh!" Priscilla cried. "You are a brute!"

The very softness of his tone—and the sudden hardness of his gaze—sent a chill over her. "I am your future husband, lass. You've been warned."

Then he was gone, leaving Priscilla to tremble in the wake of his departure. She could not believe Jake had just barged in on her, uninvited, and so presumptuously tried to take over her life. It was unnerving, especially now that she was beginning to see her journey through time as her second chance to have the lifetime of her dreams—an existence Jake Blarney clearly intended to sabotage for her! She felt frightened, deeply shaken—especially by her own devastating response to his stolen kisses. He was entirely wrong for her, yet he possessed the ability to get through to her as no other man ever had before.

"Oh, God, he's going to ruin everything!" she cried, pacing the room and wringing her hands.

He was a charmer, all right, but he was brash, dangerous, and demanding. Her father had possessed that same Irish charm—and a very volatile temper. Priscilla had no intention of ever getting caught up with a man like that, of living the hellish existence her mother had . . .

Priscilla sighed deeply as she remembered her parents' tenth wedding anniversary. For once her father had come home in a good mood—not drunk, not dragging along his obnoxious poker buddies to trash the house. He had even brought her mother flowers. The three of them had shared a civil meal together—until afterward, when Beatrice had discovered that the money she had squirreled away in a flour canister was missing.

Beatrice had turned indignantly to Whitey. "You snatched the money I was saving! You used it for your gambling debts!"

Her father's face had darkened in fury. "And why not? It's my money, ain't it? You stole it from me, right?"

"I saved it from the grocery money as a down payment on Priscilla's braces!" cried her mother, trembling with outrage.

Her father had turned to sneer at Priscilla. "You really think braces will help an ugly kid like her? She's a lost cause if I ever seen one."

Even as Priscilla had reeled from her father's cruel words, Beatrice had continued raving. "The dentist says she has to have braces! I can't believe you actually stole from your own child!"

Whitey had risen up, waving a fist. "You drove me to it, woman—you and your brat!"

The rest had been horrible—the yelling, the physical abuse, and her mother's tears. Whitey had stormed out, and Priscilla had comforted her heartbroken mother. Even now, rage welled in her at the memory of her mother and her hunched together at the kitchen table, shuddering in the wake of Whitey's departure, amid broken dishes and bitter tears. Whitey had always won that way, even when Beatrice had tried to stand up to him, by exercising his temper and his superior strength.

Ultimately Priscilla's grandmother had paid for her

braces. It had been deeply humiliating for Priscilla to know that her father hadn't cared enough to provide for his own child . . .

Priscilla shuddered at the prospect of repeating her parents' turbulent history with Jake. Granted, Jake didn't seem to possess Whitey's sadistic streak, but he *had* overwhelmed her physically today. He was strong-willed and determined to dominate her, just as her father had been with her mother. Jake would make her life an emotional roller-coaster ride, when she so badly craved safety, peace, and security.

Besides, if pushed too far, who knew what Jake Blarney might actually do? Heavens, the man had even threatened to spank her! Jake had demonstrated that he had the potential for charm . . . and danger.

Jake Blarney was engrossed in thought as he drove his buggy down the deserted beach toward his cottage. He'd enjoyed seeing Priscilla again—and had delighted in having her in his arms—although it was obvious to him now that winning over the stubborn colleen would be an uphill battle.

Why was she so determined to resist him, and to set her cap on a snob like Ackerly Frost? Why couldn't she believe they were meant to be, that it was her destiny to become his bride and a mother to his wee babes? Had he been wrong about her? Would she turn away from a match made in heaven to seek social status and wealth?

He frowned. She'd assailed him today, calling him a boor and a bumpkin, among other scathing epithets. She'd said he reminded her of someone . . . a person she refused to name. Was that her problem, then? Did she bear some scar from her past? Had some other man hurt her, a bloke who reminded her of himself? Who had wounded her so deeply that she had closed her mind to him, and to the possibility of loving a man of humble station?

One thing was certain. He should not have threatened to spank her. 'Twas not the way to ease her fears and win her trust, no matter how badly she had provoked him. Although Jake saw nothing wrong with a little good-natured wrestling with a woman in bed, strictly to enhance the enjoyment of sex, he had no respect for any man who would force a woman, or try to control her by exercising his superior strength. Indeed, Jake had never struck a woman in his life, not even Lucinda on that day, not long before she'd left him, when he had discovered she'd gone off for a stroll on the beach, leaving the babies alone, screaming and terrified, in their cradles.

Then why had he acted so menacing today? He supposed it was because the thought of Priscilla kissing Ackerly Frost as passionately as she had kissed him made him demented.

Ah, that kiss! As wonderful as it had been, 'twas not the kiss of a maiden lady, Jake mused darkly. Was Priscilla not a virgin, then? He frowned, unsettled by the possibility. What kind of mate had the tides brought him? The lass was truly an enigma . . . but her secrets would not be safe from him.

In time, he would learn everything about her, he vowed. In time, she would be his.

Chapter 9

On Sunday morning Priscilla felt consumed with excitement as she prepared for church and her outing with J. Ackerly. She had been in 1880 Galveston for several days now, and had spent much of her time exploring the community. The feeling that she was living some sort of dream was gone now. Whatever had happened to her, she seemed to be stuck in the late nineteenth century.

One of her biggest remaining anxieties concerned the pain her disappearance may have caused her mother; she missed Beatrice and remained worried about her. She feared that those she had left behind had by now assumed she had drowned—and again, she reflected that perhaps she had. Aside from her moment of weakness when she had dispatched her note to the twentieth-century Ackerly, she had begun to feel more and more that perhaps her plight was not such a tragedy. Perhaps she was still meant to become Priscilla Pemberton Frost, married not to Ackerly V, but to his great-great-grandfather, Ackerly I.

If only Jake Blarney didn't spoil her chances of success! Every time she recalled his visit several days ago, his presumptuousness and brash kisses, she became overwrought. Although his behavior had maddened her, she couldn't deny that his kisses had thrilled her to a degree she'd never before experienced. Indeed, never in her life had Priscilla been wooed by such a handsome, sexy man—and never had she been pursued by a man who was more wrong for her. She fervently hoped Jake would soon give up and stop pestering her, although she had a sinking feeling he would not. He seemed stubbornly fixated on his contention that she was his destiny, the bride the tides had brought to him—and following her own bizarre experience, she had to concede his thinking had a certain logic.

What scared her most of all was how drawn she felt toward him, even as determined as she was to resist. Remembering how he had decimated her defenses with his lips, she feared what might happen if he maneuvered her off alone again. She certainly didn't trust him—nor could she completely trust herself. Priscilla was totally unaccustomed to feeling out of control of her life or her feelings—she liked being associated with men she could control and manipulate to her purposes, men like the Frosts. Jake Blarney was one hundred percent loose cannon—dangerous, unpredictable, and potentially disastrous to her life and goals.

Priscilla stood at the dressing table eyeing her appearance critically. Days ago, Miss O'Shanahan's man had delivered the rest of her wardrobe, and now she wore her finest outfit, a forest green serge suit-dress, beautifully tailored, with braid on the lapels, cuffs, and high collar of the jacket, and with a modest bustle embellishing the straight, pleated skirt. She wore black silk stockings and shiny, high-topped black leather shoes. Her hair fell in orderly curls to her shoulders, and a small, green straw hat trimmed with silk tea roses graced the crown of her head. Grabbing her lace-trimmed dark green silk parasol and twirling about in front of the pier mirror, Priscilla decided she truly loved dressing up in such elegant, old-fashioned finery. Although she missed some of the conveniences of the twentieth century, there was much about the Victorian age that appealed to her.

Hearing a rap at her door, Priscilla called, "Come

in!" and Mary O'Brien, Priscilla's neighbor across the hallway, swept inside.

"Good morning, Priscilla," Mary remarked in her Irish brogue. "My, what a smart outfit."

"Thanks, Mary. Good morning to you."

Priscilla smiled at the young woman whom she had met in the upstairs hallway three days ago. A shopgirl at an apothecary on the Strand, Mary had gone out of her way to make Priscilla feel at home and help her get acclimated. Dark-haired, rosy-cheeked, pretty but slightly plump, Mary looked charming today in her long-sleeved, ruffled and bustled frock of brown and gold calico.

"Just getting ready to meet me aunt Phoebe for mass at Saint Patrick's," announced Mary as she joined Priscilla near the mirror and peered critically at her own reflection. She straightened her straw hat and tucked a stray hairpin into her bun.

"You look delightful," Priscilla assured her.

Mary beamed. "Why, thank you. And if you don't make a fetching portrait yourself."

"Do you really think so?" Priscilla asked wistfully.

Mary looked her over and nodded firmly. "Oh, my, yes. That outfit is perfect for you, bringing out the red in your hair and the green of your eyes." The girl shook a finger at Priscilla and grinned. "You'll be turning male heads today, I'll wager."

Priscilla laughed. "Well, I'm hoping Mr. Frost will be pleased."

"I'm sure he will be," the girl added with less enthusiasm.

Priscilla frowned. She had mentioned Ackerly to Mary several times now, and invariably the girl's attitude had grown cool on hearing his name. She hadn't as yet mentioned Jake Blarney, although she assumed the girl knew him, since they both attended St. Patrick's.

"I do so hope to make a good impression today," she confided, "since this is my first real foray into Galveston society."

"Oh, you'll do fine." Mary extended a folded fan toward Priscilla. "And here's a little souvenir for good luck."

"Oh, Mary, you shouldn't have." Taking the gift, Priscilla spread the sticks of the colorful fabric fan and stared at a lovely scene of couples waltzing at a cotillion. "How exquisite!"

Mary waved her off. "Oh, it's just a cheap little gewgaw, made of bamboo and handkerchief linen. Wish I could have afforded one of the silk and ivory ones Mr. Peebles gets in at the apothecary, but they're too dear. Anyway, I thought the scene was pretty, and when it gets hot in church, that fan will suffice as well as the most expensive ones."

Priscilla waved the fan to demonstrate. "Oh, yes. You're a dear. Thank you very much."

The girl nodded. "Well, I'd best be going or I'll miss my trolley and be late to mass. Aunt Phoebe keeps insisting I'm too young to live on my own, so I guess I'd best step lively and not give her any more ammunition."

"Let's have tea this afternoon," Priscilla suggested.

"I'd be pleased to. And good luck with Mr. Frost."

As Mary was heading toward the door, another rap sounded. Priscilla called, "Who is it?"

"Mrs. Gatling," came the cool response.

Priscilla and Mary exchanged a forbearing glance. Mary had already informed her that the other boarders disliked the overbearing, snoopy landlady so much that they called her "Gatling gun."

"Come in," Priscilla called pleasantly.

"Got to run, dear," whispered Mary, dashing for the door and opening it just as Mrs. Gatling strolled in.

Gowned in sedate black silk, Rose Gatling frowned at Mary as the girl swept past her. She settled her frosty gaze on Priscilla. "Miss Pemberton."

Determined to kill the old biddy with kindness, Priscilla replied, "Why, good morning, Mrs. Gatling. How nice to see you. Isn't it a lovely day? I was just enjoying the fragrance drifting up from the rose garden—"

"Now, none of that," cut in the widow sternly. "Miss, you are causing me no small amount of grief."

"What do you mean?" Priscilla said, bewildered. "What have I done?"

The woman waved a hand in exasperation. "What have you done? Only caused a scandal, on the Lord's day, no less. Do you realize there are two gentlemen waiting downstairs to take you to church?"

"Two?" Priscilla was flabbergasted.

"Yes—and both of them looking ready to fight a duel, I must add. I'll have you know, miss, that I run a decent establishment here. I'll not be putting up with these shenanigans."

Priscilla was appalled. "Of course not, and you are absolutely right, Mrs. Gatling. I'll deal with the situation at once—and I assure you it will never happen again."

The woman nodded in grim satisfaction. "See that it doesn't," she snapped, turning with dignity and leaving the room.

"Oh, brother," Priscilla groaned.

She grabbed her reticule and headed out of the room, wondering what horror awaited her downstairs. She had no doubt that the maddening Irishman, Jake Blarney, had shown up along with Ackerly. Oh, she should have known better after he issued his ultimatum the other day, cautioning her not to go to church with Ackerly. What a fool she had been even to tell him of her plans . . .

But she had never expected him to behave in such an audacious manner, gate-crashing her Sunday date!

She rushed down the stairs and into the ladies' parlor, skidding to a halt just inside the door. Just as she suspected, both Jake and Ackerly were present, seated across from each other in velvet side chairs near the fireplace. Ackerly wore a striped brown suit, with ascot and stickpin, Jake a less fashionable frock coat and dark trousers. Ackerly appeared irate, Jake—damn his eyes!—secretly amused.

"What is the meaning of this?" she demanded.

Spotting her, both men shot to their feet and said in unison, "I've come to take you to church."

Priscilla ground her jaw as the two men exchanged glares. She swung her fuming gaze toward Jake. "Mr. Blarney, what are you doing here?"

He grinned, and Priscilla could almost feel her blood pressure shooting up. "Why, I've come to protect your interests, lassie, since you've obviously no father or male relation to speak up for you."

Before Priscilla could respond to his presumptuous statement, Ackerly inquired coolly, "I take it you know this scoundrel, Miss Pemberton?"

"Scoundrel?" she repeated, taken aback.

Jake responded in her stead. "Aye," he said nastily to Ackerly, "the lass knows me, and bear in mind that I'm more than man enough to box the ears of a mollycoddle such as yourself."

Priscilla gasped.

Ackerly had gone livid. "You, sir, are a miserable boor, and a villain." Sternly he regarded Priscilla. "Miss Pemberton, how did you come to be acquainted with this man, and why does he presume he is escorting you to church?"

"He is doing nothing of the sort!" Priscilla retorted, fuming as she noted Jake's expression of smug pleasure. "I did meet Mr. Blarney the other day. I—I was lost and he offered me directions—"

"Directions, and a lot more," Jake put in devilishly.

Humiliated by his comment, and fully aware of Ackerly's astounded expression, Priscilla snapped to Jake, "You, sir, will cease casting aspersions on my character and leave us at once."

He shook his head. "I ain't leaving, fair Priscilla." He leveled a scowl at Ackerly. "Not until I ascertain Mr. Frost's intentions toward you. For all I know, he could be aiming to steal you off for some nefarious purpose."

"Oh!" Priscilla cried.

"My intentions toward Miss Pemberton are none of your affair," retorted Ackerly.

"Agreed!" seconded Priscilla.

Jake crossed his arms over his chest and replied belligerently, "Then I cannot allow you to escort Miss Pemberton anywhere."

"And you presume to stop me, sir?" Ackerly queried, his voice rising.

"Aye," said Jake with sadistic relish.

Ackerly took an aggressive step toward Jake. "Then it appears you have left me no alternative, sir, but to put you out!"

Jake roared with laughter. "A milksop like you couldn't put out a cat."

Ackerly raised a fist. "Are you calling me a coward, sir?"

"Aye."

"You miscreant!"

All at once, Mrs. Gatling burst into the room, eyeing the ongoing confrontation in horror. "What is going on here? Raised voices on the Sabbath, no less! I insist you two *gentlemen* settle this matter outside!"

Appearing miserably embarrassed, Ackerly turned to the landlady. "Mrs. Gatling, I apologize if we've disturbed your peace." He glanced irately at Jake, then nodded stiffly to Priscilla. "Miss Pemberton, under the circumstances, I'm afraid I have no choice but to leave."

"I understand, Mr. Frost," she conceded miserably.

A jerking muscle in his cheek betraying his agitation, Ackerly clapped on his hat and sedately exited the room. Priscilla felt mortified.

"Well, Miss Pemberton?" inquired an icy feminine voice. "Can I depend on you to see your other caller out? Or must I summon the sheriff?"

Priscilla turned to the irate landlady, who stood with hands balled on her hips near a very amused Jake Blarney. "Mrs. Gatling, kindly allow me to handle my own affairs—"

"Your affairs, Miss Pemberton?"

Priscilla's patience was wearing thin. "Mrs. Gatling, I assure you I am in no need of your assistance."

"Well, I never!" huffed Mrs. Gatling. "You, miss, will be packed and out of here by day's end."

"With pleasure—if you will refund my rent money."

"With pleasure," the woman retorted, turning on her heel and sweeping from the room.

Priscilla heard Jake's maddening chuckle behind her and whirled to face him with eyes blazing. For a moment, she was too outraged to speak.

"Ah, lass, you really put that old battle-ax in her place," he declared unabashedly. "You've such spirit—I'm proud of you."

She shook a fist at him. "How dare you even address me, you insufferable brute, when you have caused this entire debacle—and thoroughly enjoyed yourself while you were at it!"

"Aye, lassie," he conceded smugly.

"Don't you dare smile, or take pride in your infamy!" she shot back. "I can't believe you had the nerve to show up here again, uninvited and unwanted. Now you have ruined everything for me. God only knows the scandal this will cause! Why, it's the year 1880, for heaven's sake!"

"Aye, 'tis," he murmured, perplexed.

Waving a hand, she continued to rant. "Now I must even move out because of you! Not to mention what Mr. Frost must think of me. I wager he's never before been evicted from someone's parlor—and all thanks to a scamp like you. Oh! I've never been so humiliated in my entire life!"

Jake appeared unmoved by her tirade. "Bah!" he scoffed. "What do you want with a peacock such as J. Ackerly, anyway?"

"Ackerly is a gentleman."

"He's a pampered whey-face," Jake retorted. "No guts and no perseverance. Just look how he dashed out of here with his tail between his legs at the first whisper of adversity."

"Mrs. Gatling insisted he leave."

"Well, I haven't left!"

"That is because you, sir, are *not* a gentleman like Mr. Frost."

Jake waved her off. "That Nervous Nellie is as skittish as a mouse." He drew himself up with pride. "As for me, lass, you'll find staying power is my strong suit."

Priscilla felt hot color shooting up her face at his titillating remark. Somehow, she forced her words out through clenched teeth. "Of course you would reduce things to such a crude level, Mr. Blarney, since you have not an ounce of breeding or chivalry in your entire boorish body!"

At last she had raised a scowl on his handsome, arrogant face. "Lass, you can't mean that—"

"I do! When will you get it through your thick head that I want nothing to do with you, that the biggest misfortune I have ever had in my life was laying eyes on you!"

His features darkened in fury. "So I'm a misfortune for you, am I? The very man who summoned you, and rescued you in your hour of need! And you think that pious dandy is right for you?"

"Yes!"

Priscilla was stunned by what happened next. She gasped as Jake angrily crossed the distance between them. Heedless of her protests, he grabbed her wrist, dragged her out of the room, down the hallway, and out of the house. She was livid as he pulled her down the steps and through the yard; she sputtered protests and tried to dig in her heels, to no avail. He hauled her on toward the curb, where, to her horror, she spotted Ackerly and Mrs. Gatling conversing next to his handsome carriage.

As the amazed Ackerly and Mrs. Gatling looked on, Jake heaved Priscilla into his arms, ignoring her helpless shrieks and flailing limbs. With her skirts flying, he swung her high, and plopped her onto Ackerly's carriage seat.

He turned to Ackerly, nodded vehemently, and dusted off his hands. "Take her," he said curtly. "I'd say the two of you deserve each other."

All three watched in stupefaction as Jake Blarney strode off to his own buggy without looking back. Mrs. Gatling appeared so flabbergasted by the encounter that, after vainly trying to speak, she merely turned and walked off as if in a daze.

Priscilla stared sheepishly down at a grim-faced Ackerly. She knew she must look a scandal, with her clothing rumpled, her hat askew, her cheeks flushed from her breathless struggles with Jake. She spoke with heartfelt sincerity. "Mr. Frost, I cannot begin to tell you how sorry I am regarding this entire calamity. I assure you that I did nothing at all to encourage the attentions of that boor who just abused us both. However, if you no longer desire to take me to church, I fully understand."

He stared at her intently for a moment, then harrumphed and swung up to take his place beside her on the seat. "Frankly, young lady," he remarked dryly, snapping the reins, "after what I just witnessed, I would say you are sorely in need of redemption."

That was an understatement! Priscilla thought, tempted to laugh aloud as Ackerly's carriage glided away from the curb. She straightened her hat, smoothed down her skirts, and tried to calm her chaotic senses. She felt very grateful that, considering all that had transpired, Ackerly had accepted her back with panache and even a sense of humor.

For a moment they proceeded in silence, passing other gleaming conveyances filled with churchgoers dressed in Sunday frippery. At last Ackerly slanted Priscilla a bemused look. "Do you mind telling me how you came to be associated with a rogue such as Jake Blarney?"

She sighed heavily. "I assure you I am not *associ-*

ated with him, Mr. Frost. As I touched on earlier, I encountered Mr. Blarney when I first arrived here—in town."

He nodded. "That's right, Blarney delivers his jugs of milk daily to the pasteurizing plant on the Strand."

"Anyway, being a newcomer, I simply asked directions from Mr. Blarney so that I might locate Father O'Dooley, my contact here. Mr. Blarney helped me find Father O'Dooley, who in turn helped me secure lodging."

"I see."

Priscilla clenched her hands into fists. "But ever since that time, Mr. Blarney keeps showing up uninvited, pestering me. For some reason that is totally incomprehensible to me, he seems to think I am interested in him romantically."

Ackerly absorbed this information with a scowl. "I can't say I'm surprised by Blarney's audacious behavior. The man is a blackguard, brash and nervy as they come. But you must understand that a young woman such as yourself can be ruined by his unwanted attentions."

"You think I don't know that?" cried Priscilla.

"You are aware that he has a terrible reputation as a drunkard and a brawler?"

"No, but I'm not surprised," Priscilla replied, musing grimly that she had been entirely right to fear Jake was too much like her father.

"His wife left him, and it's rumored that he drove the woman away with his hot temper and disgraceful conduct." Ackerly lifted a brow sternly. "He's really quite dangerous, you know."

Priscilla groaned. "But what can I do, with him so determined to harass me?"

"Hmmmmm . . . Perhaps some legal remedy can be found for you. You must take care for your reputation, if you are to become a success in this community."

"Believe me, Mr. Frost, I'm eminently aware of that."

"That was why I was chatting with Mrs. Gatling." He flashed her a smug smile. "I think I managed to convince her to keep this entire incident quiet."

"You did? But how?"

He clucked to the horse. "The bank has been very generous toward Rose during the last year. You see, we hold the mortgage on her establishment."

"Ah, I see," murmured Priscilla. "She insisted I must move out, you know."

"Oh, I wouldn't worry on that account, since I think I've smoothed things over for you," Ackerly assured her. "Why don't you stay on and pretend the altercation in the parlor never occurred?"

Priscilla smiled brilliantly. "I am clearly in your debt, sir."

"Give it no further thought," he answered gallantly. His gaze slid over her with appreciation. "You look lovely and very elegant, my dear. It will be my pleasure to introduce you around today."

"You are too kind."

They proceeded on toward Trinity Episcopal, Priscilla feeling immensely relieved that she had survived her latest encounter with the brash Irishman without totally ruining her reputation. She felt equally delighted that she had not been denied her outing with Ackerly—even if, in the back of her mind, it bothered her that Ackerly had made no real attempt to defend her against Jake; that, just as Jake had pointed out, he had fled at the first hint of conflict. Of course, Mrs. Gatling had insisted he leave, and as a gentleman, he had likely felt he had no choice but to oblige.

What rankled even worse was that she actually felt a prickle of guilt over her diatribe toward Jake. Why? she asked herself angrily. Jake Blarney was an obnoxious boor, and according to what Ackerly had just told her, she had been entirely justified to assume he was both wrong for her and dangerous.

Why should she feel even the slightest stirring of conscience, when she was the one who had been insulted and mortified—and he was the one who had behaved like a contemptible bully?

She remembered a time when her father had embarrassed her even more. She had been ten, and her mother had thrown her a birthday party. Beatrice had invited every girl from Priscilla's class at school, but only four had attended. Just as Priscilla was opening her presents in front of her guests and their mothers, her father had come charging in, drunk and belligerent. Her friends had cried out in fright as Whitey had staggered about, knocking over the furniture and smashing the punch bowl. The other mothers, horrified, had quickly left with their panicked daughters.

Humiliated, Priscilla had confronted her father in tears. "How dare you ruin my party!"

Whitey had sneered back, "You think you're pretty fine, don't you, miss?" He'd snatched up the doll one of the girls had given her, and had shaken it at her. "You think you'll ever be pretty like this?"

Whitey had hurled the doll at his daughter's feet, and Priscilla had fled to her room, utterly devastated. The next day at school, her only real friend, Michelle, had told her, "My mama says I can't play with you anymore, 'cause your daddy's a drunkard . . ."

Even now, the memory hurt terribly. Whitey had been like that—he *always* ruined everything. He always took everything away from his wife and child—whether it be friends, self-esteem, or peace of mind.

She feared Jake had that same potential to wreak havoc in her life, just as he had embarrassed her today in front of Ackerly. Jake might not be a cruel man, but like her father, he was arrogant and often heedless of her feelings. Life with such a man would be turbulent and uncertain, robbing her of the emotional security she was so determined to attain.

But the hell of it was, she *still* felt drawn to him!

Chapter 10

Attending church at Trinity Episcopal was an enlightening experience for Priscilla. Thanks to Jake Blarney's shenanigans, she and Ackerly arrived only moments before the service began, and were forced to parade before the entire congregation toward Ackerly's pew near the front of the church. They attracted many murmurs and curious glances.

Priscilla was intrigued by the sanctuary, which was somewhat different from the Trinity Episcopal she remembered from the late twentieth century. Although the church building was the same, a plain, water-stained ceiling hung low over the sanctuary, instead of the spectacularly high, sawn-timber framing Priscilla remembered from the present. Large, obtrusive plaster pillars loomed in place of the handsome wooden columns she recalled.

As in the present, soft light sifted through stained-glass panels and shone on the handsome wooden pews and the magnificent high, carved pulpit. Otherwise, most of the appointments and all of the people were radically different. She was amazed by the mellow sounds droning from the old-fashioned pipe organ, and enthralled by the nineteenth-century finery worn by the worshipers—the women in their jacketed dresses and feathered hats; the men in double-breasted striped suits, their beaver hats in their laps; the little boys in sailor suits; the girls in frilly frocks and pantaloons. Even the mishmash of scents was interesting—the men's bay rum mingling with the women's lavender and rosewater, the sanctuary's own smells of beeswax, flowers, and that quaint Victorian mustiness that seemed to permeate all structures on the island.

Priscilla had no difficulty participating in the hymn singing, the readings, and Communion, but she found that her tight jacket collar began to chafe her badly during the interminable sermon. She was grateful for Mary's fan, which provided some relief from the warmth.

After the service, Priscilla was pleased when a number of prominent church members came forward to greet them. First came a robust fortyish man with his pretty pregnant wife and two small daughters. The man wore a handsomely tailored brown suit, his wife a voluminous frock of black silk bombazine, and the girls laced-trimmed pink silk dresses with matching bonnets.

"Well, Mr. Frost," he said, shaking hands with Ackerly, "good to see you here today." He nodded to Priscilla. "And who is the young lady?"

"Mr. and Mrs. George Sealy," said Ackerly, "I'd like to introduce you to Miss Priscilla Pemberton, who has just arrived in our community from Mississippi."

"Ah, Miss Pemberton," Sealy said. "How nice to make your acquaintance. I'd like you to meet my wife, Magnolia, and our daughters, Margaret and Ella."

"How do you do?" Priscilla asked, shaking the hands of husband and wife. To Magnolia she said, "Your daughters are adorable."

"Why, thank you, Miss Pemberton," she replied with obvious pride. With a discreet glance toward her large middle, she confided, "George and I are really hoping for a boy this next time. That would be such a nice Christmas gift."

"Indeed," murmured Priscilla, as she mused to herself that Magnolia and George might well be granted their wish. If memory served, the famous

Galveston entrepreneur George Sealy, Jr., was due to be born around this time.

"I do hope you enjoy your stay in our community, and we're so pleased to have you worship with us," Magnolia continued graciously.

"You're very kind. It's my pleasure to be here."

Next Ackerly introduced Priscilla to Reverend Albert Lyon, headmaster of Trinity Parish School. Upon learning of Priscilla's impressive credentials, Lyon expressed much dismay that there was not currently a post open for a teacher at the school. Priscilla then met Mr. and Mrs. J. M. Brown, their handsome grown son, Dr. Moreau Roberts Brown, and his wife and young son. She also became acquainted with members of the prominent Hutchings and Rosenberg families. Priscilla felt astounded to be actually speaking to historical patriarchs of the Galveston community whom she had only read about before. She was charmed by all the quaint accents she heard—the charming Swiss intonation of Henry Rosenberg, the Dutch and Polish inflections of others she met. Never had Priscilla realized that Galveston was such an immigrant community. As she visited with some of the children who echoed the speech patterns of their parents, an idea began to form in her mind . . .

At last she and Ackerly emerged into the bright sunshine. They were heading back toward his carriage when a feminine voice trilled out, "Oh, Ackerly! Is that you?"

The couple turned to watch a beautiful young woman approach, followed by a sedate middle-aged couple and a younger boy.

"Why, Winnie Haggarty!" called Ackerly with a grin. "I had no idea you were back in town. You've bloomed into a beautiful young woman, my dear."

Had she indeed! thought Priscilla with some resentment as the girl arrived at their side, in a heavy wake of perfume. Obviously no more than eighteen, Winnie was a classic beauty, with her thick, chestnut-colored hair and her face of cameo perfection, complete with pink cheeks, full red mouth, and lovely dark eyes—not to mention her hourglass figure and well-endowed bosom. Unlike Priscilla, Winnie was decked out as if to attend a garden party; she wore a frilly pink silk organza dress trimmed with extravagant satin bows and silk tea roses, a wide-brimmed straw hat sporting its own floral arrangement, pale silk stockings showcasing trim ankles beneath the hem of her dress, and handsome white kid shoes. She stood batting dark eyelashes at Ackerly and twirling the most lacy, flamboyant parasol Priscilla had ever seen. Priscilla fought back irritation at the girl's blatant flirting; Winnie was the kind of voluptuous enchantress with whom she could never compete, and yet she seemed the very type of simpering belle who drew men in droves.

Even Ackerly seemed impressed, Priscilla noted with some annoyance. "Well, well, Winnie," he said, taking and kissing the girl's white-gloved hand. "It is so good to see you again, my dear." As the rest of the Haggartys stepped up to join them, he turned to Priscilla. "Miss Pemberton, I would like to present my dear friends, the Haggartys—John, his wife, Eleanor, their daughter, Winnie, and son, Jimmy."

"How do you do?" Priscilla asked, shaking the hand of each Haggarty in turn. All of the Haggartys murmured pleasantries back to Priscilla, with the exception of Winnie, who merely flashed Priscilla an insipid smile as she limply shook her hand.

"Are you new in Galveston, my dear?" Eleanor Haggarty inquired.

"Yes," Priscilla replied, "you might say that."

"Miss Pemberton was educated at Vanderbilt, and she now desires to settle in our community and seek employment here," put in Ackerly.

"Ah," murmured John. "We are most impressed, as well as delighted, to have you among us, Miss Pemberton."

"Thank you, sir," said Priscilla.

"Our Winnie is just back from finishing school in Boston," remarked Eleanor proudly.

Ackerly smiled at Winnie, who blushed prettily in response. "Congratulations, my dear. Will your parents be announcing a stunning match for you before long?"

She giggled and twirled her parasol. "Not yet, Ackerly."

Seeming to absorb Priscilla's tense stare, Ackerly cleared his throat and nodded to her. "John and I have long been partners in a hardware business on the Strand."

"How nice," Priscilla murmured, thinking that if Ackerly and Winnie married, then the Haggartys could keep control of the entire business within the family. No wonder they were all fawning over him!

"Ackerly, would you and Miss Pemberton care to join us at home for luncheon?" asked Eleanor.

Ackerly glanced at Priscilla and must have seen the silent pleading in her eyes. "Thank you, Eleanor, but could we make it another time? I promised Miss Pemberton luncheon at the Tremont today."

"Of course," John said tactfully. "We'll do it another time."

They bid the Haggartys farewell, and soon Priscilla and Ackerly were driving off in his carriage, both rather subdued.

"The Haggartys were charming," Priscilla felt impelled to say at last, "and Winnie is a lovely girl."

He offered her a sheepish grin. "Lovely indeed, but something of a child."

Priscilla rolled her eyes. "A very voluptuous child."

He chuckled, but for once, didn't respond as his usual, reserved self. "Why, Miss Pemberton," he teased, "if I didn't know better, I'd swear you were jealous."

Priscilla flashed him an enigmatic smile and didn't comment.

She soon forgot her anxieties amid the wonder of

their arrival at the elegant Tremont Hotel. She felt awestruck from the moment they stepped inside the lobby with its spectacular rotunda, Italian tile floors, and soaring Corinthian columns. They proceeded into a lavish dining hall, where Priscilla's eager gaze drank in Persian rugs, crystal chandeliers, verdant ferns, and linen-draped tables with fine china and freshly cut flowers.

A smiling maître d' recognized Ackerly at once. As the man led them toward their table, Ackerly paused several times to introduce Priscilla to more of his friends. She met Colonel and Mrs. Moody, Harris and Eliza Kempner, and their several children, as well as the charming Nicholas Clayton, who was having luncheon with members of the board of St. Mary's Orphanage. Shaking hands with Clayton, the most brilliant architect in Galvestonian history, Priscilla almost blurted out a compliment on his most famous design, the Bishop's Palace. Thankfully, she remembered that the mansion wasn't built until the 1890s, and she instead complimented him on Ackerly's bank.

Again, although she admired Ackerly's esteemed circle of friends, it gave Priscilla an eerie feeling to be meeting all of these famous people who had been dead to her mere days ago.

"You've made quite a place for yourself in this community," she remarked a moment later as she sat across from Ackerly, unfolding her snowy linen napkin. "I'm impressed."

He smiled. "And you've made a fine impression on everyone today, as well."

"Well, I hope so," she said brightly.

Ackerly ordered their luncheon, and Priscilla found the fare extravagant and scrumptious: creamed spinach soup, lemon chicken fricassee, steamed flounder, rice pilaf, and homemade yeast rolls. To Priscilla's delight, the food tasted fresher and more flavorful than any she could remember.

"This is wonderful!" she cried as she relished a bite

of the excellent flounder. "I've never tasted food so ... authentic!"

He chuckled. "You speak as if you've never tasted fish before."

"Not like this! I wonder if it's the lack of additives and pollutants."

He tossed her a perplexed glance and continued eating.

Buttering a roll, Priscilla offered Ackerly an encouraging smile. "Tell me a little about yourself."

"Such as?"

"Your background."

"Ah, yes." He smiled proudly. "I hail from the Hamilton Frost family of New York. As I may have already mentioned, among my parents' friends were the Astors and the Vanderbilts."

"Oh, my," she murmured, nibbling at her roll.

"Unfortunately, while I was studying at Harvard, I lost my parents and my older brother in a scarlet fever epidemic. I came west several years ago with my inheritance. I met up with John Haggarty and we started our hardware business, Haggarty and Frost, together. The venture was an immense success from the outset because of all the building going on here. I branched out into other areas—investing in the railroad, a cotton compress, several newspapers—and of late, I'm a backer of the Galveston Pavilion to open at the beach next year."

"You really are an entrepreneur," said Priscilla. "How did you get into banking?"

He shrugged. "With all the port activity and trade, Galveston is rapidly becoming the financial center of the Southwest. I merely decided to follow the lead of Samuel May Williams and Henry Rosenberg, as well as the Moodys, Sealys, and Kempners, and cash in on the lucrative investment climate myself."

"It appears you've made inroads into almost every Galveston industry."

He frowned. "Not quite."

"Oh?"

Ackerly stole a glance at the gray-bearded Colonel Moody, who sat in a corner having luncheon with his wife. "I've yet to become a stockholder in the Cotton Exchange, or in the Galveston Wharf Company—and I'm not completely sure Colonel Moody and his coterie are making all the right decisions regarding our shipping industry." Leaning toward Priscilla and lowering his voice, he confided, "You know it's rumored the colonel is friends with none other than Jay Gould."

"You don't say."

"No telling what scheme those two are cooking up—though I wish the Wharf Company would think twice before raising its fees every time the wind shifts. In the long run, it could be bad for Galveston commerce."

"I see." Being from the future, Priscilla was well aware that Galveston shipping was doomed in any event, in large part due to the calamity of the Great Storm of 1900, after which Houston would rapidly overtake Galveston as the premiere port city of the Southwest. She suspected Ackerly's comments stemmed mostly from jealousy toward Moody's successful consortium, which controlled so much of Galveston's wharves and commerce. But then he was a successful businessman, and he had to stay competitive, she supposed.

"At any rate, it's wonderful that you are friends with so many prominent people," she said.

"Yes, and I suspect in time you will be, too."

"Really?"

He looked her over admiringly. "Now that I've filled you in on my background, it's your turn. Tell me more about yourself, Miss Pemberton, and why you decided to join us here on the island."

Priscilla had been fully expecting this query, and was prepared with a carefully contrived history. "Well, as you already know, I hail from Oxford, Mississippi. My father was a language professor at the university there. He died when I was only twelve, and Mother passed away while I was completing my education in Nashville. During college, I stayed with some old friends of my family's, a Vanderbilt professor and his wife. They had once summered in Galveston, and described it as an enchanting place. After receiving my master's, I was eager to make a new start . . . so here I am."

"So here you are," he repeated with a delighted grin. "And I was right about you."

"Were you?"

His nodded proudly. "From the moment I met you, Miss Pemberton, I could tell you were a young woman of great refinement and culture. It does not surprise me in the least that your father was a university professor. As I mentioned earlier, you made an excellent impression on everyone at church, and I'm sure in time you'll find your rightful place in this community."

Priscilla beamed. "I'm thrilled by your faith in me, Mr. Frost."

"And I'm honored to become something of your mentor."

"Why, Mr. Frost, I'm touched," she said graciously.

He slanted her a look of caution. "Only you must take great care, young lady. As we've already discussed, you must steer clear of scoundrels such as Jake Blarney."

"Believe me, I intend to," she replied feelingly.

He brightened. "Have you thought of what you might do as yet, my dear? It is a shame Reverend Lyon has no post open for you at the moment."

A thoughtful expression gripped her face. "As a matter of fact, a possible solution occurred to me just today. I think I'm going to rent a small shop somewhere in the center of town—preferably on the Strand—and offer elocution lessons."

He set down his coffee cup, his expression astonished. "Quite a novel idea. What inspired it?"

"Actually, all the different accents I heard after church. It occurred to me that some of the more prominent families might want their children to learn to speak with a more cultured tongue."

"Why, that is an inspired notion," he declared. "I knew you were an intelligent and resourceful woman, and your usage of the King's English is certainly impeccable. If you need any references, I'll be only too happy to oblige."

"Thank you, Mr. Frost," she said cheerily, and took a bite of cherry cobbler.

In due course, they left the hotel, and Ackerly drove Priscilla back to Rose Gatling's rooming house. "It's been a lovely outing, Mr. Frost," she said as they started up the path. "I can't thank you enough."

"We must do this again sometime," he said gallantly.

"Indeed."

At the porch, he lingered, a curious frown tugging at his thin lips. "Miss Pemberton, I've been wondering something . . ."

"Yes?"

He appeared secretly amused, his hazel eyes glittering. "When we chatted with Winnie and her parents after church, did my attentions toward her offend you?"

"I'm sure I don't know what you mean," she responded primly.

Tactfully he continued. "You must understand that when I came to Galveston, Winnie was but a child of twelve. I have watched her grow up—"

"Well, you needn't watch anymore," Priscilla cut in. "She has more than completed the task!"

"So she has." He stroked his jaw and actually winked at her. "But I do think you were a little jealous."

Priscilla grew indignant. "I was nothing of the kind—"

"And I rather liked it, my dear."

She stared up at him, pleasantly taken aback.

Before she could think of a suitable reply, Ackerly ducked down and briefly brushed her cheek with his lips. Then he turned and strode down the steps, waving his walking stick and whistling a jaunty tune.

Priscilla shook her head and smiled. He was a clever one, Ackerly Frost, and had a charming way about him. Then she remembered how cool his lips had felt on her cheek, unlike Jake . . .

Jake! She refused to allow herself to even think about that rogue!

But Priscilla was not to be allowed such a luxury. She entered the boardinghouse and almost collided with a grim-faced Mrs. Gatling. She cringed from the landlady's blistering look and muttered an apology.

"You're out to ruin me, aren't you?" the woman demanded.

"What do you mean?" Priscilla cried. "What have I done now?"

"What do you think, miss?"

Mystified, Priscilla fell silent, then groaned as she heard a male voice humming "Poor Wandering One" in the parlor. "Oh, no, not again!" she wailed.

"That's right. He's back!" Rose Gatling snapped.

Chapter 11

∼⁓∽

"What are you doing here again?" Priscilla cried. "Are you trying to ruin my life?"

When Priscilla charged inside the parlor, Jake Blarney stood with his broad back to her. At the sound of her voice, he turned, a devilish grin sculpting his handsome face, and a bouquet of red roses in his hands.

"Hello, lass," he drawled, extending the flowers. "I've come to make amends."

She groaned. "If you want to make amends, then get out of my life!"

"I ain't leaving, lassie—at least not until you accept my peace offering."

"Oh, for heaven's sake!" Priscilla charged across the room, grabbed the flowers by their bunched and wrapped stems, then sailed over to a pier table to plant the bouquet in an empty crystal vase, hoping Mrs. Gatling would take note of her gesture and have mercy on her. Still, the bouquet was beautiful, and she traitorously lingered for a moment to inhale the roses' lush fragrance. Then she remembered how her father sometimes brought her mother roses, to make amends when he had behaved abominably, and she frowned.

She heard Jake chuckle behind her, and she whirled in fury. "What is so amusing now?"

He winked at her solemnly. " 'Tis magical, isn't it, lass?"

"What's magical?"

119

His sensual gaze slid over her. "The effect the smell of a rose can have on a woman."

Priscilla blushed to the roots of her hair, as much from his disarming look as from his soulful words. "Th-That's prosperous! Furthermore, you have now attempted to make your apologies, Mr. Blarney, so kindly leave!"

He was obviously in no hurry at all as he strode over to a tufted velvet side chair and settled his large frame into it. "Sit down, Miss Pemberton."

"No!"

He raised an eyebrow. "So you mean to cause another scene when I force you to oblige me?"

Her mouth fell open. "You wouldn't!"

"I would. And frankly, dear, Rose Gatling is on such a tear at the moment, I'll wager if we provoke her again, she'll call in the sheriff."

Priscilla trembled in rage. "I refuse to bow to your bullying, sir!"

His tone brooked no challenge. "Miss Pemberton, listen to me like a good lass. *Neither* of us is leaving this room until we have us a little chat."

Realizing further protest was futile, Priscilla mouthed a curse under her breath and stormed across the room to the settee. She flounced down, glaring at him.

"That's better," he drawled, unperturbed, leaning toward her and lacing his long, tanned fingers together.

Priscilla tried to steel her floundering senses against how handsome he looked, stretched forward on the chair, with his jacket and trousers pulling at the taut muscles of his arms, shoulders, and legs, his chin set at a stern and earnest angle, sunlight dancing in his thick, dark hair.

She caught a convulsive breath. "What do you want this time? Didn't you do enough damage before?"

"How was your outing with J. Ackerly?" he asked casually.

"That's none of your damned affair."

He ignored her outburst. "Did you kiss him?"

"Go to hell!"

"Did you?" Undaunted, he leaned back in his chair and lazily crossed his legs. "I'm waiting, Miss Pemberton."

"You can wait until the Gulf freezes over!"

He laughed. "If you wish."

Priscilla could have screamed her exasperation. "Our outing was fine."

He made a clucking sound. "And you haven't answered my question."

"Correction—I answered one of your questions, and that is all you are getting, sir."

He eyed her speculatively. "You don't appear flushed—or the least bit undone. I'll wager that pansy never got close enough to touch you, much less kiss you."

"Oh!" she gasped.

"So I'm correct?"

"As a matter of fact," Priscilla fumed, "Mr. Frost very properly kissed my cheek before he left!"

"Oh, did he now?" asked Jake mildly. "You're not exactly prostrate from his amorous attentions, are you?"

She glared.

"Actually, I'm stunned to hear of such a passionate display from the likes of Ackerly Frost." He looked her over carefully, then grinned. "But at least I don't see any icicles hanging on you."

Priscilla frowned. Despite herself, she was intrigued. "What do you mean, icicles?"

"Don't you know that J. Ackerly is known in this community as 'Jack Frost'?"

Caught off guard, Priscilla fought a chortle. "You mean there are two of them?"

"Two?"

Realizing her blunder, Priscilla quickly forged on. "Never mind. I'm sure that if Ackerly is known by such an undeserved name, it's only because people misinterpret his natural reserve." She drew herself up with dignity. "Is there anything else, Mr. Blarney? I really don't have all day."

But Jake acted as if she did, pausing to brush a bit of lint from his jacket sleeve. "Did Ackerly introduce you to all the right people?"

"He did indeed—and he warned me to stay away from scoundrels such as yourself."

At first Jake appeared amused by this bit of information, then he feigned a dark scowl. "So that pantywaist was casting aspersions on me character again, was he? I must have a word with him."

"I'm sure that any *aspersions* he cast were well deserved."

Jake smiled tightly and stood, coming over to sit beside her. Priscilla tried to dash off, but Jake easily caught her wrist.

"Let me go!"

He released her, but shook a finger and warned, "Try to bolt up again, lassie, and you'll be sitting in my lap for the balance of our little discussion."

Her face flaming, Priscilla did not dare move in the wake of this horrifying—and unexpectedly titillating—threat. She ground her teeth and glowered. "You have me as your captive audience, Mr. Blarney."

Ignoring her spiteful tone, he stroked his jaw. "I can't quite figure something out here. What do you want with a milksop such as Ackerly, anyway?"

"He's not a milksop, he's—"

"Are you afraid of being with a real man?"

Priscilla gave an incredulous laugh. "Not in the least! And if you think being an arrogant bully qualifies you as a real man, then you, sir, are sadly deluded!"

Priscilla might have been expostulating to a mule, for all the note Jake took. "But you'll be needing a strong, hardworking man to provide for you, lass."

His chauvinistic remark prompted a new wave of righteous indignation. "To provide for me? Do you think I'm some helpless clinging vine? I can provide for myself quite handsomely, thank you!"

"And how do you propose to do that, lass?" he inquired.

"I have no intention of telling you!"

He crossed his arms over his chest. "Then I have no intention of leaving."

Priscilla made a sound of helpless frustration. "If you must know, Mr. Blarney—"

"I must."

"I'm planning to give elocution lessons to the children of some of Galveston's most prominent families."

He howled with laughter. "You're pulling me leg, lass!"

"I am not!"

"So you're determined to play the prig and the snob to the end, are you?" he scoffed.

"This has nothing whatsoever to do with snobbery! I simply must earn a livelihood, and Mr. Frost has generously promised to provide references."

At this, Jake got up and began to pace. His brow was knit in a murderous scowl, his hands were clasped behind his back, and he was muttering under his breath. Priscilla was thrilled to see him squirming for a change after she had been put on the hot seat for so long.

At last he turned to her. "I am sorely disappointed in you."

"I am crushed," she assured him with an air of tragedy.

"I never thought you'd sell your soul to hobnob with the sanctimonious nabobs here in Galveston."

Priscilla elaborately smoothed her skirts. "Obviously you have no appreciation of people of quality."

"I was about to say the same thing about you."

Priscilla thrust her chin high. "Then it appears you and I define 'quality' in entirely different terms, sir."

Appearing perplexed, he came to sit beside her

again. "Why do you feel you must put on airs, lass? Why can't you simply be yourself?"

Priscilla floundered beneath the unexpected and sincere query. "I—I am precisely myself!"

"No, you are not." He scooted closer to her and gazed intently into her face, making her feel agitated and rattled. "You're afraid of me, aren't you?"

"I am nothing of the sort!" she blustered.

"Oh, yes you are," he asserted confidently. "Yesterday you said I was wrong for you, that I reminded you of someone . . ."

Feeling extremely discomfited, Priscilla twisted the ties of her reticule. "I'm sure I have no idea what you mean."

"Oh, but you do."

Her heart hammering, Priscilla stole a glance at him, and felt her stomach clench at the sincere, ardent gleam in his eyes.

Softly he said, "I suspect there's a hurt inside you, girl, and you won't really be happy until you share your soul with a man. A *real* man, lass, not an ice cube like Ackerly Frost."

Now Priscilla was the one who bolted up, trembling. Jake's nearness was far too titillating, his insights unexpected and unnerving. She never would have dreamed a bumpkin such as Jake could be so perceptive, so soulful; could see through her facade and touch her own pain and insecurities.

"Mr. Blarney, I'm sure I have no idea what you are talking about," she asserted with bravado, her back to him.

But he merely crossed over to stand behind her. She winced with combined uncertainty and longing as he gently took one of her tight fists, raised it to his mouth, then kissed her tense fingers. She made a strangled sound, feeling as if a rock were lodged in her throat.

"Do you think a dandy like Ackerly Frost knows anything about wooing a spirited and love-starved lass such as yourself?" he whispered.

Priscilla whirled, her self-possession dissolving. Jake was staring at her as if he could see straight through to her soul. How could he know her most intimate secrets—especially that she felt love-starved? Was there indeed a deep bond between them that she was too frightened to acknowledge? Oh, heavens, he was too near ... she could feel his heat, his intensity.

"I—I'm not love-starved," she asserted weakly.

"Oh, yes you are, lass," he whispered huskily. He wrapped an arm around her waist, drew her against his strength, and she moaned. "Ackerly Frost knows nothing of what you need."

Priscilla could barely hear his words over the mad pounding of her heart. Why couldn't she seem to fight him? "And you think you do?"

Cupping her chin with his hand, he forced her to meet his probing stare. "Aye. You don't have to put on airs with me, lass. I like you just the way you are. I see the real woman inside you."

Priscilla floundered all the more. Never had she expected such masterful wooing from the brash Jake Blarney! Never had anyone cared about the fragile, vulnerable person inside Priscilla Pemberton, the person she tried so hard to shield, to hide away from a world that had caused her such misery. She found herself perilously close to tears.

Her voice came hoarsely, the barest whisper. "And what do you think you see, Mr. Blarney?"

He gazed down into her eyes. "I see you living the life you're meant to live."

"And what life is that?"

He gestured at the room. "I see you away from all this frippery and folderol. I see you minus all your airs, lass, stripped of all your pretensions. I see you in a lacy dress and a bonnet, amid a field of wild-flowers, picking blooms with me and the wee babes."

Priscilla was unexpectedly entranced by the images. "A nice pastoral scene," she acknowledged.

Gathering her closer, he leaned over and pressed

his mouth against her temple. She shuddered with helpless longing. "I see the two of us alone—me wooing you with wine and poetry, and helping you heal that aching inside you."

Priscilla was rapidly losing control of her emotions. "Mr. Blarney, please!"

Yet he continued talking, his sexy voice hypnotizing and electrifying her. "I see you in my bed, lass, wearing a lacy white gown that's open to the waist, with your breasts free and your nipples puckered like tiny rosebuds, begging for me lips."

"Mr. Blarney!" The protest came weak and breathy.

"I see you beckoning to me with arms held wide."

Priscilla was near panic. "Please, you must stop—"

"I see you with me wee son suckling at your breast—"

She was struggling to get free, fighting herself more than him. "Please, this is indecent."

"No, lass, 'tis inevitable." He reached out and touched her bright cheek. "Look at me, lass."

"No."

"Look at me."

She complied, wincing at the passion in his eyes.

"Just the thought of what we'll share has made you all hot and flushed," he whispered seductively. "Unlike when you're with Jack Frost. We both know damn well he will never put that heat in your cheeks—or in your blood."

She made a sound of shameless yearning, and he pulled her close again. He tucked her head beneath his chin, and the tenderness was near agonizing for Priscilla.

"I'm adding us a bedroom onto the house," he said.

Fascinated, she stared up at him.

He ran his tormenting finger down her throat. "It won't be proper for the babes to see what we'll be doing, you know. I've ordered us a big brass bed from Marx and Kempner, and they'll be shipping it here all the way from France—"

"You are insane!"

He shook his head solemnly. "If you like, lassie, I'll order us a mirror, too, to hang over the bed. There will be no shame or modesty in what we will share as husband and wife."

At last Priscilla broke away from him, struggling to hold on to her own emotional equilibrium. Never in her life had she been shaken this badly—and by mere words! Jake Blarney hadn't even kissed her. If he did kiss her again . . . She hated to even contemplate the mess her life would be in.

"Mr. Blarney, please leave!" she begged hoarsely. "This is impossible."

"Why, Priscilla?"

"Because we're too different."

He shook his head vehemently. "Nay, we're precisely alike—passionate and needing love, the both of us. Only, you're too scared and proud to give yourself to a man who will demand all of you. You'd rather hide your true feelings behind a milksop like Frost, who will never even prick the surface of you."

Priscilla gasped. To Jake she barely managed to say, "This discussion is at an end. Good day, Mr. Blarney."

But as she attempted to exit the room with some modicum of dignity, he grabbed her arm. His voice, which had been so beguiling before, took on a hard edge. "Then you won't agree to see me again?"

"I can't," she whispered in desperation. "Please let me go."

"No, lass." Even as she struggled, he held her fast. With soft menace he asked, "What do you think the society queen bees here would say if they knew how you really arrived here—and that you spent your first night under me roof?"

She pivoted to face him, aghast. "You are determined to ruin me!"

"I'm determined to save you from yourself, to bring you to your senses, and to make you admit that your destiny is as my bride."

"My destiny is nothing of the sort," she retorted, infuriated. "And I refuse to bow to your blackmailing. Go ahead and spread your treason. I'll withstand it!"

"Will you?" he asked with a smile, clearly not fooled by her bravado. "You know, as I mentioned the other day, I still have that scandalous little frock and those risqué drawers you wore when you arrived, dripping and bedraggled, on my stoop. They might prove interesting conversation pieces here locally."

She went wide-eyed. "You wouldn't!"

He spoke huskily. "Of course, you're welcome to retrieve your garments, any time. Under the proper circumstances, I might be enticed to relinquish them."

"You are depraved!"

"Aye."

She flung a hand heavenward. "What do you want from me, Mr. Blarney? Will you never be satisfied short of making a debacle of my entire life?"

He chuckled. "I think you'll find satisfying me at this point to be relatively easy . . ." He stared meaningfully into her eyes. "That is, until you beg me to make it very hard."

She gulped, her heart thundering. She was sorely tempted to beg him right now. Her voice quavered. "Tell me what it will take to keep you from wreaking havoc on my reputation."

He was in his element, grinning his triumph. "Very well, lass. If you'll allow that milksop to court you, you'll allow me to woo you, as well."

She mouthed a blistering curse.

He shook a finger at her. "I mean it, Priscilla. I'll be courting you, too, or you'll be ruing the consequences."

"Then do your worst, sir, and I no doubt shall rue away!" she declared.

He called her bluff with ease. "In that case, I'll be

stopping on me way home to have a little chat with Miss Fannie Bastion. She's the biggest gossip on the island, in case you haven't heard."

"Oh!"

Once again, Priscilla resorted to pacing about the room, trying to think of some way to outfox him, while he watched her with a look of patient indulgence.

At last, acknowledging her defeat, she turned. "Very well, Mr. Blarney, I will allow you to call on me. But there must be a time limit to this insanity. Two weeks."

"Six," he said.

"That is ludicrous! Four."

"Eight," he said.

"Eight? But you're going the wrong way. I'll take six."

"Ten," he said.

"Ten!"

He rocked on his heels and flashed his perfect white teeth. "The more you argue, lass, the more demanding I intend to become."

"Oh, for heaven's sake! I'll take—"

"Twelve. You must at least allow me to court you through Christmas. 'Tis me final offer."

Priscilla could have strangled him. But he had her, and he knew it. "All right! And remind me never to play poker with you—"

"Oh, I'll be finding some suitable games for us to play, lass."

"I just bet you will. And I won't see you every day."

To her surprise, he concurred. "Twice weekly should do it, for now. I'm a busy man, you see."

"You are insufferable!"

"But don't fret, darlin'. I'll make time for you. And we must plan our first excursion."

"In public."

"If you wish. We'll picnic on the beach."

"Bring the babies."

"Why, lass, are you afraid to be alone with me?" he teased.

"Didn't you say the girls miss me?"

"Of course. I'll bring them along." He stepped closer. "Now give us a kiss."

"Drop dead."

He merely grinned and clapped on his hat. "Until Wednesday, lass. Two o'clock."

"Three."

"One."

"Oh, you're infuriating!"

"One, lass."

Then he was gone, whistling a jaunty tune that made her wonder what sort of emotional catastrophe she was letting herself in for. She was scared to death. For in truth, it wasn't Jake's threats that had swayed Priscilla—it was the way he'd touched her vulnerable soul. How had he managed so quickly to see through her facade to the hurt and insecurity deep inside her? Why was it she couldn't seem to hide her true self from him? Whatever the reasons, his ardent, beautiful words and Irish charm had melted her.

And aroused her! With just a look or a word, Jake Blarney could make her feel desire more intense than she had felt while ostensibly in the throes of passion with Ackerly V!

She realized Jake had made one valid point. Perhaps Ackerlys and passion didn't mix. But, even with all the excitement he stirred, Jake Blarney was clearly wrong for her! He was the very man with the power to destroy her, and yet, without even touching her, he could strip her emotions bare.

Oh, what was she to do? If she didn't take greater care, she was bound to repeat the mistakes of her parents' marriage.

She groaned as she remembered one time at home when things were particularly bad. Whitey had hit

Beatrice again, and Beatrice and Priscilla had taken refuge with a neighbor, a divorcée with three small children who could ill afford to offer them shelter. Whitey came over to offer his wife flowers—he was all charm, just as Jake was today.

Whitey cajoled his wife, with her swollen face and look of fear. "I didn't mean it, Bea," he said contritely. "Please come home. I miss you. It won't happen again, I promise."

After much pleading, Beatrice gave in, as she always did. Later at home, as Priscilla lay shuddering in bed, she heard her father shouting, and her mother's cry as Whitey blackened his wife's other eye. Priscilla wrapped a pillow around her ears and sobbed, promising herself that she would *never* let herself become vulnerable to that sort of misery. She hurt for her parents, for herself, and especially because the love she felt for her father would never be returned. She actually hated herself for loving him, for being unable to shield herself from *feeling* . . .

As time passed and the turmoil increased at home, Priscilla became more and more locked up in herself and safe from the world, safe from her feelings. She became resigned to living her life that way, to marrying a man like one of the Ackerlys who would leave her emotions unscathed.

Yet Jake Blarney—damn him!—could pierce her armor and threaten all her painfully learned convictions. And the rogue had just hustled himself the right to see her for the next twelve weeks!

Late that afternoon, Jake sat in his cottage, rocking his babes. A crisp sea breeze wafted through the curtains, filling the room with the scent of the surf.

Mrs. Braunhurst had left only moments earlier, after Jake had thanked her for forgoing her Lutheran services this once in order to sit with the girls. Normally on Sundays, Jake took the twins with him to mass at St. Patrick's, leaving them in the church nursery. But today he had skipped services in order to see Priscilla. After all, he had rationalized, wasn't it more important that he pursue a mother for his poor babes than that he attend mass this once?

He stared down at his darlings. In the crook of one arm, dear little Nell dozed with her thumb in her mouth, while Sal rested in her pa's other arm, drowsily humming to herself and playing with the cuff of Jake's shirt. Bless the mites' little souls—their mum had deserted them when they were but three months old. Nell had taken it the hardest. Even now, Jake felt a tear stinging as he recalled how the baby had resisted the nursing bottle, spitting out the nipple and shrieking inconsolably, almost starving herself, so badly had she missed her faithless mother's tit. Sal was the tougher one, always full of cheer and laughter. She had taken to the bottle with ease, hardly seeming to notice Lucinda's departure.

Nevertheless, both girls sorely needed a mum, and Jake was determined that the bride the tide had sent him would be brought around to his way of thinking. He smiled, recalling his moments with Priscilla today. She was a feisty one, hell-bent on resisting him, but he had definitely won this round. Now he would be allowed his chance to court her—and Jake intended to woo and win Miss Pemberton in short order.

As for Ackerly Frost, that dandy would prove scant competition, Jake was certain. A few passionate kisses would divest Priscilla of her fascination with that jellyfish. If kisses alone didn't work, Jake was not averse to tossing up Priscilla's skirts and getting her in a family way, compelling her to the altar. Indeed, he would enjoy seducing her immensely, and he was convinced now that the lass could be successfully enticed.

Jake had learned much about Priscilla today—the most encouraging revelation being that a real woman's heart lay beneath that prim and cool exterior. He knew he had flustered her, probed her soul a bit, made her feel shaken and vulnerable. That was exactly how he wanted her. He was more convinced than ever that she had been badly hurt in her past, and had erected barriers to shield herself from further assaults on her heart. Jake intended to tear down those walls and expose the passionate, caring woman inside Priscilla. She would be frightened and uncertain at first, but she would learn to trust him. Aye, 'twould be his pleasure to teach her!

If he didn't press her too hard, scare her off, ruin it all. But then, pressing hard seemed to be Jake Blarney's style. And time was of the essence. How long could his motherless babes wait?

How long could *he* wait?

Shifting Sal slightly, Jake reached over to the tea table close by and picked up the charcoal sketch he'd done earlier of Priscilla. At once Sal tried to seize it with her chubby fingers.

"No, lassie," he chided, lifting the sketch out of reach. "Look at this with your pa."

With a coo, Sal obliged, staring solemnly at the sketch. 'Twas not a bad likeness of Priscilla, Jake mused. The strongly etched portrait well displayed her darling, upturned nose, large eyes, wide mouth, strong chin, and that riot of curly hair.

Surely she had a touch of the Irish in her, with that temper of hers, that spirit that set his blood on fire!

Sal gurgled and again tried to grab the sketch. Jake shifted it once more.

"See, darlin'?" Jake asked, holding the sketch aloft. "Mama."

Sal turned her adorable face up to Jake's. "Mama!" she chortled.

"No, not me, minx," he admonished, laughing. Carefully he tapped one of Sal's fingers on the sketch. "Her. Mama."

Sal stared solemnly at the sketch and cooed, "Mama!"

"That's right, angel, now you've got it."

Jake leaned over and kissed the cherub's curly head. Sal babbled happily, then settled back to yawn as her father continued to rock her.

Chapter 12

Monday, Priscilla began implementing plans for her new career. When she took the trolley into town, she already had a lead on a location for her elocution studio. Late yesterday afternoon during tea with her new friend Mary O'Brien, Priscilla had mentioned her intention to give private lessons in town, and Mary had excitedly informed Priscilla that her employer had a small shop for rent next door to his apothecary.

On the Strand, Priscilla strolled along until she located the small vacant storefront, situated in a strategic spot near the corner of Strand and Twenty-second Street. Priscilla found the architecture of the shop to be handsome and whimsical, complete with redbrick facade, half a dozen tall Romanesque windows, and mock columns with heavily carved capitals.

Satisfied with the outward appearance of the property, Priscilla went next door, where Mary introduced her to her employer, Mr. Peebles. The kindly little man showed Priscilla the empty shop, which contained one large room with plastered walls and stone floor, and a small anteroom in the back. Priscilla decided that, although the store was very grimy and musty, it would definitely suffice.

Priscilla gave Mr. Peebles a bank draft for the deposit and the first month's rent on the property. At her landlord's suggestion, she went down the street to a secondhand store and purchased the modicum of furniture she would need before hanging out her shingle. Her accoutrements included several frayed but presentable Belter side chairs, a plain but hand-some Federal writing table with chair, and, to add touches of warmth, a couple of framed watercolors of the Gulf and a worn Persian rug. By the time Priscilla located a sign painter on Market Street and arranged for him to paint her shingle, and went by the *News* office to purchase an ad offering her services, her lit-tle nest egg was running low. She consoled herself with the cliché "It takes money to make money," and hoped potential students would soon appear!

Since her sign would not be finished, and the ad would not appear, until Thursday, Priscilla did what she could to enhance word-of-mouth news of her new venture. Mary had already gotten her started there, by promising to tell all the apothecary custom-ers about her lessons. And when Priscilla dropped in to see her friend Sarah O'Shanahan, the dressmaker was so delighted to hear Priscilla's news that she promised to put a notice in her window regarding the lessons, and also vowed that her niece's children would become Priscilla's first pupils. Priscilla then stopped by the Frost National Bank to see Ackerly. Although he was busy and seemed harried, he, too, expressed pleasure at her news and promised he would do his part to ensure the community became aware of her services.

Tuesday, when her furnishings arrived, Priscilla spent much time arranging her shop, as well as cleaning and dusting the little store, and washing the front windows with a solution of vinegar and water. Mary stopped by at noon, kindly sharing her box lunch with Priscilla and even helping her brush cob-webs from the ceiling.

Ackerly surprised Priscilla by stopping by early in the afternoon. When he strode inside looking so dap-per in his smart suit, Priscilla was on a stepladder she had borrowed from Mr. Peebles, cleaning one of the grimy windows for the second time.

"Why, Miss Pemberton," Ackerly called, glancing up at her. "You do look industrious."

She laughed and stepped down from the ladder, musing that Ackerly couldn't have come calling at a worse time. She was grimy, her coiffure disheveled, her white muslin apron smeared with dirt. Tossing her rag into the bucket, she remarked awkwardly, "It's nice of you to stop by, Mr. Frost."

"My pleasure," he replied, taking out his handkerchief and handing it to her. "By the way, you have a bit of a smudge on the tip of your nose."

Self-consciously Priscilla took the handkerchief and wiped her face. "Thank you." She glanced around and grimaced to avoid sneezing. "I don't think I've ever seen a dustier establishment. I'm wondering if I'll ever get it truly clean."

He stared about them. "You seem to be making very good progress, however."

"Well, I do hope so."

He began striding about the small expanse, eyeing the arrangement of her furnishings, amusing Priscilla as he paused to line up a chair here, to straighten a picture there.

Scowling at one of her watercolors of the Gulf, he remarked, "This property has been vacant for some time, and was a bookshop before, as I recall. Still, the location is a good one, and I predict your enterprise will flourish."

"I sincerely hope so," Priscilla replied feelingly. "My ad and shingle won't premiere until Thursday, and I do need students."

"Ah, yes, the reason I stopped by," he continued, flashing her a smug smile. "Eleanor Haggarty was just by the bank with Winnie, and when I mentioned your elocution lessons, Eleanor promised to bring little Jimmy by to see you."

Priscilla's joy at this bit of news was tempered by the annoying mention of Winnie. Nonetheless, she feigned her most gracious tone with Ackerly. "Oh, how nice. I really can't thank you enough."

"Glad to oblige." He took out a carved gold pocket watch, flipped it open, and stared at the dial. "Well, I do have an appointment ..."

Priscilla walked with him toward the door. "Again, thank you for stopping by, Mr. Frost."

"I'm always one to encourage new commerce in our island community," he replied.

"I'm sure you are."

He stared at her thoughtfully for a moment. "By the way, Miss Pemberton, I almost forgot ..."

"Yes?"

"Would you care to accompany me to my prayer group tomorrow evening? It would be a good opportunity for you to meet more of the movers and shakers of this town."

She smiled brilliantly. "Why, Mr. Frost, I'd be delighted."

"Good. May I call for you at seven o'clock then?"

"Perfect."

As she showed him out, Priscilla's smile faded. Tomorrow was also her date with Jake. Thank God he had moved their appointment back to one P.M. With any luck, Jake would escort her back to the boardinghouse before Ackerly appeared, in time to prevent another altercation between the two men, she fervently hoped. Otherwise, if Ackerly discovered she was still seeing Jake Blarney ... he would doubtless drop her like a hot potato.

Wednesday brought many surprises. When Priscilla arrived to unlock her shop on the Strand, she already had customers waiting. She stared in pleasant surprise at the young, red-haired matron who stood near the door with two children, a boy and a girl. Both children were red-haired and freckle-faced, appeared about ten years old, and so closely resembled each other that Priscilla knew at once they were twins. Like their mother, the children were nicely dressed and regarding Priscilla anxiously.

"May I help you?" she asked.

"Would you be Miss Pemberton?" the woman inquired in a heavy Irish brogue.

"Yes, I am."

"Good," the woman said. "I'm Polly Carmichael, Sarah O'Shanahan's niece, and these be me twins, Shannon and Devin. They both attend Saint Mary's Parochial School."

"Why, I'm most pleased to meet all of you," said Priscilla, shaking the hand of each Carmichael in turn.

The woman broke into a bright smile. "Blimey, me twins is late for school already, wouldn't you know, and it'll take some doing to keep them strict nuns from rapping their little knuckles. But me auntie insisted we must stop off here first. Me aunt told me you might give me twins lessons on how to spake proper like."

It appears you could use a few lessons yourself, Mrs. Carmichael, Priscilla thought dryly. To the matron she said pleasantly, "Why, of course, I'd be delighted to discuss the matter."

Almost defensively, Polly pressed on. "Me husband, Mr. Carmichael, he owns a brickyard, so there'll be no problem with yer fee now."

"I never dreamed there would be," Priscilla replied smoothly, opening her reticule. "Just let me find my key, and we'll all have a nice long chat."

As she fished for the key, the little boy asked wistfully, "Miss, do you really thank you can teach Shannon and me to spake proper?"

"Of course," said Priscilla, smiling at the boy.

She tried to put her key in the lock, but this time the little girl grasped her arm. "And will the other children quit laughing at us then, miss?"

"You can be assured that they will," Priscilla responded firmly, and all three Carmichaels beamed with happiness.

Inside, Priscilla continued visiting with the Carmichaels. She soon surmised that the twins had accents every bit as pronounced as their mother's. It did sadden her to realize the children were being ostracized because of their speech—yet this circumstance also made her determined to help them. She signed the twins up for lessons every Tuesday and Thursday after school, and she even managed to lasso in the mother, when she pointed out to Polly that she might benefit from a few lessons geared at helping her children practice at home. Priscilla marveled at her own ingenuity in signing up her first adult student without wounding the woman's pride. She and Polly settled on a weekly fee for the three of them, and Polly gave her a deposit for the first two weeks.

As soon as her customers were out the door, Priscilla shrieked with joy and danced about her studio with Polly Carmichael's bank draft in hand, celebrating her feat. When at last she came to a stop, she had to laugh aloud at her own gleefulness. She wondered how Ackerly would have responded if he had seen her cavorting about like a madwoman. Of course, he might not understand such undignified exuberance. Oddly, she ached to share her small triumph with Jake, for she somehow sensed he would empathize and even share her joy as Ackerly never could.

She banished the traitorous thought at once.

Less than an hour later, Eleanor Haggarty entered the studio, tugging along her young son, Jimmy. Priscilla greeted her guests warmly, then the three settled around her desk to discuss business.

"I must say I'm impressed by your establishment, Miss Pemberton," Eleanor began, glancing about her.

"Thank you."

"Have you signed many students as yet?"

"I signed my first three this very morning," Priscilla related proudly.

"Congratulations. I'm very impressed," said Eleanor. "And Ackerly Frost assures us your credentials are impeccable. Vanderbilt, I believe it is?"

"That's correct."

Eleanor gestured toward her son. "John and I have

decided Jimmy might benefit from your services. Our boy's marks in grammar and reading at Trinity Parish School are excellent, but he's very shy about speaking up or reading before the class."

Priscilla smiled at Jimmy. "Would you like to take lessons with me, young man?"

He nodded shyly. "Yes, ma'am. Mother says you'll teach me to talk like a real gent."

"Well, I'll certainly try my best," assured Priscilla.

"And if Jimmy progresses well," Eleanor added, "I'll be certain to inform all my friends."

"You are too kind," said Priscilla.

Thus, before noon, Priscilla had four students signed up—and her room and board money for the following week! She was feeling eminently proud of herself when she closed up shop at noon and went home to change for her outing with Jake. The way her new career was progressing, she might well face a real flood of students tomorrow, when her shingle was hung and her ad appeared in the *News!*

Chapter 13

For the picnic, Priscilla changed into a lacy white eyelet Victorian frock with low neckline, long, puffed sleeves, a blue satin sash at the waist, and a slightly flared skirt minus a bustle. She donned white silk stockings and blue satin slippers, arranged her hair in curls about her neck and shoulders, then used several hairpins to anchor a straw hat on her head.

Eyeing her reflection in the pier mirror, she had to smile. True, she wasn't beautiful, but the elegant, old-fashioned finery suited her well. She looked . . . pretty.

A thoughtful frown drifted in. Considering that her date was with Jake Blarney, why had she primped so? As badly as she wanted to discourage him, she should have worn a gunnysack! And yet she perversely relished the possibility that her appearance might please him. Had he really meant what he'd said on several occasions when he had insisted she was pretty? She couldn't be sure, but she'd savored his compliments much more than she cared to admit.

Rather than risk another unpleasant encounter with Rose Gatling, Priscilla crept downstairs and stood tensely waiting for Jake beside the front door, peering through the oval glass panel. Within moments, she saw his buggy pull up outside the gate. Next to him sat Mrs. Braunhurst holding both babies. Good—perhaps the housekeeper would be going along on their picnic!

Priscilla rushed out the door and down the steps just as Jake was striding up the walkway to meet her. They met beneath the shade of a magnolia tree, he towering over her.

Priscilla had to admit Jake looked marvelous in his long-sleeved white shirt and dark trousers, and he smelled fresh and clean. Around them, the air was mild and fragrant—an excellent day for an excursion, she decided. Although she knew she should resent his having forced her along on the outing, she found herself sadly lacking in moral outrage.

"Good afternoon, Mr. Blarney," she greeted him rather breathlessly.

Jake looked her over with an appreciative gleam in his eyes. "Good afternoon, lass. My, but you look fetching."

"Thank you," she responded self-consciously. She glanced toward the conveyance. "Is Mrs. Braunhurst coming along on our outing?"

"Nay, I'm just giving Bula a ride home—her buggy still isn't repaired, you see. And I needed another set of hands to hold the wee babes on our way into town."

"Oh, I see." Oddly, Priscilla felt both disappointed and perversely pleased that they would go to the beach unchaperoned—except for the babies.

He took her hand and grinned. "Come along, then, lass."

Priscilla felt secretly thrilled by that smile, and the strength and warmth of Jake's rough fingers clutching hers. He led her through the gate to his buggy. Before she could protest, he caught her about the waist and easily lifted her onto the seat, then went to adjust the gray horse's harness.

Settling herself next to the housekeeper, Priscilla smiled at the hefty German woman, who was struggling to contain the two rambunctious babies. The girls did look adorable, both dressed in lacy white dresses, matching bonnets, and precious crocheted booties tied with little blue ribbons. Upon spotting her, Sal cooed and held out her arms, while Nell stuffed her thumb into her mouth and eyed Priscilla solemnly.

"Good afternoon, Mrs. Braunhurst," Priscilla greeted the woman pleasantly.

"*Guten tag*," she huffed back.

"May I take one of the babies for you?"

"*Ja*," the woman said, obviously relieved.

Priscilla took Sal, and when Jake slid in beside them, it was really a tight squeeze with all five of them wedged together on the narrow seat. Tucked between Mrs. Braunhurst and Jake, Priscilla felt his arm muscles rippling as he worked the reins, and the heat of his vibrant male body seeping into her.

Thankfully, it was only a few blocks to Mrs. Braunhurst's modest cottage on Church Street. There was much more room on the seat once the hefty woman alighted, but then Priscilla was left to hold both babies, who were gurgling and squirming, obviously thoroughly enjoying their outing . . . and giving Priscilla one devil of a time trying to contain them!

"You really do need car seats, Mr. Blarney," Priscilla scolded as they started off again.

He tossed her a perplexed look. "What are they?"

She laughed, realizing her faux pas. "I'm simply saying that it doesn't seem very safe for us to be rocking along in this buggy, with only me to hold these babies."

"You're the one who insisted I bring them along," he pointed out.

Priscilla grimaced as Sal tried to wiggle out of her embrace. "You're right. I apologize."

"You ain't thinking you'll be dropping them now?" he added sternly.

"Of course not. Perish the thought." Priscilla clamped an arm more securely around each baby. "Don't worry. We'll be fine."

After eyeing her askance, Jake drove south until they reached the beach. Priscilla spotted a couple wading in the surf—the man in a navy blue knit shirt

and matching short pants, the woman in a voluminous bathing cape with ruffled cap. Priscilla could
only shake her head at the sight as Jake wheeled the
horse to the west. They continued at a fine clip for
several more miles, passing his farm and a few more
scattered cottages. She particularly enjoyed watching
the birds—the sandpipers, yellowlegs, and herons
near the ponds, the gulls and curlews flying over.

At last they arrived at a dune facing the Gulf and
sheltered by a small stand of oaks. "What a lovely
spot," she said, glancing at the graceful trees whipping in the wind, and the waves lapping the shoreline beyond.

Jake hopped down, came around the buggy, and
reached up to take the babies from Priscilla. " 'Tis
Lafitte's Grove, lass."

"Lafitte's Grove!" Carefully transferring the girls to
their father's arms, Priscilla gaped about them. "You
mean the very spot where it's rumored Jean Lafitte
buried his treasure?"

Jake chuckled. "Many have sought the pirate gold,
but none have found it. 'Tis rumored Lafitte and his
men once battled Karankawa Indians on this site."

"Oh, my." Priscilla slipped to the ground, following Jake as he headed toward the trees with the girls.

"At any rate, we'll be needing the shade of the
trees to keep the wee ones from getting their rosy
skin burned," he called.

Priscilla mused that, despite his brashness, Jake
Blarney really was a fine man to show such fatherly
concern for his children. Beneath the shelter of the
oaks, she held the babies while he finished unloading
the buggy. He spread out a large blanket for them all,
and fetched a cradle and a picnic basket. Priscilla was
grateful to be able to put the girls down on the blanket, but the babies proved rambunctious as puppies,
crawling off numerous times and forcing Jake and
Priscilla to chase them down. Priscilla felt astonished
that Nell, normally so restrained, seemed caught up
in the fun, scampering all over the blanket and chor-

tling in glee. Sal was busier than the sorcerer's apprentice, constantly scrambling away to dig in the sand and shower Priscilla and Jake with the grit. Retrieving her, Jake quipped, "Mayhap she'll find some of Lafitte's doubloons," even as the baby kicked her feet and squealed to get free.

Priscilla, who had just corralled Nell for the sixth time, tossed Jake a beseeching glance. "Why are they so active?"

Jake lifted Sal high in his arms. "What is it you want, darlin'?"

"Bath!" she gurgled, kicking her plump little feet.

He laughed, then lowered the child to his lap and glanced at Priscilla, who was trying without success to interest Nell in a silver rattle she had found in the cradle.

"I think the wee ones want us to take them wading in the Gulf," Jake said. "Wee Sal and wee Nell love the ocean, you know."

"But won't they burn?"

"Nay." He leaned over to kiss Sal's flushed cheek. "They have their little dresses and bonnets to protect them. And we'll make it just a wee dip." He gently laid the baby down on her back, and as she began waving her arms and legs, he untied her booties. "Doff your shoes, Pris," he directed, "and wee Nell's booties, as well."

The babies continued to giggle, coo, and kick exuberantly as their booties were removed, and Priscilla found their spirit of fun infectious. She removed her own shoes and stockings, blushing as she caught Jake's frankly curious glance at her ankles and calves. Within moments, the four of them linked hands and headed for the water, the babies toddling between Priscilla and Jake.

All sense of order dissolved the minute they arrived at the edge of the surf. With cries of zeal, both girls plopped down on their bottoms in the shallow waves and enthusiastically splashed themselves, each other, and Priscilla and Jake.

"I'll say they like the ocean," she remarked to him, observing Sallie crawling along, squealing, as waves sluiced over her. "They are ruining their outfits!"

He shrugged. "Nothing a good laundering won't fix. Besides, I've fresh diapers for the wee ones in the picnic basket. We may as well wear them out, so they'll take a good nap."

They allowed the girls to cavort for less than ten minutes, all the while keeping eagle eyes trained on them, and seeing that they remained in the shallowest water. By the time Jake and Priscilla, each toting a wet baby, headed back for the blanket, both girls were relaxed and yawning. A good six inches of Priscilla's skirts were drenched and caked with mud, but she didn't care. She couldn't remember when she'd had more fun.

They sat down together on the blanket, both laughing, the content babies in their arms. "Looks like we tuckered them out," Jake announced proudly.

He and Priscilla removed the girls' wet clothes, dried them off, powdered them, and dressed them in fresh diapers. Then Jake fed Sal her bottle while Priscilla fed Nell.

It was a purely familial scene to which Priscilla was far from immune. Poignant emotion welled in her as she sat with the precious child in her arms. Nell wore only a diaper, and her skin was heavenly soft. Equally irresistible was her baby scent of fresh talcum and milk. She was staring up at Priscilla so solemnly, so trustingly, her tiny fingers possessively twisting a strand of Priscilla's long hair.

Even more disarming to Priscilla was the sight of Jake feeding Sal, rocking her in his arms and humming to her softly. Evidently feeling her perusal, he glanced up, and when she smiled at him, he gave her an intimate wink that made her heart race. Oh, why did he have to be so appealing, so handsome—the strong lines of his face such classic perfection, and the blue of his eyes so electrifying? Never in her wildest dreams would Priscilla have imagined such a gorgeous man would look at her with such devastating tenderness.

"I'd forgotten how soft babies are," she murmured, stroking Nell's soft little foot. "It's been ages since my cousin's children were this small . . ."

Her slip of the tongue brought a scowl to his face. "Then you have more relations than you've owned up to so far, lass?"

"Er . . . yes." Uncomfortable with the subject, Priscilla nodded toward the pile of soggy baby clothes. "You must remember to bathe both girls tonight, and shampoo their hair. Otherwise, the salt may chafe their skin, and the grit can't be good for their hair, either. And don't forget to rinse out their clothing."

He chuckled. "Aye, aye, ma'am. You're sounding like their ma already. You're welcome to come along to supervise, lass."

Priscilla felt heat rising in her cheeks—for she had indeed sounded like the girls' mother. "I—I can't," she muttered.

They fell into silence for a moment. Little Sal soon dozed off, and Jake placed her in the cradle and covered her with a light blanket. He nodded toward Nell, who was also asleep, cuddled against Priscilla's bosom with the nipple of her bottle in her mouth, her little lips still working as she dozed.

"Shall I put her to bed with her sister?" he whispered.

"Oh, no," said Priscilla. "I can't bear to let her go."

Delight shone in his eyes. "That's the idea, lass. These babes are me pride and joy—as you are, girl."

Though it was very difficult, Priscilla managed to slant him a chiding glance. "You're using your children to woo me."

His grin was unrepentant. "Absolutely. But mind you, my dear, you *are* the one who insisted they come along."

"True." That had been her greatest mistake, albeit a thoroughly delightful error. Seeing Jake's devotion toward the children made him all the more irresistible to her.

He turned and opened the picnic basket. She inwardly winced as the action pulled loose one of the buttons on his shirt, giving her an enticing glimpse of the coarse, dark hair on his chest.

"Well, sweet Pris," he was murmuring, "since you don't want to put down wee Nell, I suppose I'll have to be feeding you your luncheon, then."

Priscilla could hardly protest, yet it was sheer torture to have Jake feed her bits of ham, bites of German potato salad, grapes, and pieces of biscuit, all the while staring into her eyes and singing the poignant tune "Ah, So Pure" in his heavenly tenor voice. Priscilla felt herself blushing crimson when he soulfully intoned, "Oh, so mild, so divine . . . She beguiled this heart of mine."

At last she breathlessly held up a hand as he would have plopped another grape in her mouth. "You sing very well, Mr. Blarney. Have you ever thought of joining the opera?"

"Bah!" he scoffed. "That's a pantywaist's dream. I sing for meself, for me wee babes, to praise God at mass"—he paused to wink at her—"and to woo fair colleens."

By now, Priscilla was all but squirming, and grateful when Jake turned away to pour them some wine. He lifted a goblet toward her lips. "Here, lass, have a drink of this."

Priscilla took a sip of the sweet brew, then felt a drop of wine trickling down her chin. Jake reached over to wipe up the droplet with his forefinger, then stared into her eyes as he solemnly licked the wine off his fingertip.

Priscilla's blood was roaring so loudly, she was surprised smoke didn't come pouring out of her ears.

Desperate to distract them both from the electricity sizzling between them, Priscilla miserably cleared her throat. "I—I signed up my first four elocution students this morning," she stammered.

For a moment Jake appeared taken aback, then he grinned. "Did you now, lass? Why, I'm proud of you. I meant to ask about your new venture."

"It's coming along very well," she told him. "I've already rented a small studio along the Strand. I found the shop on a tip from one of my neighbors at the rooming house, Mary O'Brien."

"Ah, yes, Mary," he murmured.

"You know her?"

"From Saint Patrick's."

"That's right, you do both attend the same church." Shifting the baby slightly, she continued, "Anyway, I'm thrilled to have students already lined up, especially since my shingle and the newspaper ad won't even appear until tomorrow."

He frowned. "Then how did you acquire your first four students?"

Priscilla was beginning to feel uncomfortable again. "Oh, word of mouth."

"Whose mouth, lassie?"

Terrified he would learn more of her relationship with Ackerly Frost and his encouragement of her venture, she blurted, "Just the shopkeepers in the area. Plus, everyone seems impressed by my degree from Vanderbilt."

He appeared amazed. "You were educated at Vanderbilt, lassie?"

Priscilla could have kicked herself for her latest blunder. Every time Jake asked one of his pointed questions and she tried to dodge him, it seemed she only made matters worse by revealing something else she didn't want him to know. "Er . . . yes."

He was scowling deeply. "You're pulling me leg again, aren't you, lass?"

"No, not at all!" she protested.

"Then you're saying you've figured everything out?"

"What do you mean, figured it out?"

"That you're no longer confused? That you know

now where you came from, and where your people are?"

Priscilla was silent for a long moment. Oh, Lord, how could she answer *this*? After thinking fiercely for a moment, she said carefully, "Actually, I think I have pretty much solved the mystery . . . but if I told you the truth, you'd never believe me."

"No doubt," he responded solemnly.

She frowned. "What do you mean by that?"

"I mean, lass," he drawled sardonically, "that you've got more hot air in your head than a carnival balloon."

"Oh," Priscilla cried, outraged. "Well, I never!"

"Educated at Vanderbilt, my foot," he sneered.

"But I was!" she cried.

He howled with laughter. "Shall we be dispatching a letter to them to confirm it?"

Priscilla went pale. Jake Blarney might be a bumpkin, but he was no fool. "You wouldn't."

He wagged a finger at her. "Ah, so I've caught you in a lie, have I, lassie? You'll be paying me a hefty price for that one. And you've given me a wee bit more leverage to use the next time you balk at one of my requests."

"Oh—that is contemptible."

He grinned. "Easy, lass. Your secret will be safe with me—assuming you're halfway biddable. Otherwise, I don't really care about your background."

She was mystified. "You don't care?"

He set down his wine and leaned toward her earnestly. "What I mean is, it don't matter to me if you hail from humble circumstances—which I suspect you do—or even if you're running from a shameful past—which I suspect you are. I'd guess that's precisely how you ended up in Texas."

"Well, you are wrong!"

He made a low, clucking sound. "You can go right ahead and put on airs with everyone else, pretend you are from some exalted society family, that you were educated at Vanderbilt, or that you are Queen

Victoria's cousin. But you can't hide who you really are from me, lass. It won't work."

Priscilla reeled, again wondering how this man, who knew so little about her, could know so *much* about her! It was unnerving to think that earthy, simple Jake Blarney held the power to strip away all her pretensions—especially when she needed those very pretensions so badly to survive, to shield herself from being hurt!

"Well, lass?" he prodded.

At last Priscilla managed to take charge of herself. "Your discretion is appreciated, Mr. Blarney. Beyond that, I think you've had me on the hot seat quite long enough."

He chuckled.

"Now I think it's time to learn a little more about you."

She felt relieved when he stretched out lazily, supporting his weight with an elbow. "Why, lass, I'm thrilled by your interest. What do you want to know?"

She frowned, trying hard not to think how sexy he looked, with a dark curl tossed over his forehead, and his clothing pulling at the solid muscles of his reclined body. "Well, how did you happen to immigrate to this country?" she asked. "Was it the potato famine?"

He hooted a laugh. "The potato famine was in forty-five. Where have you been, lass?"

Where indeed? she thought. "I suppose my grasp of Irish history is somewhat lacking."

"Aye, 'tis."

She shooed away a fly that was making a dive toward Nell. "What brought you here to America?"

He sighed. "Me people were dairy farmers in Ireland. Me pa owned a wee bit of land on Saint Finian's Bay, County Kerry. After me ma and pa both died, I decided to sell out and start over here."

"But why?"

He regarded her earnestly. "Because I wanted to

live in a country where I could practice my religion freely, and not support the Church of England through its unjustly charged land rents."

"Ah," she said, concentrating to remember her English history. "You are speaking of the entire Irish Home Rule issue—Parnell and all that?"

He grinned. "Perhaps you're better educated than I thought, lass."

"You have no idea," she murmured ironically. "For that matter, the struggle in Ireland is still going on to this day."

He glanced at her quizzically. "Aye. 'Tis."

"Do you miss your homeland?"

He considered that for a long moment. "Sometimes I get melancholy when I remember the rolling hills and the beautiful coastline, the mists and the heather. But good riddance to the cold and the rain. As for living beneath the iron fist of tyranny—that, I'll never again yearn for, lass."

"You are a fierce nationalist, then?"

"Aye."

"But happy to be settled here in Galveston?"

"Aye." He glanced out at the Gulf. "I have the sea, and the satisfaction of living by the labors of me own hands." He nudged her slipper with his boot. "With your brains and me brawn, lass, we'll do well together."

"Mr. Blarney, really!"

"Have some more wine, lass," he urged, lifting the glass to her mouth.

She took another sip, then gazed down at the baby. "She sleeps so peacefully."

He nodded. "She's made for your arms, lass. She took it the hardest, losing her ma."

"Do you mind telling me a little more about that?"

His expression grew wistful. "Me babes were only three months old, not even weaned, when it happened. I don't know what possessed Lucinda to run off as she did."

"Perhaps it was postpartum blues."

He frowned. "Whatever. But off she went with this bloke in his wagon, as if me and the babes were nothing to her. Oh, the drummer had been round before, the rascal, and I'd seen him making eyes at me missus. But this time the two of them lost their heads. I was in the barn with a sick cow late that night when she left with him. I went back into the house and found me wee babes alone, frightened and wailing."

Priscilla reached over Nell to touch his arm. "Jake, I'm so sorry."

His expression went hard. "I don't know why me wife and that scoundrel couldn't have committed their adultery here on the island. But no, the imbeciles had to try to row over to the mainland. No more ferries that night, I reckon. Anyway, that was their mistake. Their bodies washed up off San Luis Pass the next morning."

Priscilla groaned. "How awful."

He reached out and touched the baby's foot. "Of course, there was a terrible scandal. But I didn't care about that. I cared about me babes. Nell there wouldn't eat from missing her mother's breast. I couldn't find her a wet nurse, so I was up to all hours trying to coax her into taking the bottle."

Priscilla fought tears at the image of this proud Irishman as a forsaken, distraught father. "I bet you were scared to death."

He gave a shrug. "Aye. But we made it. Then right after the funeral, Lucinda's sister Octavia spoke out. Said she'd be taking the babes—and I said 'twould be over me dead body. 'Twas a scene the two of us made, until I bodily threw her out of me house. She still comes round on occasion to make trouble."

"It would be better, then, if you had a wife," Priscilla said without thinking.

He reached over the baby to stroke her cheek. "Aye, lass. 'Twould be better."

By now, Priscilla felt very unnerved and vulnerable, almost tempted to volunteer as stepmother to his babies. "I—I think you'd better take Nell, now," she stammered. "If you'll put her in the cradle with Sal, I'll help you pack up. I need to get back."

"Already?" he cried, indignant.

"Really, Mr. Blarney, we've been gone for hours. You must escort me back to the boardinghouse before you start home with the babies, and if you wait any longer, it's bound to be twilight by the time you reach your farm."

He breathed a great sigh. "Aye, you're right. It's just hard letting you go, lassie."

Priscilla lowered her gaze. Although she couldn't dare admit it to Jake, it was difficult for her to see the outing end, as well, so special had been the time she had shared with Jake and the babies. Jake's charm, and especially his restraint in not pressing her today, had proven devastating.

She forced a smile. "Please tell Mrs. Braunhurst the picnic meal was delicious." She bit her lip and started to hand Nell to Jake, then abruptly laughed. "Well, look who's awake."

Both glanced down at the baby as she solemnly whispered, "Mama."

Priscilla gasped and stared up at Jake through sudden tears. "She called me 'Mama.' How adorable!"

The stark joy reflected in his eyes made more poignant feeling well up inside her. "Aye, lass," he whispered. "The wee mite needs you—as I do."

Jake leaned across the baby and caught Priscilla's lips in an exquisitely gentle, almost reverent kiss. Only their lips touched as the surf roared beyond them and the wind caressed their bodies. With Jake's mouth on hers and his baby in her arms, Priscilla exulted in the sweetest, dearest moment she had ever known. The intense emotion was almost more than she could bear.

At last, as Nell began to squirm between them, they drew apart and laughed.

"Guess I'd best be getting you home, lass," Jake

teased, reaching down to tweak Nell's nose. "That is, if you can bear to part with her."

Staring down at the precious baby, Priscilla mused that she could hardly bear to part with any member of this endearing little family . . .

But ultimately she did.

Later, Jake Blarney felt pleased with himself as he drove his children home. He'd done well today in wooing Priscilla, and the lass was coming around. In due course, she would discover there was no fighting destiny—or him!

Even if there was still much about the girl that confused him—her claims that she had been educated at Vanderbilt, her reluctance to answer his questions about her family and where she had come from. Although it dismayed him to see her putting on airs, he truly didn't care about her past, as long as she accepted that he was her future.

Of course, using his girls to woo her had been naughty. He glanced at his darlings as they dozed in the cradle, securely wedged on the floor beside him. They were worth it, he decided with a catch in his throat. He would do anything, be utterly ruthless in winning himself a wife and his daughters the stepmother they so desperately needed.

Priscilla Pemberton was the bride the tides had brought him, and Jake Blarney would *never* give her up.

Chapter 14

Bible study Wednesday night turned out to be a real anticlimax for Priscilla. Normally she would have been fascinated with the home where the circle met—a sweeping, pillared Greek Revival mansion surrounded by stately oaks, with a fabulous interior sporting high fretwork ceilings and posh velvet furniture. At any other time, she would have been enthralled by the attendees, couples representing some of Galveston's most esteemed families—the Sealys, the Browns, the Rosenbergs, the Hutchingses, and the Haggartys, minus Winnie and Jimmy. Even the subject matter, "Are you a soldier of the cross?" paraphrased from the hymn, should have stirred a more zealous response in her.

Instead, sitting with the others in the huge parlor of the Swan home, Priscilla found her attention endlessly wandering. More than once she failed to answer a question from the group leader, Mr. Earnest Swan, and she couldn't find her place in the Bible as her turn came up to read. She kept remembering her magical hours with Jake and his adorable babies. She felt a lump in her throat every time she recalled holding sweet, soft little Nell, and the way that darling child had opened her eyes, smiled up at Priscilla, and called her "Mama." The moment when she and Jake had kissed while she held his baby had been so poignant that her heart tripped with emotion each time she remembered it. She was clearly falling in love with Jake's babies ... and quite likely with him, as

157

well. It terrified Priscilla to feel so drawn to a man who was dead wrong for her, who had the ability to make her look inside herself at the person she really was, who could probe her own needs and vulnerabilities. But she could not deny the intensity of her own longing.

Even when Jake had brought her back to the boardinghouse, she had fretted so much about his getting safely home with the sleeping twins that she had almost stood Ackerly up in order to help Jake fetch the children home. But Jake had managed to securely wedge the cradle with the two dozing babies on the floor of the buggy beside him, and he had assured Priscilla that he would stop the buggy at once should either of the girls stir. At last Priscilla had reluctantly let the small family go, but not before Jake had exacted a promise that she would see him again on Saturday. He had invited her to have an early supper with him, the girls, and Mrs. Braunhurst at the cottage. He had also announced that afterward, while Mrs. Braunhurst sat with the children, he intended to take Priscilla for a sunset ride along the beach. "You'll be enjoying that, lassie, I promise," had been his parting words.

Remembering the passionate glint in his eyes, she mused that she would no doubt enjoy herself a lot more than she wanted, just as she had today. Indeed, throughout the rest of Bible study and the social afterward, Priscilla could think of little else except her upcoming date with Jake . . .

Later, Ackerly commented on her distracted state as he escorted her toward Rose Gatling's door. The two paused at the base of the steps, their forms awash in the gaslight spilling from the sconces on the porch.

"Miss Pemberton, you didn't seem quite yourself tonight," he said solicitously. "I hope nothing is amiss?"

Priscilla touched his sleeve. "I'm sorry, Mr. Frost. It

was truly kind of you to introduce me to your Bible study group."

"It was my pleasure."

She sighed. "I suppose I bordered on rudeness tonight, didn't I?"

"I'm sure we all have a bad day on occasion," he responded tactfully.

"I didn't mean to act so aloof toward everyone," she said contritely. "I suppose my focus is somewhat divided at the moment, since I'm trying to get my new business off the ground and all."

"I see. How is that progressing?"

"Pretty well. In fact, I wanted to thank you for helping to get Jimmy Haggarty lined up as one of my first students."

He smiled. "You're welcome. Eleanor mentioned to me tonight how excited Jimmy is regarding the lessons. Have you acquired any additional pupils?"

"A few. I'm hoping for more of an influx after tomorrow, when my shingle is hung and my ad comes out in the *News*."

He nodded. "I'm sure a woman of your accomplishments will attract numerous students. And by the way, Priscilla ... Er, may I call you that?"

"Of course. And may I call you Ackerly?"

"Certainly. I was wondering if you would care to attend church with me again on Sunday."

"I'd be honored."

He coughed. "I trust the hooligan Jake Blarney will not be lurking about this time?"

Following an afternoon spent getting better acquainted with Jake, Priscilla was sorely tempted to snap back that Jake Blarney was neither a hooligan, nor did he lurk. But she stopped herself, not wanting to alienate Ackerly. Besides, to be fair, Jake *had* behaved like a ruffian around Ackerly—and around her at times, as well!

Stiffly she replied, "You trust right."

Eyeing her strained expression, he flashed a cajoling smile. "I hate to speak ill of anyone, my dear, but

Blarney really is a dangerous character. Why, I've even heard he's spent a few nights in jail following his . . . er . . . what is that word the Irish use?"

"Donnybrooks?" Priscilla provided.

"Yes, that's it. You'd be well advised to steer clear of him."

"So it appears," muttered Priscilla. Feeling sobered by Ackerly's not-unexpected revelations, she forced a more pleasant expression. "Until Sunday, then?"

"Of course." Ackerly leaned over and pecked her cheek. "I shall call for you at ten-thirty."

Upstairs, Priscilla found herself agonizing over her relationships with both Jake and Ackerly—Jake, whom she craved but could not trust; Ackerly, whom she trusted but did not crave. Certainly she couldn't deny that Ackerly Frost was a nice man—perhaps even a better man than his great-great-grandson. Indeed, he'd been indulgent toward her tonight, considering that she *had* acted rude during Bible study. Even his warnings about Jake had seemed motivated more out of concern than mean-spiritedness.

But the thrill simply wasn't there as it was with Jake, and this bothered her. Nevertheless, she knew she would continue to see Ackerly because she needed him—needed his help in accomplishing her goals here in nineteenth-century Galveston. The admittedly mercenary nature of her motives sometimes made her dislike herself. On the other hand, she suspected he might harbor at least some ulterior motives in seeing her. Obviously Ackerly needed a refined, socially adept wife in order to further his ambitions, just as she needed his contacts to penetrate the upper crust of Galveston society.

Cold-blooded though the arrangement might seem, it did make sense to Priscilla. As far as her future was concerned, she was determined that her head would rule her heart. In time she might even marry Ackerly, even though—just as with Ackerly V—she doubted she would ever love him. But he was her type, from her world . . .

Unlike Jake Blarney, who doubtless had spent a few nights in jail, who likely had learned those pretty songs at a seamy grogshop. Not Jake Blarney, whose reputation would only weigh her down in this community. Not Jake, whose unpredictable, volatile temperament would surely break her heart. Even if his two children badly needed a mother ... even if he inspired in her the most devastating passion, and perhaps something far deeper ...

Priscilla's mother had married for love and passion. Priscilla remembered her own humiliation, even as a child, when she had gone with Beatrice to bail Whitey McCoy out of jail, after he had gotten in another fray at a bar. She recalled the cruel taunts of the other children at school, when gossip about her father's exploits had gotten around. The boys at school had acted particularly vicious toward her, running away when she appeared, screaming, "Jailbird, jailbird!" and flapping their arms like wings. Some of the girls had ridiculed her, too. It had been deeply humiliating for Priscilla, and she had run off to sob in the girls' rest room more than once.

At home, Priscilla's mother had been too caught up in her own troubles to give her daughter the comfort she needed, as Whitey had disgraced them again and again. And then one day he had walked out, never to return, leaving Priscilla and her mother destitute.

She would not repeat that tragic history with Jake Blarney, who was just the kind of passionate bounder to dish it up in full measure. Of course, there were differences between the two men, Jake being by far the better man. But she and Jake responded to each other on that same emotional, tempestuous level as had her parents, and she could too easily picture him humiliating her in a dozen ways, even holding her up to scorn in the community. She could also picture herself shamelessly going off to jail to rescue him following one of his debacles.

Heaven forbid! She would stick with Ackerly

Frost, even if her decision left her in terrible turmoil and self-doubt—for she was fighting for her own future and emotional survival. Never again could she endure the ostracism and mental anguish she'd known as a child. Far better not to give her heart at all than to give it to a man she could never trust.

Nonetheless, for the balance of the week, Priscilla found herself anticipating Saturday's date with Jake much more than Sunday's appointment with Ackerly.

Chapter 15

The next day, more students began to trickle in for Priscilla, although not the flood she had hoped for. She signed up the children of three new families that day, and acquired five new students the next. She was particularly pleased on Thursday to welcome young Isaac Herbert Kempner, son of the prominent Harris Kempner, as one of her pupils. On that same afternoon, she began giving her first elocution lessons to the Carmichael twins, Shannon and Devin.

Although teaching children was a novelty to Priscilla following three years of experience at the university level, she felt at least marginally qualified in elocution, since she had taken some communications courses while pursuing her baccalaureate degree. Realizing that she could not teach any of her students how to properly project their voices, or to speak in public, before she evened out their accents, she had already planned to center her curriculum on the International Phonetic Alphabet. While taking some linguistics courses for her masters program, Priscilla had learned that anyone could be taught to speak with any accent—or without it—through learning to use the alphabet. And in this case, she would approach the subject matter in its purest form, since she was teaching English precisely as it should be spoken. Doubtless no one here in Galveston had even heard of the International Phonetic Society, but the twins seemed to find the various symbols interesting.

She confined their first lesson to a few basics, as well as suggestions for practice at home; when Polly Carmichael stopped by to collect the children, she seemed thrilled that they had already learned to say "have" instead of "hae," and "get" instead of "gat."

On Friday Priscilla acquired her first teacher's pet. Around fourteen years old and almost pathetically thin, the boy walked in wearing a frayed suit two sizes too small for him, and a tattered cap. Despite his near-pitiful attire, he carried himself with great dignity. With his red hair, freckled face, and green eyes, he looked like Tom Sawyer—but Priscilla soon discovered he was pure Cockney.

"Hallo, miss," he greeted her, yanking off his cap. "Would ye be the lady what's larnin' folks t'spake?"

Priscilla had to struggle not to laugh as she rose from her desk. "Young man, you are definitely in the right place."

Priscilla offered her guest a chair, and they chatted for some moments. She learned his name was Willie Shrewsbury, that he and his family had emigrated here from the East End of London several years ago, and that his father had been tragically killed in an accident at the Galveston docks last year.

"Me mum takes in laundry to keep a roof over our heads and bread on the table," Willie confided. "So I be paying for me lessons me own self. I work the docks after school each day, unloading freighters."

"I see." Priscilla smiled quizzically. "Why do you want lessons, Willie?"

He glanced away, a muscle working in his thin cheek.

"Willie, if you don't have a good reason, I'm afraid this won't work."

He nodded with grim determination, though his eyes gleamed with pride. " 'Twill work, miss, and I'll try hard for ye. I just want for the other kids at school to quit tormentin' me."

"Oh, Willie." Having as a child experienced such

cruelty herself, Priscilla found her heart going out to this needy lad.

He held up a thin hand. "Now, I ain't askin' for yer pity, miss, only yer instruction—and I'm aimin' ter pay." He took out a silver dollar and shoved it across the desk with his callused fingers.

Priscilla felt very touched. "Really, Willie, you don't have to give me money right away—"

"But I be wantin' me first lesson straightaway, miss."

"Now?"

"Aye, we've not a second to waste. Next month, there's to be a contest for all the city schools, in el—elo—"

"Elocution?" Priscilla provided.

He grinned. "Aye, miss. In that. And I'm aiming ter win first place and make me mum proud."

Priscilla beamed her pleasure. "Willie, I think if we both work hard, we may be able to do just that. Now, tell me, where do you go to school?"

"Trinity Mission School, miss," the boy said, lowering his gaze.

Realizing he must be a charity student, Priscilla felt a new surge of sympathy for him. "And you say all of the schools in Galveston community will be involved in this contest?"

"Aye, miss. Saint Mary's Parochial School and Ursuline Academy, the Collegiate Institute and the German Lutheran School . . . All the schools in town will be there."

"And where will the contest be held?"

"At the Tremont Opera House, I reckon."

"How interesting." Priscilla's mind was humming with anticipation of the forthcoming contest as a boon to her enrollment campaign, assuming her students performed well—and she would ensure that they did!

Willie stretched forward anxiously in his chair. "Can we get started then, miss? We've not a second to waste!"

"Indeed," murmured Priscilla.

She gave Willie his first lesson, feeling much like Professor Henry Higgins with Eliza Doolittle.

By Saturday, Priscilla's fortunes had increased to the point that she easily paid her room and board, and also splurged on a new dress for her outing with Jake. The garment was a mouthwatering long-sleeved frock of green and white lawn, with a green satin sash at the waist and green ruffles on the cuffs and hem. She also indulged herself with a new wide-brimmed straw hat decorated with silk roses, and a lacy green and white parasol.

At mid-afternoon, she was dressed in the frock twirling before her mirror, when she heard a knock. "Come in!" she called.

Mary O'Brien stepped inside and at once smiled from ear to ear. "Ah, Priscilla, dear, you do look a picture."

"Thanks, Mary. Please come in."

She stepped inside, closed the door, and plopped herself down on the low divan. "How did the rest of your week go?"

Priscilla beamed. "Splendidly. Twelve students in all signed up."

Mary clapped her hands. "Oh, love, that's wonderful!"

"I decided to celebrate by purchasing this dress," Priscilla confided.

"And it suits you so well. Are you stepping out with Mr. Frost again?"

Priscilla laughed dryly. "Don't tell Mrs. Gatling—"

"That nosy biddy? I wouldn't dream!"

"But I'm going out with Mr. Jake Blarney. You know him, don't you?"

Mary's mouth dropped open. "Him! Attends mass with us at Saint Patrick's, he does. Him and his wee babes—"

"I know. Aren't they precious?"

"Aye." The girl frowned. "But I must warn you,

Jake Blarney has a bad reputation. Course, he's so wickedly handsome, he gives all the ladies palpitations anyhow, but there's no doubt he's a wild 'un."

Priscilla sighed. "I'm afraid that's no news to me. What have you heard about him?"

"Oh, the usual—that he frequents the grogshops, has been known to gamble and pinch the derrieres of barmaids, or swing his fist at a sailor or two, when the drink is in him."

Priscilla rearranged a curl and frowned.

Mary rose and moved toward Priscilla. "Why are you stepping out with his kind, Priscilla? Not that I'm overly keen on your Mr. Ackerly Frost, but he seems more your type, all refined and such. And here you are trying so hard to make your place in the community. Why risk scandal with a man like Blarney?"

"It's a long story, Mary," Priscilla confided ruefully. "You really don't have a very high opinion of Jake, do you?"

Mary mulled over that question with a scowl. "Truth to tell, Priscilla, Jake Blarney may be a mite unruly, but I suspect his heart is in the right place. Just needs the right woman to reform his wayward ways, he does. To be frank, I'd take Jake any day over ten J. Ackerly Frosts."

Priscilla smiled in pleasant surprise. "Why, Mary! Are you interested in Mr. Blarney yourself?"

The young woman blushed. "Why, I never said that!"

Priscilla touched her arm in reassurance. "Sorry, Mary, I didn't mean to put you on the spot." Under her breath she finished, "It's just that, before this is over, I may need to find the man a wife."

When Jake Blarney called for Priscilla, she was waiting for him on the front porch, her parasol tucked beneath her arm and two small, wrapped packages in her hands. He sprinted up the steps toward her, looking dashing and a bit rakish in his flowing white shirt and dark pants—an ensemble that seemed to be his uniform, and suited him so well. With the weather still so mild, he wore no jacket.

He cast his vibrant gaze over Priscilla, and she didn't protest when he leaned over and pecked her cheek. "My, what a pretty sight you are!" he declared. "You've bought another handsome new frock, I see. And what do you have in the packages?"

Priscilla laughed, feeling breathless at his intent perusal. "Oh, just some small gifts for the girls."

He regarded her quizzically. "You must be doing quite handsomely, lass, to be splurging on such finery."

She nodded happily. "I've acquired twelve new students this week."

"Twelve! My, my, but you are the ambitious one." He wagged a finger at her. "Just don't become so preoccupied with your new duties that you forget your obligations to me and the wee babes."

His comment was presumptuous, but Priscilla felt too charmed by his teasing to scold him right now. She took his arm and let him escort her down the steps, through the yard, and to his buggy. As he had the other day, he effortlessly lifted her up onto the seat.

They were clattering away when Priscilla happened to glance back at the house and was certain she glimpsed a curtain moving in an upstairs window. "You do know Mary O'Brien, don't you, Mr. Blarney?"

He scowled. "Ah, yes, the shopgirl who attends my church. What makes you mention her again?"

"Oh, nothing, really. Mary's another boarder at Mrs. Gatling's house, and she and I have become friends." She flashed him a simpering smile. "She's *awfully* nice, you know—and she's Catholic."

He gave her a stern glance. "You wouldn't be trying to steer me toward someone else, now would you, lass?"

"Moi?" Priscilla protested.

He reached out to graze her warm cheek with his fingertips. "Me mind's made up—you're the one for me, lassie. Summoned by me in my despair, and dispatched by the tides to save me from hopelessness. You'll see in time that we are meant to be, that there will be no fighting the fates."

Her heart hammering at his ardent words, Priscilla was very much afraid Jake's prophesy would prove true. Jake Blarney might be brash and unpredictable, but at times he could speak with more earthy eloquence than many of the master poets she'd read.

Embarrassed, she asked, "Where are the girls?"

"At home, with Bula. Saints be praised, Bula's conveyance has at last been repaired. So, if you don't mind, lassie, I'll have her fetch you home later. That way I won't have to disturb the wee babes."

"Of course, I don't mind at all."

He flashed her a wicked grin. "We'll still have plenty of time alone, lass ... during our ride."

The lustful gleam in his eyes left Priscilla raising a hand to her fluttering breast. Jake looked entirely too sexy, with the wind tousling his dark hair and tugging at his clothing. He'd rolled up his shirtsleeves, and she could see the hard brown muscles of his arms working as he snapped the reins. His powerful legs were slightly spread, his thigh intimately pressing into hers, his boot close to her slipper. Yes, this man exuded a raw sensuality, a vigorous physicality ... His lustiness bespoke that he was a man whose hands could skillfully ply the earth or tenderly ply a woman. Every time she was in his presence, she was reminded that he stirred a response in her that Ackerly Frost never could.

She knew she was taking a big chance seeing him again today. By Victorian standards, her visit to his home would likely be considered scandalous—despite the presence of Mrs. Braunhurst as chaperon. Of course, being seen with him in town might cause even more of a stir. She knew that if she continued dating Jake, sooner or later Ackerly was bound to find out.

Yet how could she stop seeing him, when he might make good on his threat to ruin her reputation? Still, she recognized that his blackmail was not the only reason she continued to see him.

After all, an unwilling captive would hardly spend hours shopping for a new frock to impress her captor, or buy gifts for his children, or squander half the afternoon arranging her coiffure with an old-fashioned curling iron heated on the globe of a lantern! An unwilling captive would not dream of strong arms she ached to feel holding her, or passionate kisses that she knew could turn her emotions inside out.

The truth was, Priscilla Pemberton had not indulged in great sex in a long time—correction, she had *never* indulged in truly great sex. And this man, even if he was lying through his teeth every time he tried to charm her, made her *feel* sexy with his stirring words and burning looks. If only Jake were the type to indulge in a casual affair with someone besides a harbor strumpet ... If so, she would snap him up in a instant. But Jake considered her a lady, and in these times, if she, a lady, went to bed with a man such as Jake Blarney, he would consider that her signal that she was ready to be prodded to the altar.

She almost laughed aloud at that image. She wanted prodding from Jake, all right, but not *that* kind! If only she and Jake shared more in common, beyond the devastating cravings he stirred!

As they left Galveston proper behind and traveled down the sun-swept beach, they chatted about their week, Priscilla relating anecdotes about her first days teaching elocution, Jake describing the various antics of the twins. He told of how he had taken both girls with him to the kitchen one morning and was busy cooking their cereal when they discovered the sack of dried oatmeal he had unwittingly left on the table. " 'Twas raining flakes all over the place," he informed Priscilla. "Thought I'd never get the sticky mess out of the wee lassies' hair—or mine."

Priscilla was splitting her sides laughing as they pulled up to Jake's cottage. She paused to take her first really good look at the farm. Her gaze swept past the homey cottage to the barnyard where chickens scurried about, the crude corral where a large horse lapped at a water trough, the long, weather-beaten dairy. Cows roamed in the distance, grazing on grass near a pond where red-breasted mergansers floated about and roseate spoonbills and blue herons fed in the shallows. Glancing back toward the house, she noticed a freshly planted garden and the beginnings of framing for an add-on room on the far side of the cottage.

She regarded Jake in puzzlement. "What's that?"

He winked at her devilishly. "Didn't I tell you, lassie? 'Tis our future bedroom."

Her face went crimson. "You aren't serious!"

He leaned toward her intimately, and spoke with an electrifying huskiness. "Aye. I'm very serious where our forthcoming marriage is concerned."

Jake hopped down and reached up to grasp Priscilla around the waist. She went quietly insane as he lowered her to the ground, his body brushing against hers. He took her chin in his fingertips and tilted her face toward his. When she saw the stark longing reflected in his bright blue eyes, she panicked, the potency of her desire for him shaking her to the core of her being. And that was before he started lowering his intent, handsome face toward hers.

"Please," she protested breathlessly.

"Don't mind if I do," he teased back with a perverse smile, leaning over to kiss her.

Priscilla couldn't seem to stop trembling, until Jake caught her gently against him and he became her mainstay in a reality spinning out of control. How could she object to a kiss that was so tender, so sweet; a kiss that communicated so poignantly that she was the woman Jake Blarney wanted to marry, perhaps even the woman he loved? The scent and taste of him excited her deeply, and his arms felt so warm and strong around her, she mused that he could easily become her entire world.

Oh, Lord, this was getting way too serious! She nudged him away while she could still gather the courage. "We . . . must go inside."

His gaze slid lazily over her. "You shouldn't dress so temptingly, lass, if you don't mean to invite my kisses. Why the rush?"

"The babies."

He chuckled, reached up onto the buggy seat to get her packages, and placed them in her hands. "Very well, Pris. But you won't be fending me off so easily later when we're alone."

Priscilla was already eminently aware of that!

Jake took her arm and escorted her up the steps and into his cottage. Mrs. Braunhurst was setting the table, and the babies were standing in their cradles across the room.

The instant they spotted Priscilla, both girls began bouncing up and down, holding out their arms and squealing, "Mama!"

Charmed to the bottom of her heart, Priscilla none-theless shot Jake a suspicious glance. "What is this 'Mama' business? Don't tell me you've been training the girls—manipulating them at their early age?"

"Me?" he answered. "Certainly not. Besides, the wee ones are far too young to be trained. Have minds of their own, the wee lassies do. And it appears they're telling us in no uncertain terms that they want you for their ma."

She frowned at him, still dubious, but floundering for her emotional equilibrium.

Thankfully, Mrs. Braunhurst stepped forward, end-ing the awkwardness. "I see you have returned with your guest, sir."

Priscilla smiled at the woman. "Hello again, Mrs. Braunhurst."

"*Guten tag*," she replied stiffly, and turned to Jake. "Would you like me to fetch in supper now?"

"By all means."

Mrs. Braunhurst lumbered out the front door. Observing Priscilla making eyes at the girls, Jake clapped his hands. "Sit down in the rocker, lass, and I'll bring wee Sal and wee Nell to you. They'll be making quick work of those packages you've brought, I'm betting."

She laughed. "Oh, thanks. I can't wait to hold them—and to give them their presents."

Priscilla settled herself in the rocker, and Jake brought over the babies and put one in each of Priscilla's arms. He knelt beside the chair and helped the girls open the presents. Amid much laughter, cooing, and gurgling, the twins uncovered identical baby dolls with angelic bisque faces, dressed in knitted gowns and bonnets.

" 'Twas sweet of you to treat them, gal," Jake said, watching Nell kiss her baby doll's face.

"It's my pleasure," Priscilla replied, laughing as Sal chortled and bounced her doll on a chubby knee.

Jake went to sit across from them near the hearth. He watched Priscilla rock the girls as they played with their new toys. After a moment, Nell cuddled her doll, began sucking her thumb, and fell asleep, while Sal squirmed, and even tossed her doll on the floor.

"I think she wants to get down," Priscilla whispered to Jake.

Jake got up, took the baby, lifted her high, and kissed her cheek while she giggled and flailed her arms and legs. Then he set her down on all fours. " 'Tis all right, lass, we'll keep a good eye on her."

Priscilla rocked Nell and watched Sal, and felt Jake staring at her. As before, the intimacy of the domestic scene was almost too much for her. For a moment she could almost pretend she and Jake were married, and the twins were their darling children—

A dangerous pretense indeed!

"Why are you staring at me so?" she demanded of Jake at last.

"Because you look so beautiful holding me wee babe," he replied tenderly.

"For the last time, I—I'm not beautiful," she denied, in quivering tones.

He appeared incredulous. "But you are, lass. Especially holding me wee one. Why do you keep denying your own charms? To me you'll always be as lovely as the roses of Tralee, as vibrant as the heather when it blooms in County Kerry."

Embarrassed, she glanced away and watched Sal pull a piece of parchment from beneath the table next to her. She frowned at Jake. "What does she have?"

Before he could retrieve the child, Sal quickly crawled over to Priscilla and plopped the piece of paper on her lap. "Mama!" she gurgled.

Priscilla picked up the paper and stared in amazement at a pencil drawing of her face—and not a bad one at that! She glanced at Jake, noticing the twinkle in his eyes and his unrepentant grin. "A picture of me? You drew this?"

"I'm a talented fellow, ain't I, lass?"

"You're—oh! Diabolical is more like it! You used the picture to . . . You *have* been training these babies to call me 'Mama'! Why, you stinker!"

He glowered magnificently. "Are you implying that I smell, woman?"

"Not at all. I'm saying you are . . ."

"Yes?"

"A very clever scoundrel!"

He chuckled, got up, and scooped Sal into his arms. "Ah, me wee one, you've gotten your pa in big trouble now." He glanced at Priscilla. "And what are we going to do about it, lassie? You can't disappoint the babies after I've spent all this time training them, can you?"

"You rascal!"

"Mama!" cried Sal, clapping her hands and struggling to reach for Priscilla.

Jake placed the baby against Priscilla's free arm. "Well, Pris, what do you say?"

Her lips twitched. "I say these two are too adorable."

"Aye," he agreed, leaning toward her and quickly kissing her lips. "And you're looking at the man who can give you at least a dozen more. Just say the word, lass."

Priscilla stared up raptly at him, fearing she might blurt out the very words he wanted to hear.

"Dinner is here, sir," called out Mrs. Braunhurst as she moved through the front door with a large tray.

Priscilla's gaze still hadn't left Jake's. She had suddenly lost her appetite—for food, that is!

The meal was great fun, with the twins getting more of the sausage and sauerkraut on each other than in their stomachs. Jake and Priscilla laughed over the girls' mischief, while Mrs. Braunhurst tried her best to mop up spilled milk and spattered food.

When the meal was finished and Jake announced it was time for his and Priscilla's ride, Mrs. Braunhurst insisted Priscilla should wear a shawl. Since she hadn't brought one along, Jake went over to his sea chest, and Priscilla followed him. She felt rather uneasy as she watched him dig through various female attire, since she realized all of the items must have belonged to his wife. Then she watched, wide-eyed, as he uncovered a framed photograph of a strikingly beautiful dark-haired, dark-eyed woman.

Priscilla gasped. "Who is that?"

Jake hastily turned the photograph over, shut the trunk, and shoved a white wool shawl into her hands. " 'Tis Lucinda," he said gruffly.

Priscilla went pale. "But why ... ?"

Jake appeared equally discomfited. "I kept the photograph and a few of her things for the girls, lassie, so they'll have something of their ma to remember her by when they're grown."

"I see," Priscilla replied, draping the shawl about her shoulders and flashing him a frozen smile.

Although Priscilla could understand Jake's logic in keeping the items for his girls, and she was convinced he had spoken honestly, her glimpse of the photograph had been sobering indeed. She'd always assumed the girls had gotten their good looks from their father, but now it was obvious that their mother had contributed plenty to their loveliness, as well.

She wondered why Jake wanted her so much, besides the obvious conveniences that taking a second bride would bring him. How could she ever hope to compete with the memory of such a ravishing beauty?

Chapter 16

"**Y**ou can't mean to take me for a ride on *that!*" Priscilla exclaimed moments later.

"And why not?" answered Jake. "Clyde is as gentle as they come."

Moving to the edge of the porch, Priscilla watched, flabbergasted, as Jake trotted the huge work horse up to the cottage steps. The enormous reddish brown animal seemed to tower at least six feet in height at his massive shoulders. His muzzle and flowing mane were white, as were his fetlocks, hocks, and shaggy hooves. Priscilla was certain the gargantuan beast must weigh at least a ton.

"Well, come on, Pris, have a better look at him," Jake encouraged. "He won't bite."

Tentatively she started down the steps, the horse looming larger with every step she descended. "What manner of breed is he?" she asked, squinting up at Jake in the saddle.

"An English shire, lass," he replied amiably, stroking the horse's flank. "Now, are you going to climb up here behind me, or stand there babbling away the fine evening?"

"Are—are you sure we'll be safe?" she asked skeptically.

"Safe? Clyde wouldn't hurt a fly."

Watching Clyde's impressive tail soundly swat a horsefly, Priscilla grimaced. "I'm not so sure I want to go for our ride, after all. I hadn't realized you meant for us to ride double, on such a huge beast. I assumed we would be riding normal horses—"

"Normal horses?" Jake threw back his head and laughed. "This is a working farm, lass, and I don't breed Kentucky thoroughbreds." Removing his boot from the stirrup, he stretched an arm down toward her. "Now, place your little slipper in the stirrup, lass, and give me your hand, before I come down there and fetch you."

Grumbling under her breath, Priscilla had little choice but to comply. After tying her shawl securely about her shoulders, she slipped her foot into the stirrup and took Jake's hand; a second later, amid her smothered cry, he hoisted her onto the blanket behind him. Priscilla felt very awkward sitting sideways on the huge horse; her position flanking Jake seemed precarious, to say the least. Clyde showed no reaction to her added weight, other than to bat his tail at another horsefly. But this action alone was enough to prompt Priscilla to squeak in anxiety, flail her arms, and grab two handfuls of Jake's shirt.

Jake twisted about to raise an eyebrow at her. "Why so skittish, lass? A body would think you'd never sat on the back end of a horse before."

"Actually, Mr. Blarney, I've never sat on any part of a horse before."

"You must be jesting!"

She shook her head.

"You speak as if you were raised on another planet," he said incredulously.

She laughed. "You may not be so wrong."

He rolled his eyes. "Now, hold on tight, lassie. Clutching my shirt won't help you at all if Clyde decides he wants to chase the moon."

Hearing him cluck to the horse, Priscilla quickly wrapped her arms about Jake's waist. She heard a contented sigh escape him.

The work horse began to plod away from the house toward the beach. At first the ride was fairly agreeable, once Priscilla grew accustomed to the jolting movements of the horse's huge legs. She did enjoy feeling the cool sea breeze on her face, watching the sun-gilded waves roll toward the beach, seeing seagulls swoop about, while sandpipers skipped through the waves and black skimmers glided close to the surf, dipping for fish with their curved beaks. Most enthralling of all was Jake's closeness, the strength and heat of his back against her breasts, the seduction of his male scent.

When Clyde abruptly lurched into a gallop, Priscilla found herself clinging to Jake's waist for dear life, her breasts slamming provocatively against his back with each powerful, rhythmic lunge of the horse. She knew she should be terrified, scandalized, yet instead she felt exhilarated, and even laughed aloud as they glided along the shoreline. What a picture the two of them must make, she mused, with the giant horse leaping through the surf, the two riders melded together, their hair and clothes tangling in the wind. Priscilla gloried in the joyous, unfettered moment . . . She was unaccustomed to such feelings of freedom, of leaving all her troubles behind her. The vibrant seascape, the magnificent horse, the sexy man riding with her, all seemed part of the sensuality and euphoria she felt.

She was half-dizzy by the time Jake finally pulled the horse to a halt in the grove of oak trees where they had picnicked with the babies earlier that week. "Why are we stopping?" she asked breathlessly, watching him dismount.

"And I thought you were afraid of the horse, lass," he teased, pulling her down to the ground beside him. He stroked her flushed cheek and winked at her tenderly. "I knew you'd take well to the ride."

Floundering at the sexual innuendo in his words, Priscilla avoided his eyes. It was almost too much for her, the sea breeze whipping Jake's clothing about his powerful body, the passionate way he was looking at her, the spectacularly romantic sunset . . .

She cleared her throat. "You still haven't explained why we stopped."

He nodded toward the trees, then turned to pull a blanket and a bottle of wine from the saddlebags. "I thought we'd chat awhile and watch the sunset."

You mean you thought you'd seduce me, Priscilla added to herself with burgeoning excitement.

Jake took her hand and grinned. "Come along, lassie. Let's become a wee bit better acquainted."

"Right," she murmured drolly, letting him lead her to the dune.

They paused beneath the largest oak tree, where Jake set down the bottle of wine and spread out the blanket. Priscilla plopped to the ground beside him and removed her shawl. Clyde ambled off to nibble on some grass.

Priscilla watched Jake pull the cork from the bottle with his teeth. "What, no glasses?"

"They would have broken in the saddlebags."

"Not if you had wrapped them in the blanket."

He wagged a finger at her. "Now, don't be contrary, lass. Besides, it's sexier to share the same bottle." He extended the wine toward her. "Here, have a sip."

"I'm not sure I should."

"Of course you should. It's fine, aged Madeira."

"Well, if you insist . . ." She accepted the wine and took a gulp of the rich brew. "Time in a bottle," she murmured, handing it back to him.

He frowned and took a drink himself. "You are an odd one, lass."

They reclined together on their elbows, sipped the wine, and enjoyed the setting—the roar of the surf and sweet smell of the sea breeze, the delightful pastel palette of the skies, the chatter of mockingbirds and blue jays in the tree branches over their heads.

Passing the bottle back to Jake, Priscilla stretched luxuriantly. She was enjoying this outing, and Jake Blarney's company, far too much. Would J. Ackerly Frost—in either century—be content simply to sit with her on the beach and enjoy the sunset? Of course, she and Ackerly V had gone bird-watching together on Bolivar mudflats. But it hadn't been romantic like this, not when they'd tramped through the marshes, meticulously adding names of birds to their ornithological life lists!

Jake wrapped an arm about her shoulder and kissed her cheek. "What are you thinking, lass?"

She smiled at him. "Do you honestly want to know?"

"Do you think I want you to lie?"

She shook her head. "Actually, when I look at the sea like this, I often think of Matthew Arnold."

Jake fell quiet a moment, scowling, and she half expected him to react in ignorance or jealousy, to demand to know who this new romantic competition was.

Instead, he stared out at the sea and quoted softly and poignantly, " 'Come, dear children, come away down; / Call no more! . . . She will not come though you call all day; / Come away, come away!' "

" 'The Forsaken Merman'!" Priscilla cried, astonished. "It's one of my favorites! I had no idea you were familiar with Arnold's poetry!"

"Aye, you think I'm a real bumpkin, don't you?" he asked cynically.

Priscilla felt rather ashamed. "No—it's just that one doesn't exactly expect a dairy farmer to recite poetry."

"I wasn't reared in a cabbage patch, lass," he informed her irritably. "Me mum was convent-educated in Dublin, and taught me to read and write and appreciate some of the finer things. I've still some of her books, which I cherish, I'll have you know. Wordsworth and Robert Browning, and Bobby Burns."

"But I saw no books in your home!"

"I store them in a trunk up in the loft, lass, to keep the damp and mold at bay."

She fell thoughtfully quiet, watching him gaze abstractedly out at the Gulf. "You must have really loved your wife, to quote 'The Forsaken Merman.' "

He shrugged a shoulder.

"Did you, Jake?"

He smiled bitterly. "Me marriage with Lucinda was more a matter of a wee nip too much in the moonlight. Her father was a tavern master on Smokey Row, you see, and Lucinda was one of the serving maids. That's how I met her. After I got her in a family way, the three of them came calling."

"Three?" asked a perplexed Priscilla. "You mean her mother came as well?"

"Nay, her ma passed on long ago. I mean Lucinda, her pa, and his shotgun."

Despite herself, Priscilla giggled.

Jake's expression grew wistful. "What could I do? Lucinda was a flighty, irresponsible lass, but she carried me dear twins even then. So it was off to the church for the three of us—"

"With the twins, wouldn't that have made five of you?" she teased gently.

He playfully tweaked the tip of her nose. "Aye. So we married . . . and you know the rest."

She regarded him thoughtfully. "What will you tell the girls about her when they're older?"

"That she died in an accident," he said tightly.

"Do you ever see Lucinda's father?"

"Nay," Jake responded with contempt. "After she died, he moved to the mainland. He never showed any interest in the girls . . . I'm thinking he only forced the marriage out of pride, and not wantin' to take responsibility for a pregnant daughter."

"I'm so sorry," Priscilla replied. "So you've had sole responsibility for the girls, and really no family to help."

"Aye." Again he gazed poignantly out at the sea. "After Lucinda left and the wee ones were so forlorn, I used to quote 'The Forsaken Merman' to them while I rocked them on the porch, with the sea a-roaring just beyond us: 'There dwells a loved one,

/ But cruel is she! / She left lonely for ever / The kings of the sea.' "

The sound of Jake's dramatic voice put chills down Priscilla's spine, and she could only stare at him in awe. "You really do love poetry! No wonder you penned a poetic note after you lost your wife. And then the sea brought you a replacement."

He turned to stare at her intently, almost reverently. "Aye, sweet Prissie," he murmured huskily, thrusting his hand beneath her hair and caressing the nape of her neck. "And this time, lass, I won't be losing her."

Jake crushed his lips over hers, and Priscilla could only moan in abandonment. He tasted of wine and delicious sexual need. The moment was so magical, with the sound and scent of the sea surrounding them, the music of the wind rustling the oak leaves above them ... Priscilla felt as if the two of them were locked together in a warm, sensual cocoon, and she found herself mightily tempted to surrender to Jake's drugging passion.

When his hand cupped her breast and giddy desire threatened to melt all her inhibitions, she managed to gather the strength to pull away. "Please."

Undaunted, he grabbed the wine bottle. "Have another swig, lassie."

"Mr. Blarney, you are trying to get me tipsy!" she accused.

His eyes twinkled with mischief and amusement. "Quit this 'Blarney' nonsense and call me 'Jake.' "

"Very well. *Jake*, you are trying to get me tipsy."

"Aye," he murmured, pressing the bottle to her lips.

She took a small sip, then protested, "But we mustn't swill too freely—"

"And why not?"

"B-Because we won't be able to find our way home."

He laughed heartily. "Clyde knows the way."

"Oh, I suppose he does." She bit her lip, unable to deny his logic.

He set down the bottle and drew her into his arms again, stroking her back reassuringly. "Relax, lassie," he coaxed. "I won't be hurting you, you know."

She tried to object, but Jake's mouth smothered her parted lips, then his hot, rough tongue plunged into her mouth . . . and then she forgot what she wanted to protest! They tumbled to the blanket together, kissing feverishly, her arms curled about his neck. Priscilla mused that it should be a sin for any man to taste so seductive, to smell so wonderful, to feel so hard and sexy. Jake Blarney might be all wrong for her, but in her arms he *felt* so right!

"Ah, lassie, darling lassie," he murmured, burying his lips against her throat.

Priscilla shivered as his skilled lips tortured the sensitive flesh of her neck. She groaned as his teeth nipped her gently. But when his fingers began toying with the buttons at the collar of her dress, she realized things were getting out of control, and grabbed his wrists.

"We must stop."

He easily pulled free, reaching out to undo another button and holding her captive with his fervent gaze. She trembled in his arms and could not force herself to resist.

"Lie here with me awhile, Pris," he whispered in a tormenting, sexy tone. "Just let me hold you. Talk to me."

"About what?" she whispered, her heart hammering.

Staring solemnly into her eyes, he brushed a wisp of hair from her brow. "About why you won't trust me, girl, why you're afraid of me. I know my kisses excite you, but you keep pulling away."

Gazing up at his ardent face, she hesitated, fearful her sharing might give him too much power over her. Yet his searching expression compelled honesty.

"I don't think I'm afraid of you, Jake," she began

quietly, "or I wouldn't have come out here with you tonight."

He ran his fingertip over her lips, and she struggled not to moan. "But you're afraid of giving yourself to me."

"Yes, of course I am," she admitted with a quavering laugh. "Because if I do, you'll just drag me off to the altar, won't you?"

"Aye, I will," he admitted unabashedly. "I'd love to drag you there right now."

She smiled with sadness and regret. "I know you would, Jake—but I can't go."

He pressed his lips to her hair. "Why, lass?"

She drew a deep, bracing breath. "Because I think you're determined to marry me for all the wrong reasons—mainly to find a stepmother for your girls."

He pulled back to glower. "That's not true."

"Then why would you want me?" she asked in a small, anguished voice. "I'm not the ravishing beauty Lucinda was."

He pressed his fingers to her mouth and spoke with great fervor. "Oh, but you are. To me you are everything I've ever wanted—spirited and proud and needing love, as I do. Inside you're beautiful, lass. And if you won't let me say it, by Saint Brendan, I'll have you over my knee. You have a real woman's heart, girl—Lucinda had none."

Priscilla shuddered in the wake of his soulful, vehement words. "You're very passionate, Jake, very persuasive," she conceded quietly. "But you're also rash and unheeding. You became involved with your first wife on a whim. Then, the instant I arrived on your stoop, you set your sights on me. Who knows what you may think you want tomorrow?"

He eyed her with burgeoning suspicion. "So that's it? You'll not have me because you think I'm reckless?"

She nodded hesitantly.

"Bah!" he scoffed. "There's more to it than that, lass. You've closed your mind and heart to me. I know there's something you're hiding, something that's tormenting you, and you won't be happy until you share it."

Yes, there's something I'm hiding, Priscilla thought with irony. *The truth is, I'm from one hundred and fifteen years in the future.*

But she knew what Jake really meant, what he truly needed to hear. Even though she feared exposing her deepest fears to him, perhaps it was best that she get her feelings out into the open now, rather than continue to give him false hope.

"Lass?" he prodded. "Why won't you let me close?"

She hesitated for a long moment, then glanced up at him and said heavily, "There's someone you remind me of."

"Who?"

"My father, Whitey McCoy."

Jake snapped his fingers and regarded her in astonishment. "I *knew* you had a bit of the Irish in you!"

"I have a lot of Irish in me," she admitted ruefully.

"But your name is Pemberton ... Don't tell me you've been married before, that you've already taken another bloke's name?"

She shook her head. "No, my parents split up when I was only twelve, and my mother and I had our names legally changed back to her maiden name of Pemberton."

"But why?"

"Bitterness, I suppose. My father walked out on us."

He gave a groan. "I'm sorry, lass. Then you were forsaken, just as I was by Lucinda?"

"Yes."

"Tell me about it."

She sighed. "Whitey McCoy was a drinker and a gambler, very short-tempered, always ridiculing me and my mother. My childhood was miserable because of him, as was my mother's entire marriage.

We lived in a small, conservative community. From the time I was little, I remember the other students taunting me for my father's drinking, the scraps he got into at the bars, the fact that he never paid his bills on time . . ."

Jake hugged her reassuringly. "Oh, lass, how terrible for you."

"Then one day my mother and father had a huge fight, and he just left. I wish I could say things improved for us then, but it took a long time. I had to help my mother suffer through losing our home, a divorce . . . It was devastating."

He kissed her cheek tenderly. "Bless your heart, lassie. But I think I knew this all the time."

"Knew what?" she asked.

"Knew you came from modest circumstances, and that you'd been badly hurt. That's why you won't trust me, girl—or believe in yourself."

"What do you mean, I won't believe in myself?" she asked, intrigued.

Solemnly he explained, "You say your pa disgraced you, tore you down. You say you suffered and did without. So now you think if you can get all the things he denied you, you'll be truly happy. That's why you're so determined to become a society queen, isn't it?"

Priscilla felt her hackles rising. "If you mean I'm determined never again to be poor, never to live in a community where I'll be ridiculed, where I'll have no prestige, then you're absolutely right."

"And that's why you don't want to marry a humble man such as me?"

"Yes," she admitted guiltily.

He shook his head. "Oh, lass, you are sadly deluded."

"What do you mean, I'm deluded?"

He stared into her eyes and spoke soulfully. "Happiness don't come from wealth, or from signing your name in the social register—it comes from the heart, girl."

Although Jake's words were both fervent and compelling, Priscilla felt unconvinced, her features tightening in remembered pain. "My mother followed her heart ... straight down the path of destruction."

"But, lass, is it fair to blame me for another man's sins?" he beseeched.

She bit her lip, feeling torn. "Perhaps not. You're a better man than Whitey McCoy was, Jake—there's no doubt about it. But you also remind me of him. You're quick-tempered, impetuous—"

"But me heart's in the right place," he cut in earnestly.

She smiled sadly. "You're a charmer, all right, but it takes more than good intentions to make a lasting marriage. There must be shared sensibilities and goals."

"You think I'm going to heap scandal on you like your pa did to your ma?" he asked.

"I'm convinced you have that capacity, Jake. I've heard things about you—"

"Such as?"

"That you've been known to frequent the grogshops, to get in fights, even to spend a few nights in jail—"

He nodded ruefully. "Aye, I'll not deny going on a bender or two and getting in some donnybrooks, especially right after Lucinda left me."

Vehemently she declared, "But I cannot live with a man with those destructive tendencies!"

"But, love, I'd never disgrace you that way," he argued earnestly, squeezing her hand.

"You might not want to, Jake, but I firmly believe that most people with such propensities simply do not change. And I cannot live with a man who may hold me up to public ridicule, whom I may have to bail out of jail."

His features mirrored deep disappointment. "So you're saying you won't trust me, lassie?"

"I can't afford to, Jake. We're too different. The things we want are diametrically opposed. You obviously want a simple existence on your dairy farm—I want a much more elegant and refined way of life. In the long run, we'd make each other miserable."

"What exactly are you telling me?" he demanded darkly.

"I—I'm saying we've given this a fair chance, but now I think we both need to quit while we're ahead."

Thunderclouds loomed in his eyes. "Oh, do you?"

Though it was terribly difficult, Priscilla forged on. "Yes, I do. You're wrong for me, and God knows I'd make a wretched dairy farmer's bride. It's time to call off this doomed relationship before we risk either of us getting badly hurt."

His spoke hoarsely. "What about destiny, lass? What about the note that brought you to me?"

She lowered her gaze. "I—I can't explain that."

He grasped her chin and tilted her face, forcing her to meet his impassioned countenance. "Aye—because the most powerful reasons a man and woman are drawn together can't be explained by your cursed logic. They're felt, lassie . . ." He pressed her palm to his heart. "Felt here. You can't deny it, girl—if you'll just tell the truth."

Indeed, Priscilla could feel the hard thump of Jake's heart beneath her fingertips, could see the need burning in his eyes, and every inch of her ached to acknowledge that need and respond to it. But she couldn't. She couldn't face the potential pain and hurt again—not after she'd fought so long, so hard, to become a safe and secure person.

"I know we're attracted to each other," she cried. "But physical compatibility alone is not a strong enough bond—"

"You're wrong, lassie," he whispered fiercely. "That and what's in the heart and soul are the strongest bond of all—the *only* reason that makes sense for bringing a man and woman together."

Even as Priscilla stared at him in terrible turmoil, Jake caught her close and kissed her, devouring her mouth with hungry lips and thrusting tongue. Priscilla could not think or breathe, his arms were so tight about her, his desire—and her own—so all-consuming.

At last, when he moved his tormenting lips to her hot cheek, she tried to push him away. "This is . . . getting out of hand."

"That's the idea, lass," he rasped. "I think you need to lose control quite badly."

"I think we both need to stop."

He chuckled, a low, wicked sound as he nuzzled her chin. "And you're expecting me to just let you walk out of my life unscathed?"

A small gasp escaped her. "I don't think you'll ruin me, if that's what you're hinting. Only a cruel man would do that. And you're not that ruthless."

"Oh, I'm not?" Abruptly he rolled her beneath him on the blanket. His gaze burned down into hers. "A ruthless man might make you fess up to what you're really feeling, lass," he whispered, and began unbuttoning her bodice again.

"Stop," she whispered, electrified to feel his hard, heavy body crushing her, his rock-solid erection bruising her pelvis.

"Stop me," he whispered, and they both knew she couldn't.

Indeed, Priscilla could only shudder as Jake's tormenting fingers moved down her bodice, unbuttoning one tiny button after another, a delicious death by inches. He drowned her tiny protests with a deep kiss. He arched his hips, rubbing his enticing hardness provocatively against her, and she dug her fingernails into his shoulders, feeling the feminine center of her go hot, moist, and achy, eager to receive him.

Then his fingers slipped inside her dress, to touch her nipple through her chemise, and Priscilla writhed from the sweet torment. She felt her nipple pucker and tingle at his touch, and she arched her back in pleasure.

"A ruthless man might seduce you, Pris," he mur-

mured, staring down into her eyes, "and force you to
the altar in the family way."

"You're not that ruthless," she murmured.

"Aye." But his next ravenous kiss clearly bespoke
otherwise.

Soon his skilled lips moved down her throat again,
to her breast. His fingers gently nudged aside her
chemise. When she felt his hot breath on her exposed
nipple, she squirmed, fighting the overwhelmingly
erotic sensation. He easily restrained her and slowly
drew the little peak into his mouth. Priscilla went insane, whimpering with delirious pleasure as Jake alternately sucked and flicked his tongue over the
throbbing peak. She pounded a fist on his back in
frustration, and heard his low chuckle. He was
pleased—the rogue!

"Sweet little buds," she heard him whisper, and
her fist relaxed, her fingers caressing the strong muscles of his spine.

He nibbled at her, tasted her at his leisure. When
she was breathless and frantic, he planted tormenting
kisses all over her breast, then repeated the entire,
agonizing ritual on the other one.

When his hot mouth mated with hers again, when
she felt his bold hand raising her skirt, his fingers
reaching for the ties on her drawers, at last she
seized control of herself, although her frustration was
nearly agonizing.

Desperately she pushed him away. "Please, Jake,
we must stop!"

He stared at her, breathing hard, like a man roused
from a hypnotic state.

"Please," she beseeched, "we must get back. The
girls . . . Mrs. Braunhurst."

He spent another tense moment collecting himself.
At last he murmured, "Very well, lassie, we'll go. But
only if there's no more talk about calling this off."

"All right," she conceded.

He studied her skeptically for a long moment before rolling his body off her. "When will I see you again?"

She was struggling to button up her bodice. "I—I'm not sure."

"Come with me and the wee babes to mass tomorrow," he suggested.

His unexpected invitation set her reeling. "I can't."

He scowled suspiciously. "And why not?"

Priscilla was still trying to avoid his demanding gaze. "B-Because I'm Episcopalian."

He grasped her face in his hands. "You're not still seeing Ackerly Frost, are you?"

"That is none of your business," she asserted with bravado.

His eyes clouded with anger. "With your skirts just hiked and your breast in me mouth, miss, it's very much my business."

"Oh!" She shoved him away and sat up. "You are crude!"

He shook a finger at her. "And you, miss, had best not be playing me falsely, or there will be the devil to pay. I'll not be betrayed again by some heartless strumpet."

"Heartless strumpet! How dare you imply—"

He stood and pulled her to her feet beside him. "I ain't implying a thing, Pris, only giving you fair warning. I'm not a man to be trifled with, and you'll rue the day you try it. Now, let's get you back before I'm tempted to. wallop some sense into you."

With few words and many angry glances, they gathered up their things and started back toward the cottage on Clyde. Priscilla couldn't believe the mess she was in. She seemed hopelessly caught between excitement and sensibility, between logic and lust. Jake had even managed to make her feel hellishly guilty for seeing two men at once—when he'd blackmailed her cooperation! If she didn't guard her emotions better, she would soon be hauled off to the altar by him—and likely in a family way, to boot. She must not lose her resolve, yet all she could think of was the tormenting, unfulfilled aching inside her ...

Jake, too, was furious and bemused. He understood Priscilla better now, but was disappointed that she seemed determined to allow her ambitions to overrule her heart. He knew she had been hurt before, but why couldn't she trust him? Why was she blaming him for her father's transgressions? Why couldn't she see that they were meant to be, that what really mattered was their love, their destiny together ... and not her place in Galveston society?

Could he have been wrong about her? Was she a heartless deceiver, after all? He shook his head. No, from the moment she'd appeared on his stoop, he'd known Priscilla Pemberton was the one true love he'd been waiting for. He'd been cruelly forsaken before, and surely this time the fates would remedy the injustice. Surely in her heart of hearts, Priscilla was merely scared, hurting, and confused, not calculating and mercenary as she sometimes seemed.

He smiled ruefully. Truth to tell, he could give the girl a lot more material security than she knew. The irony was, he might be able to outshine even Ackerly Frost as a marriage prospect.

Yet he yearned to hear her say that she would be content to become Priscilla Blarney, a humble dairy farmer's bride and stepmother to his children. Was it wrong of him to want to be loved for himself?

Chapter 17

Priscilla found herself living a double life—seeing Ackerly on Wednesdays and Sundays, dating Jake twice weekly at other times. Since most of her excursions with Jake were away from town at the beach or the farm, she was able to keep her appointments with him secret from Ackerly, and vice versa. However, she knew it was only a matter of time before each discovered she was going out with the other.

She did feel conflicted about dating two men at the same time. And despite Jake's blackmail, she continued to feel guilty about seeing Ackerly behind his back! Intellectually she knew Ackerly was the right man for her—yet emotionally she felt more drawn toward Jake with each passing day.

Following her magical moments on the beach with Jake, she was beginning to suspect that it might be only a matter of time before she succumbed to his masterful sensuality. For this reason she tried to avoid being alone with him, and sometimes even rented a small buggy and ventured forth on her own to see him and the girls at the cottage while Mrs. Braunhurst was present. Thankfully, Jake's housekeeper seemed very loyal to Jake and the girls, and not inclined to gossip. Priscilla also showed Mrs. Braunhurst numerous kindnesses, helping her tidy up after meals and sometimes offering her transportation to and from the Blarney farm.

Yet even when others were present and Priscilla

was "safe" from Jake's actual advances, she was far from immune to his magnetic appeal; his presence dominated all her thoughts. Each time she visited his farm, she would note that he had made further progress on constructing the bedroom addition—*their* bedroom addition, according to him—and this reality jarred her at a gut level as she found herself irresistibly fantasizing about what the room would look like when completed ... especially with her and Jake alone and naked on that magnificent brass bed he had ordered all the way from France! She tried to sweep such traitorous longings from her mind and heart, but she couldn't seem to escape them, especially late at night, when she lay alone in bed at the boardinghouse.

The more time she spent with Jake and the children, the deeper the fascination she felt with all of them. Often, as she sat rocking the babies, he would pull out a book of poetry and read aloud, enthralling Priscilla with his deep, mesmerizing voice. Hearing Jake read Whitman or Arnold or Browning in his rich Irish brogue made Priscilla dizzy with desire. More and more, she realized this Irishman she had considered to be such a bumpkin had real soul—even if it was a raw, passionate, earthy soul. At times she sorely wished they were not so many worlds apart. She wanted to live her life free of pain and turmoil, respectably ensconced in the grandest mansion on Broadway, not entangled in a potentially tempestuous marriage on a dairy farm. Yet she found herself spending some of her most cherished moments with Jake and the girls.

Priscilla tried to give her relationship with Ackerly Frost a fair chance. He was doing a commendable job in helping her establish strong ties in the community. She enjoyed his company in an intellectual sense, when they discussed issues confronting the community or a novel they had both read. She knew that as far as their backgrounds and aspirations were concerned, they had much in common and could build a strong marriage in many ways. But Ackerly simply did not excite her as Jake did. She endlessly wondered why forbidden fruit always seemed sweeter!

While Priscilla was torn between the two men, she no longer felt so conflicted over the fact that she was living in nineteenth-century Galveston. With the passage of time, she realized that perhaps she was destined to spend the rest of her life here. She could not begin to understand the mystical forces that had hurled her backward through time, but she sensed strongly that she might never see the present again. She still fretted over and missed the mother she had left behind, and she sometimes wondered if she would ever receive a response to the note she had dispatched to Ackerly V in her hour of despair, begging him to rescue her. As the days passed, any hope that she might be able to reach her mother or the *other* Ackerly began to fade with the growing awareness that she really was establishing a new life here.

Priscilla continued to build her student base in elocution, and also began tutoring some of her more struggling students in English, math, and history. She tried to coordinate her curriculum through the local private schools; she made courtesy calls on the directors of Ursuline Academy, St. Mary's Parochial School, Trinity Parish School, and several other institutions in town. In exchange for her own charm and tact toward the educators, Priscilla was rewarded with a number of current textbooks to use for her own reference, and a promise that at least some of her students would be granted release time during school hours in order to attend her sessions. The concessions on release time were a big boon to Priscilla's enterprise, since otherwise she would have had to stop enrolling students as soon as the after-school and Saturday hours were filled.

As for the curriculum itself, it very much amused Priscilla to be teaching history from books that ended their accounts shortly after the Civil War. The math texts were so basic that they covered little beyond the principles of addition, substraction, and multiplication; thus Priscilla, who had hardly been a wizard at balancing her own checkbook back in the present, could tutor students in math even at the high school level.

Priscilla prepared a number of her older students, including the Carmichael twins, for the city-wide elocution contest to be held in early November. Through talking with local educators, she learned more details about the upcoming event at the Tremont Opera House, which was sponsored by the Histrionic Society, a group of young thespians who performed at the theater. There were to be three prizes, first prize being a twenty-dollar gold piece as well as a blue ribbon.

That was the prize young Willie Shrewsbury coveted. Ambitious and hardworking, Willie had become Priscilla's pride and joy. She took delight in his tireless efforts and unfailing good humor. She encountered none of the difficulties of Henry Higgins with Eliza Dolittle, as Willie was quick to add the hard "h" sounds Priscilla intoned for him, to substitute "who" for "what" and "my" for "me" whenever appropriate. Indeed, Priscilla was delighted when Willie burst through the door for his second lesson and happily recited: " 'Hark, hark! The lark at heaven's gate sings!' " Priscilla was so thrilled by his progress that after their lesson, she took him next door to the apothecary, treated him to an ice cream soda, and bragged to her friend Mary of his accomplishments. She also spent much time selecting a poem for Willie to recite at the elocution contest, and finally settled on Blake's dramatic "Tiger, Tiger."

Late in October, Ackerly invited Priscilla to attend an important benefit, a supper and ball at the Galveston Cotton Exchange, hosted by the Galveston Wharf Company to benefit St. Mary's Orphanage. Excited by his prediction that "all the right people will attend," Priscilla eagerly accepted.

The following morning, Jake Blarney shocked Priscilla by dropping by her office on the Strand. It was still early, no students having yet arrived, when he abruptly burst in her door, wearing rumpled dungarees, a work shirt, a sheen of sweat, and a lusty grin.

"Good morning, lass," he called, whipping off his cap and starting toward her.

At her desk poring over her lesson plans, Priscilla stared up at him, fighting her secret pleasure at his presence. She was surprised to see him here, since they had an appointment for the following day. Although she was aware that Jake drove into town daily to deliver his milk, he had never before stopped at her studio.

She stood. "Jake—this is quite unexpected. What are you doing here?"

He arrived at her side and caught her close. "I couldn't wait till tomorrow to see you, love." He leaned over and kissed her ardently.

Blushing, Priscilla pushed him away. "Jake, really. This is a public establishment—"

"And you think I don't want the public to know you're mine, lass?" he teased.

"I'm not yours, Jake," she replied, fighting a smile.

He appeared wounded, forlornly pressing a hand to his heart. "That's not how it seemed when you kissed me good night on Saturday—"

Priscilla wagged a finger at him. "Mr. Blarney, I'll have you know *you* kissed *me* good night!"

"Really, lass? I could have sworn 'twas you."

"My, your modesty is so becoming!"

"Not nearly as becoming as the pretty blush I've put in your cheeks," he teased back.

She attempted an admonishing glance. "Jake, you are a bundle of charm as usual, but my schedule is really very pressing today, and you still haven't told me why you have burst in on me this way."

He glanced around the studio. "Well, lass, I was just delivering me milk to the pasteurizing plant, and thought I'd have a look at the place where you conduct your business."

She fought secret amusement. "So have a look if you must. Only, step lively. My first student is due at any moment."

"Step lively, eh?" he repeated cynically.

Deliberately taunting her, he strode slowly about the room, hands clasped behind his back and a scowl knitting his handsome brow. Reminding Priscilla of Ackerly during his first inspection tour, Jake carefully scrutinized a book here, a paper there, and took a long moment to straighten an antimacassar draped over the back of a chair.

"Jake, please!" she pleaded.

He turned and grinned. "So this is where you practice your fine university degree, eh, lass?"

"This is it."

"Well, you won't be needing the place once we're wed."

She groaned. "Jake, you're making a pest of yourself—and being a chauvinist."

"What's that?"

"Consider your irrepressible self to be the perfect definition," she quipped back.

Scowling slightly, he asked, "Tell me exactly what you do here, darlin'."

Realizing he was determined to assuage his curiosity, she replied with forbearance, "Essentially, I teach my students to speak correctly."

"I bet you think I could use some help there," he said drolly.

Priscilla smiled. "Actually, I think it would be a sin to spoil your charming Irish inflections."

"Then why are you teaching the others?"

"Because some of the children have accents so bad, they're being ridiculed at school. I understand how harmful that can be."

"Ah, I suppose you would," he replied. "But you think I'm a lost cause?"

"In many ways," she said dryly. "Look, Jake, this has been delightful, but I really am pushed for time right now. So unless there's something else you want, could you please let me attend to my business?"

He came to her side, hauled her close, and winked. "What I'm wanting, lass, will be spoiling all your business for this day and many more to come."

She broke free again, her voice rising. "Jake, I am about to lose my patience!"

The devil only crossed his forearms over his chest and chuckled. "Actually, darlin', I was just about to head home when I had me a thought. The weather's still so beautiful, with Indian summer lingering into late October. Why don't we plan an excursion with the girls on Saturday? We'll all take a steamer over to the mainland, and spend the day picnicking on Virginia Point. We may be late getting back, but I'm sure 'twill be worth missing your Saturday night bath."

Priscilla felt the color drain from her face. "You're asking me to spend Saturday with you?"

"Aye." He frowned at her wan expression. "Look, if it's the proprieties that are fretting you, we'll take along Bula. That may be best in any event, since 'twill likely be dusk before we return. Then on Sunday, I'm counting on you to come out to the farm house and help me and the babes bob for apples and keep the Halloween ghosts and goblins at bay."

Priscilla took a deep, bracing breath. "Jake, I'm very sorry, but I can't see you on Saturday—or on Sunday, either."

His gaze sharpened with suspicion. His voice came very soft. "And why not, darlin'?"

"Because I have other plans."

"What other plans?"

"That's none of your affair!"

He seized her by the shoulders. "What other plans?"

"Let go of me!" she ordered furiously.

"You're seeing Jack Frost, aren't you?" he demanded, his eyes gleaming with anger.

"What if I am? And his name is J. Ackerly Frost."

"Why, you two-timing little schemer!"

"I'm nothing of the sort!"

"You're stepping out with two men at the same time."

"Yes—but only because you blackmailed me into seeing you, Jake. Otherwise, I would be seeing only one man—"

"Jack Frost?" he roared.

"Yes."

"And you think he's the right man for you?"

"Yes. We're alike. You and I . . . have nothing in common."

"Nothing in common?" he repeated, staring at her meaningfully.

"Nothing enduring," she asserted with bravado, despite the color rising in her face.

"Oh, really, lass? Then how do you explain this?"

Priscilla realized his brash intention too late. Before she could duck away, Jake grabbed her and kissed her, bruising her lips with his, plundering her mouth with his tongue. Priscilla was enraged by his audacious conduct. She knew he was trying to insult and humiliate her, and she tried to fight back, tried to pound his back with her fists, but he was simply too strong, the ox! Jake kissed her until she was desperate, dizzy, and had no choice but to cling to him or else collapse at his feet. She despised him for exposing her weakness, yet her traitorous body still wanted him. He knew it, too, the devil! He plunged with his tongue, seduced with his lips, until at last she responded. He left her no pride. When his mouth finally released hers, she heaved in her breath, feeling both feverish and furious.

"Well, lass?" he asked in triumph.

Were she not assured of even worse retaliation, she would have slapped his arrogant face. Instead, trembling with passion and mortification, she said hoarsely, "Besides that."

He shook a finger at her. "*That* is what the best marriages are made of—"

"According to you! I'll decide what makes a good

marriage for me, thank you very much! And for me, it's not brute force!"

Jake's countenance grew murderous. "I didn't force you—"

"The hell you didn't!"

"I warned you not to see him, girl."

Priscilla stamped her foot in fury. "Believe it or not, Mr. Blarney, I, and not you, am in charge of my life. You've coerced me into seeing you, but that does not give you the right to control everything I do. So, despite your endearing caveman tactics, I'll see whomever I damn well please!"

The big lummox didn't even blink. "Where is he taking you on Saturday?"

"Get out of here and leave me alone!"

He grabbed her shoulders again and shook her slightly. "I said, where is he taking you?"

"To the Cotton Exchange Ball!" she all but screamed.

"So you can lord it up with the high and mighty?" he sneered.

"It's an important benefit for Saint Mary's Orphanage."

"You mean a benefit for the vanity of you and your hoity-toity friends."

With deadly calm she said, "I'm telling you one last time to get out of here and leave me in peace."

His fiercely determined features brooked no challenge. "And I'm warning you one last time not to do this."

She said nothing, but her eyes blazed with defiance.

"You've just made a big mistake, lass," he said, and left.

After he was gone, Priscilla paced about her studio in terrible turmoil. On one level, she could understand Jake's anger over her date with Ackerly—but what else should he have expected, after he'd blackmailed her cooperation? He'd had no right to behave like such a beast, forcing another kiss on her, making her respond on that same emotional level she so feared. He reminded her of Whitey when he had tried to charm her mother; when charm hadn't worked, her father had resorted to coercion, threats, and intimidation. Just like Jake today!

Well, it was over now. Doubtless, after revealing her plans with Ackerly, she had chased Jake away for good. She should feel relieved. She should be grateful that there would be no Jake Blarney around to penetrate her facade and expose her true feelings, to make her vulnerable.

Instead, it was all she could do not to burst out sobbing.

Jake fumed as he stormed out of Priscilla's studio and headed back for his wagon. Was Priscilla a heartless two-timer after all? Why was she seeing Ackerly Frost when he was certain the man inspired no true passion in her? Why couldn't she see what truly mattered between a man and a woman?

Obviously his bride-to-be was still determined to fight the strong bond between them, still obsessed with gaining Frost's wealth and prestige. It hurt Jake terribly that Priscilla was seeing another man, when he was the man who understood her best, the man who was ready and willing to help her heal her pain and fill the emptiness inside her. Why wouldn't she trust him?

One thing was certain. He was not about to be bested by that mollycoddle, Jack Frost. He'd be shoveled six feet under before he allowed that whey-face to steal the woman destiny had brought him. *His* woman, by damn!

Perhaps Priscilla needed to be shown a bit more dramatically that the two of them were meant to be . . .

Chapter 18

Priscilla did not see Jake for several more days. She tried to tell herself it was inevitable that he found out about Ackerly, and that the two of them should arrive at a parting of the ways. And surely their breakup was for the best. After all, he had behaved like a bully when he showed up at her studio—trying to tell her what to do, forcing his attentions on her. His actions had proven he was far too brash, too unpredictable, too dangerous, to be considered a fitting suitor. Intellectually she knew she should consider herself lucky to be rid of such a male chauvinist . . .

Yet emotionally she didn't feel so lucky, for she missed Jake and the girls terribly, and even felt guilty for rejecting him. Sometimes she wondered if what he'd said the night she had arrived on his stoop had been true—that she couldn't fight destiny. She knew he was entirely wrong for her, yet she craved him more every day.

Priscilla tried to stay busy, hosting a small Halloween party for her students, giving them apples and nuts and candy. Anticipation of the Cotton Exchange Ball at the end of the week also provided some welcome distraction. Right after Ackerly had invited her, Priscilla had ordered a custom ball gown from Sarah O'Shanahan, and the seamstress did a masterful job on the formal frock. Priscilla oohed and aahed over the garment when she picked it up from Sarah's shop on Saturday morning.

On Saturday evening, after Priscilla had spent many hours bathing, dressing, and styling her hair, she swept out of her room and crossed the hallway to show her friend Mary her fabulous gown. But a rap on Mary's door brought no response. After a moment, Priscilla peeked inside, and found the room perfectly in order, but no Mary in sight. She frowned. It was unlike Mary to leave for the weekend and not tell Priscilla, and actually, the girl had seemed preoccupied and distant much of the week. She hoped Mary was not embroiled in some crisis, and unwilling to share her troubles with Priscilla.

Closing the door, she heard a familiar female voice call up from the stairs, "Miss Pemberton, Mr. Frost has arrived."

Priscilla peered over the railing to see Rose Gatling standing on the landing. "Thank you, Mrs. Gatling. Please tell him I'll be right down."

If Mrs. Gatling was at all impressed by Priscilla's costume, she showed no sign, merely turning and descending the staircase. Feeling jittery, Priscilla ducked back inside her room and eyed herself in the mirror one last time. How she hoped and prayed her image would pass muster tonight! She would doubtless meet many more distinguished Galvestonians, and she was determined to make the best impression.

She scowled at her reflection, smoothing down a ruffle here, a pleat there. She still wasn't beautiful, nor would she ever be big-busted, she mused with regret. But she had to admit she had never looked better. She wore a sweeping, tight-waisted gown of pale green taffeta, with a pleated underskirt of pink crossbar lawn. Her double-poufed train was graced by green satin ribbons and pink silk roses. Her hair was upswept in a bun decorated with flowers, and she had laboriously curled a few loose strands about her brow, earlobes, and the nape of her neck. She wore pearl earrings and a matching choker that accented the décolletage of her frock. Elegant white gloves covered her bare arms past the elbows, and she carried a stylish rose silk fan with ivory sticks.

She might as well face the lions, she mused. Before she could lose her nerve, she grabbed her beaded reticule and white cashmere shawl, and left her room.

The moment she swept past the landing and heard Ackerly's astonished whistle, she knew she had scored a hit. She smiled down at him, feeling keenly relieved at his enthralled expression. He stood by the newel post watching her descend, looking dashing in his formal black cutaway with white linen shirt and black cravat.

He was literally beaming when she arrived at his side. "My dear, you look a vision!" he cried, kissing her gloved hand.

"Why, thank you, Ackerly. You look quite dapper yourself."

"I'm sure we'll be the most admired couple at the ball," he declared, offering his arm.

Priscilla forced a smile as they left the rooming house together. Yes indeed, they would make a fine impression tonight. Ackerly was just the type of refined, sophisticated man she belonged with . . .

Then why did she miss Jake so much?

The trading room of the Cotton Exchange fascinated Priscilla from the moment she and Ackerly strolled through its ornate portal. The ballroom appeared to be at least sixty by eighty feet, with a three-story-high, heavily carved ceiling, from which were suspended massive wrought-iron chandeliers fitted with gleaming gaslights. A mock wrought-iron balcony encircled the entire second story, with beautifully arched windows opening off the railing to offices on that level.

The main floor, inlaid of oak and walnut, glittered with humanity—dashing gentlemen in black cutaways waltzing lovely ladies in vibrant ball gowns of silk and satin and velvet. Tiaras sparkled from the crowns of elaborate coiffures, diamond studs twinkled from impeccably tailored shirtfronts, and scintillating laughter and elegant music filled the air, along with the delicate scents of flowers, pomade, and expensive perfumes. On a dais in a back corner, a small orchestra strummed Strauss's "Roses of the South," while toward the front of the room was laid out the long, lavish buffet table, with several uniformed stewards serving punch, carving roast beef, or dishing out delicacies ranging from oysters Bienville to crabmeat crepes and pickled herring. The table sported decorations that included jack-o'-lanterns and cornucopias spilling forth fruit and nuts, in keeping with a Halloween theme.

"Well, Ackerly, Miss Pemberton, how good to see you here," a deep male voice boomed out.

Priscilla turned to see Colonel and Mrs. Moody standing just inside the doorway. She remembered chatting briefly with the couple several times when she had dined with Ackerly at the Tremont Hotel. Moody had graying hair, a long beard, and piercing eyes; his smiling wife was gowned in elegant black silk. Ackerly at once extended his hand. "Well, Colonel Moody, Mrs. Moody, what a pleasure."

"The pleasure is ours, Ackerly," Moody replied. "And, Miss Pemberton, you look a vision."

"Thank you, Colonel," said Priscilla, offering her hand.

"We've heard such good things about you, Miss Pemberton," said Mrs. Moody. "We do hope you're enjoying our community."

"Oh, I am," Priscilla assured, shaking Mrs. Moody's hand. "Everyone here has been most gracious to me."

"You hail from Mississippi, I understand?" inquired Mrs. Moody.

"That's correct. From Oxford."

"Priscilla was educated at Vanderbilt," Ackerly said proudly. "She's a true asset to our community."

"And now I hear Miss Pemberton is tutoring the

children of some of our best families," remarked
Moody.

"Indeed she is," Ackerly acknowledged happily.

"Colonel, it ⁓⁓⁓s so good of the Wharf Company to
sponsor this wonderful event," Priscilla said, gesturing toward the ballroom.

"Yes—we're only too happy to help the orphans of
our community." Moody winked at Priscilla. "You
two have a fine time, now."

"Oh, we shall," Ackerly assured him.

"And, Mr. Frost," Moody added, "one of these af-
ternoons you must join George and John Sealy, Harris Kempner, and myself for coffee on the veranda of
the Tremont Hotel."

"Colonel, I'd be honored."

Ackerly was all but glowing with pride as he escorted Priscilla to the buffet table, and they were
served. They nibbled on the excellent fare, all the while
greeting other esteemed guests—George and Magnolia
Sealy, James and Rebecca Brown, Harris and Eliza
Kempner. John and Eleanor Haggarty paused to visit,
John and Ackerly discussing business while Eleanor
lavishly praised Priscilla for Jimmy's progress in elocution.

An awkward moment ensued when Winnie Haggarty swept up to join them. The young woman
looked gorgeous in a low-cut, bustled gown of sapphire blue satin. Her rich chestnut curls were piled
in an elaborate coiffure on top of her head, and fabulous sapphire and diamond jewelry graced her ears,
throat, and hands.

She made a beeline for Ackerly. "Ackerly, you look
divine!" she preened, dimpling prettily.

"As do you, my dear," answered Ackerly gallantly
as he leaned over and kissed Winnie's gloved hand.

Priscilla felt irritation rising at the young belle's
blatant flirting with her date. There was no doubt as
to who Winnie Haggarty had set her cap on!

Winnie spotted Priscilla, and flashed her most sim-

ering smile. "Oh, hello, Priscilla, dear," she said
almost as an afterthought. "What a sweet little
frock."

"Hello, Winnie," Priscilla replied with equal insin-
cerity. "My, aren't you a picture tonight." *A picture of
the scheming femme fatale!* she added to herself.

Winnie continued to chat with Ackerly, tempting
Priscilla to ask the little tease why she hadn't batted
her eyelashes or waved her fan at him yet. Instead
she smiled benignly, noting to her further annoyance
that Ackerly seemed flattered by the young co-
quette's attentions.

Thank heaven Winnie's escort, a flustered-looking
young man with blond hair and blue eyes, soon appeared to whisk her onto the dance floor. John and
Eleanor drifted off, and Ackerly introduced Priscilla
to some other good friends of his, Claude and Helen
Durant.

"Helen is on the board of the Tremont Opera
House," Ackerly informed Priscilla before turning to
chat with Claude.

"Oh, really?" Priscilla asked Helen, smiling at the
tall, slim, middle-aged woman who was exquisitely
attired in a black velvet gown accented by diamond
jewelry. "I'm so impressed to hear that, Mrs. Durant."

"We are equally impressed to hear of your elocution
lessons, Miss Pemberton," Helen responded warmly.
"Tell me, are any of your students participating in the
contest at the Tremont next weekend?"

"Why, yes, several!" declared Priscilla. "I understand the event is sponsored by the Histrionic Society?"

"Yes, they're a very promising group of young
thespians associated with the theater. The Histrionics
sponsor frequent dramatic presentations between our
scheduled operas. We've actually had some world-
class events at the Tremont—including performances
by Jenny Lind and Sarah Bernhardt, Barrett and
Booth and Edwin Forrest."

"Oh, how fabulous! I simply adore opera."

"Do you? Have you attended the Tremont yet?"

"No, but I can hardly wait."

Helen continued excitedly. "You know, we're currently restaging the successful *Maniac Lover* from the late sixties, as well as casting for our next production, *Samson and Delilah*. Tell me, Miss Pemberton, do you sing? We're always looking for talented additions to our chorus."

Priscilla laughed. "Mrs. Durant, let me assure you that my singing talents would only cause a run on rotten eggs for your subscribers."

"Miss Pemberton, I'm sure you exaggerate."

"I wish I could agree."

Laughing, Helen glanced about the room. "You know, we really need a talented tenor, as well. I wish we had Jake Blarney. Perhaps I can have a word with him tonight."

Priscilla peered about in astonishment, struggling to keep her mouth from dropping open. "Jake Blarney is here?"

Helen nodded toward the buffet table. "He's right over there with his young lady."

"His *young lady*?"

Priscilla glanced across the room, and felt flabbergasted to view Jake, dressed in formal black, handing a glass of punch to none other than her own friend Mary O'Brien! Mary, dressed in a modest but presentable frock of yellow satin, was smiling back at him, obviously thoroughly enjoying herself. As Mary began to sip her punch, she spotted Priscilla staring at her and turned to give a little wave, along with a guilty smile. Then Jake also spotted Priscilla and greeted her with a brash grin and an exaggerated salute.

Outraged, Priscilla quickly glanced away. Oh, the nerve of that rogue! He had actually taken her best friend out on a date! At first she felt tempted to charge across the room and set them both in their places—but she quickly realized she had absolutely no right to do so. After all, she had just broken up with Jake, and was attending this event with someone else. Jake had every right to do the same—even if he was making her boiling mad! As for Mary, it did seem unlike her to do something like this, when she had to have known that stepping out with Jake might cause Priscilla pain. Why had she done so? Perhaps Priscilla should give her friend the benefit of the doubt until she spoke with her . . .

"Miss Pemberton, are you all right?" she heard Helen ask.

"Wh-Why, yes," Priscilla stammered, flashing the matron a frozen smile. "I just had no idea Mr. Blarney would be here."

"Do you know him?"

"Vaguely." By now Priscilla's hands were trembling so badly that she gratefully dumped her dinner plate and punch cup on a tray offered by a passing servant.

"Then perhaps you can help us approach Mr. Blarney for the opera," Helen asked.

Priscilla regarded the woman quizzically. "Why do you want him so badly?"

"Why, his heavenly voice!" Helen cried. "That tenor of his is one in a million. You see, Claude and I attend Saint Patrick's with Mr. Blarney, and we've heard him sing many times. As Father O'Dooley has so often said, not even the angels can match Jake Blarney when he sings "Agnus Dei.""

"Why, I had no idea he was *that* talented," Priscilla muttered, though she was not really surprised. Jake's voice was marvelous—she had been favored to hear it on many occasions now.

Helen was regarding him with an appreciative eye. "He's an extraordinary example of manhood, isn't he?"

Feeling put on the spot, Priscilla glanced covetously at Jake and toyed with her pearl choker. "Well, I suppose . . ."

"He attends the opera, you know," confided Helen.

"He what?" Priscilla regarded Helen wide-eyed.

She nodded smugly. "I've spotted him up in the balcony several times. How I wish I could get him to try out for *Pirates of Penzance* next spring. With his dashing good looks and remarkable voice, he'd make a perfect pirate king, you know."

Priscilla was too mystified to respond.

After a moment, Helen drifted off with Claude, and Ackerly rejoined Priscilla. Eyeing her pale countenance, he inquired, "My dear, are you unwell?"

She forced a smile. "Not at all. I just saw . . . someone I didn't expect to see here, that's all."

His gaze swung about the room and settled on Jake. "Well, I'll be deuced—the milkman, Jake Blarney. Imagine his nerve showing up here."

Priscilla felt somewhat irritated. "Isn't this benefit open to anyone who can afford the price of the tickets?"

Ackerly snorted in disdain. "My dear, the tickets are deliberately priced high to exclude such riffraff and to ensure that only the right class of people attends."

His snobbishness aggravated her. "My word, Ackerly, are you sure you should have escorted *me*?"

Her sarcasm seemed lost on him as he continued to stare rudely at Jake. "And he's escorting that shabby little drugstore clerk, Mary O'Brien."

Despite Mary's possible disloyalty in attending the event with Jake, Priscilla was affronted by Ackerly's tacky remark. "That shabby little drugstore clerk happens to be my best friend!"

Ackerly had the grace to look embarrassed, and quickly patted her hand. "I'm sorry, my dear. I never intended to insult a friend of yours. But a young lady of your refinement and gentility should be able to cultivate friends in the highest circles, don't you think?"

Even as Priscilla frowned back in perplexity, Ackerly turned away to chat with Nicholas Clayton. The orchestra started up a lilting rendition of "Poor

Wandering One," and that was when Priscilla could *feel* someone staring at her.

Heart hammering, she turned to watch Jake Blarney stride purposefully toward her, looking splendid in his black cutaway, with the gaslight gleaming in his thick, dark hair, and the determined glint shining in his eyes. He appeared like a magnificent dark predator stalking her, and she was surprised she was able to hang on to the undigested supper already churning in her stomach. She looked wildly for an avenue of escape. But there was none, short of turning and running across the ballroom, amid the certainty of his pursuit, a debacle that would surely earn them both an exalted place in the Histrionic Society.

He paused to bow before her, and the scent of his bay rum wafted over her. As he straightened, his brilliant blue eyes seemed to impale her, increasing her agitation. Oh, Lord, he was utterly devastating!

His voice oozed charm. "Miss Pemberton, I believe they are playing our song. May I have the honor of this dance?"

That drew Ackerly's attention, and he turned to glare haughtily at Jake. "Sir, I must insist that you remember your place and not annoy Miss Pemberton."

Jake's intense gaze never wavered from Priscilla, and she knew he was well aware of the high color blooming in her cheeks. "Is the lass annoyed?" he asked softly. "I believe she can speak for herself."

Ultimately it was all too irresistible to Priscilla, the opportunity to dance with Jake and set Ackerly in his place for acting the pompous snob. After all, the orchestra *was* playing her and Jake's song—the very song that had brought her across time to him.

Without even looking at Ackerly, Priscilla perched her fingers on Jake's arm. "Mr. Blarney, I'd be honored."

She heard Ackerly call her name, quite irritably, as Jake escorted her to the dance floor, never taking his eyes off her. They were the first couple to arrive on the floor for the new selection, and she knew they were causing a stir, no doubt a scandal. But she didn't care. She had missed Jake terribly, and he looked so handsome and smelled so good—even though she could strangle him for taking out Mary and cruelly raising her friend's hopes.

He pulled her into his arms and swept her about to the buoyant melody. Oh, he could dance! He waltzed divinely, whirling her about as if they were floating on a cloud! Would he never cease to amaze her?

"You look wonderful, Priscilla," he whispered.

She glanced up at his dark, ardent face, and decided he was sincere. "Thank you."

"Are you surprised to see me here?"

That question roused her righteous indignation. "Actually, you have no business being here, Jake Blarney, splurging on such high-priced tickets . . . and that divine suit."

"Do you think I look divine in it, lass?" he teased.

Priscilla felt herself blushing at her own unconscious slip. "I-I'm simply making the point that the money could have been much better spent on the girls. And by the way, how are they?"

He laughed. "They're fine, only they miss you terribly."

She glanced away miserably. She missed the babies, too—as much as she had missed Jake.

"So you think J. Ackerly Frost is the only man on this island with enough money to attend this event?" he asked.

She groaned. "You just had to prove your point, didn't you?"

"What point is that, Miss Pemberton?"

"You know good and well what point! You had to show me you're as good as Ackerly, and never mind who you hurt in the process. Furthermore, you were cruel to invite Mary here, and raise her hopes, when you know you're not interested in her."

His eyes twinkled with devilment. "What makes you think I'm not interested in her?"

Even as his skilled riposte had her gasping, Priscilla was tempted to knock some sense into his hard head. "Oh—you're impossible. You know Mary is my friend—and you know you're using her tonight to try to get to me—"

"Aye. And I told her as much, lass."

"Told her what?"

"That I was inviting her along to make you jealous, of course," came the unabashed reply.

"You didn't! You scoundrel!"

He grinned, totally unrepentant. "Would it have been better to lie to her?"

"N-No, but ..." Exasperated, she demanded, "What did Mary say when you so bluntly laid out your motives?"

"Well, after I convinced her that my intentions toward you are completely honorable, she admitted that she'd be happy to get to attend the Cotton Exchange Ball, whatever the reason. And she agreed that Ackerly Frost is wrong for you. I believe her words were that you could use a good prodding, stubborn as you are—"

Despite herself, Priscilla laughed. "That does sound like Mary."

He drew her slightly closer and whispered wickedly, "Well, is the ploy working, sweet Pris?"

Her heart was hammering wildly. "Is what ploy working?"

"Did I make you jealous by bringing Mary tonight?" he teased. "Will you become more jealous still if I kiss her good night?"

"You wouldn't!" she cried.

"On the cheek," he murmured back, "like a proper friend." He skillfully maneuvered her past another couple, his arms tightening around her. "Although, of course, that's not how I'm aiming to kiss you, lass, or where ..."

Priscilla felt deliciously mortified, especially as she

noted a number of people staring at them. "Jake, please, you're holding me much too close—"

"Not as close as I soon will, fair Prissie." His gaze slid to her bosom, and his voice grew husky. "You shouldn't come here dressed like such an enchantress if you aim to keep me at bay. Ackerly now, he'll take you home with every curl and ribbon in place. But if you were out with me tonight, love, I'd take you home all ashambles, and begging to be undone even more."

"Jake, please." His words were incredibly sexy, and Priscilla was reeling, to the point of pleading.

But he only continued in an adamant, deeply impassioned voice. "I warned you, lass. We're meant to be. You can't fight it."

He swung her about, and she found herself wondering if she could fight the fates. The waltz was long, agonizingly so. Jake's nearness and charm were making her demented—

Then they almost collided with Ackerly and Winnie Haggarty. Jake deftly maneuvered Priscilla out of range; Ackerly glowered at them both, and Winnie smirked as the other couple swirled off.

"Oh!" Priscilla exclaimed. "Ackerly is dancing with—that child!"

Jake laughed. "That pretty child could use a prisspot like Jack Frost. Don't look at them. Look at me."

Priscilla did so, and felt herself floundering all the more at the hunger burning in his eyes.

As the song reached a crescendo, Jake smiled at her and softly sang:

> "If such poor love as mine
> Can help thee find
> True peace of mind,
> Why, take it, it is thine."

The music ended. At the center of the room, they stopped, still regarding each other raptly. The tension seemed to stretch out over an eternity. Convinced she was about to melt into a puddle at Jake's feet, Priscilla stammered, "Y-You sing beautifully, Jake. Mrs. Durant says you attend the opera."

He frowned, taken aback. "Does she, now?"

"She wants you to try out for *Pirates of Penzance* in the spring."

"Well, she had best not hold her breath."

"You know you have a splendid voice. Would you be ashamed to go onstage?"

He drew himself up with pride. "I ain't ashamed of what I am, lass. And it ain't no dandified opera singer."

"But you could share your talents with the world."

He winked at her tenderly. "I'm aiming to share them only with you, lass."

Priscilla was at a loss for words, though a wince of longing escaped her.

The other dancers had left the floor now, and most everyone in the room was avidly observing the lone couple standing at center stage with eyes only for each other. In full view of everyone, Jake leaned over and graced Priscilla's lips with a gentle, tantalizing kiss. Then he straightened and grinned at her intimately.

"There's a good sample of me talents, lass. You can have the rest any time. I'm yours for the taking."

Priscilla stood spellbound.

Reality at last intruded as Ackerly stormed up, trembling with anger. To Jake he snapped, "Manhandle Miss Pemberton again, you hooligan, and I'll call you out."

Jake glanced at Ackerly, then laughed. "I'll save you the trouble, Mr. Frost."

And before Priscilla's horrified eyes, Jake swung back his fist and punched Ackerly squarely in the face, easily sending him crashing to the floor. Priscilla flung a hand to her mouth as a collective gasp rippled over the crowd.

Priscilla could have died on the spot. In the space of a split second, the romantic spell Jake had cast about her had been cruelly shattered. Utterly humiliated, near tears, she turned and soundly slapped Jake's face.

"You obnoxious brute!" she said in a mortified whisper. "Look what you've done! I hope I never lay eyes on you again!"

For a moment he glared back at her, appearing so indignant that she feared he would strike her back. Then he turned on his heel, went to grab Mary, and quickly escorted her out.

Several men rushed forward to help Ackerly, who had come to and was glancing about in befuddlement, shaking his head. Hearing the scandalized murmurs flitting through the room, observing the many eyes focused on her in shock, pity, and even revulsion, Priscilla wished she could sink through the floor.

Thus the Cotton Exchange Ball ended in a shambles.

The mood was somber half an hour later as Jake Blarney escorted Mary O'Brien through the yard to her aunt Phoebe's house on Seventeenth Street. Jake's expression was utterly dour, Mary's a picture of distress.

"I'm really sorry, dear," he told her sincerely. "I turned your lovely evening into a calamity, and likely ruined your friendship with Priscilla, as well."

At the base of the steps, she touched his arm in reassurance. "You meant well, Jake. We both thought a nudge in the right direction might help bring Priscilla round."

"Aye, but now me fine scheme has backfired in both our faces," he admitted morosely. He clenched a fist in frustration. "If only I hadn't lost my temper and punched Ackerly Frost! But when that pantywaist called me a hooligan and insisted I couldn't touch Priscilla, well, I suppose I took leave of me senses."

"I understand, Jake," said Mary sympathetically.

He sighed. "Now there will be no hope for Priscilla and me."

Mary gasped. "Don't say that!"

" 'Tis true. If Frost and I had had our donnybrook in private, that would have been one thing. But now I've disgraced Priscilla before the entire community. She sets great store by her reputation, and she'll never forgive me for heaping such scandal on her."

They trudged up the steps to the porch, and stood beneath the yellow light of the gas sconces. Eyeing Jake's tragic face, Mary implored, "Please don't give up."

He forced a grin. "I'd best be going—Bula and her husband are sitting with me wee twins." He leaned over to peck her cheek. "Thanks for coming out with me, love. Sorry the evening didn't turn out better."

As Jake turned and retreated down the steps, Mary stood rubbing her cheek and wistfully watching him. "Oh, Priscilla, love," she murmured sadly. "You've chosen yourself the wrong man."

Back at her room at the boardinghouse, Priscilla was distraught. Ackerly hadn't even spoken with her when he had dropped her off. She had never been so mortified in her entire life! She felt hurt, devastated, and humiliated by Jake Blarney's unheeding actions.

Indeed, she was so overwrought, she was on the verge of hyperventilating. She rushed outside onto her balcony, in the cool air, and took several deep breaths to try to calm her raging senses.

She wondered if she would ever recover from the disgrace Jake had heaped on her tonight. She felt as if she had just relived all the agonies of her miserable childhood.

Her features clenched in bitterness as she recalled a similar incident instigated by her father. Priscilla, Beatrice, and Whitey had attended a church dinner together, and things had gone well until after the meal, when the three of them had visited the dessert table. Whitey had run across a man he'd done business with, the president of a local finance company. The two men greeted each other tensely, then the businessman said apologetically, "Whitey, I'm really sorry I had to repossess your tractor—"

Those had been the last words to leave his mouth as Whitey had knocked the poor man unconscious, in full view of the horrified minister and all the members of the church! Priscilla and Beatrice had been utterly humiliated. Priscilla would never forget the shocked murmurs, the pitying looks she and her mother had received—

Just like tonight! Jake Blarney was destroying her reputation in this community! He was determined to take everything she valued—security, prestige, peace of mind—away from her! He was hell-bent on driving her down the same perilous path that had destroyed her mother . . .

And the agony of it was, despite everything, she *still* wanted him!

Chapter 19

The president of the Frost National Bank of Galveston had quite a shiner.

Early Monday morning, Priscilla sat across from Ackerly at his desk, struggling not to wince as she regarded his battered face. The purplish bruise curving beneath his left eye and extending high onto his cheekbone stood out in stark contrast to his formal demeanor and understated banker attire.

For at least ten minutes, Priscilla had been imploring him to forgive Saturday night's debacle. Following the reprehensible scene Jake Blarney had caused, Priscilla had decided once and for all that she wanted nothing more to do with the brash Irishman who promised to take her life—and her reputation—straight down the road to destruction. The passion he stirred be damned! Ackerly Frost—with his sophistication and good sense—was the right man for her.

"Ackerly, I can't begin to tell you how sorry I am," she repeated for at least the sixth time.

"You weren't so sorry that you refused to dance with Jake Blarney," he responded sternly.

Priscilla groaned, for Ackerly had a valid point.

"You might give a thought to my reputation in this community, Priscilla," he continued. "Great Scot, the man kissed you, on the mouth, in the presence of at least a hundred of Galveston's most esteemed citizens."

"I know," she conceded miserably.

"Under the circumstances, it's difficult for me to believe you've done nothing to encourage him."

"What was I supposed to do, cause a scene by refusing to dance with him?" she asked with an exasperated wave of her hand.

"You caused more of a scene by consenting!"

"Yes, but I didn't know I would at the time!" She glanced away guiltily. "Look, Ackerly, it's possible I may have inadvertently encouraged Mr. Blarney. Of course, I dislike being rude or cruel toward anyone. But believe me, I have learned my lesson. In the future, I won't do so much as to grant him the time of day. Jake Blarney showed everyone his true stripes on Saturday night."

Ackerly studied her skeptically. "Well, I'm relieved to hear you at least acknowledge your folly. After listening to you defend the man at the ball, I was almost convinced you were enamored of that rogue."

"Don't be ridiculous!" she exclaimed. "And I really wasn't defending Jake Blarney so much as taking issue with ... well ... your apparent class snobbery, Ackerly."

He slammed shut a ledger, his hazel eyes gleaming with outrage. "My class snobbery? So now I've been assaulted physically by Blarney and verbally by you. Have you any more insults to hurl my way? I do have a very busy schedule, and I'm not sure I can abide any more of your goodwill this morning."

Priscilla groaned, drawing a gloved hand to her brow. "I seem to be saying everything wrong this morning."

"Yes, you are," he agreed.

She leaned toward him and spoke earnestly. "My purpose was never to insult you, Ackerly, only to try to explain. Once again, I'm very sorry for what happened Saturday night."

"Very well, I accept your apology," he said with strained patience. "Is there anything else?"

Although the thought of retreat was appealing, Priscilla was determined to stay her course. "Actually, there is another matter . . ." Bucking up her courage, she said brightly, "I was wondering if you would escort me to the elocution contest at the Tremont Opera House on Saturday night."

He appeared incredulous. "You must be jesting. Surely you must realize that, following the calamity at the Cotton Exchange Ball, our association must end."

"You can't mean that!" she cried.

"I most assuredly do," he replied. "After all, I must safeguard my good name in this community."

"So you're afraid I'll ruin a grown man such as yourself? Don't you have things somewhat backward?"

He began to blink rapidly. "That is entirely enough, Priscilla! You were supposed to be my companion on Saturday night, and you heaped disgrace on both of us by dancing with that ruffian!"

"Well, you can't claim to be as pure as the driven snow in that regard," Priscilla shot back. "You're the one who was fawning all over Winnie Haggarty."

Flustered, Ackerly glanced at a customer and Mr. Fitzgerald, both of whom were observing them aghast from the next desk. "Kindly lower your voice! Furthermore, I did not fawn! And Winnie asked me to dance."

But Priscilla knew she had the advantage, and she was not about to back down. Feigning a pout, she declared, "You all but drooled on her. You obviously prefer that simpering, voluptuous child to me."

Dark color shot up Ackerly's face. "Priscilla, I cannot believe you are making such appalling accusations. I'll have you know Winnie does not simper—"

"Nor is she voluptuous?" Priscilla cut in with an air of hurt.

Ackerly was squirming in his chair. "That is beside the point. Winnie is too young for me. Furthermore, I never judge a woman by looks alone."

Priscilla gave an astounded laugh. "That line is older than the hills."

He regarded her in consternation.

She flung her hands wide and spoke with theatrical despair. "Very well. Cast me out of your life simply because I became Jake Blarney's unfortunate victim at the ball." With less emotion, she continued. "But have you thought of the loss of face you'll suffer in this community when everyone realizes you allowed Jake to best you? That all it took was one black eye to scare you away?"

Ackerly's features went pale, but his eyes seethed with turmoil.

"Well, Ackerly?" she pressed. "Are you going to give Jake Blarney exactly what he wants by letting him chase you away with your tail between your legs?"

"He hasn't chased me away!"

"Oh, yes, he has! He's trying to make a fool of you, but only you can allow him to do so. Surely you must realize that now is when we must stand together, to let the gossips see that Jake Blarney's reprehensible conduct has had no effect on us?"

Rapping his fingertips on the desk, he appeared extremely agitated. "Well, perhaps you have a point—"

"Of course I do!"

"But why the elocution contest?" he inquired.

She smiled, recognizing victory within her grasp. "It's the first time my students will perform in public."

He scowled. "I'm surprised you haven't lost students after Saturday night. Why, right before we left the Cotton Exchange, Eleanor Haggarty informed me she'll likely withdraw Jimmy now that you've been tainted by scandal."

Priscilla felt the color drain from her face. She was already terrified of losing much of her student base over Saturday night's calamity, and this sobering threat made her even more furious with Jake. Indeed, she had arrived at her studio earlier this morning to find a note from the mother of one of her students, canceling the boy's nine A.M. appointment.

But she was not about to admit to Ackerly that she was experiencing the least difficulty. That would certainly not further her cause with him!

Calmly she stated, "Although it is true that I may have some fence mending to do in the community, I'm confident I shall weather this small crisis just fine. I am eager to demonstrate to everyone that I have nothing to hide, nothing to be ashamed of. After all, I'm not the one who became violent on Saturday night—it was Mr. Blarney."

"Well, I suppose that's true ..."

"As for the contest itself, I think Willie Shrewsbury has an excellent chance of winning first place. And I would assume you would want to attend in any event, Ackerly. Since this is a city-wide competition, all of the private schools will be represented."

Ackerly's gaze narrowed, and Priscilla could almost see the wheels of his mind turning. "Which means all the prominent families will be in attendance?"

She stared him straight in the eye. "But of course. This is not an occasion to be missed by the socially conscious."

"And you believe one of your students may win?"

"Absolutely."

Ackerly was silent for a long moment, then finally he conceded wearily, "Very well, Priscilla. We'll go."

Priscilla arrived back at her studio to find Mary O'Brien standing outside next to the locked door, wringing her hands. The November morning was briskly cool, and Priscilla judged that the high color staining Mary's cheeks emanated either from the blustery wind or, more likely, from embarrassment.

Wanting to reassure her friend, she smiled. "Hello, Mary."

Mary's gaze beseeched Priscilla's. "Priscilla, I'm so

sorry," she began in a rush. "May I come inside and have a word with you?"

"Of course. I have a cancellation, so we'll have time to visit." Priscilla unlocked the door. "By the way, where have you been? You weren't at the boardinghouse all weekend long."

"I know—I spent the weekend with Aunt Phoebe," the girl admitted. "I just felt so guilty about . . ." Her voice trailed off and she grimaced.

"Please, don't feel guilty." Priscilla opened the door and gestured for Mary to precede her inside.

Once both women had entered, Mary stood rubbing her arms to stave off the cold, while Priscilla went over to light the gas stove.

Anxiously Mary called, "You say you have a cancellation? I do hope you're not losing any students because of Saturday night."

Priscilla turned and blew out a match. "Well, it's not the end of the world, although I'll likely have to smooth down the feathers of a few local matriarchs." She gestured toward the chair in front of her desk. "Won't you sit down?"

Mary twisted her gloved fingers together. "Thank you, but I prefer to stand."

Priscilla stepped closer. "What did you wish to discuss?"

"I just wanted to tell you again how very sorry I am," Mary stated. "I never should have gone along with Jake Blarney's scheme."

Priscilla studied Mary's face, which mirrored both sincerity and regret. "Mary, please, there's no need to apologize. I know you would never deliberately set out to hurt me. But what was Jake's scheme? At least, according to you. I've already heard his version, by the way."

Mary nodded. "Jake came to me and told me he was hopelessly in love with you—"

"He *what?*" Priscilla gasped.

"Aye, those were his exact words. He said, 'Mary, dear, I'm hopeless in love with Priscilla, but she's determined to marry that diamond stickpin, Jack Frost.' "

Priscilla had to struggle not to laugh. The comment sounded just like Jake, and Mary had repeated his words so earnestly. "Go on."

Avoiding Priscilla's eye, Mary muttered, "So Jake asked me to accompany him to the Cotton Exchange Ball to make you jealous, and I agreed."

Priscilla nodded. "That's pretty much how he outlined his motives to me."

Mary stepped forward and solemnly crossed herself. "I swear by all the saints that Jake would give me no peace until I promised to help him out. I went there with the best intentions, and never thought you'd be caused such embarrassment or pain. And I promise you Mr. Blarney never touched me—except to do all the gentlemanly things, to hand me in and out of his buggy and such, and peck my cheek good night, just like my cousin Teddy does." Mary heaved a great sigh. "Had I only known he would strike Mr. Frost, I never would have stepped out with him."

"Oh, Mary, I certainly realize all this," put in Priscilla sympathetically.

Mary grimaced. "How bad is the damage—to your reputation and such?"

Priscilla sighed. "I'm not sure yet. I may lose some students—but I do think I've managed to smooth things over with Mr. Frost."

"Oh, thank goodness." Mary frowned. "Then you still think he's the one for you, and not Jake?"

Priscilla laughed ruefully. "Yes indeed, I think Mr. Frost is exactly the one for me—now more than ever."

"But you don't love him, do you, Priscilla?" Mary asked gently.

"No, but we want the same things—unlike me and a certain impudent Irishman."

Mary laughed. "Well, you can be assured of one thing—I'll never again step out with that impudent Irishman."

Priscilla hesitated a moment, then said bravely, "You can have him if you want him."

Mary went wide-eyed. "You must be jesting!"

Despite the lump in her throat, Priscilla solemnly shook her head. "Not at all. There's definitely no future for me and Jake, so if you want him, you may as well pursue him."

Mary grew silent for a long moment, biting her lip, as if she were dying to say something else.

"Come on, Mary," Priscilla prodded. "What aren't you telling me?"

"Well . . . you know, Jake's taken this awful hard."

"*He's* taken it hard?" Priscilla exclaimed.

"I saw him yesterday at mass, and he seemed very down in the mouth. He repeated what he told me Saturday night—that he's ruined his chances with you."

"Well, at least he's man enough to put the blame where it belongs," Priscilla replied. "And if he's morose, it's his own damn fault for acting like such a beast. I am pleased to know that at least I won't have to worry about his blackmailing me any longer."

Mary went pale. "Blackmailing you? What do you mean?"

"Never mind," Priscilla quickly replied, realizing she had said more than she had intended.

Mary stubbornly set her jaw. "Priscilla, please don't leave me in suspense when I already feel wretched about this whole affair. What is going on between you and Jake Blarney that you're not telling me? Why is it you're so set against him?"

Priscilla hesitated for a long moment, not sure she could share with Mary—or with anyone—the bizarre tale of her journey through time, of how she'd arrived on Jake Blarney's stoop, and how he'd subsequently blackmailed her into seeing him.

But she did owe her friend some sort of explanation. "I'll tell you one thing, Mary. I can never live with a man like Jake Blarney. He's too much like my father—a hothead and a brawler. Saturday night's scene was just like one of the stunts my father used to pull—acting temperamental and belligerent, becoming violent at parties and social events, causing me and my mother untold anguish and humiliation. I watched my mother go through hell because of my father's excesses, and I've no desire to watch history repeat itself. Besides, Jake brings out the worst in me—he makes me respond in an emotional way that I don't care for. With him, I can look forward to a lifetime of histrionics and low-class scenes."

"Ah," Mary murmured, her eyes bright with realization. "So that's what's eating at you, is it, Priscilla? You can't trust Jake, and you think Ackerly Frost is the one to give you what you need?"

"Yes. You can be sure Ackerly Frost will never humiliate his wife and children. He could never afford to—unlike Jake, who seems to have nothing to lose. Ackerly represents all I want from life—emotional stability, security, prestige."

"But not love?"

Priscilla drew a convulsive breath. "If I have to live without love, then so be it. As I've pretty much stated, I think love is overrated."

Mary shook her head. "And I still say I'd take Jake Blarney over a dozen Ackerlys, any day."

Priscilla was surprised to feel bitter tears burning. "Then take him. He's yours!"

Mary's expression was filled with compassion and regret as she stepped forward to embrace Priscilla. "Oh, my poor, dear friend. We both know Jake Blarney will never be mine. His heart is taken—and you're the lass holding it in your hands."

Priscilla managed to keep her emotions in check until Mary left. Then she sat down at her desk, buried her face in her hands, and shook with silent sobs.

Chapter 20

❧ ∽❤⌒∽ ❧

Priscilla muddled through her week, preparing her students for Saturday night's elocution contest, even running her entire group through a couple of rehearsals at the Tremont Opera House. She also did some fence mending with several mothers of her charges, calling on ladies who had canceled their children's lessons. During the visits, Priscilla cleverly manipulated the issue of the calamity at the Cotton Exchange Ball to her own advantage. She told each woman that she had only meant to be polite to Jake Blarney and had never anticipated he would behave in such an abominable manner, and asked the ladies' advice for dealing with any such future social challenges she might face. With few exceptions, the mothers were flattered to have the obviously distraught Priscilla seek their counsel; Priscilla received several impassioned lectures, and made half a dozen new friends. When all was said and done, her net loss of students was only three.

On Saturday night, Priscilla felt filled with excitement and pride as she and Ackerly climbed the steps to the elegant Tremont Opera House, with its wrought-iron-embellished first story and Mansard roof. The evening was chill and bright, and beyond them, Market Street gleamed with gaslight.

In honor of the occasion, Priscilla had purchased a new ensemble. She wore a braided gold wool opera cloak over a sleek evening gown of mauve velvet. She had also donned elbow-length white gloves and had arranged her hair in a bun accented with pink silk roses.

Ackerly, at her side, wore a Prince Albert coat and a silk top hat, and carried an ebony walking stick. His attire was dapper and his expression pleasant, but Priscilla sensed tension lingering between them. He had acted distant from the moment he had called for her at the boardinghouse, and he hadn't even complimented her on her stylish new attire. So far they had exchanged only the briefest and most superficial of conversation.

Oh, well, she thought, his attitude toward her would change once her students won a smashing victory tonight!

Just inside the door, Ackerly handed their tickets to a young usher, who gave them each a program. They moved into the opulent lobby, which was empty except for several people heading into the auditorium. As she had already done a couple of times this week, Priscilla marveled at the gorgeous green faux marble pillars, posh green carpeting, and a spectacularly high ceiling with a gilded cast-plaster frieze and sparkling crystal chandeliers.

Ackerly flashed Priscilla a kindly smile. "I see we are still early, my dear. If you've no objection, I'll go downstairs and see if I can find my friends in the bar."

Priscilla had already heard about the Tremont's bar on the first floor, where gentlemen of the community gathered to share drinks and conversation before and after performances, and at intermission. "Yes, do go on," she replied graciously, "and I'll check on my students."

"I'll meet you in the auditorium, then," he said.

They parted company, and Priscilla headed toward the wings, which teemed with young people and their parents or teachers. The corridors rang with the sounds of young voices performing last-minute rehearsals of poems, speeches, and dramatic monologues. She spotted her own students grouped together outside one of the dressing rooms, under the watchful eye of Willie Shrewsbury, who had acted as unofficial major domo for Priscilla during rehearsals.

"Well, hello, everyone!" Priscilla called gaily.

All ten of Priscilla's contest entrants rushed forward to greet her, exclaiming cheerful hellos and buzzing around her like little bees. Priscilla regarded her charges with pride. The Carmichael twins looked adorable, Shannon in a Bo-Peep–style shepherdess dress with bonnet, and Devin in a shirt, vest, short pants, and feathered cap. Willie Shrewsbury looked handsome in his brown twill coat and trousers, with his face scrubbed clean and his hair slicked back. Seven-year-old Isaac Kempner and ten-year-old Jimmy Haggarty both looked precious in sailor suits, complete with knickers and straw hats. All of the children seemed filled with restless energy; the Carmichael twins were hopping up and down.

"Miss Pemberton, we're so glad to see you," announced Willie.

"Are all my little stars ready to shine tonight?" Priscilla inquired brightly.

"We're nervous," admitted Shannon.

"What if I forget my poem?" asked Isaac.

Priscilla smiled down at their anxious, precious faces. "You'll all do just fine, I'm certain of it."

"Can you stay with us, Miss Pemberton?" pleaded Devin.

Priscilla shook her head. "I'm sorry, but the rules allow no parents or coaches to remain in the wings once the contest begins. The ushers will be in charge of you, and will let you know when it's your turn to perform."

"I'll keep everyone in line, Miss Pemberton," promised Willie.

"I'm sure you will. And, all of you, remember my instructions. Pretend the audience isn't there. And don't forget to project your voices, and to breathe properly."

"We'll do you proud, Miss Pemberton," Willie assured her.

"I know you will. Well, break a leg, everyone."

Ten young faces stared at her blankly.

Priscilla laughed, realizing the children had no idea what she meant. "That's theater talk for good luck to you all!"

This time a chorus of smiles and thank-yous greeted her words. Priscilla hugged each of her charges, and as an usher called out that curtain call was in five minutes, she hastily took her leave with the other coaches and parents.

Back in the lobby, she ran across several parents of her students, and paused to chat briefly with John and Eleanor Haggarty, as well as with Sarah O'Shanahan, her niece Polly, and Polly's husband, Sean Carmichael. By the time she entered the auditorium, the posh velvet seats and beautifully carved private boxes overhead were filled with elegant humanity. She recognized a number of prominent families among the attendees, but didn't spot Jake Blarney anywhere. His absence made her feel not nearly as relieved as she should have.

At last Priscilla joined Ackerly in their orchestra box seats. This time he greeted her with a smile, and even helped remove her cape.

His words, and a whiff of brandy, floated over her. "Well, my dear, it appears you were right about this occasion. Many pillars of the community are present. In fact, I had a very nice chat with Harris Kempner down in the bar. It seems Harris's wife, Eliza, is very pleased with young Isaac's progress under your tutelage."

Priscilla smiled, relieved that she was one step closer to redeeming herself with Ackerly. "Isaac is a dear, bright child who I'm sure will perform splendidly tonight."

They chatted until the auditorium lights went down and the stage lights came up. Reverend Albert Lyon, headmaster of Trinity Parish School, took the stage to act as emcee. He introduced the judges, who included nuns from Ursuline Academy and St. Mary's Parochial School, and the headmasters from several other institutions. Lyon then began calling up the contestants to do their recitations.

The program that followed was enjoyable, with students from the various city schools intoning everything from the prose of Shakespeare and Milton to the poems of Wordsworth, Longfellow, and Whitman. Priscilla could not have been more delighted with her own students' performances. Shannon and Devin Carmichael did a charming dual recitation of William Blake's "Little Lamb." Isaac Kempner was flawless and winsome in his recitation of Shelley's "The Cloud." Jimmy Haggarty poignantly intoned Browning's "Song from Pippa Passes."

But it was Willie Shrewsbury who captivated the audience with his dramatic recitation of Blake's "Tiger, Tiger." Willie's enunciation was perfect, his projection excellent. His stage presence was awesome as he made his delivery with sweeping gestures and fiery eyes, and his voice rang with the resonance and vision of Blake's poem. When the boy finished, the audience came out of its seats for a standing ovation, and even Ackerly acknowledged Priscilla's triumph with an approving nod.

Priscilla almost wept with pride when Willie was awarded first place, the blue ribbon and the coveted twenty-dollar gold piece; never had she seen a dearer sight than the look of stark joy on young Willie's face. Second place went to a female student from St. Ursuline's, and third to Isaac Kempner. Priscilla was thrilled once more when Devin and Shannon Carmichael, as well as Jimmy Haggarty, were awarded honorable mentions.

Out in the lobby afterward, Priscilla and Ackerly were mobbed by her students and their proud parents, along with other members of the community who came forward to congratulate her on her students' feats.

While Ackerly spoke with John Haggarty, Sarah O'Shanahan rushed up to Priscilla with the entire Carmichael clan. "We're so proud of Shannon and Devin!" she exclaimed, her face aglow.

Priscilla winked at the twins, both of whom sported broad smiles and colorful yellow ribbons. "Yes, weren't they wonderful tonight? They thoroughly deserve their award."

"And the twins have been invited to a Christmas party for a cousin of the Sealys!" Polly announced gaily.

"I'm so thrilled for them."

Polly nudged the children. "Now, what do you say?"

"Thank you, Miss Pemberton," Shannon and Devin cried in unison.

Priscilla laughed. "You're most welcome."

The family group trooped off, and Priscilla turned as an attractive older couple stepped up to join her. "Why, Mr. and Mrs. Brown, how nice to see you."

"You've caused quite a stir in this community tonight, young lady," Brown told her with a twinkle in his eyes. "My sincere congratulations."

"Thank you, sir," Priscilla said, shaking his hand.

"We were just speaking with the Kempners, and they are beside themselves with joy over Isaac's performance," added a smiling Rebecca Brown. "I shall tell our son, Moreau, that he must enroll our grandson, James, for your lessons."

"I'd be honored to have him," Priscilla replied.

As the Browns moved on to speak with Ackerly, Willie Shrewsbury came racing up to Priscilla sporting a huge grin and a blue ribbon. "Ma'am! I won!"

"I know, and you were wonderful," Priscilla replied, giving him a fond hug.

A meagerly dressed middle-aged woman tentatively stepped up to join them. She possessed a sad, pinched face and was trying her best to avoid Priscilla's eye. Priscilla spotted a familial resemblance between the woman and Willie, and knew she must be his mother. She felt sorry for the pathetic creature in her ragged coat and droopy hat.

Willie turned to put an arm around the woman, then smiled at Priscilla. "Miss Pemberton, meet me mum—that is, my mother."

Priscilla shook the little woman's hand. "How do you do? I'm so proud of Willie."

"Thank you, ma'am," the woman mumbled, staring at the floor. "Willie done me proud tonight."

"Well, congratulations, young man," Ackerly said to Willie, offering his hand.

Suddenly the boy's countenance went cold. "I won't be needing your congratulations or shaking your hand, Jack Frost."

"Willie!" gasped Priscilla, gazing from the irate boy to his mother, who appeared even more miserably put on the spot than before.

"I ain't apologizing, Miss Pemberton," said Willie, hurling a glare at Ackerly. Reverting to his Cockney speech in his anger, he accused, " 'E's the one what threw me and me mum out of our house after me dad died."

Priscilla glanced horrified at Ackerly. "Is this true?"

"I'll not be discussing the bank's business in public," he replied coldly.

"Never you mind, Miss Pemberton, we're going," said Willie, sneering at Ackerly. "I'm shocked at ye for associatin' with 'is kind."

Willie tugged at his mother, and Priscilla at once confronted Ackerly. "Did you force that boy and his mother out of their home?"

"I don't think that is any of your affair, my dear," he reiterated.

"I'm making it my affair."

"Do you think the Frost National Bank is a charitable institution?"

Priscilla already had her answer. "Definitely not!"

He groaned. "Priscilla—"

Before he could explain, Colonel and Mrs. Moody

walked up, beaming. "Miss Pemberton, what a masterful job you have done with your students!" the colonel said to Priscilla.

"You are a miracle worker, young lady," added his wife.

Her argument with Ackerly was momentarily thrust aside as Priscilla visited with the Moodys and the Kempners, who also stopped by to praise and thank Priscilla. She tried her best to be gracious to one and all, even though she was still very upset over Willie's revelations. She noted to her irritation that Ackerly was only too glad to help her accept all the accolades.

At one point she observed George Sealy pounding Ackerly across the shoulders, and heard him say, "An unfortunate incident at the Cotton Exchange Ball Saturday night, wasn't it, Mr. Frost? But we're all grateful Miss Pemberton has you to protect her from that rascal Jake Blarney."

Hearing Sealy's remark and taking note of Ackerly's smug grin, Priscilla almost laughed aloud. Ackerly was so busy gloating, he had utterly forgotten that he had actually "protected" her while he was lying on the floor of the Cotton Exchange!

Priscilla was not about to drop the incident concerning Willie Shrewsbury. As Ackerly drove her home in his buggy, she said, "About your evicting my prize student and his mother—"

Ackerly's exasperated sigh cut short her words. "Priscilla, you must realize I run an enterprise, not a charity. I must protect the interests of our depositors."

"I realize this. But to evict a new widow and her child—"

"The Shrewsbury note was one of several I acquired from Hollis Ford when he retired last year from his exchange business. At the time, the note had already been in arrears for many months. I tried to work with Mattie Shrewsbury, but the widow was unwilling to set up even the most modest repayment schedule. If I may be frank, I think she has a drinking problem, as did her husband. Ultimately I had no choice but to foreclose."

Priscilla was silent, brooding. Remembering how her father had once had his tractor repossessed because he hadn't paid his note on time, she could understand Ackerly's perspective.

"Do you think I like having to take such steps?" he continued with frustration. "Everyone wants the bank to be profitable, but no one wants to make the unpleasant choices that are crucial to keeping such an institution solvent."

"I suppose you have a point," she conceded.

He smiled. "Now, no more of this. Let's talk about you. Weren't you the toast of the town tonight?"

She smiled. "I'm so proud of my students."

"And from what I observed, any ground you may have lost at the Cotton Exchange Ball was more than made up tonight."

"I suppose," she murmured.

"You're too modest," he assured her. "Why, you stood the town on its ear, your students triumphing over contestants from the best institutions in town. And if I'm not mistaken, you've now acquired at least four more pupils—from some of the island's finest families, I might add."

"I would treasure them just as much if they weren't from some of Galveston's finest families," she replied defensively.

He pulled his conveyance to a halt before Rose Gatling's boardinghouse and glanced at her in mystification. "Priscilla, what is ailing you tonight? Is this 'rake Ackerly over the coals' week?"

She had to laugh at his humor.

"I've been humiliated, knocked to my heels by a brash hooligan, accused of treachery toward my mortgagees . . ." He smiled. "You know, I'm really not such a dastardly fellow."

"I know," she admitted with a laugh.

"And I thought it was important for you to be seen with me," he continued with an air of injury. "I thought you truly wanted to establish your place in this community."

"Oh, but I do," she quickly reassured him.

"And you have." Taking a deep breath, he announced, "I think we should become engaged."

"What?" she cried, flabbergasted.

"It can't come as so great a shock," he continued earnestly. "We've been seeing each other for several weeks now, and we do have much in common. We want the same things out of life—especially to cultivate the same social circles."

"That's true. B-But engaged! We haven't even kissed yet!"

Ackerly drew himself up with dignity. "I should hope not. We haven't become properly affianced as yet."

She shook her head in disbelief. "Why are you proposing now?"

He straightened his lapels. "I suppose I'm simply at that stage in life where I need to settle down. The most prominent men in this town have wives and children, and I think that in the long run, the lack of a suitable mate could diminish my chances for continued success."

"I must say you're being rather cold-blooded about choosing a spouse," remarked Priscilla. *As I am,* she admitted to herself in honest self-reproach.

"Perhaps I simply believe such decisions are best made without undue passion," he replied. "I think we must be frank regarding our needs and aspirations. You and I are obviously a good match. And as you've already pointed out, don't you think we should do our part to keep the gossips quiet?"

"Well, I suppose," she said, frowning.

"Then the answer is yes?"

"May I think about it?" she asked.

"Of course."

When Ackerly escorted Priscilla to the front door,

he lightly pecked her lips, for the first time. Priscilla walked inside feeling very confused. At last she had the proposal she had coveted. Then why didn't she feel more thrilled? Why wasn't she jumping at the chance to snap up Ackerly's bait?

In the days that followed, Priscilla stalled when Ackerly again brought up the subject of matrimony. She even found herself breaking dates with him, so mixed were her emotions regarding his proposal. They did attend a couple of parties heralding the beginning of the holiday season in Galveston. Their relationship was back on an even keel, but she couldn't commit to him. On the one hand, his proposal offered her everything she had always wanted, her chance to secure her place in society; on the other hand, her prospective bridegroom still left her cold, and after knowing Jake, the thought of living in a passionless marriage had lost a great deal of its appeal. It frustrated her that her emotions could so cloud her better judgment, when logic argued that she should seize her chance for emotional safety and security.

Priscilla kept busy with her students, but found she missed Jake and the babies more and more with each passing day. She had glimpsed a world that she knew was wrong for her, but she found herself wanting that world, nonetheless. She often stopped in at the apothecary next door to have lunch with Mary, and invariably couldn't resist asking for news of Jake and his children. "I saw Jake and the babes at mass," Mary would say. "Looked awful melancholy, he did."

Priscilla wondered how she could feel so guilty over Jake's state of mind, when he was the one who had disgraced her, and acted like such a brute!

Then early one morning, Mary burst into Priscilla's studio while Priscilla was tutoring Shannon Carmichael. "Priscilla, I must speak with you at once!" she cried.

Mystified by the intrusion, Priscilla excused herself

and swept over to the door. "Mary, I have a student—"

"Priscilla, I thought you'd want to know Jake's babies are ailing," Mary cut in urgently.

Priscilla's heart did a nosedive. "What? When did you learn this?"

"About an hour ago. I came here soon as I could get away. Anyhow, Jake arrived the minute we opened, asking Mr. Peebles for something to give the babies for their fever. Seemed awful worried, he did. Said Mrs. Braunhurst was under the weather, too, but was sitting at the farm with the girls till he gets back. Jake was all in a rush to get home to tend his girls, and to let Bula's husband fetch her back to town."

Priscilla was wringing her hands. "Oh, this is terrible."

"I thought you'd want to know."

"Thanks, Mary."

Anxiously Mary added, "What will you do, Priscilla?"

She hesitated for less than a second. "What do you think?"

Mary smiled.

As soon as Mary left, Priscilla turned to her student, who appeared confused. "Shannon, I apologize, but can we finish this another day? You can wait for your mother at Great-Aunt Sarah's shop, can't you?"

"Of course, Miss Pemberton," the girl replied graciously.

After seeing Shannon safely over to Sarah O'Shanahan's shop, Priscilla locked up her studio, posted a note for Shannon's mother and her other scheduled students, then raced down to the stable to rent a horse and buggy. Within ten minutes she was in the conveyance, clipping toward Broadway, and feeling sick with fear.

The babies were sick! They needed her! Jake needed her! What a fool she had been! Her wounded pride and affronted dignity seemed so trivial now!

Oh, Lord, people still died of fevers in this day and age, didn't they? Should she fetch a doctor? But didn't some doctors still bleed people in 1880? If only she knew the formula for acetaminophen!

Forty-five minutes later, Priscilla was half out of her mind with worry when she finally arrived at Jake's cottage and raced up the steps. She pounded on the door for a long time before he answered—

The sight of him made her gasp. He was unshaven, his clothing rumpled. And she could see at once in his bleary eyes his terrible fear.

"Jake . . . you need help."

"We don't want any two-timers here," he greeted her belligerently.

"The babies are sick," she replied frantically. "Damn it, I'm here to help you!"

"We don't want your help."

Priscilla was near hysteria, her eyes gleaming with tears as she shook a fist at him. "Well, I'm here and I'm helping, and you're going to have to shoot me to stop me, Jake Blarney!"

He glowered a moment.

"Why are you standing there like an idiot, when Nell and Sal are sick and they need me?" she screamed.

He scratched his jaw. "I'm trying to recollect where I stashed me pistol."

Not at all moved by his humor, she angrily shoved at his solid chest. "Move aside, you stubborn Irishman. I'm coming in."

Muttering a curse, he finally stepped back. She strode in, and for a wrenching moment they stared at each other starkly. A split second later, she was in his arms.

"I need you, girl," Jake whispered.

Chapter 21

For a moment they clung to each other, two very frightened human beings seeking comfort in the bond between them.

Then Priscilla broke away. "The girls!" she cried.

Jake took her hand and led her across the room toward the cradles, and it was then that she noticed how warm the house was, with a huge fire blazing in the grate.

"They're sleeping now," he said, "but still burning up. The fever just won't break."

Priscilla gasped as she viewed the girls in their small beds. Both were asleep, with bright faces, wispy damp curls clinging to their foreheads, and wool blankets swaddling their bodies.

"No wonder they're burning up with fever!" she exclaimed. "You're smothering them, Jake!"

He appeared incredulous. "But they must be tightly wrapped to keep them from taking a chill—and to break the fever."

"No, no!" she insisted, gesturing distraughtly. "We must cool them off or they won't have a chance."

Even as she reached for the nearest child, Jake caught her wrist and glared at her. "I won't have you telling me how best to care for me own children."

"Do you want to lose them?" she asked plaintively.

"No, but—"

"Think a minute," she implored. "How can their body temperatures go down with the room so hot,

243

and them bound up like mummies? They'll become dehydrated in no time."

His agonized features reflecting his horrible indecision, Jake drew his fingers through his rumpled hair. "Lass, I know no other way—"

"There *is* a better way!"

"What are you suggesting?"

Urgently she said, "We must take everything off them but their diapers, sponge them off with cool cloths, and get liquids down them."

His mouth fell open in horror. "It'll be the death of them."

"No, it won't. It's their only chance."

"But how can you know this?" he cried.

"I just know. I—I come from a place where I was taught such things."

"You mean your highfalutin college?" he scoffed.

"No." She grabbed him by the forearm. "Jake, please stop arguing with me. While we're standing here wasting time, we could lose both babies due to your stubbornness. Your treatment for these girls is only worsening their fever. You're going to have to trust me and try things my way. You know how much I love Sal and Nell. Believe me, I'd never suggest anything that would hurt them."

He eyed her impassioned face for a long moment, then sighed heavily. "Very well, girl. We'll give your way a try."

"Good. We haven't a second to waste." Pulling off her cloak and rolling up her sleeves, she jerked her head toward the fireplace. "Kindly put out that fire and open some windows. And please lay out on the dining table a quilt, some clean rags, and a bowl of cool water. I'll get started with the girls."

"Aye, lass." He rushed off.

Priscilla unwrapped both babies and removed their gowns. At once, Sal and Nell began to cough and whimper, making Priscilla feel heartsick at their misery, and guilt-ridden that she had been compelled to disturb them. "Poor darlings," she murmured, kissing and cuddling them by turns.

Once Jake had cooled down the room and arranged a sort of work station for them on the dining room table, the two of them carried the girls to the table and laid them down on the quilt. The girls continued to fret as Priscilla sponged them down with damp, cool cloths. Jake prepared them bottles of cold cistern water. Afterward, she sat in the rocking chair feeding Nell her water, while Jake sat across from her on the daybed, trying to coax Sal into taking a few drops from the bottle.

"They're both still so red and hot," Priscilla fretted, touching Nell's warm little face. "What started the illness, anyway?"

"Well, Bula has been sneezing and sniffing for days, then all at once, she and both girls took ill."

"It must be some sort of cold or flu," said Priscilla as she felt Nell's brow. "But it's the fever that's so worrisome. Fevers can run so dangerously high in young children. I remember when my cousin's little boy was five and he suddenly developed a fever that shot up to a hundred and four. What was really strange was that he displayed no other signs of illness. We had to put him in ice water to keep him from going into convulsions."

"*Ice water?*" Jake appeared amazed.

Priscilla touched Nell's hot cheek and grimaced. "Jake, we mustn't rule out dunking them in the Gulf if we can't cool them down otherwise. I don't suppose you have a thermometer?"

He solemnly shook his head.

"Has a doctor seen them?"

He frowned. "I don't hold by such, lass. When me mum was so ill back in Ireland, that charlatan me aunt called bled her to death, I think."

Priscilla shuddered. "You're probably right to be cautious. Was the druggist of any help?"

Jake nodded toward the dresser. "He sold me some cough elixir and fever powders."

Priscilla frowned. "That may help a little. I just wish we had some acetaminophen."

"What is that, lass?"

"Oh, just a very effective painkiller and fever reducer we used where I came from. Aspirin was another miracle drug, but it is not always the best choice for babies or children."

"And there is no way we can acquire these marvels here?"

Priscilla stared down at Nell's vulnerable, flushed face. "God, I wish there were. I wish I were a chemist, or had thought to bring a lot more things here with me."

Jake regarded her in perplexity, then became distracted as Sal whimpered.

In the next hours, Priscilla and Jake anxiously tended the babies. That afternoon, noting how drawn Jake looked, Priscilla asked him how long he had been on his feet, and when he admitted that he had been up with the babies for over thirty-six hours, she insisted he must rest on the daybed. After arguing the point, he finally obliged, and her heart twisted with tenderness as she observed him lying there, his expression fraught with anxiety even in sleep.

Priscilla kept coaxing liquids down the girls, sponging them off, and giving them their prescribed medicines on schedule. By midafternoon, blessedly, both seemed cooler and not nearly as fretful. At last she laid them both down for a nap and covered them with light blankets.

She did not realize she had dozed in the rocking chair until she felt Jake gently shaking her arm. She blinked to see him standing over her, staring down at her with incredulous joy.

"Lass!" he cried excitedly. "The fevers have broken!"

Priscilla bolted up from her chair and crossed over to the babies, feeling the girls' foreheads. Both were sleeping peacefully, their coloring normal, their skin cool to the touch.

Priscilla straightened and exultantly thrust herself into Jake's arms. "Thank God! The crisis is over."

Squeezing Priscilla, Jake leaned down to replace the blanket Sal had just kicked off. "You were right, lass, to keep them cool as you did."

"I'm just incredibly relieved that they're better."

"As I am, love." Jake hauled her close and she could feel him trembling. His voice was thick with tears. "Thank you, lass. Thank you for me wee babes."

His heartfelt words affected her deeply, and she hugged him back. "Thank you for trusting me."

He buried his lips in her hair. "Oh, lass. I thought I was going to lose them both—and I thought I'd lost you, too. 'Twas unbearable, darlin'."

"I know—but I'm here now. Everything will be fine."

He drew back slightly, staring down at her, and her own eyes filled with tears at the sight of the poignant emotion reflected on his face. Gently he caressed her cheek.

Soulfully he whispered, " 'Twas love that brought you here, lassie—love for the babes, and for me. And 'twill be love that will make you stay, I reckon."

"Oh, Jake." She stretched on tiptoe just as his warm mouth descended on hers. They shared their overwhelming joy and relief in a long, tender kiss.

Afterward, he smiled and took her hand. "Come along, lassie. There's something I've been meaning to show you."

Bemused, she let him lead her toward some curtains that hadn't been there during her last visit. He pulled aside the panel and tugged her into a room that also hadn't been there the last time she visited.

"You completed the bedroom addition!" she cried.

"Aye, lassie," he declared proudly.

"I was so preoccupied when I arrived, I didn't even notice!"

He grinned. "Well, have a look now."

Priscilla gaped about her in amazement. The room

was small but cozy, the walls wainscoted in white, with delicate, floral-patterned green and white wallpaper above. A handsome dressing screen stood in one corner, covered with fabric that matched the wallpaper. A carved mahogany dresser rested against one wall, and a rose-and-green-patterned carpet covered the floor. But the true centerpiece of the room was a huge brass bed with crimson satin counterpane. The sight of it set Priscilla's blood on fire.

"Oh, Jake!" Her face was as bright as the girls' had been hours earlier.

"I did it all for you, lassie," he replied huskily, moving purposefully toward her. "I never gave up on you—I knew you'd come to me."

Priscilla's emotion was such that she couldn't even speak, but could only gaze at him, riveted.

"Mary helped me make some of the selections—the wallpaper and such. Are you pleased?"

"Overwhelmed is more like it!"

He curled an arm around her waist and began maneuvering her toward the bed. "Overwhelmed is just the way I'm meaning to keep you, love. I'm dying to kiss you again—and much more."

Priscilla's knees had gone wobbly. "B-But the girls. I . . . er . . . shouldn't we check?"

"Their fevers have broken, and they've both healthy sets of lungs." He eyed her burningly. "I've waited for you too long, lassie. I can't wait any longer."

Priscilla gulped. Although she had a strong notion she would regret this tomorrow, she doubted she could wait, either. Jake was so near, the scent and heat of him inflaming her senses. She had wanted him desperately for so long. She realized the emotion and intimacy of the hours they had spent caring for his babies had built to a fever of longing for them both. And now there was no more potent aphrodisiac than knowing Jake had built this room for them to share, that he had bought this scandalous bed for them to lie upon together and consummate their love, that he had painstakingly selected the boards for the floor, the paper for the walls, the lace doilies on the dresser. Never had she felt closer to him, or more deeply touched.

"I—I still can't believe you did all this," she stammered. "No one has ever done anything like that for me before."

He gazed at her tenderly. "Lass, I've only begun to do things for you. And to you."

Reeling, she gestured about her. "But an entire room, the bed, that sinful satin spread—"

He hauled her close. "Quit talking about it, lassie, and let's try it out. Let's see how that hot satin feels against our naked flesh."

"Oh, God." She stared at him, uncertain but also wildly aroused. Then his lips caught hers in a fiery, captivating kiss that seemed to last forever.

Even as she stood panting for breath, he released her, went to sit down on the bed, and pulled off his boots. He regarded her with such love that she felt not the least bit threatened. She felt needed, cherished . . .

His soft, ardent words drifted over to her. "Here's the room I have built for us, lass. Here is the bed where I hope we will share our love. You're free to come to me, you know. Or you're free to go. Only, if you're leaving, lass, I'd advise you to do so now, for I've developed a powerful aching for you. I'm not sure I can keep my hands off you for another instant if you stay."

The stark honesty and passion in his beautiful blue eyes proved Priscilla's undoing. She shuddered, then went over to stand between his spread knees. With a groan, he curled his arms about her waist, pulled her close, and rested his cheek against her bosom.

"Your heart's pounding, lassie," he whispered. "Hammering something fierce."

"For you," she murmured.

A split second later, they tumbled onto the soft mattress together, the springs groaning in a sensual echoing of their own need. Jake rolled Priscilla beneath him, gently kissed her lips, and stared searchingly into her eyes.

"Oh, lassie, lassie," he breathed, brushing his lips across her cheek, her throat. "I've dreamed of this day so. You in my arms, and loving me so sweetly."

"Me, too."

Their mouths met in an ardent kiss. Jake's face was prickly with two days worth of beard, and his skin felt rough, wicked, sensual, against her own tender lips and smooth cheek. His tongue slashed inside her mouth with a demanding passion that heated her blood and left her throbbing between her thighs. She gloried in the sheer masculinity of him, the crushing weight of his robust body on hers. She kneaded his shoulder muscles with her fingertips and kissed him back fervently.

He moved his lips down her throat while unbuttoning her bodice. She moaned with delight as he uncovered her breasts and stared at them.

"Such lovely, precious little mounds," he murmured, kissing each breast in turn, driving her insane with the erotic abrasion of his unshaven face. "I've been dying to suckle them again for so long. Ever since that night at the beach. Remember, lassie?"

How could she ever forget! Priscilla thrust her fingers into his silky hair and panted in pleasure. "Were you really afraid you had lost me?"

"Aye, lass. But you're all mine now, you know."

She was his. At least for today. It was electrifying, frightening . . . but right now Priscilla didn't care about all the implications, or tomorrow. She only knew she had to have this man, or she would surely die. She wanted to surrender entirely to Jake, to the powerful feelings he alone stirred. When his teeth nibbled at her nipples, when his tongue flicked across the turgid peaks, tormenting her unbearably, she wondered how she had ever resisted him for so long.

His lips moved down her body, kissing her midriff

and belly, making her shiver and burn. His hands impatiently tugged aside her clothing, and being undone by him felt so glorious. Never had any man stirred Priscilla so. She wondered for a moment of near-panic how he would react when he discovered she was not a virgin, but she didn't allow herself to dwell on that either, so overpowering was her desire. She ripped at the buttons on his shirt and slipped her hands inside, feeling his hard, warm, corded shoulders, and the rough hair, the smooth muscles, of his chest. She stroked and caressed him; he groaned and slid his body upward to reward her with a demanding kiss.

His hard, naked chest crushed her breasts so sensually that she squirmed in delirious arousal and anticipation. A moment later, he was staring down at her starkly, his eyes near-black with desire, and his breath coming in hard heaves.

"My God, lassie, this is going too fast."

"I want it fast," she said recklessly, reaching down to stroke him though his trousers and glorying in the way his features clenched in savage need. "I want you. I've wanted you for so long that—"

His ravenous kiss drowned the rest of her words as one of his hands began sliding up her leg. He undid the tie to her drawers and tugged them down. She writhed as he stroked her between her thighs with exquisite tenderness, his skilled, sensitive touch causing her to whimper frantically ... He caressed her delicate folds until she was moist, ready for him. Then he was probing against her, hot and rigid, and she felt herself aching to receive him. He nudged her thighs farther apart, then pressed. She gasped.

"Easy, love," he murmured, and thrust powerfully.

The breath was sucked from Priscilla's lungs. Her fingernails dug into Jake's rigid shoulders. She had never felt anything like this, like him. He was so solid, unyielding, inside her, so young, splendid, and strong, and her tight flesh ached and throbbed exquisitely about his heat. Although he was only half-way inside her, she climaxed.

She heard him chuckle. "Patience, darling. Wait for me."

His hands slid beneath her, cupping and lifting her bottom. Staring into her eyes, he plunged deep, filling her to the hilt with wrenching, unbearable pleasure. She cried out, her lips feverishly seeking his, her legs coiling high about his waist to give him greater ease. Their mouths mated in a frenzy of need. Jake withdrew and thrust vigorously again, all the while lifting her higher and higher. The rapture became so intense that she tore her lips from his, calling his name as she was hurled toward the next glorious, devastating pinnacle. His mouth roughly seized her breast, sucking powerfully, and she sobbed and tossed her head. Never had she felt more shattered or more fulfilled.

Indeed, she couldn't wait for Jake that time, or the next, until at last their bodies melded in an explosion of rapture that left both of them shuddering.

Chapter 22

"**Y**ou mind telling me who he was, lass?"
Jake stood just inside the doorway to the bedroom, wearing only his trousers. He had just gone to check on the girls, who were still sleeping peacefully, and now he had a thing or two to discuss with Priscilla. Claiming her at last had been glorious; he'd found utter paradise in joining himself with the woman he loved. Only now it appeared she wasn't entirely his, that she'd given her innocence to another before him. The fact that his future bride had come to him less than chaste made him feel hurt and uncertain. Even though he had suspected before that she might not be pure, his manly pride was badly chafed.

Across the room, Priscilla stood regarding Jake in indignation and uncertainty. She had just emerged from behind the dressing screen, after cleansing herself and righting her clothing as best she could. To have Jake ask her such a crude and unfeeling question at a time when her emotions were still raw from their lovemaking made her feel hurt and angry. She had just given herself to him in a very special way, had just experienced the most shattering orgasm of her entire lifetime. How dare he ask her such a thing?

"How are the girls?" she asked tensely, trying to ward off the looming explosion.

"They're fine. Now, answer me question. Who was he?"

"That's none of your business."

"It's damn well me business!"

Jake took an aggressive step toward her, and Priscilla gulped as she watched the light play over the harsh planes and angles of his face, the magnificent muscles and tufted dark hair of his bare chest.

"I can't believe you're asking me this!"

"Well, I'm asking. You didn't bleed, lassie," he stated bluntly. "You were not a virgin."

Priscilla struggled against an instinct to slap his arrogant face. "Oh! Only an ungallant boor would point that out!"

He scowled. "If I'm to become your husband, lass, I've a right to know who took your innocence."

"And who in hell says you're to become my husband?" she retorted. "Perhaps I have no desire to marry a Neanderthal such as yourself!"

He set his jaw stubbornly. "Then you should have thought of that a mite sooner. We've no choice but to marry after what we just shared."

"Or course we have a choice."

"Oh, do we? What if there's a wee one?"

Priscilla felt the blood drain from her face as she considered her own carelessness. She had definitely not brought her diaphragm to the past. She hurriedly calculated the date of her last period, and realized with relief that the timing of their lovemaking would likely not produce a child this time. "Let's not get precipitous."

He crossed over to her, grabbed her arm, and glowered down at her. "Was it Ackerly?"

She shoved him away. "I've already told you that's none of your damned affair!"

"Now, don't you go getting sassy with me," he snapped.

"Why don't you give me the names of every woman you've ever bedded?"

He smiled. "A man is expected to have certain dalliances—"

"And a woman is not?"

The scowl returned, more fearsome than ever. "Certainly not."

"Talk about the double standard!" she raved. "I should have expected such an outmoded attitude from a nineteenth-century chauvinist such as yourself."

He appeared confused. "Are you saying I've no right to expect chastity from a nineteenth-century woman such as yourself?"

"I'm *not* a nineteenth-century woman!" she blurted without thought.

"Oh, you're not," he mocked. "Then whence do you hail, lass—from some other planet?"

"Well, perhaps I do!"

He shook his head in incredulity. "And I presume *that* is where you're claiming to have mislaid your innocence?"

"As a matter of fact, it was."

He flung a hand outward in exasperation. "That's the most ridiculous claim I've ever heard."

"Damn it, I'm telling you the truth."

"You're lying through your teeth."

"I am not!"

He crossed his arms over his chest and glared. "Then, pray tell, explain. If you can."

Priscilla hesitated. Should she tell Jake her secret, how she had come here from another time? Would he even believe her? But how else could she make him understand that she wasn't a jezebel? Did she even care what he thought? Unfortunately, she found she did care. Good grief, she had just made uninhibited love with this man, had just given herself to him as she never had before with any man. Wasn't it time she leveled with him—and let him know how different they truly were, whether he chose to believe her or not?

Priscilla took a deep, bracing breath and stared him in the eye. "Well, if you must know, I'm not a virgin because I came here from a time and place where a woman's sexual celibacy prior to marriage was no longer an issue."

He snorted in disbelief. "And where was that, lassie? On the moon?"

"Actually, it was right here on earth, but a hundred and fifteen years in the future."

Jake howled with laughter. "Lass, that is preposterous."

"It may sound bizarre, but I tell you, it really happened." Priscilla touched his arm and spoke vehemently. "I probably should have explained this before now, but I've been afraid you wouldn't understand."

"I don't understand, lassie."

"Think, Jake," she insisted. "Don't you wonder how I came to know about miracle drugs, and why I was able to help you save Sal and Nell? Well, it's because I'm from the future, where we've learned about such things."

"Bah!"

"Will you please listen?"

He glared.

She paused to take a bracing breath. "The time I come from is so complex and amazing, I can't even begin to make you understand it just yet. Nor can I explain why this has happened—whether it was magic, the fates, or whatever, that brought me here. But I will tell you this, Jake—your note drew me across time to you—from the year 1995."

For a moment he stared at her in consternation, as if wavering. Then he threw back his head and laughed. "From 1995? Lass, you are demented!"

"I am not!"

"You must have taken the girls' fever, for you're spouting the most addlepated nonsense."

"I am not!"

"You are!"

"You don't believe me," she accused.

He rolled his eyes heavenward. "Not a word. Travels through time, me rosy behind! I think you're only inventing this folderol to excuse yourself for being a bad girl ... and you're not getting off the hook with me."

"Oh!"

"Well, ain't I right?"

"No, you couldn't be more wrong," she retorted through clenched teeth. "I'm not making excuses at all, only trying to make you understand that where I come from, women are not ostracized for having love affairs. And I'm also trying to make you see that, while I don't regret making love with you, I can't marry you. We're simply too different."

"Oh, we are?"

"Yes. For one thing, a hundred and fifteen years is a *lot* to overcome."

He pointed angrily at the bed. "We just overcame everything that matters right there, lassie, with your legs wrapped around me waist, and me buried inside you."

"You are crude!"

He waved an arm. "I am speaking the truth, by Saint Brendan! Furthermore, I'm through listening to your demented ramblings and poppycock excuses. You're mine now, and you'll rue the day you try to deny it. If you're wise, you'll heed my words and redeem yourself with me."

"*Redeem myself?*"

He shook a finger at her. "What I'm expecting of you, miss, is no more mischief. I'm marrying you at once, you understand, since it's high time someone made an honest woman out of you."

"An honest woman?" she shrieked.

"You may be a soiled dove, but you're the one the tides sent me, so it's done."

For a moment Priscilla's outrage was such that she couldn't even speak. Then she began pummeling Jake's chest with her fists. "You, sir, are an arrogant brute! If those are your true sentiments, why would you even want me?"

He grabbed her wrists, jerked her close, and spoke

with fire blazing in his eyes. "Because I love you, lassie, and so do the girls."

Even as hurt and furious as she was, Priscilla almost relented at Jake's ardent declaration. "If you love me, you have a fine way of showing it!" she accused.

"Oh, I'll be demonstrating me feelings to your satisfaction, lass," he murmured in an impassioned way that made her toes curl. "But I'll be tolerating no more flirting, no more Ackerly, ever. If I catch you even looking at another man, I'll have you over me knee in an instant and put a stop to your nonsense posthaste, let me assure you."

"You are insufferable!"

"You're very fortunate I haven't disciplined you already," he shot back. "You're getting off with no more than a slap on the wrist this time, lass. But let me tell you, girl, I dealt with one faithless wife, and I won't be tolerating a second. I'll have me eye on you every minute, so you'd best toe the mark."

"I'll do nothing of the kind!" She struggled unsuccessfully to get free.

Undaunted, he merely looked her over thoroughly, his lustful gaze lingering meaningfully on her rumpled bodice and bruised mouth. "You're obviously a passionate sort," he whispered huskily. " 'Twill be best to keep you bedded well, I reckon—and pregnant much of the time. We'd best be about it, then. Come back to bed with me."

Seething with anger, Priscilla at last shoved him away, turned on her heel, and charged for the doorway. "Why don't you just drop dead, you obnoxious beast! I think you've insulted me quite enough! I'm leaving now."

He was after her in a flash, and easily caught her arm. Even as she struggled and squealed with indignation, he flashed a charming smile and spoke cajolingly.

"Lassie, lassie, now, don't go running off in a snit.

Why don't you just take your medicine like a good girl, and let's kiss and make up?"

She tried to kick his shin, but he skillfully danced out of range. "I'd just as soon kiss Clyde's back end!"

The maddening devil only chuckled. "That's not how it seemed a few moments ago."

To her horror, Priscilla found she was close to tears, as mad at herself for letting him get to her as she was with him. "That was before you insulted me from bow to stern!"

"Now let me kiss you from bow to stern," he urged with a sexy wink.

"No!"

"Yes." He pulled her roughly against him, but his voice was soft. "Let me show you the reward nice girls get for being good."

"I *am* good!" she declared.

"Of course you are, darlin'," he whispered sympathetically. "Good, you are—and nice, too."

At her wit's end, Priscilla gave a little squeak—all the encouragement Jake needed. He crushed her close and passionately kissed her. Her outrage faded with the demanding thrust of his tongue in her mouth, and the magic of his hand stroking the curve of her hip.

Somehow, she gathered the strength to wrench her lips away from his. "No, no, I can't do this—I'm still angry at you!"

Jake was fervently kissing her throat. "Priscilla, love, don't be a sore loser. You won't be angry when I'm done with you, girl . . . I promise."

"That's what I'm afraid of," she whispered, shuddering.

"Why should you be afraid, love, when you know this is the only way to make things better?"

"Because I don't want to make things better! I want to kill you!"

He laughed again, raising one of her trembling hands and kissing the soft fingers. "You know you rushed me the first time, love, and I didn't get to do all the wicked things I wanted to do to you."

She froze, staring up at him in fascination.

He slid a sensual finger down her hot face and flushed throat, then began undoing her bodice. "We never got to feel our bodies naked against that satin spread, now did we, lass?"

"No, I—I suppose we didn't," she stammered, floundering.

He drew her hand to the front of his trousers, and she moaned helplessly as she felt his solid arousal. He gazed deeply into her eyes. "And I never got to kiss you where I really wanted to."

Priscilla totally lost it then. Her cheeks burning, she whispered, "Neither did I."

Priscilla caught only the briefest glimpse of the naked joy flaring in his eyes. Jake crushed his mouth on hers. She flung her arms about his neck. All at once, they were like two wild animals, tearing at each other's clothing between delirious, desperate kisses. A moment later, they fell naked together across the incredibly wicked satin coverlet. The tactile contrast between the cool, silky texture of the spread and the hot, rough man who held her was enough to drive Priscilla over the edge then and there.

She moaned as Jake pressed his prickly face between her breasts. She stretched forward to kiss his soft, thick hair, and inhaled the musky scent of him.

"Should I shave, love?" he asked, tonguing her tight nipple.

"No, don't. I like you just as you are."

"I'll put my mark on you," he warned.

"You already have."

He looked up, flashing her a devilish grin. His lips moved down her belly. Priscilla cried out at the erotic abrasion of his rough face on her skin. Slowly he moved lower, his fingers caressing the curls at the joining of her thighs. Even as she tensed in anticipation, his hands parted her, then his lips followed. She sucked in a frenzied breath and bit her fist . . .

Jake gloried in his taste of Priscilla, in getting to place his stamp of ownership on the feminine center of her. He gently parted her velvety folds, and flicked his tongue across her tiny, swollen nub. To his delight, she went insane, writhing and trying to wiggle her hips free from the sweet torment. He chuckled, held her fast, and used his tongue to torture her at his leisure.

The sounds of her torrid cries made his chest ache with emotion. She may have been had before, he thought with possessive triumph, but he reckoned she'd never been had quite this way. And Jake intended to claim her thoroughly, to make her climb the walls. He buried his face against her intimate parts, delving deeper to suck gently, then ravenously . . .

At the shattering stimulation, Priscilla grew frantic, struggling between ecstasy and fear. Jake's rough face felt wickedly abrasive against her tenderest parts. Never had she expected him to take her with such uninhibited passion. Never before had she given herself to any man so intimately. Jake was demanding her body and soul, and it was frightening to give in to such intense feelings, for this meant giving herself over to him, holding nothing back. Then she would be his forever—if she wasn't already!

She pounded her fist on the coverlet. "Jake, please, please . . ."

He looked up to smile at her, his fingers stroking where his mouth had been. "Relax, lassie, 'twill do you no good to resist. I'm not stopping until I've had my fill of you . . . and given you yours."

"Oh, God," she groaned.

Then his tongue performed its scandalous dance again, and Priscilla sobbed with pleasure. Soon she was totally without shame. Jake's tongue flicked, his mouth drew, until she gave in to all the ecstasy she felt and arched into his bold, relentless strokes, crying out wildly, letting his love consume her and drive her to the devouring pinnacle. She tossed her head and sobbed her pleasure until she was drained, replete.

His body slid up hers, and she felt his hard manhood probing insistently. Mindless with hunger for him, she called his name and struggled to take him inside her.

But he held back, grabbing her about the waist. His gaze smoldered into hers. "Promise me you'll never again take another inside you, lass."

Her expression was miserably torn. "Jake, I can't."

"Promise me."

She shuddered. Hell, he was worth it. "I promise."

Priscilla caught a glimpse of a smile so glorious, it seemed to light up her entire universe. Then Jake impaled her greedily, and she moaned in abandonment, so full of him, she could not bear the riotous rapture.

Jake had found his own paradise in the hot center of the woman he loved. He slid upward until he completely buried himself in her warm, tight sheath, and felt her fingernails dig into his shoulders. He drove into her slowly, again and again, savoring the velvety constriction of her, determined to bring her to madness once more before he gave her pleasure. He did. At his unhurried deep thrusts, the lass grew tormented, brazenly rolling her hips, inviting his unbridled plunder. He reveled in her response, drinking in the desperate passion in her eyes, the frantic sounds rising in her throat, the tightness of her red nipples. He didn't want to push her too far. Ah, but the lass was game, so sweet and willing that he was rapidly losing control! All at once he could not get enough of her, could not catch his breath, could not still his raging heart. Even as he thrust into her with consuming need, he felt her softening, melting into his lusty possession, and heard her ragged sobs of surrender. He caught her to him for a fevered kiss as they both scaled the gates of heaven.

Chapter 23

It was difficult to think rationally when one's head was so filled with passion. This was Priscilla's thought an hour later when Jake returned to the bedroom with a bottle of wine and two glasses. She pulled the covers up to her neck and smiled at him shyly, and he winked back. Her pulse surged wildly. He did look terribly rakish, dressed only in his trousers, with the golden light of sunset filtering through the curtains and outlining his magnificent physique.

He set the tray on the bedside table, poured her a glassful, and after tenderly kissing her lips, handed it to her. "How are you faring, lassie? Have I worn you out yet?"

"Don't worry about me," she replied, taking a sip, then putting down her glass. "What about the girls?"

"I checked on them. They're still sleeping like babies, and cool as cucumbers."

"My, but you use a lot of clichés."

"And you're a sassy wench, too." Taking a sip from his own glass, he sat down beside her on the bed and wrapped his free arm about her shoulders. "It's getting toward sundown, darlin'. For the sake of your reputation, perhaps you should soon be heading back to Rose Gatling's place."

She raised an eyebrow at him. "You mean to say you are actually concerned for my reputation?"

He grinned. "If you're volunteering to stay the night, darlin', you'll not hear a protest from me." He kneaded one of her breasts and finished wickedly,

"Though you may be squealing a mite by the time I'm done with you, love."

Priscilla attempted an admonishing look that soon dissolved into a sigh of pleasure. "Actually, I suppose you're right. As long as the girls are okay, it's best that I do start back."

"But we'll be together soon enough, darlin'," he assured her, kissing the tip of her nose. "I'm aiming to apply for our license tomorrow."

Priscilla groaned. "Jake, didn't you hear anything I said earlier?"

He eyed her sternly. "I'm only hearing what you said when you were in my arms, lass. You said you're mine now, that no other man will touch you as I have."

She glanced away miserably. "I was ... er ... under duress at the time."

"Duress, eh?"

She grinned crookedly. "Well, in the throes of passion."

He chuckled, and leaned over to nibble at her jaw. "Where I'm aiming to keep you, love."

She shuddered, pulling away from him. "I—I think we're rushing into the possibility of marriage too quickly."

"And I think we have no time to spare."

Priscilla bit her lip. "Jake, I don't want to give you false hope. I can't promise I'll marry you."

"And why not?"

"Haven't we had this conversation before?"

"Not in bed, we haven't!"

Priscilla struggled not to laugh, for he looked so irate. "I suppose you have a point. What we shared was beautiful, but it doesn't change the fact that we're too different."

"That again!" he exclaimed in frustration.

"You know it's true, Jake. We're from different worlds."

"Ah, yes—you're from a hundred and fifteen years in the future," he mocked.

"I am!"

"And I'm from the kingdom of Lilliput!"

In her frustration, she dug her fingernails into the satin coverlet. "Jake, you have no idea what kind of world I came from."

"Damn it, girl!" He set down his wineglass and glared at her. "I'll hear no more of this demented talk—you traveling through time and such. Why, it's downright sacrilegious and just a flimsy excuse for not marrying me."

"Then I'll give you a better one. We have nothing in common."

He laughed. "Nothing?"

"Well, almost nothing." Her face smarting, she forged on. "Jake, a solid marriage must be based on more than just great sex."

Wickedly he drew her fingers to the bulging front of his trousers. "Aye, darling, there's solid sex, too."

"Will you stop it?" Blushing furiously, she snatched her fingers away and punched him in the shoulder, but he only laughed. "What I'm saying is, you'll never want the things I want—culture, a place in society. Indeed, you constantly scoff at my aspirations."

"You're speaking of outward trappings only," he declared heatedly.

"And there you go, doing it again!" she cried, flinging a hand outward. "You're denigrating what I want by implying my own goals are superficial."

"But they are, lass."

She pounded him with a pillow. "You are impossible!"

He grabbed the pillow and they faced each other over a shower of tiny feathers. "Lass, all I'm trying to say is that it's what's in our hearts that counts."

"Perhaps. But even in our hearts, we want different things. And to me, outward trappings are important."

"So you won't have me because I'm a dairy farmer?" he asked darkly.

"Jake, we've been over that before, too. It's not that simple."

"You're still afraid I'll be like your pa?"

She nodded.

"Why won't you trust me?"

Priscilla took a long moment to collect her tumultuous feelings. "After my father deserted my mother and me, I promised myself I'd never marry a man like him—that I wouldn't spend my life in that kind of pain and emotional upheaval, that I would only marry a man who was revered in the community and would always provide well for me."

"Ah, so now I understand. You still think I'm going to bring you disgrace?"

"I think you could, Jake. I think our relationship would continue to be very tempestuous, and in time you'd grow bored with me. After all, I'm not a beauty like your first wife."

"Now who's accusing who of being superficial?" he demanded. "How many times must I tell you you're beautiful to me?"

"But don't you think a big reason you find me appealing is because you think the fates brought us together, and because you need a mother for your girls?" she argued. At his indignant look, she held up a hand. "I'm not saying motherhood isn't a noble undertaking, just that necessity alone is not a good basis for a lasting marriage."

Quietly he asked, "So you didn't listen when I told you I love you?"

Put on the spot, she glanced away. "I don't think you'd be the first man blinded by passion or poor judgment. I—I need something more enduring."

"And you think Mr. Pantywaist can give you what you need?"

"I think he and I have much more in common."

Jake's laughter was cynical. "He has no heart, girl, and you're a fool to trust him. I'm the one who can give you what you need—including my heart and my loyalty. You're simply going to have to take a leap of faith and trust me."

Miserably she stared at her lap. "I can't. I don't regret what we've shared, but I can't give you the commitment you want."

Scowling, he stood. "Get dressed, lassie. I've something to show you."

She regarded his dark, intent face in confusion.

He leaned over, scooped up her camisole and bloomers and tossed them onto her lap. "Just do as I say. You'll see."

They both put on their clothes and went out to the parlor. While Priscilla checked on the babies, she was puzzled to note Jake removing several loose boards from the floor. A moment later, he placed a small, plain wooden chest on the table.

"Come here, lassie."

Her expression quizzical, she moved to his side. "What is that?"

He grinned. "You think I cannot provide for you, eh?"

Jake flung open the lid of the chest, and Priscilla gasped as she viewed the velvet-lined interior—which was piled high with glittering gold and silver coins.

She stared at Jake. "My God! That looks like—well, like Jean Lafitte's treasure!"

"So 'tis, lassie," he rejoined solemnly.

Her eyes went wide. "You have uncovered part of Jean Lafitte's plunder?"

He chuckled. "Why so stunned, lassie? It's long been rumored Lafitte left behind enough booty in these parts to pave Broadway in gold."

"But . . . how did you come into possession of all of this?" She snapped her fingers. "Did you find the treasure in Lafitte's Grove?"

He winked at her. "Mayhap I captured a leprechaun, lassie."

Priscilla rolled her eyes. "Come on, Jake! This

much gold didn't just materialize out of thin air. Fess up."

He scratched his jaw and fought amusement. "Truth to tell, I'll admit to having done a bit of poking about at the Grove over the years."

"My heavens, you actually did it!" cried Priscilla. "I remember even in the present, people were always digging around for the pirate gold—and to think that you found it!"

He eyed her in perplexity.

Returning her attention to the treasure, Priscilla picked up a gold doubloon and examined it carefully. Not quite perfectly round, the shiny piece was encircled by ancient writing. At its center was inscribed a Gothic cross surrounded by various insignia, including a lion and a castle. Priscilla presumed she was staring at some sort of ancient coat of arms. She laid the doubloon down and sifted through more of the booty, studying a larger silver coin with a crown and shield that she guessed was a piece of eight, and a smaller gold coin etched with a ship.

"Amazing," she murmured, running her fingertips over the glittering heap and listening to the sounds of the coins jingling together.

"So you think I cannot provide for you, lassie?" Jake repeated, his eyes gleaming with triumph as he gestured toward the mound of pirate treasure. "Well, here's proof that I can."

She dropped a coin and regarded him irately. "There's surely a small fortune here, Jake. Why don't you have this in the bank?"

He waved her off. "I don't hold with such."

"B-But what if this chest were stolen? Think of the loss to the girls—"

"No one knows about it but you and me."

"That's beside the point," she exclaimed. "You're a fool to leave a bonanza in gold under your floorboards."

He ignored her comment, saying proudly, "Marry

me, lass, and 'twill all be yours. I'm betting Ackerly Frost will never match it."

She was stunned. "Are you trying to buy me, Jake?"

"If that's what it takes, darlin'. You set a high store by riches, don't you? With this gold, you'll be secure. You won't be needing your hoity-toity friends, or to be selling your services on the Strand."

She went pale. "Now you're making me sound like some sort of prostitute!"

He drew himself up proudly. "As Jake Blarney's wife, you won't be selling anything, lass. Everything you need, you'll be getting right here on this farm."

Jake's words both hurt and appalled Priscilla. Did he really think she was so shallow that she could be bought off with a chestful of pirate coins? Couldn't he understand that her aspirations in life went beyond material security, that she needed friends, a place in society, a husband she could always depend on to help her maintain that station? Couldn't he see that the idea of loving a brash, unpredictable, volatile man such as him still scared her to death?

She remembered the disgrace Jake had heaped on her at the Cotton Exchange Ball. She didn't doubt he would do it again. She very much feared she was in love with him, and she certainly adored his children; yet Jake remained the antithesis of everything she had ever wanted. Now he seemed to be asking her to give up everything that mattered to *her*.

A bitter revolt welled up in Priscilla. Her mother had lived her life that way. Her father had been so demanding and domineering, and he had alienated so many people, that Beatrice had never really had a life of her own until after Whitey had left. Priscilla was not about to follow in her mother's footsteps and marry a man who would both dominate her life and make her miserable. She felt agonized, especially for the sake of the twins, who so badly needed a mother, but unable to deny the sobering truth.

"Lass?" he prodded. "Well, what do you say?"

Priscilla blinked back tears and spoke in a quavering voice. "Jake, you're so blind. You think all it takes is gold to convince me to give up all my dreams. Even if you are rich, you can't change what you are. You're simply not the right man for me. And I'm not going to spend the rest of my life here with you, milking the cows."

Before he could comment—before she could catch a last glimpse of the babies and lose her resolve—Priscilla ran for the door.

Hours later, Jake stood by the front window, holding Sal and staring desolately out at the Gulf. Both girls had awakened soon after Priscilla left; they had been free of fever, but starved. Nell had been satisfied by a bottle, and had quickly drifted back to sleep. Sal, as usual, was restless, so after feeding her, Jake had walked the floor with her.

His emotions felt raw. He was deeply grateful that the girls would recover, but devastated that he had lost Priscilla. She had come to him, saved his children, made incredible, beautiful love with him, and she had left him. He had declared his love and devotion, and she had thrown both back in his face.

He felt so confused, so hurt, so frustrated. He knew he understood Priscilla better than any other man, yet she persisted in not trusting him and thwarted his every attempt to get through to her.

Other aspects of her behavior baffled him. Why had she come to him at all, if she saw no future for them? Why hadn't she been a virgin? Why had she claimed to have come here from a hundred and fifteen years in the future?

That possibility boggled Jake's mind. Although he had insisted Priscilla's claim was blarney, in truth, he couldn't be sure what he believed. Was it possible the note he had sent had brought her here across time? Had the fates conspired to set aside the laws of the universe? The prospect was truly awesome. But if such a miracle had occurred, why wouldn't she believe that they were meant to be together? Surely only the greatest of all love could draw two people to each other across the vast gulf of time.

On the other hand, if some mystical force had brought her to him, couldn't that same force snatch her away? That particular prospect was terrifying, and Jake was sure his fear of losing her was at the root of his inability to even discuss the daunting notion with her.

But hadn't he lost her anyway? Anguish assailed him as he envisioned the lonely years stretching ahead of him without her sweet loving. After having known the paradise of making her his own, the agony of losing her was all the more unbearable. But it was clear to him now that the girl had needs he could never fulfill. She was convinced that being his bride and the mother to his babies would never be enough for her. Of course, he'd been stubborn, insisting she must give up her friends and her promising new career. But he'd been so afraid that those duties, and the Galveston social scene, would take her away from him . . .

Now it appeared he'd been right.

Sal began to squirm and let out a demanding cry. Jake kissed the child's dear little brow, then began walking the floor with her again. Softly he sang the lullaby "Sweet and Low." Once the baby dozed in his arms, he returned to the window and stared again at the billowing sea. The sea that had brought his true love to him. The sea that mocked him now.

"She's gone, Sal," he whispered, his voice breaking. "I don't know what brought her here, and I don't understand why she wouldn't stay. I need her—we all need her, you know. I thought it was riches she wanted, but I was wrong. It's *me* she doesn't want. I tried to win her, but I've lost her now."

Only the mournful waves answered.

Chapter 24

Priscilla was distraught and still disheveled an
hour and a half later when she entered the
boardinghouse. After turning in the horse and buggy
at the stable, she had caught the last trolley home.

She tried to enter the house quietly, but Rose Gatling emerged from the parlor to give her a stern look.
"Miss Pemberton, I do hope nothing is amiss."

"Good evening, Miss Gatling," Priscilla replied, resisting the urge to nervously smooth down her coiffure. "Why would anything be amiss?"

"You appear rather . . . agitated."

"I'm sure you're mistaken."

Her head held high, Priscilla rushed for the stairs.
Oh, what an emotional roller coaster this day had
been! She barely held in her tears until she got into
her room and shut the door. Then she leaned against
the panel and sobbed. It had torn her apart to leave
Jake after all they had shared . . . but she remained
convinced he would break her heart in the long run
if she stayed with him.

Momentarily she heard a rap, and uttered a cry of
outrage. That nosy biddy must have followed her
upstairs. "Who is it?" she called irritably. "I prefer to
be left alone, thank you."

" 'Tis Mary," came the tense reply. "I'm sorry if I
disturbed you."

Priscilla flung open the door. "Mary, please, come
in. I didn't mean to sound so peevish, but I thought
you were Gatling Gun."

Mary was staring aghast at Priscilla's distraught face. "What's wrong, love? I heard you crying as I passed through the hallway." She gasped. "Is it Mr. Blarney's wee ones? Have they taken a turn for the worse?"

"No. Actually, they're fine now."

Mary heaved a sigh and crossed herself. "Saints be praised."

"Amen." Priscilla pulled Mary into the room and shut the door. "It's really rather personal, I'm afraid."

"Is it about you and Mr. Blarney?" Mary touched her arm. "Look, Priscilla, if you don't want to confide in me, just tell me it's none of my business. But you do look rather down in the mouth, dear."

"I know." Priscilla gestured toward a Queen Anne chair next to the bed. "Would you sit with me for a moment?"

"Of course."

Mary sat down on the chair, and Priscilla perched herself on the edge of her bed. She brushed a strand of hair from her eyes and braved a smile at her friend. "Can you keep this entirely confidential?"

Again Mary crossed herself. "You have me word."

"I'm afraid I may have just made a terrible mistake."

Mary frowned. "But how, love?"

Priscilla bit her lip. "Will you *really* promise never to tell anyone?"

"Priscilla, you can trust me," admonished Mary.

"I know." She drew a shaky breath. "I'm afraid I just ... er ... committed an indiscretion with Mr. Blarney."

"Ye gads!" Mary gasped, her hand flying to her mouth. "Do you mean the brute took advantage of you?"

Priscilla felt color shooting up her face. "Er ... no. It was a mutual indiscretion."

Mary's mouth dropped open. "I never knew anyone who committed one of those before."

Priscilla wrung her hands. "It was the babies, you

see—all the tension of worrying about them. We nursed them together all day, and finally, when their fevers broke, we were so relieved and, we just got . . . carried away with emotion." Priscilla burst into new sobs.

Mary rushed over to comfort her, sitting down beside her and patting her heaving shoulders. "And now the scoundrel refuses to take responsibility?"

"Oh, no," Priscilla replied, waving a hand. "He's more determined than ever to marry me."

Mary laughed. "Then it's all fixed, love. Why are you crying?"

"Because I can't marry him!" Priscilla burst out.

"And why not?"

"It's just . . . He's not my kind, and I really can't trust him."

"Just because a man's of humble circumstances doesn't mean he's of questionable character," Mary pointed out.

"I realize this, but—"

"And do you have a choice after what happened?"

"One always has a choice," said Priscilla.

Mary sadly shook her head. "Not a lady, love. You're ruined now, and if you're smart, you'll marry Mr. Blarney."

"I'm not going to marry him simply because of some outdated double standard," Priscilla declared.

Mary stared at her blankly.

"Don't you understand?" Priscilla continued in agitation. "Jake is not my kind—we have nothing in common. You told me yourself he has a bad reputation—"

"Aye, but many a bad'un shapes up just fine with a good righteous woman to keep him in line."

"Well, it won't be this woman. I grew up with a mother who tried to redeem the man she loved, and her efforts brought her nothing but grief. I must have a man I can depend on never to disgrace me. I just can't live through that kind of pain and humiliation again."

Mary sighed as if she understood. "Ah—so it's
Mr. Ackerly Frost you're wanting—with all his
wealth?"

"It's not just money at issue," Priscilla argued, remembering Jake's doubloons, and how he had tried
to buy her. "It's my emotional well-being, my peace
of mind—a serenity I'd never have with Jake. Besides, Mr. Frost and I can make something together
in this community."

"Aye," said Mary ruefully, "you'll make a very
cold bed, I would reckon."

Priscilla regarded Mary in anguish. "If you were in
my shoes, what would you do?"

Mary nodded with determination. "That's simple,
love. I'd marry Jake Blarney in an instant—and I'd
never trust Mr. Frost."

Time passed, and Priscilla did not see Jake. She did
learn, with a keen sense of relief mingled with lingering disappointment, that she was not pregnant.
Funny, she had never thought much about her own
future children until she had met Jake and his babies,
and now, at times, she still found it difficult to think
about anything else. Even after she walked out on
him, fantasies of familial bliss with him and the girls
haunted her. However, despite her more poignant
feelings, despite the fact that she missed Jake and the
twins intensely, she remained convinced that she had
made the only right decision for herself as a person.

She continued to see Ackerly, though not as often.
Although she had cut her ties with Jake, she felt
guilty for seeing another man when so many of her
emotions still seemed tied to the Blarney farm. She
did attend a few holiday parties and socials—
sometimes with Ackerly, more often without him.
When he questioned why she didn't want to see him
as much, she cited the demands of her career, and he
reluctantly accepted her explanation. Actually, her
enterprise was flourishing; following her triumph at
the elocution contest, she had gained another dozen

new students, and her reputation as a tutor grew by leaps and bounds. Her account at Ackerly's bank grew fatter, too.

When they were together, Ackerly continued to press Priscilla for an answer on his marriage proposal, and she continued to hold him off. Finally she placated him by promising him her answer before Christmas. Ackerly even seemed pleased that she was stalling. "We've been invited to a caroling party at the Sealys on Christmas Eve," he informed her. "That would be a most fitting time to announce our engagement to our friends, don't you think?"

Actually, Priscilla doubted she could commit to Ackerly even then. In her heart of hearts, she knew what the problem was. Jake Blarney. She missed him, couldn't stop thinking about him, and was surely in love with him. Yet as the days and weeks passed, she received alarming reports of his behavior that seemed to reinforce her previous doubts about him. When Ackerly mentioned having heard that Jake was involved in a drunken brawl at a grogshop on Postoffice Street, Priscilla at first doubted the account. But when similar reports starting cropping up from other, more reliable sources, Priscilla grew very concerned.

First, Mary dropped a broad hint one November day when Priscilla stopped in for lunch at the apothecary. Leaning over the counter toward Priscilla, the girl confided, "Jake Blarney was in here earlier, buying a new kerosene lamp. Said he broke the other one."

Priscilla frowned. "Broke it?"

" 'Twas no wonder if you ask me," Mary went on. "He looked a terrible sight. Like he hadn't shaved in a week. All bleary-eyed, too, and he reeked of whiskey."

"No!" Priscilla gasped.

"Aye. I'm thinking he's been on an eight-day bender . . ."

The next dire report Priscilla received was from the

mother of one of her newest students, Chester Snodgrass, whom she'd acquired following the elocution contest. Priscilla didn't much care for Chester's mother, Delia, who seemed condescending as well as a mean-spirited gossip. But Chester was a promising student, and the Snodgrasses were prominent.

One day as Delia came to collect Chester, the tall, thin, sharply featured woman confided to Priscilla, "Well, Miss Pemberton, have you heard the latest about that irascible Irishman, Jake Blarney?" With a nasty smile she finished, "I do believe you're acquainted with him."

Priscilla smiled poisonously. "You and everyone else who attended the Cotton Exchange Ball."

"Well, yes. Anyway, Durwood and I were asleep the other night when we heard that demented Irishman driving his buggy down Broadway, singing at the top of his lungs. 'Poor Wandering One,' I believe it was."

"How apt," muttered Priscilla.

"Disgraceful is more like it. He awakened our entire household. Durwood almost went for the sheriff, but at last the abominable man passed." She stared sternly at Priscilla. "I've half a mind to inform my friend Octavia Overstreet, in Houston, about Mr. Blarney's disgraceful shenanigans. She's the twins' aunt, you know, and is most concerned for their welfare."

Priscilla was tensely silent.

"As for you, young lady," Delia continued severely, "you do have to watch who you associate with in this town."

Priscilla responded coldly. "Actually, as much as I appreciate your help, Mrs. Snodgrass, I am perfectly capable of handling my own associations."

"Well!" Delia summoned her son, who had been listening intently. "Come along, Chester . . ."

The next day brought Father O'Dooley. "Miss Pemberton, I'll be having a word with you!" he announced as he burst in her door on the Strand.

Priscilla was tutoring Willie Shrewsbury. She excused herself and rushed to the door. "Father O'Dooley," she whispered urgently, "I have a student."

In his agitation, he took no note of her protest, but began to pace about and wave his hands. "Young woman, I'm worried about Jake Blarney. You must do something about him!"

Priscilla was trying her best to follow him. "Why me?"

He slanted her a chiding glance. "You know very well why you. You have a responsibility to the man. He hasn't attended mass in weeks, and I've heard scandalous reports about him. I went out to call on him and he wouldn't even let me in the front door. Sounded half-drunk, too."

Priscilla felt intensely torn. "Father O'Dooley, please, there's really nothing I can do—"

He shook a pudgy finger at her. "You and I both know better than that, young lady! At this rate, Jake is going straight to hell, and it'll be on your head!"

Soon thereafter a distraught Bula Braunhurst made an unexpected appearance at Priscilla's studio. Thankfully, this time Priscilla was between lessons. Bula sat before Priscilla's desk, sobbing and twisting her handkerchief.

"Mr. Jake is not the same," she lamented. "Gone to all hours, and drinking worse than a sailor."

Priscilla grabbed the woman's sleeve. "What about the girls? Are they all right?"

She nodded. "Oh, *ja*, he sees they are not lacking, but 'tis not the same, miss. I'm there to all hours sitting with the little darlings while he's out carousing— and my husband, Walter, is on the verge of apoplexy to have his wife never home. Can you do something to help, miss?"

"What could I do?"

Bula touched Priscilla's hand. "Talk to him. Please, miss."

She bit her lip. "I'll see what I can do. If you need help with the girls, you let me know."

"Ja, miss."

Priscilla agonized, wondering what she should do. She was worried about the girls, but afraid that if she ventured out to Jake's cabin again, she might end up in his arms. Hell, she was certain of it!

Nonetheless, she awakened quite early the next morning convinced that she must take the bull by the horns and see Jake, insist that he shape up for the girls' sake. She went into town very early, hoping to catch him when he made his daily delivery to the pasteurizing plant on the Strand. She had just arrived in front of her studio when she spotted his work wagon two blocks away. Jake was driving a team of two large horses, and his dray was loaded with huge jugs of milk.

What luck to find him! she thought. She started briskly toward him. "Jake Blarney, you stop right there! I need to talk to you!"

Ignoring her, he did not even slow his horses! Furious, she ventured out into the middle of the street, heedless of the huge conveyance rattling toward her. This time he did react. Indeed, he was barely able to reign in the powerful work horses before they would have trampled Priscilla. She stood her ground, trembling badly, especially as the huge beasts stood snorting and stamping their shaggy hooves mere inches away from her!

Jake jumped down to confront her, his features ashen. "Are you insane, woman? You could have just been killed!"

She looked him over and found he appeared as bleary-eyed and unshaven as Mary had insisted—and damned sexy, in spite of it all! She stiffened up her spine and retorted, "You look like hell."

"And you almost got yourself dispatched to the nether regions!" he snapped back, grabbing her arm and pulling her over to the shell walkway. "Explain this demented behavior!"

She braced herself with a deep breath, and plunged in. "Jake, I've been hearing terrible things about you. That you've been drinking, gambling, starting fights, that you haven't been to mass—"

His features contorted in fury. "What in hell do you, an Episcopalian, care about whether I attend mass? And what business is it of yours how I live my life, after you walked out on me?"

"It's the principle of the thing," she argued, struggling to hold on to her resolve. "You're setting a terrible example for the girls."

"My daughters have everything they need," he ground out.

"Except a father," she retorted. "And they sorely need one."

He grabbed her by the shoulders, his bright, wounded gaze boring into hers. "They need a mother, too, but *cruel is she.*"

Fighting humiliating tears, Priscilla shoved him away. "How dare you sanctimoniously quote Arnold's poetry to me at a time like this! You're the one who has neglected your duties, Jake Blarney, and you're not going to pin the blame on me! Do you know Delia Snodgrass is thinking about informing the twins' aunt in Houston of your disgraceful conduct of late?"

"She already has," Jake sneered. "I received a nasty letter from Octavia's lawyer just yesterday. She's demanding that I relinquish custody of the twins."

Priscilla was astounded and alarmed. "Jake, you must take this seriously!"

"Ah, hogwash." He waved her off. "That biddy's been trying to intimidate me ever since Lucinda walked out on me. I've cast Octavia out of me house so many times that now she hides behind her slimy paid weasel and gets him to harass me. She knows I'll strangle her with me bare hands before I allow her to touch me precious babes. As for Delia Snodgrass and her role in this—she's an interfering, lying bitch."

"Is everyone lying, Jake?" Priscilla demanded in exasperation. "Father O'Dooley, Mrs. Braunhurst, and, well, a lot of people are growing very concerned about you."

"Are you concerned about me, lass?" he inquired cynically.

Even as his question battered her with guilt, she whispered plaintively, "I certainly wish you no ill."

"Well, you have a mighty fine way of showing it."

"Jake, I want you to be a good father to the girls," she pleaded. "I want you to be responsible . . . and happy."

"And what about what I want?" he asked, looming over her in hurt and anger. "I want you in bed with me from now till sundown—nay, from now until the end of time. Then maybe I'll be happy."

Priscilla's knees had gone weak, as had her resolve. "This is getting us nowhere. I must go."

"That's right," he mocked. "Run away. Just like last time."

She was backing away, blinded by hot tears. "You take good care of those girls, Jake Blarney, or I'll kill you."

He strode after her and grabbed her arm, restraining her. "Not that it's any of your damned affair, but I *always* take good care of me daughters."

"I don't believe you!" she cried, struggling to get free.

He hauled her against him, his impassioned face looming very close to hers. "Well, if you want to be sure, lassie, you know just what it's going to take."

He released her, turned on his heel, and stalked off.

Jake delivered his jugs of milk to the Strand Pasteurizing Plant, and loaded up the cleaned, empty ones to carry home to the dairy and fill with milk tomorrow. He was in a foul humor as he drove his team back through town toward the beach. How dare Priscilla chide him for being a poor father, when she was willing to accept no responsibility for the twins herself!

Still, he had to admit that her words had chafed badly because they had a ring of truth. He knew he was out of control these days, spending far too much time in grogshops, drinking and gambling, his mean temper getting him into donnybrooks. But he'd seen to it that his girls had not suffered—except, as Priscilla had bluntly pointed out, through his absences.

Damn her, anyway! Seeing her just now had been torture, making him relive the agony of her desertion, when she'd told him he would never be good enough for her, that she would never trust him, that she placed pompous jackasses like Ackerly Frost and her exalted Galveston society far above him and anything he could ever offer.

How did she expect him to react under the circumstances? Yes, she was heartless and cruel, but she'd been sweet and loving, too; after believing she was his for one glorious afternoon, he wasn't sure he would ever recover from the heartache of losing her.

Chapter 25

Another week passed. An agonizing week. Reports of Jake's shocking behavior continued. Delia Snodgrass gleefully informed Priscilla that Jake had been spotted on a recent night staggering down Postoffice Street, with a woman of ill-repute dangling over one shoulder, kicking and screaming. Father O'Dooley returned to the studio and paced about, ranting and raving over Jake's refusal to attend mass or accept his counsel. Mrs. Braunhurst dropped in once more to alternately wring her hands and sob for half an hour. The twins were fine, she reported; she and Walter were keeping them at their house most nights now. But Mr. Blarney was driving her insane with his outlandish behavior: staying out to all hours; drinking; coming home battered and bleary-eyed. Bula didn't know how much more she could take.

Priscilla, too, was almost at the breaking point—sick with fear over the twins and ready to do almost anything to ensure that they were all right, and not suffering due to their father's lapses. She told Bula to call on her at any time if there were any problem with the girls or their care.

Of course, all of these accounts reinforced Priscilla's conviction that Jake was wrong for her; but this time she took no satisfaction in being right. Indeed, the possibility that he had been seen with a prostitute—if Delia Snodgrass was telling the truth—was intensely disconcerting. Even if she and Jake

283

weren't compatible, even if he was a man she could never completely trust, she couldn't help the fact that she cared for him deeply and her arms ached to hold his precious babies again. More than once she walked past the Braunhurst cottage, wondering if Sal and Nell were inside. More than once she almost went to the door; but she held back, fearing that if she took those precious angels in her arms again, she would become Jake's bride before Christmas.

Adding to Priscilla's frustration was the fact that Ackerly Frost kept pressing her for an answer to his marriage proposal. Instead of seeing him as her salvation, she felt more confused than ever and found herself breaking more dates with him. When they did attend holiday events together, rather than getting caught up in the spirit of the season and enjoying Galveston's most splendid mansions all decked out for Christmas, she found herself feeling preoccupied, fretting over Jake and the babies.

She knew she was developing new doubts about Ackerly. She'd seen a hint of social snobbery in him at the Cotton Exchange Ball, when he'd criticized Jake and Mary. More and more she suspected he was a shameless social climber, and he wanted her because she fit in well with his plans. The fact that her own motives in seeing him had been equally mercenary only heightened her doubt and self-recrimination.

She became particularly annoyed with him soon after Helen Durant sent her two tickets to the premiere of *Samson and Delilah,* at the Tremont Opera House on Thanksgiving eve. Priscilla invited Ackerly to go with her to the performance, but he demurred, pointing out that they'd been invited to the Moodys' that night for a tree-trimming party. "I'm finally making inroads with the colonel and his group," Ackerly announced. "Of course, it was kind of Helen to send us the tickets, but attending the Moody soirée that night is by far the more socially expedient choice."

Although Priscilla protested, Ackerly proved adamant. They went to the Moody gathering, and Priscilla thought of Jake and the girls all night. On Thanksgiving day Ackerly took her to the buffet at the Tremont Hotel, which he assured her was the place to be. Priscilla picked at the fabulous fare and wondered what Thanksgiving was like at the Blarney cottage. Ackerly spent the meal cataloging all their remaining invitations for the holiday season, and informing her which ones were the most socially advantageous to accept. Priscilla pleaded a headache and asked him to take her home early.

Priscilla found his posturing irritating, and she was honest enough to admit that perhaps she was beginning to see too much of herself in Ackerly Frost. If his values were shallow, then what did that say about some of her own goals? Was attaining her craved place in society not worth the cost of living without love? She wasn't sure what the solution was for her life anymore; but she did know her victory had a hollow ring without Jake.

Late one early December night, Priscilla was lying in bed, tossing and turning, when she heard a loud commotion out on her balcony. Instantly alert with terror, she jerked upright, certain someone was trying to break into her room. She had just grabbed a vase from the bedside table when she heard a familiar voice—it was Jake Blarney, yelling like a madman through her French doors!

For a futile moment Priscilla prayed her ears were deceiving her. But no, it definitely was Jake, bellowing poetry at the top of his lungs!

Appalled, she listened:

"Open the door, some pity to show
Open the door to me
Though thou hast been false, I'll ever prove true,
Open the door to me."

"Oh, my God!" she gasped, panic-stricken. "He's going to wake the dead!"

Priscilla set down the vase and bolted out of bed. Stumbling on the hem of her flannel nightgown, she rushed over to fling open the French doors. A gust of chill wind battered her, along with the overwhelming presence of Jake Blarney, who tottered before her in the moonlight, dressed in a wool jacket, dark trousers, and a ratty cap.

"Jake! What on earth are you doing here!" she cried.

"I'm reciting poetry, lass," he shouted drunkenly. "I'll quote Bobby Burns to you, even if he is a damned Scot!"

"B-But how did you get here?"

He flung out a hand and almost lost his balance. "I climbed yon trellis—"

"Then you may leave here by yon trellis at once!" she hissed. "Where are the girls, for heaven's sake?"

"They're spending the night with Bula and Walter." He wobbled a step closer and leered at her lecherously. "And you're spending the night with me, lassie."

Priscilla shrank away from him in horror. "No! You're going to ruin me!"

"You've ruined me already, lass!" he declared, waving a hand wildly. "You've driven me to the Devil with your cruelty!"

Priscilla was feeling desperate. "Jake, please, stop this at once!"

To her chagrin, he only ignored her, pressed a hand to his breast, and began hollering poetry once again, reinforcing his words with melodramatic gestures.

> "Cold is the blast upon my pale cheek
> But colder thy love for me.
> The frost that freezes the life at my heart
> Is naught to my pains from thee."

Priscilla beseeched him frantically. "Jake, please get out of here before you wake up Mrs. Gatling!"

"I ain't leaving, lass! I'll fling myself from your balcony if you don't let me in!"

Wide-eyed, Priscilla watched him stumble about and try to clamber up onto the balcony railing. Certain she was about to witness his suicide, she firmly grabbed his arm and hauled him into the room. He staggered against her, almost knocking her over.

"You idiot!" she snapped, turning and shutting the French doors.

But he only pulled her close, and buried his face in her hair. The smell of brandy, the manly scent of him, enveloped her as treacherously as his embrace.

"Lass ... oh, lass," he whispered achingly. "I've missed you so ..."

All at once Priscilla became very aware that she was wearing only a nightgown, that she was pressed scandalously against Jake, that his hand was massaging her bottom ... and that she was loving it!

Trembling, she shoved him away. "Stop this at once! Come with me to the hallway, and I'll pray I can sneak you out of here before Mrs. Gatling summons the sheriff."

"Not until you give me a kiss, lass."

"I— That's out of the question!"

He flung back an arm and scowled, and Priscilla was certain he was about to start bellowing Bobby Burns again.

"Very well!" she cried.

She was unprepared for what happened next. Jake caught her close and kissed her ardently, plunging his tongue inside her mouth. Despite all her doubts and fears, his nearness, after their agonizing alienation, was rough, potent magic, and she moaned in helpless abandonment. The fact that he was unshaven only excited her all the more, intensifying the scandalous, illicit thrill she felt.

"Oh, lassie, darling lassie," he murmured, kissing

her face and neck, roving his hands boldly over her, hiking up her gown.

Passion mingled with panic swamped Priscilla as he ran his hand over her bare bottom. She struggled against him, mostly fighting her own weakening will, her devastating need for him.

"Jake, no, we mustn't ... You said one kiss ..."

He pressed his lips to her ear, and she heard his tortured voice. "No, lassie. Please don't fight me. Not when I need you so much."

A knot of poignant longing seemed to burst in Priscilla, and she hesitated for the briefest moment. Jake backed her toward the bed, pinning her against the bedpost with his aroused body and kissing her with devastating need. She heard a tiny rip, felt Jake's hot mouth possessively taking her breast, and she was lost. Chills racked her and hot desire sizzled deep inside her. Even as she floated, panting, in a delirium of desire, Jake's skilled hands quickly gathered her gown high above her waist, and his rough fingers parted and stroked her. Priscilla couldn't believe this was happening to her, yet never had she wanted anything more! And the shock of the cool air hitting her bare thighs seemed very real! When he thrust two fingers inside her, probing and stretching her taut flesh, she dug her fingernails into his shoulders and squirmed helplessly.

"Easy, love," he whispered, holding her firmly against him while penetrating deeper with his fingers, and caressing her with his thumb.

Priscilla was reeling, frantic. "Oh, Jake ... oh God."

"Easy," he whispered, taking her trembling lips as he stroked her relentlessly to ecstasy, stretching out the moment until she let him push her over the edge into riotous rapture.

When at last he withdrew his fingers, they fell across the soft mattress together. She ripped at his jacket, his shirt, finally contacting the warm flesh of his chest. She caressed his muscles and buried her

lips against his neck, thrilling to his moan of pleasure.

A moment later, she felt hotter than she had ever
dreamed possible as Jake pounded himself into her
with a passion so fierce, so powerful, she was sure
she might faint of it. He felt so hard and vibrant inside her, his thrusts filling and stretching her, lifting
her off the bed. She whimpered desperately, and he
smothered her moans and drove deeper. He murmured soothing words, all the while pressing her
higher and higher toward exquisite, pulsating release. She writhed, half-frightened by the intense sen-
sations threatening to consume her, to swallow up
her own will. Jake held her fast until she moved with
him, arching into his demanding strokes, giving herself to him entirely. He savagely seized her lips as
they climaxed together . . .

It was a long time before Priscilla returned to
earth. Jake was still inside her, his weight sweetly
crushing her. He hadn't even removed his jacket, and
she could feel the rough wool abrading her exposed
breasts. She tenderly stroked his hair and kissed his
forehead.

In anguish she asked, "Jake, why are you behaving
this way? Drinking, carousing to all hours?"

"You've broken me heart, lassie," he murmured
thickly. "When an Irishman's heart is broken, he
drinks."

Tenderly she caught him to her, her voice breaking.
"Oh, Jake. I'm so sorry."

Priscilla was crying, but not for long. Jake was
kissing her again . . .

Priscilla awakened in the predawn. She could hear
birds singing out in the garden. Since the room was
extremely cold, she got up, shivering, donned her
gown, and went over to light the gas heater. Teeth
chattering, she scurried back into bed and slipped in
beside him, absorbing the heaven of his warmth.

He still slept peacefully beside her, looking like a

handsome, roguish angel with a very dark five-o'clock shadow. She roved her gaze over the splendid lines of his face and strong neck, then moved the coverlet slightly and sneaked a peek at his muscled chest. An ecstatic sigh escaped her. She remembered that dark, coarse chest hair rubbing her breasts so pleasurably last night. Mercy! They had made love practically the whole night through! The things she had said . . . and done! They had devoured each other. She had gloried in it, she still felt tender all over . . . and yet she was starved for more.

Heavens, what was happening to her? In one brief night she had gone from being determined never to marry Jake Blarney to being just as convinced that she couldn't live without him. What was she to do?

She glanced toward the French doors, watching the first mellow rays of dawn filter through lacy panels. For now, she must get Jake out of here before they were discovered. She also needed to get him out of her hair for a while, so she could sort out her jumbled thoughts and emotions.

She shook his shoulder gently. "Jake! Jake, it's almost morning! You must go!"

He stirred, and she found herself staring into his vivid blue eyes. "Lass," he murmured, hauling her close for a kiss.

Priscilla fought the wave of desire and tenderness that his closeness and burning kiss stirred. "Jake," she repeated breathlessly, bracing a hand on his chest. "The sun is rising! You must leave before someone discovers us!"

He yawned, then frowned at her sleepily. "Not quite yet, lass. We need to have a little chat, you and I."

"Not *now*, Jake!" she beseeched.

"Aye," he replied stubbornly. "*Now.*"

"Jake—be reasonable!"

He shook his head. "I'm not leaving until this is settled, lass. So if you want me out of here quickly, you'd best hush and listen."

"Jake, I promise I'm going to think about us, but I'm not ready to have this conversation."

"And I say we're going to face this now, together."

"Oh, very well," she conceded, exasperated. "But please try to be brief."

He grinned. "That's better." He sat up against the headboard and patted the place next to him. "Come sit here, lassie."

Reluctantly she complied.

He looked her over. "Why the gown? I thought I got rid of that impediment last night."

"I was cold."

"I'll warm you," he said lecherously, reaching for her.

"Jake, please!" She swatted his hands away. "At this rate, we'll never talk."

"You're right," he acquiesced with a disappointed sigh.

"What do you want to discuss?"

He turned slightly to stare into her eyes. "I want to know why you ran away from me after we first made love."

"Oh, that."

"Yes, that."

"I . . ." She gestured helplessly. "I guess I'm afraid of commitment."

"Not with Ackerly Frost," he pointed out reproachfully.

She thought over his words, and sighed. "Ackerly is . . . a known quantity. He's reliable, predictable, like the northbound train or the milk delivered each morning."

"Ah, you can control him—but not me?"

"I can depend on him . . . and I sure as hell can't control you."

"You still won't trust me?"

She flung her hands outward. "Well, look at your behavior over the past weeks. Drinking, gambling, brawling—and God knows what else! Why, I even heard you were spotted carrying a—a woman of ill repute down Postoffice Street, and her kicking and screaming!"

"I was, lass," he admitted with a chuckle.

"Oh—you cad!" Outraged, Priscilla began pummeling his shoulders with her fists.

Glowering, he caught her wrists. "Wait a minute! Listen to me, lass! She was only seventeen."

Priscilla was horror-stricken, struggling to get free. "That's even worse! It's depraved."

"Damn it, girl, I took her home!"

Priscilla froze. "Home where?"

"To her mum."

Priscilla was mystified. "Explain that."

"The lass was a babe in the woods, out trying to earn her ma the rent money along Smokey Row. When she tried to peddle her wares to me, I recognized she was a novice. So I took her home to her mum, and I gave them the rent money."

All of Priscilla's anger faded in a surge of tenderness. "Oh, Jake! That was so dear."

"You've spoiled me for other women, lass," he replied with a charming grin.

"But what about the rest ... the drinking, the fights?"

"The rest is your fault," he informed her sanctimoniously.

"Oh, no you don't!" she cried. "You can't blame me for your own lapses."

"Oh, but I am. You broke me heart."

She bit her lip, not knowing what to say.

He leaned toward her, staring soulfully into her eyes, cupping her breast with his large, rough hand. Despite the tension between them, Priscilla began to tremble anew with desire.

" 'Tis true, lassie," Jake whispered. "In all the weeks we've been apart, I could not even look at another woman. You've bewitched me, girl. And I love you so."

"Jake, please, don't say that," she pleaded miserably.

His hand slipped inside her gown and his fingers caressed her tautened nipple. She groaned and clenched shut her eyes.

"And all this while, you've been stepping high with Jack Frost, driving a knife into me heart. How do you think that makes me feel, girl? Knowing he's with you, touching you—"

"We haven't even kissed yet!" Priscilla burst out defensively, only to sigh again as Jake kneaded her breast. "At least, not really."

He scowled murderously.

"Don't you believe me, Jake?"

"Then he wasn't the one?" Jake asked in perplexity.

Going insane with desire, she curled her arms around his neck and impudently kissed his mouth. "You're the only one ... that matters. No one has ever made me feel the passion that you make me feel."

"Is that so?" he asked with amusement and pride.

She grinned crookedly. "There's really no man who can compare to you, Jake."

A smile tugged at his mouth, but his voice turned ominous. "Then I'm giving you fair warning, lass."

"Yes?"

He touched the tip of her nose. "This is the end of Ackerly Frost. Is that clear?"

She hesitated a moment, then nodded. "You're right. I can't be having a love affair with you, and also seeing Ackerly. It's dishonest."

"Damn right it is," he agreed. "And furthermore, this ain't no bloody love affair. We're marrying at once, girl."

Now Priscilla did protest. "Oh, no, Jake. Not yet. I promise I'll see you ... to find out where this leads. I promise that as long as we're together, it will be monogamous—"

"What in hell is that?" he demanded with a scowl. "It sounds downright sinful."

She laughed. "I'll be loyal to you, Jake. For as long as we're together, there will be no one else."

"Damn tooting."

"But I can't promise that I'll marry you. It will still take time for me to be sure you're right for me. And you'll have to clean up your act, too."

He chuckled. "You mean no more drinking and gambling, eh?"

"I mean precisely that," she informed him primly. "I mean no more rescuing would-be hookers, either. I think we can leave those sorts of activities to the Ladies Rescue Mission."

Melodramatically he pressed a hand to his heart. "Ah, lass, you slay me."

"And I mean staying home nights to care for the twins."

He nuzzled her cheek. "As long as you come visit us, angel."

"I . . . er, of course I will."

"So I'm to persuade you that we're right for each other?" he inquired huskily.

"Er . . . yes."

He boldly lifted her gown, and reached down to caress between her thighs. "I'm very good at persuading, you know."

She squirmed in ecstasy. "I know."

"Like this little problem you're having with commitment," he continued. "I think I can ease your doubts, love."

To Priscilla's delight, he quickly brought her astride him, then eased her down on his manhood so slowly, so thoroughly, that both of them shuddered with pleasure.

Jake grasped her face in his hands. "Do you still feel a lack of commitment, darlin'?"

She shook her head.

"Are you sure?"

"I . . . Oh, God, yes."

He withdrew slightly, then clamped his forearms at her waist and brought her down forcefully, wrenching a delighted gasp from her. *"That's* what total commitment feels like."

He was right. Priscilla could feel him to her soul. She eagerly sought his lips as together they succumbed to a sweet delirium of passion.

Chapter 26

Priscilla had always heard it was best to break up with a boyfriend/girlfriend in some public place, to lessen the likelihood of a scene ensuing. Thus that morning at nine A.M., she was seated before Ackerly's desk at the bank.

He appeared distracted as he sifted through a stack of documents. "Priscilla, must we talk now? As I've already mentioned, I have a critical appointment in fifteen minutes, and I'm trying to get everything organized."

"I'm really sorry, Ackerly, but I'm afraid it's rather urgent."

He pulled off his reading glasses. "Very well. But please, do be brief."

She took a deep, bracing breath. "I've come to tell you that I ... well, I really regret this, Ackerly, but I'm afraid I'm having second thoughts about us."

He appeared perplexed. "Second thoughts?"

"Yes. I—I really can't accept your proposal of marriage, after all, and I think perhaps it's best we stop seeing each other."

He went ashen. "What? You must be jesting!"

She soberly shook her head. "I'm afraid not."

He fell back in his chair and gazed at her in astonishment. "But what brought about this abrupt change of heart? We're practically engaged!"

She stared at her lap. "Actually, I've had doubts all along."

"Why?" he cried.

"Because . . ." Miserably she admitted, "I think I went out with you for misguided reasons."

"Such as?"

"I thought we'd make a good match."

"So did I, Priscilla."

"I realize this." Earnestly she continued. "But expediency is really not enough, Ackerly—not for either of us. You need a woman who can love you as you deserve to be loved, and I'm just not that woman. Although I've enjoyed knowing you and have appreciated all the things you've done for me, I simply have not developed strong, enduring feelings for you. There's just no real feelings of . . . well, passion between us. Thus, this would not be a love match, but one effected strictly for practicality."

"But aren't all good marriages just so?"

"No, I don't think so."

He leaned toward her and lowered his voice. "Won't this . . . passion you speak of come in time?"

She shook her head. "I'm afraid it doesn't work that way, at least not for me. I tried to tell myself that our shared interests were enough, but now I know differently."

"Now you know differently." All at once he appeared suspicious, rapping a pencil on his desk and gazing at her narrowly. "What changed your mind, Priscilla?"

Guiltily she glanced away. "Nothing."

He shoved aside the papers. "Don't lie to me! I think at this juncture, you at least owe me the truth."

"Very well." She met his eye bravely. "I can't see you again because I—I think I'm in love with someone else."

"Who?" he demanded.

"Ackerly, must you?" she pleaded.

"*Who*, Priscilla?"

Miserably she admitted, "Jake Blarney."

"*What?*" His features a picture of disbelief and outrage, he bolted to his feet. "You're in love with that— that bounder? You're turning up your nose at all I have to offer, in favor of a no-account hayseed with two sniveling orphans?"

Priscilla also shot to her feet, trembling with shock and indignity, very tempted to slap his insolent face. "How dare you call him a hayseed! Or insult those darling children of his!"

He appeared stunned. "I can't believe I'm hearing this!"

"Well, believe it. And it's over between the two of us."

He regarded her with distaste. "Why, you cunning little jezebel! After all I've done for you!"

"You've benefited from our arrangement, too!"

"Not as much as you have!" Ackerly spoke in full-blown fury, a muscle jerking in his cheek. "Here you were, a total outsider and newcomer in our community, yet I was generous enough to take you under my wing and help you establish yourself in the best circles. This is the thanks I get ... you scorning all I have to offer and taking up with that ruffian, behind my back. I should have known better. I never should have forgiven your indiscretion at the Cotton Exchange Ball, but I was a fool, bewitched by your feminine wiles. Mother always told me that, in the final analysis, class will always tell, and she was right. You, my dear, obviously have no class at all, and you belong with trash like Blarney. I should have realized long ago that you're not good enough to be associated with people of quality."

Although she wanted nothing further to do with Ackerly, Priscilla found his unexpectedly mean, contemptuous words stabbed at her own vulnerabilities and smarted terribly. She had tried to let him down gently, and the cad had turned on her!

Her voice trembled as she retorted, "To think that I actually respected you, Ackerly. I should have known you're no better than the rest of your clan! And now you're only behaving like a jackass because you lost out to a much better man."

"*That* comment is too laughable to even dignify with a response!" he declared.

"Then I won't wait for one," she replied, turning to leave.

He tore after her, stepping in front of her to block her path. "You heartless conniver! You used me to establish yourself here, and now you're casting me away! Mark my words, Priscilla! Take up with Jake Blarney and you're going to ruin your reputation in this community."

She shook a finger at him. "My reputation will be just fine, thank you, Mr. Frost. And by damn, if you do *anything* to try to defame me, or Jake and his girls, I swear I'll retaliate in a manner you will never live down!"

Ackerly hastily stepped aside as Priscilla would have mowed him down. She left the bank feeling extremely grateful she had shed Ackerly Frost—especially now that he had revealed his true colors. He and his great grandson were obviously cut from the same cloth—and it was a very cheap blend indeed!

That evening at sundown, Priscilla stood on the beach in front of Jake's house. The dying day was cold but clear, and she wore a heavy shawl around her shoulders. Beyond her, foamy breakers pounded at the shoreline, while gulls swooped and cawed in the red-gold light.

Priscilla had been at Jake's cottage for about three hours, playing with the girls and thoroughly enjoying their and Jake's company. A moment ago, while Jake rocked the babies, she had excused herself and come outside, taking an object from her rented buggy.

She held that item in her hand now—a corked bottle much like two others that had once bobbed about in the Gulf, a vessel she'd bought today at the china shop in town. She mused ironically that a lifetime seemed to have passed since she'd watched that first bottle wash up on a lonely shore in a distant time, a distant world. Now she was here in the year 1880, caught up in a totally new life.

Tonight, in many ways, Priscilla had reached a turning point, and she was ready to tie up some loose ends. After breaking up with Ackerly, she had remembered the note she had cast adrift in another bottle so many weeks ago, in which she had begged Ackerly's contemporary counterpart, Ackerly V, to come rescue her. It all seemed absurd now, but since a note in a bottle had brought her through time, the last thing she needed was for Ackerly V to come after her—especially not now that she was so happy to have shed Ackerly I, and to be with Jake! Although she would always miss and worry about the mother she'd left behind in the present, she recognized increasingly that *this* was where she was meant to be—her chance for a truly new life—and if so, there really was no turning back. It was time to cut her ties with the present.

Thus, she had penned a second note today, and she pulled the scrap from her pocket. "Jake Frost, get lost," it read. She laughed aloud at the silly, terse missive. But the rhyme very much summed up her feelings toward both Ackerlys at the moment. She found it truly mind-boggling that in one day she was breaking up with two quasi-fiancés in two different centuries!

She folded the note, pulled the cork from the bottle, and slipped it inside. She stepped out a bit and tossed the bottle into the tide. She watched the playful waves take it way.

"Good riddance," she yelled to the wind.

Then she heard Jake's voice from the porch, calling her name. "Girl, get your sweet self back inside here. The girls miss you. I miss you, love."

Priscilla rushed back to Jake's waiting arms.

Chapter 27

⟋◝◜◞◟⟍

Priscilla began to burn her candle at both ends, sneaking out to Jake's cabin at night to make love with him, driving back to the boardinghouse before first light, so exhausted that she was grateful for the birds she spotted along the way to help her keep alert. Later she would fall asleep while trying to give elocution lessons! She knew she was out of control. She was clearly in love with Jake, yearning to become his wife and stepmother to his babies. For the first time in her life, she was behaving heedless of her own doubts and fears.

But as the days and weeks passed, it also became clear that Jake was making a valiant attempt at reform. He no longer frequented grogshops, and limited his drinking to a glass of wine with dinner. Other than to make his deliveries, attend occasional lodge meetings for the Order of the Hibernians, and take the girls into town for mass, he rarely ventured away from the farm.

Yet Priscilla retained doubts about marrying him. Jake remained a handsome charmer with a mercurial nature. Could she really trust him to love her, to be faithful to her alone, and not to betray her during the marriage? Would he be content to abandon seamy temptations for the rest of his life? Would their relationship disintegrate into the emotional quagmire that had characterized her parents' marriage?

Priscilla also continued to fear Jake was deceiving himself as far as his feelings for her were concerned.

That night when she had arrived, bedraggled, on his doorstep, he had instantly decided they were "meant to be." How much of that sudden devotion had been based on the fact that he badly needed a wife and a mother for his children? And could he not just as quickly and whimsically change his mind again and pursue another woman? He had certainly rushed into his relationship with Lucinda impetuously, his head turned by a ravishingly beautiful woman— could such a creature lure him away from her?

The progression of holiday festivities in Galveston proper reinforced Priscilla's doubts ... for here was a world she could not share with Jake, at least not yet. On the one hand, she found to her delight that, although she had shed Ackerly, she still received a number of invitations for important Christmas socials from prominent mothers of her students. She also realized that, even minus Ackerly, she attached great importance to her place in Galveston society. Priscilla made a point of attending all the strictly female activities—the teas and luncheons, and the Ladies Guild meetings at Trinity Church held to prepare baskets for the poor. But she declined on most evening invitations that would have required an escort, such as the Sealys' caroling party, or the dinner party hosted by the J. M. Browns on St. Lucia's Day, to honor some guests from Sweden.

Actually, Priscilla would have loved to invite Jake to squire her about to the parties, but she held back due to uncertainties regarding how he would respond to her friends. Jake had always displayed a jaundiced attitude toward the Galveston upper crust, and she feared that if they did step out together on important occasions, he might scoff or ridicule some of her friends, or even resort to violence as he had at the Cotton Exchange Ball. She realized that in time, Jake would have to accept more of her world, or the two of them likely wouldn't make it. But she wasn't sure their fragile relationship could endure such a test just yet.

Although she had to question whether there was a true meeting ground between her and Jake, on a deeper level she was beginning to feel ashamed of some of her own prior, shallow values, especially her having wanted to marry Ackerly Frost, in either the nineteenth or twentieth century. Occasionally she still passed Ackerly on the Strand, and the cold, contemptuous looks he cast her way made her furious, and not quite able to understand the depth of her own anger, or why his attitude should rankle at all any longer.

Finally, after some soul-searching, Priscilla realized she felt threatened because Ackerly seemed to be saying what he'd said when they broke up—that she had no class, that she had never been good enough to associate with his kind. And there, Priscilla had to admit, she still felt vulnerable. Given the bitter wounds from her childhood, part of her remained scared to death to become a dairy farmer's bride, possibly even to sacrifice the inroads she'd made in Galveston society in order to have a successful marriage with Jake. She wasn't ashamed of Jake, not at all; but his volatile nature clearly threatened all her hard-won accomplishments.

Because of her misgivings, Priscilla tried to get Jake to use birth control. She persuaded Mary to buy her some rubber condoms at the apothecary, and her friend brought them over to the studio one day as Priscilla was about to lock up.

"My boss caught me ringing up the English armor and tried to give me a lecture," Mary confided with a giggle, slipping a small box and some change into Priscilla's hand. "So I told him they were for my cousin, Teddy. Now he intends to give Teddy a lecture."

Mary and Priscilla laughed over the incident. But that night at Jake's house, when the babies were asleep and Priscilla made her shy request in the bedroom, Jake was outraged.

"Where in God's name did you learn about that?"

he demanded, staring in horror at the small box in
her hand.

She smiled. "In the future."

He waved her off. "You're not starting that future
babble with me again."

"Very well. Don't believe me. Just use the condoms."

He regarded her in smoldering suspicion. "How
did you acquire protective sheaths, woman?"

"At the apothecary."

"You know the Church highly disapproves of such
contraptions."

Priscilla was rapidly losing her patience. "And I
highly disapprove of seeing myself become
pregnant—out of wedlock."

His eyes danced with amusement. "You know the
solution to that, lass. A proper marriage, followed by
a proper marriage bed. You won't risk disgrace and
I'll remain a good Catholic."

Exasperated, she shoved the box into his hand.
"Well, if *this* good Catholic wants inside *this* good
Episcopalian, he's going to wear a condom!"

He glowered.

Deciding to try charm in the face of his rebellion,
she moved closer. "I'll put it on you."

He appeared stunned. "You wouldn't!"

"Wouldn't I?"

Flashing him a sultry smile, she began unbuttoning
his trousers. He stayed her fingers, but she managed
to stroke him, nonetheless. He groaned, then ripped
open the package . . .

Thereafter, Jake practiced birth control if Priscilla
insisted, but he also perversely resisted whenever the
opportunity presented itself, trying to distract her
until it was too late—something he was a master at
accomplishing. She knew he'd be pleased as punch
to get her pregnant and force their nuptials—and this
knowledge both thrilled and frustrated her.

Indeed, she managed a few slips herself. This was
especially true one night when they sat together in

bed naked, and Jake read Priscilla poetry. Inspired by his stirring intonations of Bobby Burns, Priscilla began kissing his strong jaw and smooth shoulders, his sexy chest, until he gave up, tossed aside the book, and pulled her into his arms.

"So you've a mind to make love to me now, eh?" he teased, stroking her spine.

"Indeed, I do, sir," she responded saucily.

"Was it me or Bobby Burns who stirred you?"

She wrinkled her nose at him. "You decide."

Priscilla worked her lips slowly down Jake's body, wrenching several tormented grunts from him. But when, on an impulse, she lowered the sheet and kissed him more intimately, he flinched and grabbed her by the hair.

"What in the name of heaven do you think you're doing?" he demanded, scowling at her.

She glanced up at him, taken aback. "I just wanted to kiss you there."

"And who taught you that?"

"No one," she replied. "I just wanted to because ... well, you've done it to me, and ..."

"Aye, I have," he agreed huskily. "But I didn't think proper ladies did such things."

"Well, maybe I'm not so proper, after all," she teased impudently. "Besides, are you saying you can but I can't?"

A roguish grin sculpted his handsome features. "I didn't say you couldn't, darling." He caught her beneath the arms, pulled her up his body and cuddled her close. "Tell me why you want to do it."

Relaxing in his masterful arms, Priscilla caught herself in time, before she blurted out, *Because I love you*. She wasn't quite ready to make that gigantic leap of faith. Instead, she said, "Because I really thought you would enjoy it."

He winked at her. "Aye, mayhap I would, after you pulled me down off the ceiling from the shock of it."

"Then prepare to climb the walls," said Priscilla wickedly.

But when she tried to slide away, he held her fast. "First a kiss," he insisted. "Several kisses."

Priscilla lovingly complied as Jake crushed her beneath him on the mattress, devouring her mouth and kneading her breasts. Moments later, when she nudged him onto his back and again started moving her lips down his body, he chuckled in devilish delight. This time he didn't protest when she boldly took his phallus into her mouth. She heard his transported moans, felt his fingers slide into her hair, felt him throb and grow rock-hard in her mouth. She tantalized him with her tongue.

She heard his agonized cry. "Sweetheart, have a care. That's not how I'm aiming to spend myself."

Priscilla only chuckled wantonly and began running her lips and tongue all over him. He responded with tortured breathing and ragged supplications to most every saint she had ever heard of. She loved what she was doing to him—loved watching him struggle for control and, time and again, almost lose it. His groans became frenzied and she was surprised he did not burst in her mouth.

A moment later, she was pushed forcefully onto her back to stare up at Jake's passion-clenched features. Priscilla was in for a few shocks herself as he tossed her ankles over his shoulders and devoured her with rapacious thrusts. Before it was over, she was the one who had to be practically pulled off the ceiling. The lamps burned as brightly as her flaming face as Jake propelled her into a rapture she could not bear and could not resist. The frenzied ecstasy brought her to tears of wild joy, and she forgot all about protection until she felt Jake spilling his seed inside her. They fell on the bed, entwined, kissing deeply and tenderly.

Much later, he murmured against her ear, "Ah, shucks, darlin', we forgot all about the condom. We'll do better next time, won't we, love?"

Impossible, Priscilla Pemberton thought.

* * *

Priscilla spent all of Christmas eve with Jake and the twins. She came to the cottage early, helping Mrs. Braunhurst clean and stuff the huge turkey Jake had killed on the far west end of the island. Once the bird was in the oven, Bula presented the twins with their presents—lace-trimmed green velvet Christmas dresses she had made for them. While Priscilla dressed the girls in their Yule finery, Jake gave his housekeeper a cash gift, and then a very happy Bula went home to celebrate Christmas with her husband.

Priscilla, Jake, and the girls were alone for the balance of the day, much of which was spent out back in the stone kitchen. Priscilla was ready to do Christmas baking, having solicited recipes from friends at every holiday social she had attended. As Jake watched and the twins "helped," Priscilla baked Christmas cookies and steamed plum pudding on the iron stove. She also basted the turkey and chopped mounds of vegetables for Christmas dinner.

After most of the baking had been completed and everyone returned to the main cottage, Jake and Priscilla took turns running back to the kitchen to baste the turkey and check the side dishes simmering on the stove. In the main room of the cottage, the twins had a marvelous time "helping" to decorate the sugarplum tree—which turned out to be sadly lacking in sugarplums, as tiny fingers plucked at treats and eager mouths devoured.

The four had Christmas dinner at a festively set, candlelit table. All four popped open their traditional Christmas crackers and donned the jaunty paper hats that had been hidden in the colorful cylinders. Using mostly their fingers as implements, the twins gobbled down turkey and cranberry salad, and Jake and Priscilla laughed as they watched the girls decorate their faces with their meal. At dessert time, the twins watched in awe as their father soaked the plum pudding in brandy and set it afire. As Jake held the flaming pudding aloft, Priscilla stared lovingly at the girls and mused that she would never forget the looks of wonder reflected in those dark, bright, angelic eyes.

When the meal ended, Jake and Priscilla sat sipping coffee as the girls scampered about, ripping open their presents and dumping out their Christmas stockings. The girls chortled over the jack-in-the-boxes and the stuffed rabbit toys their father had given them. But Priscilla had really gone overboard, presenting each girl with a sweater and matching bonnet, a stuffed clown, several handsome books of fairy tales and poetry, and a toy wicker doll carriage.

"Lass, you shouldn't have done all this!" Jake exclaimed, watching Sal as she gurgled happily and kissed her clown doll on the mouth.

"It's my pleasure," Priscilla told him. "I can't remember when I've had more fun."

"You'll spoil them badly," he scolded.

"Oh, I intend to."

Soon Nell proudly toddled over to Priscilla with a book in her hand and her clown doll tucked under her other arm. Slamming the book down in Priscilla's lap, she demanded, "Read!"

Laughing, Priscilla picked up the child. "Hey, Sal," she called. "You want me to read to you, too?"

The baby grinned up at Priscilla, then grabbed as many toys as she could carry and toddled over. Laughing at the sight, Jake scooped up Sal and placed her against Priscilla's other arm.

Balancing the babies and the toys in her arms as best she could, Priscilla read "The Night Before Christmas." Soon both babies dozed against her, Sal tenderly clutching her doll, and Nell sucking her thumb. Rocking the little angels, Priscilla felt as if she were in heaven.

Jake came over to smile at her tenderly. "You've got quite an armful there, lass."

Priscilla kissed Sal's hair and gazed down at both girls, at their rosy faces complete with button mouths and long eyelashes resting against their cheeks, the toys clutched in their chubby arms. Her voice came choked with emotion. "They've changed so much, Jake, just since I've been here. They've grown and developed, and they use more new words every day. It's truly a wondrous time for them, and I'm sorry I missed even a minute of it."

Jake leaned over and kissed her. "You won't miss a second, lass—not ever again."

After they put the girls to bed, Jake and Priscilla sat by the fire and exchanged their own presents. He gave her a lovely silver necklace with cameo charm, which she exclaimed over at length. She gave him a sturdy wool greatcoat, which he stared at in awe.

"I've noticed you don't have a really good coat," she said almost shyly.

He leaned over to kiss her, and when he spoke, his voice caught with emotion. "It's a fine present, lass. But the best Christmas gift is you."

Deeply touched, Priscilla threw her arms around his neck and kissed him.

Later he whispered, "You know, lass, the twelve weeks is over now."

"What twelve weeks?" she asked.

"The twelve weeks in which you agreed to see me."

She laughed. "You know, you're right. I agreed to see you through Christmas. I'd quite forgotten."

He feigned a scowl. "You're not going to try to get away from me now, are you?"

"Do I look like I'm going anywhere?" She turned wistful. "Do we need to agree to another twelve weeks?"

He tenderly nuzzled her cheek. "Care to make it forever yet?"

Priscilla might have said yes, but her lips were blissfully occupied . . .

New Year's passed, then came the cold, bright days of January. The idyllic period continued for Priscilla, Jake, and the girls. Priscilla knew that in many ways, she and Jake were living in a dream-world. Sooner or later, they would have to confront the prospect of their future and their role in the community. Status no longer seemed as critical to her—but she remained determined to maintain the place she had established in the Galveston community, to continue to have friends and a social life. And if she and Jake did eventually marry, she wanted only the best for the girls, as well.

Thus, when the mother of one of her students, Maude Waverly, invited Priscilla to a dinner party at her home on Broadway, Priscilla knew it was time for her and Jake to take a test run in Galveston society. She finally got up her nerve to ask him one chill January morning. Just past first light, she was preparing to leave for town, and went out to the dairy to speak with him. She found him in a stall milking a huge brown and white Guernsey cow—one of a dozen animals housed in the large shed.

Spotting her, he frowned as he pulled at the cow's udder. "Where are the wee babes? You didn't leave them alone, darlin'?"

"No, of course not." Priscilla laughed. "Bula just arrived—and she gave me a pretty funny look."

He laughed. "Don't worry, love, Bula would be the last person on earth to spread gossip."

"Good—because she'd have plenty to say about us."

He eyed her curiously. "What are you doing here in the dairy? Did you forget something?"

Priscilla chuckled. Jake knew the dairy was not her favorite place. "Yes. Mrs. Waverly has invited us to her house for dinner next week. Her daughter, Charlotte—one of my best students—will entertain us on the piano following the meal, and her older son, Horace, Jr., will also perform with his string quartet. I think we should go, don't you?"

His jaw dropped. "You must be jesting, darlin'! I'd just as soon face a firing squad as endure Maude Waverly and her hoity-toity friends."

"That's not fair," Priscilla argued. "Maude is a very nice woman, very genteel."

"Hah!" he scoffed, getting to his feet and dusting off his hands. "She's bloody British aristocracy. The whole town knows she and Horace trace their lineage back to the duke of Derby."

"So what if they do?"

"It's their kind that have enslaved me homeland," he retorted vehemently.

"Oh, for heaven's sake!" Priscilla protested. "You've been in this country for over ten years, Jake. Isn't it about time you abandoned this pointless fixation with class struggles?"

"It ain't pointless to the farmers starving back in County Kerry," he interjected angrily. "And I'm staying with me own kind."

"But where does that leave me?" she cried. "Jake, I sell tutoring services to the public. I have a place to maintain in this community—"

"Well, you won't be selling nothin' once we're wed," he cut in.

"Are you saying you won't allow me to have a profession?"

He stared at her intently. "I ain't forbidding it, lassie, if that's what you're asking. Leastwise, not until you're expecting. I ain't asking you to cut off the rest of your life for me. But I do say we don't need Maude Waverly and her kind."

"You're wrong. I do need them."

"Why?"

"Aside from my professional obligations, I need friends, a sense of community, and a social life. I grew up without all those things, Jake, and I'm not willing to become a pariah for the rest of my life. Furthermore, I need a man who isn't ashamed to listen to Bach or socialize with intelligent people."

"Bah!" He waved her off. "Don't give me that sanctimonious babble—"

"It's not sanctimonious babble! It's what I am, Jake."

"Oh, is it now, darling?" He pulled her close. "And if that's what you are, what about the brazen wench who had her mouth on a most risqué part of me anatomy for half the night?"

Although her cheeks went hot, she faced him with pride. "That's part of my nature, too, an aspect I'm not ashamed of. But don't you dare think that just because I know how to make love to a man, I can't appreciate an intelligent conversation, or a beautiful piece of music."

He sighed heavily. "Why can't what we have be enough, darlin'? You know I've toed the mark for you—"

"I know. And I treasure every moment with you and the girls. But we need to start thinking about them, too. As they grow, they'll need help in establishing their own place in this community, and they'll never have a chance if their father is an outcast."

"Anyone who would shun those girls, I don't need!" he declared hotly.

She took his hand and spoke plaintively. "Jake, we can't pretend the rest of the world doesn't exist. If we are to make it in the long run, we must find our place in society . . . for us, and for your children."

"*Our* children," he corrected.

She faced him down with absolute conviction. "If that's the way you want it, Jake, then you're going to have to meet me halfway."

"Very well." After uttering a perfunctory growl, he pulled her close and actually chuckled. "Darlin', believe it or not, I'm in this all the way."

With his demanding lips on hers, Priscilla had to agree.

After Priscilla left, Jake felt bemused as he continued his chores, milking the cows and loading up the jugs to take into town. He felt threatened by Priscilla's insistence that they attend the Waverly dinner party, that they find a place together in Galveston society. Why couldn't what they had now be enough for her?

The two of them were building a good world here with the girls. They were becoming a true family—Christmas together had been wonderful, and every day since had only gotten better. Yet now Priscilla was demanding more, that they hobnob with cultured, educated types Jake could never compete with, simple man that he was.

Again, it bothered him that Priscilla had needs he alone could not fulfill, that she still balked at marrying him. She was insisting he change, that he take her out into the glittery world she craved. Yet how could he transform himself for her, when he so feared that very world might eventually take her away from him?

Chapter 28

On a cold night in January, Priscilla tried to control her anxiety as she stood on the porch of the stately, pillared Waverly mansion with Jake. He looked dashing in his black greatcoat and beaver hat, and she felt pleased with her own choice of a tailored, rose-colored silk frock with small bustle, worn beneath her heavy wool cloak. She had arranged her hair in a bun garnished by a small floral wreath.

Yet, from the moment Jake had called for her, he had appeared tense and distracted, and it was obvious that he was escorting her tonight under duress. Remembering her last encounter with him at a social event, when he had punched Ackerly to the floor during the Cotton Exchange Ball, she shuddered and said a silent prayer that they would get through the evening minus another debacle. This was her and Jake's first foray as a couple into polite Galveston society, and Priscilla was prepared to endure some awkwardness or even embarrassment. But she was not sure she and Jake could survive another social calamity. And what if Ackerly was in attendance tonight? Without some sincere effort and restraint on Jake's part, another scene might ensue, and she and Jake could well lose whatever ground she had so far gained in the community.

Even as Priscilla wrestled with these worries, the handsome oaken door creaked open, and tall, slender Maude Waverly, looking regal in a gown of striped blue and white taffeta, appeared before them. After

314

observing Jake's presence with some astonishment, she forced a bright smile. "Well, good evening, Miss Pemberton, Mr. Blarney. Jason is busy putting away hats and cloaks, and must not have heard your knock. Do come in."

"Thank you," Priscilla murmured.

They moved into a charming Victorian foyer with Persian runner, heavily carved rosewood tables with marble tops, gilded mirrors, and crystal chandeliers. Above walnut wainscoting, green silk brocade covered the walls, and handsome plaster fretwork cascaded about the ceiling. The smells of freshly cut flowers and spicy pomander balls mingled in the air; the sounds of conversation, laughter, and music spilled out from the parlor.

"You've not been here before, have you?" Maude asked.

"No—and we're so thrilled to have this opportunity to enjoy your lovely home," answered Priscilla.

"The pleasure is all ours."

The besieged butler, Jason, now rushed up. "May I take your wraps, sir, miss?"

Priscilla was pleased when Jake at once helped her remove her cloak, then handed it to the servant along with his own hat and greatcoat. She glanced appreciatively at him in his black suit with ruffled white shirtfront and black string cravat. Priscilla felt proud that Jake had made such a sincere effort to appear genteel.

"Won't you both join us in the parlor?" Maude asked. "Dinner will be served shortly, and everyone is visiting over drinks and hors d'oeuvres first."

They followed Maude into a huge, high-ceilinged parlor furnished with red velvet rosewood furniture, gold rococo mirrors, sumptuous crystal chandeliers, and windows done in fringed and brocaded portieres, with handsome roller shades adorned with flowers and birds providing a charming counterpoint. Vivid Minton tiles lined the handsome marble-manteled fireplace, and a blue and gold Persian rug covered the floor. Priscilla judged that at least fifteen formally attired guests were chatting in the room, nibbling on crawfish balls and expensive cheeses, and sipping punch. Several of the attendees glanced at the newly arrived couple with curiosity.

Maude led Jake and Priscilla over to a tall man with a long, aristocratic face and a handlebar mustache. "Horace, dear, it's Charlotte's elocution teacher, Miss Pemberton, and her friend, Mr. Blarney."

Horace Waverly beamed at Priscilla. "Why, Miss Pemberton, how good to see you! You've been a godsend to our shy little Charlotte."

Priscilla shook Waverly's hand. "Your daughter is a wonderful pupil, Mr. Waverly. And I cannot tell you how delighted Mr. Blarney and I are to be in your home tonight."

Horace nodded to Jake and extended his hand. "Welcome, Mr. Blarney."

After hesitating a moment, Jake accepted the handshake. "Thank you, Mr. Waverly," he said stiffly. "A pretty place you have here."

"Thank you, sir."

Priscilla breathed a sigh of relief that at least Jake was being passably polite to their hosts, despite his stated resentment of the Waverlys' highborn heritage. After they had chatted briefly with the Waverlys, she maneuvered Jake away so they could circulate through the room. Priscilla did observe a few raised brows from guests noting Jake's presence at the elite gathering, but everyone greeted him politely. Priscilla introduced him to George and Magnolia Sealy, Harris and Eliza Kempner, and Henry and Letita Rosenberg. Jake was courteous to all, but continued to act ill at ease, not joining in on the conversations, often standing apart from the others with his hands stuffed in his pockets.

At least Ackerly Frost was not present, a big stroke of fortune as far as Priscilla was concerned. She wondered if perhaps he had not attended due to the lack of a suitable female companion.

Soon Claude and Helen Durant stepped up to
greet them. "Why, Miss Pemberton, Mr. Blarney,"
Helen said with a twinkle in her eye. "The last time
I saw you two out in public at the same time, it was
a memorable occasion."

For a moment the two couples stared at each other
awkwardly, then all four burst out laughing.

"Memorable occasions are me specialty, ma'am,"
Jake bragged to Helen.

"I would imagine so," she rejoined dryly. "Mr.
Blarney, you do know my husband, Claude?"

"Aye, from church." Jake pumped the other man's
hand. "Good to see you again, Mr. Durant."

"And you, Mr. Blarney," said Claude.

To Priscilla Helen said, "I've been telling Claude
how I wish Mr. Blarney would relent and come to
our spring tryouts for *Pirates of Penzance*."

Priscilla glanced at Jake and watched a predictable,
stubborn scowl spread across his face. "What do you
say, Jake?"

"I say I sing only for the cows—or for me own true
love here." He wrapped an arm about Priscilla's
waist and winked at Helen.

Laughing, she shook a finger at him. "Mr. Blarney,
you are a devil. Can't we even convince you to sing
a song or two for us tonight?"

"Not unless the lot of you grow udders," came his
unabashed reply.

At this off-color remark, Helen gasped and fought
a smile, Claude chuckled, and Priscilla brought her
heel down on Jake's instep.

Wincing slightly, Jake glowered at Priscilla, then
glanced across the room. "Ah, I see my friend Kirby
Cassidy over there."

"You know Kirby?" asked Claude.

"Aye, Kirby's pa owns the pasteurizing plant that
buys me milk, and all three of us are members of the
Hibernians. Wonder what a young lad like him is
doing here tonight?"

"Kirby is in the string quartet of the Waverlys' son

Horace, Jr.," Helen explained. "I understand they'll be performing Bach three-part inventions after dinner."

Jake's jaw dropped. "You mean to tell me that lad is using his fine fiddle to play Bach? Why, 'tis a sacrilege, I tell you. Kirby gets the lads doing a fine gig down at the pasteurizing plant."

The Durants both chuckled. "I'll bet he does," said Claude.

Jake nodded decisively. "Think I'll be having a word with old Kirby, I will." He glanced at Priscilla. "That is, if you'll excuse me, darlin'?"

"Of course," she muttered.

Watching Jake stride off, Priscilla turned to Helen Durant. "I'm sorry, Mrs. Durant. Jake is ... well, quite irrepressible."

She patted Priscilla's hand. "Actually, I think your Mr. Blarney is a charmer, despite his raising a few eyebrows hereabouts. By the way, he *is* your Mr. Blarney now, isn't he?"

Priscilla smiled. "We are ... seeing each other, if that's what you mean."

Leaning toward Priscilla, Helen said confidentially, "If you want to know the truth, dear, I like him better than Ackerly Frost."

"As do I," added Claude. "Jake Blarney is a genuine character. Our town has gotten a bit stuffy of late—as if we're all blood kin of the Astors and the Vanderbilts. I think we need to remember that Galveston was built by strong, outspoken men like Jake Blarney."

"You're both very kind," said Priscilla, hoping that the rest of Galveston society would receive her irascible lover with an equal measure of tolerance and good humor!

"Just see if you can talk him into trying out for the opera," Helen implored. "To waste a magnificent voice like his is a sin."

"I'll try," murmured Priscilla, staring across the room at Jake. He was at the punch bowl with the red-haired, freckle-faced Kirby, gulping the brew that she already knew was spiked with rum. She was not getting a good feeling about how the evening was progressing. Then she spotted her young student, twelve-year-old Charlotte Waverly, standing apart from the others in the corner, and appearing miserable. Excusing herself, she went over to speak with the shy, plain girl.

"Charlotte, you look wonderful tonight!" she declared, admiring the girl's burgundy velvet dress with lace apron, her fair hair arranged in elaborate sausage curls and interlaced with tiny silk flowers.

"Miss Pemberton, I'm so nervous," the girl confided. "Not only must I perform on the piano tonight, but Mother has insisted I recite the sonnets you taught me—in front of everyone!"

Priscilla squeezed the girl's hand. "Now, Charlotte, you'll do just fine. Just look at me, and pretend we're at the studio alone."

"Oh, Miss Pemberton, that's a wonderful idea!" Charlotte's eyes lit with happiness, and she impulsively hugged Priscilla. "You're the best teacher I've ever had!"

Priscilla beamed back at the child. It was good, she mused, to feel accomplished at something tonight. As far as introducing Jake into Galveston society was concerned, she was hardly feeling a smashing success.

She continued to chat with Charlotte, and felt relieved when the butler called everyone in to dinner— since at least Jake would now be removed from the punch bowl! She was seated at one end of the huge Queen Anne table, near Horace Waverly and Claude Durant; Jake was seated across from her, between Helen Durant and Eliza Kempner.

Priscilla did enjoy the meal, high Victorian dining at its best. The table was magnificently set with Irish linen, gold-trimmed Bristol china, Sheffield silver, Baccarat crystal, and gleaming candelabra. The fare was delectable—crawfish bisque followed by veal stuffed with oysters, eggplant soufflé, creamed peas, and hot fresh bread. The conversation began on a general theme—excitement over the forthcoming electrical cooperative and telephone exchange, and various complaints regarding Texas's latest governor, Oran M. Roberts, whose attempts to cut government costs and balance the budget had backfired due to his pardoning of dangerous criminals and reduction in manpower of the Texas Rangers guarding the frontier. Several of the men predicted that if something was not done soon, Texas would return to frontier days, with wild Indians raiding homesteads and dangerous desperadoes robbing stages.

During a lull in the conversation, Maude Waverly smiled at Jake and said, "Mr. Blarney, our oldest daughter, Sophie, has just married a very fine Irishman, Michael O'Connor. They're in Paris now on their honeymoon, but they plan to stop off in Ireland to see his people in County Galway before they return home."

"Why, how lovely!" chimed in Magnolia Sealy. "When will Michael and Sophie return from their tour?"

"We're hoping before Saint Patrick's Day," replied Horace Waverly. "In fact, Maude and I are planning to host a reception in their honor on March seventeenth, a traditional Irish *ceilidh*. All of you are invited to come, of course—and to wear the green."

Even as happy comments spilled forth, an angry-faced Jake abruptly shot to his feet, prompting a sudden, tense lull in the conversation. "What nonsense is this?" he demanded of Horace Waverly. "English throwing a Saint Patrick's Day celebration, when Irish troops fighting for the British crown were forbidden to wear the green? I suppose all of you fine English will come decked out in four-leafed clovers, thinking they're shamrocks?"

Stunned silence filled the room as everyone stared at Jake. Priscilla was horrified.

"Mr. Blarney, we meant no disrespect," said Maude

tactfully. "We simply wish to honor the heritage of our new son-in-law."

"Then let him celebrate the day in his own way, with his own kind—at traditional Irish parades and the like," Jake retorted with an impassioned gesture. "Only the Irish should celebrate their special day. They deserve it, and they've shed enough blood for the right . . . at English hands, I might add."

A gloomy cloud seemed to descend over the gathering as Jake finally took his seat. A maid appeared with dessert, a huge cheesecake covered with blueberries. Part of the tension was relieved as many of the guests complimented their hostess on the lavish treat. But Priscilla wished she could crawl under the table, so embarrassed did she feel over Jake's acrimonious outburst.

Afterward, the guests returned to the parlor for the music. Seated next to Jake on the settee, Priscilla whispered tensely, "Did you have to subject everyone to that diatribe over dinner?"

"Our hosts were in sad need of educating," he retorted.

Priscilla could have shaken him. "Oh! I never thought I'd live to see the day when *you* behaved like a sanctimonious prig!"

Jake scowled at Priscilla, but was unable to reply as Maude Waverly called everyone to attention and announced that Charlotte would now entertain them on the piano and afterward recite some Shakespearean sonnets her tutor, Miss Pemberton, had taught her.

Several approving glances were directed at Priscilla as the girl went to the piano. Jake continued to glower, the grooves along his brow only deepening as Charlotte played a Haydn arietta with seven precise and uninspiring variations. After she took her bows on the piano performance, the girl's recitation of three Shakespearean sonnets was equally flat, although Priscilla did take pride in her student's impeccable enunciation.

Jake began to squirm and toy with his watch fob.

Once the poetry recitation was over, Horace, Jr., Kirby, and the two other members of the string quartet came forward to set up their chairs. The quartet then launched into a sixty-minute concert of chamber music, including selections from Bach, Beethoven, and Mozart. By now, Jake was grinding his teeth and thrusting his fingers through his hair. Even Priscilla had to admit that after a while, the precise rococo music tended to become monotonous: she could even hear John Hutchings snoring at the back of the room. She attributed the rather tiresome repertoire to the high Victorian climate of the day.

As Mr. Waverly got up to announce yet another Beethoven minuet, Jake cupped a hand around his mouth and called, "Hey, Kirby, give us a jig on your fiddle."

Gasps were heard and heads turned to regard Jake Blarney in shock.

"Mr. Blarney, please," protested Horace Waverly with a scowl. "Our son and his group have practiced for months for this recital—"

"It's all right, Father," cut in Horace, Jr., with a grin. "If Mr. Blarney wants to hear a jig, the others of us could use a break."

"Very well," said a clearly irritated Horace Waverly. "If it's all right with Kirby."

Kirby grinned and stood with his violin.

Jake also stood and called to Kirby, "These folks want some Irish? Let's give 'em some Irish, Kirby. Play 'The Washer Woman.' "

To the amazement of one and all, Kirby launched into the lively tune and Jake Blarney strode out into the center of the room. "This is for you, darlin'," he called to Priscilla with an exaggerated bow, and began dancing a jig.

A thoroughly astounded Priscilla watched Jake step, cut, jump and hop, stride and swing, keeping his arms at his sides as he expertly performed the quick, energetic steps of the spirited traditional dance. The expressions of the guests ranged from astonishment to amusement to disapproval. Seeing him leap from side to side, skip and break, in steps and rhythms slightly reminiscent of twentieth-century tap dancing, Priscilla had to admit that Jake was a master at the intricate jig—however inappropriate it might be to launch into it during an evening of chamber music! Nevertheless, when Jake and Kirby finished, everyone applauded.

His color high and several curls dangling rakishly over his forehead, Jake grinned and bowed to one and all. To their hostess he called, "Mrs. Waverly, Miss Pemberton and I thank you for a splendid evening. But I'm thinkin' I'd best fetch me lassie home now that I've publicly wooed her. I've courting left to be done tonight, you see."

That remark was met by muffled laughter from the men and embarrassed titters from the ladies. Priscilla felt mortified by Jake's words, which by Victorian standards were crude, to say the least. Under the circumstances, however, she had little choice but to leave with him, while every eye in the parlor raptly observed their departure. Priscilla's face burned, and she was in such a state of agitation that she couldn't bear to look at Jake.

Priscilla blew her stack the minute they were safely away from the Waverly house, clipping down Broadway in Jake's buggy. "What on earth was the meaning of that little stunt back there?"

He chuckled, exacerbating her ire. "You mean the jig?"

"Yes, the jig! You just had to humiliate me, didn't you?"

"Humiliate you?" he cried. "Why, I was courting you, darlin'. That's the traditional way an Irishman woos his lass, by dancing a jig for her."

"Nonsense!" Priscilla scoffed. "That feeble excuse is only a smoke screen. You were strutting about like a damned peacock, trying to make fools of everyone there—including me!"

"Bah!" He waved her off. "The rest of the dinner guests were delighted to be rescued from death by twelve-part invention."

"How do you know they were bored? I for one was enjoying myself—"

"You were squirming like you had a nest of ants in your bustle. The truth is, I have no patience with folk who put on airs like that—"

"So you must insult them? No one insulted your heritage!"

"They did so smartly by presuming to celebrate Saint Patrick's Day—a bunch of lily white English peerage who no doubt trace their roots back to the Plantagenets."

"Do you think you are the only one with nationalistic feelings?" she argued, exasperated. "There are English who have died at the hands of the Irish, too, and you might consider that it's good of the Waverlys to bury the hatchet, so to speak, and honor your people."

"I can do without their honor!"

"Jake Blarney, you are a bigot!" she declared.

"I'm nothing of the sort."

"Then why did you have to show contempt for everyone there, including me?"

"I didn't show contempt for you!"

"You did! Everyone was laughing at me. It was just like—"

"Just like what?" he pursued.

"Just like my father used to do," she accused passionately. "I can't be married to a man who humiliates me that way, who sets me up for public ridicule!"

"That is absurd! You weren't ridiculed, love. And if you were, who needs the louts, anyway?"

"I need them!" she cried.

Heatedly he demanded, "Why can't what you and I have be enough? Why must you hobnob with snooty highbrows who spend their time listening to chamber music and putting on airs?"

"Jake, they are good people and I like them," she informed him through clenched teeth. "Furthermore, if you and I are going to make it together, we can't just hide our faces in the sand and pretend the rest of the world does not exist."

He snapped the reins. "That would be fine by me, darlin'."

"Well, it won't fly with me!" she snapped. "Furthermore, if the Waverlys do host their Saint Patrick's Day celebration, I'm attending! And if you don't care to escort me—*and* join in on the festivities in the proper spirit—then I'll go without you."

He regarded her with angry suspicion. "Are you saying you would take up with Ackerly again?"

"No. I'm saying I'm going to the gathering—with you or without you, Jake Blarney. I've shared your world with you, Jake. You have to admit that—"

"Aye, darlin'," he cut in softly, reaching over to caress her cheek.

She shrank back, determined not to let him stay her from her purpose. "But if you can't share my world with me, then there's no hope for us."

He frowned. "You can't mean that, darlin'."

Her voice was hoarse, but vehement. "I mean it, Jake."

That remark reduced Jake Blarney to glowering silence, and the two exchanged not a single word as he dropped her off.

Jake was in a turbulent mood as he drove home alone. Priscilla had been right—he had deliberately misbehaved tonight, scoffing at her friends and her high society.

Actually, he was scared to death—still frightened that people like the Waverlys and Ackerly Frost would ultimately steal away the woman he loved. He knew he could never compete with such aristocrats. Even if he could quote Bobby Burns or Will

Wordsworth, he lacked their pedigree, their culture and sophistication. That was why he'd tried to force Priscilla's hand tonight, to make her turn her back on her cherished Galveston society and admit that what he offered was enough. He'd also been afraid she would judge him against others far more refined, and find him sadly lacking ...

He laughed bitterly. That much, he had managed to accomplish through his own stupid, boorish behavior! He bemoaned his own bungling. Rather than making Priscilla his, the ploy had backfired miserably, reminding Priscilla of the disgrace her father had heaped upon her. She had risen up to defend the very ones he had scoffed. With his failure had come the sobering realization that the woman he loved truly needed a life beyond him and his children, that she required friends and a sense of community. But how could he fulfill her needs for culture and society without emphasizing even more his own inadequacies ... and eventually losing her?

Chapter 29

March came, and the trees of Galveston began to bud. The cold days of winter gave way to brisk, sunny days with an occasional cold snap.

Priscilla continued to see Jake and the twins; she enjoyed his company and delighted in hearing the girls speak in their first sentences, watching them progress from toddling about the house to running gleefully down the beach. Even though the time was idyllic for them all, Jake and Priscilla did not again venture forth in society together, and this troubled Priscilla. She remained determined that she and Jake should at least try to find their place in the Galveston community, but he was as resistant as ever. She continued with her own activities in the community, and was honored when she was named chairwoman of the Trinity Ladies Guild, a most prestigious post.

A particular bone of contention between her and Jake was the upcoming St. Patrick's Day celebration the Waverlys were hosting in honor of their returning daughter and son-in-law; Priscilla had been invited and wanted Jake to escort her, but he steadfastly refused. Jake planned to participate in the traditional "Wearing of the Green" parade on the Strand, sponsored by the Hibernians, but he denounced any celebration hosted by a family of English heritage on this day he considered to be sacrosanct to the Irish. Priscilla suspected Jake's true resentment was toward the English crown and peerage, who collectively had repressed Jake's homeland for many centuries.

A couple of weeks before St. Patrick's Day, Priscilla was having luncheon with Jake at his house when an unexpected knock came at the door. Priscilla, Jake, the twins, and Mrs. Braunhurst were all seated at the table eating chicken and dumplings.

Jake frowned, tossed down his napkin, and stood. "Wonder who that could be," he muttered, heading for the door.

Priscilla heard the door open and heard Jake ask nastily, "Octavia, what are you doing here?"

Priscilla twisted about to see a tall, thin woman standing in the portal. Appearing to be about thirty years old, she was conservatively gowned in black silk, and might have been pretty except for her sallow complexion and sour frown. Next to her stood a short, weasel-faced man with greasy dark brown hair; he wore a brown suit and held a bowler hat in his hand.

"This is not a social call, Jake," the woman replied shrilly. She strained past him to get a glimpse of the girls at the dining table. "Although I would like to see my nieces ... to ensure they have not been abused."

"Your nieces are doing just splendidly, thank you," Jake retorted, "and I'm sure they will continue to do so as long as they're not subjected to the likes of you! In case you haven't forgotten what I told you the last time you appeared here, you are not welcome in this house!"

"Well, I never!" gasped the woman, flinging a hand to her breast.

Fearing Jake was about to blow his stack, Priscilla sprang up and rushed over to join them. Arriving at his side, she glanced quickly from the woman to the man, then offered Jake a pleading look. "If this woman is the twins' aunt, shouldn't you at least invite her in?"

Jake glowered back. "I'll deal with this, thank you, Priscilla."

While Priscilla ground her teeth at Jake's sharp rebuke, the woman glanced at her with suspicion and distaste. "Who is this woman, Jake, and what is she doing in your home?"

"That's none of your damned affair," he snapped.

The man extended some papers toward Jake and spoke in a high, grating voice. "Then you can answer the judge, sir. I am Mrs. Overstreet's attorney, Stanton Smead, and I am here to inform you that my client is bringing suit against you to gain guardianship of the twins. Here is your copy of the petition for custody and a summons to appear."

While Priscilla uttered a low cry of horror, Jake grabbed the papers and glowered at the man. "This is absurd! On what grounds are you seeking custody?"

"Oh the grounds of your own gross moral misconduct and total lack of suitability as a parent for these children," the lawyer informed him.

"Bah!" scoffed Jake.

"Your charges are preposterous, sir," chimed in Priscilla. "Jake Blarney is a wonderful parent."

Octavia sniffed disdainfully at Priscilla. "Attested to by whom ... his mistress?"

"Oh!" she gasped.

Jake shook a fist at Octavia. "I'll thank you to quit insulting the lady and get the hell out of here, before I throw you out!"

"We'd be delighted," said Octavia.

"The hearing will be held in Judge Thurstan Briggs's court at 10 A.M. on the seventeeth," added Smead.

"We'll be there," snarled Jake. "Indeed, Octavia, it will be a pleasure to be rid of you once and for all."

With those words, he slammed the door in their faces.

There was a moment of stunned silence as Priscilla and Jake stared at each other. Then, from the table, Bula called out, "Sir, would you like me to fetch coffee and dessert?"

"Of course," muttered Jake.

She left, and Priscilla gazed poignantly at the twins

in their matching bow-back Windsor high chairs. Sal was singing to herself and pounding her palm on an unfortunate biscuit; Nell was sucking on her bottle. Anguish and outrage assailed her at the prospect of those darlings being wrenched away from all they held dear. Her misery only intensified at the thought of Jake losing his beloved daughters.

"Jake, what are we going to do?" she asked.

He waved her off. "Ah, that bitch Octavia is all bark and no bite. Don't worry about her."

"Don't worry?" Priscilla asked in a hoarse whisper. "But she's brought suit against you! This is really serious."

He didn't reply, but his fearsome scowl as he stroked his jaw bespoke that he, too, was aware of the true threat.

"What will you do?" Priscilla repeated. "You'll need a lawyer, you know."

He nodded. "I'm friends with Mike Mulligan. He's in the Hibernians with me, and he's a good bloke."

"Then you must see him at once. You've only two weeks to prepare."

He flashed her a brave smile. "I'm sure he'll agree with me that Octavia has no case."

"No case! Are you so sure?"

"Aye—I'm the twins' father—"

"What about all those weeks you spent carousing and brawling all over Galveston?"

He shrugged. "Only a momentary lapse, darlin'. I'll just explain to the judge that I was in love—"

"Jake, that won't get it done," she cut in vehemently. "You'll have to be on your best behavior— bring in character witnesses such as Father O'Dooley—and convince the judge you're a model father." She bit her lip. "And it may not be easy, after what just happened."

"What do you mean?"

She regarded him with exasperation. "Jake, they saw me here with you, and Octavia has already accused me of being your mistress."

"So what if she did?"

Priscilla spoke in a tense undertone. "Well, it's the truth! I know we've been careful, but what if they can find some witness who has seen me stealing out here to be alone with you? You could lose the suit on the grounds of . . . moral turpitude or whatever."

"Priscilla, you are making too much of this—"

"I'm not. I think we must marry at once."

"What?" He chuckled. "You, offering marriage? Now, that's a refreshing change."

She glanced again at the babies. "We have no choice if we want to ensure that you retain custody of the twins. You'll have a much better case if you can bring a wife to court, to prove to the judge that you can provide a stable home for your children."

Jake frowned formidably. "I don't think so, darlin'."

Priscilla was flabbergasted. "B-But you've been begging me to marry you for months now—"

"Aye, but now you're offering yourself for all the wrong reasons," he cut in, pride gleaming in his eyes. "I don't need you to help me keep me children—and until you offer yourself simply because you love me as much as I love you, then I don't want you, lassie."

Her jaw dropped. "I can't believe I'm hearing this! You would risk the twins' future—just for the sake of your vanity?"

He pulled her into his arms and regarded her sternly. " 'Tis not vanity. I won't settle for having less than all of you, lassie. And I think if you're to become stepmother to me babes, then they, too, deserve a mother who's fully committed to this marriage."

"But I am fully committed!"

"That's not how it sounded to me."

"Jake, we'll either have to marry at once, or we can't risk seeing each other before the hearing," she pleaded.

"And why not?"

"Gossip, of course! We can't take any chances, for the girls' sake!"

Jake regarded the twins with concern.

She grabbed his sleeve. "Jake, please reconsider."

He touched her cheek and smiled at her sadly. "It's not up to me, lassie. You're the one who must decide what's in your heart and what you truly want."

Soon after Priscilla left, Jake took the girls to the beach. The afternoon was mild for March and Jake had decided to allow them to cavort in the surf awhile. The mites looked adorable in the navy and white bathing dresses Priscilla had recently given them. The outfits included gathered hats and short skirts that left the babies' chubby legs free to romp in the sand and surf. Now Sal was playing with her toy boat at the edge of the water, while Nell sat digging in the sand with her little bucket and small shovel. The beach toys were also gifts from Priscilla—she seemed to bring the girls some new bauble every time she visited.

"Papa, see!" called a gleeful voice.

Jake grinned as he watched Sal dip her little boat in the surf, then dump water over her head amid a chortle of glee. Chuckling, he called out, "Yes, I see, darlin'. The water's fun, but don't venture out into the waves. The mean old jellyfish will bite your big toe!"

"Baaaad jedyfish!" Sal called with an exaggerated grimace. She grinned, leaned over to refill her little boat with water, and this time toddled over to dump the contents over Nell. Water pouring from her bathing cap, Nell turned to give her father a bewildered look.

Jake laughed over the sight until tears sprang to his eyes. Priscilla was right that the girls changed with every passing day. Watching them grow and develop was truly wondrous. A lump swelled in his throat at the thought of losing them. Damn that busybody Octavia and her troublemaking attorney! Had he been too proud earlier, when he had declined Priscilla's offer to wed him in order to forestall his legal troubles? Perhaps so, but he still felt she had to come to him strictly out of love for him and the girls, or their union would be doomed.

Yet he had taken a terrible risk. What if it turned out he had gambled and lost? He would never forgive himself.

During the next ten days, Priscilla stayed away from Jake's farm, fearing gossip, though it was torture being apart from him and the girls. She missed all three of them terribly, and agonized over the upcoming custody hearing. She endlessly wished Jake would agree that they should marry at once. However, when she thought about it, she realized he was right; if their marriage was to endure, she should be offering herself because she loved and wanted him, not strictly to save the twins. Of course, she did love and want him ... yet she couldn't deny that she retained doubts about their relationship in the long run.

Her mind was very much on these problems one early spring day when she went to the apothecary for lunch. At once she noted the worried look on Mary's face as the shopgirl spotted her coming through the door. She went over to the counter and sat on a stool.

"How are you, Priscilla?" Mary asked, handing her a glass of water.

"Oh, going crazy missing Jake and the girls." She eyed Mary with concern. "What about you? You look preoccupied."

"Oh, I'm fine," she said without conviction.

"No you're not," scolded Priscilla. "You're hiding something from me."

"Well, I did see Jake a bit earlier," Mary confided. "He came in because one of the girls has a rash, and he asked Mr. Peebles for a remedy."

"Oh, no!" cried Priscilla, suddenly all but panicstricken. "It could be measles or scarlet fever!"

"No, no, I don't think it was anything that serious," Mary quickly reassured her. "Jake didn't mention a fever."

"Then why do you look so anxious?"

Mary sighed and reached across the counter to pat Priscilla's hand. "It's you who may feel troubled, love, when I tell you what else happened this morning."

"What do you mean?"

"That busybody Delia Snodgrass was just in here buying cough elixir for her husband," Mary related with disgust.

"I know—isn't she insufferable?" Priscilla replied. "If her son, Chester, weren't such a sweetheart, I'd refuse to tutor her children. Didn't I tell you she's the one who wrote to Octavia Overstreet about Jake, and started all this trouble in the first place?"

Mary nodded grimly. "Aye, but you haven't heard the worst of it, love."

"Go on."

Mary leaned over the counter and whispered, "Delia was bragging about how she's responsible for giving that rounder Jake Blarney his comeuppance. And she said Mr. Ackerly Frost will be testifying against Jake at the hearing."

Priscilla gasped. "No!"

"I'm afraid 'tis true," said Mary.

"That jerk!" cried Priscilla. "Oh, I can't believe he's actually doing this—the cad!"

"You know he must be sore about losing you to Jake."

"I suppose . . ." Frowning distractedly, Priscilla donned her gloves. "Mary, you'll have to excuse me. I must have a word with that scoundrel at once."

"Of course. Good luck, love."

Priscilla rushed out of the apothecary and hurried the several blocks to Ackerly's bank. She found the lobby all but deserted. She questioned the elderly clerk, Fitzgerald. At first he couldn't remember where Ackerly was, but when Priscilla pleaded, he snapped his fingers and said, "I know—Mr. Frost mentioned he was having luncheon at the Tremont today."

Priscilla was off again, walking briskly to the Tremont a few blocks away. She rushed through the lobby and straight into the dining room.

The maître d' dashed up. "May I help you, miss?"

"Thank you, I'm looking for someone." Craning her neck, she glanced about until she spotted Ackerly. She stifled a cry of shock. He was seated with Winnie Haggarty and the two were laughing, their heads together. Although she no longer cared about Ackerly, it was annoying to realize he'd likely had his eye on the vapid beauty all along.

"Is something wrong?" asked the maître d'.

"Excuse me," muttered Priscilla, starting off.

Winnie, looking stunning in a lace-trimmed gown of coral silk, spotted Priscilla's approach first. Regarding the newcomer with barely repressed hostility, she murmured, "Why, Ackerly, look who's here."

Glimpsing Priscilla, Ackerly rose and stared at her with a combination of irritation and embarrassment. "Miss Pemberton, this is something of a surprise."

"Mr. Frost, I must speak with you at once," she replied coldly. "Will you kindly step out to the lobby with me for a moment?" She flashed Winnie a smile. "That is, if you will excuse us, Miss Haggarty?"

Ackerly drew himself up with dignity. "As you can see, this is an inopportune moment—"

"And shall I create an equally inopportune scene if you refuse to speak to me?" Priscilla countered sweetly.

Ackerly glanced about the room at the many prominent citizens who were already staring at them, including Colonel Moody and his associates. Grinding his jaw, he turned to Winnie. "My dear, if you will excuse me?"

Winnie waved a breadstick at him. "Oh, go speak with her, Ackerly, and be done with it. Everyone knows she has no class."

Priscilla raised an eyebrow at Winnie. "I've noticed

how the most ill-bred people are always the first to criticize others."

Winnie gasped. "Oh!"

Ackerly groaned. "Let's get this over with."

"By all means," said Priscilla.

They trooped out to the lobby in silence. Ackerly pulled out his watch and snapped it open. "Very well, Priscilla, what is it? I'm on a very tight schedule today—"

"Not so tight that you can't have lunch with Winnie," she said pleasantly. "I must say she suits you."

"Will you kindly get to the point?" he inquired with exasperation.

"Very well. I need to know whether it's true that you're planning to testify against Jake Blarney at the custody hearing on the seventeenth."

He smiled nastily. "Of course I'm planning to testify against that bounder. The man is a hooligan who assaulted me in public. Furthermore, the Snodgrasses are one of the bank's biggest depositors as well as personal friends of mine. When Delia informed me that Octavia Overstreet could use some help in her suit against Blarney, I was only too glad to oblige."

Priscilla regarded him in openmouthed horror. "You would try to crucify a man simply out of pure, mean-spirited revenge?"

"No. Try out of civic responsibility."

"Don't give me that claptrap!"

He snapped shut his watch and replaced it in his vest pocket. "Is there anything else, Priscilla? Perhaps you don't mind being rude to Miss Haggarty, but I assure you, I do."

She grabbed his sleeve and glowered. "If Octavia Overstreet has her way, Jake Blarney could lose his children. Do you honestly want that on your conscience?"

He sneered. "From everything I've heard and seen, a change of guardians would only be to the children's benefit. And if you're smart, Priscilla, you'll take a hint from this tawdry incident and avoid the man permanently."

"Not on your life!" she snapped.

"Suit yourself, then," came his cool reply. "If you're determined to ruin your reputation in this community, then there's nothing the rest of us can do to save you." Cynically he finished, "And to think of all I was willing to offer you, and you were too foolish to appreciate my proposal of marriage."

"I was foolish ever to consider it!" she retorted. "Or to ever look twice at a snake in the grass like you!"

His cheek twitched. "If you'll excuse me, Miss Pemberton, I prefer to spend the remainder of my lunch hour with a woman who appreciates my many virtues and actually has some human warmth and compassion to give in return."

Priscilla was incredulous. "Some human *warmth*? You have no idea what warmth is, Jack Frost! At least we never need fear you'll go to hell, because you'd definitely freeze the damned place over!"

Ackerly was speechless, trembling with anger. After tossing Priscilla a look of blistering contempt, he turned on his heel and walked off.

Chapter 30

Following her confrontation with Ackerly, Priscilla made a critical decision: She was going to marry Jake. Indeed, she wondered at her own foolishness in not pledging her heart to him fully before now. He was the genuine article, even if a diamond in the rough; men like Ackerly were no better than cheap paste.

Of course, Priscilla was very much aware that she was taking a risk in giving her heart to Jake; if he was unwilling to compromise, her goals for the two of them and the girls in the Galveston community might never be realized. Also, she still had no guarantees that Jake would be content with her, or would be faithful to her, over a lifetime.

But this last week and a half spent apart from him had taught her something. Being without Jake was such hell that she was willing to risk the pain and uncertainty of being with him. At this point she was willing to risk almost anything—heartbreak, social ruin. She simply loved Jake and the girls so much that life without them was unbearable.

She also felt as if she would burst if she didn't share her feelings with him, and she decided she must risk going out to his cottage just this once to see him and to check on the girls. She could hardly wait for her last student to leave that day. She rushed to the stable right before it closed and rented a horse and buggy. She drove out of town, her heart racing with anticipation as the conveyance clipped toward Jake's farm.

A sunset shower was beginning to fall, the ocean shimmering with gold, as Priscilla disembarked, raced up the steps, and pounded on Jake's door.

Momentarily he opened it, staring at her in some consternation. She drank him in lovingly, noting he looked much as he had that first magical day she'd arrived on his stoop. He was dressed in dark pants and a flowing white shirt, partially unbuttoned to reveal his very sexy chest hair.

Exclaiming his name in delight, she thrust herself into his arms, filling her senses with the male essence, the warmth, of him.

He hugged her back, then held her at arm's length, gazing into her face with concern. "Is something wrong, lass?"

"Are the girls all right?" she asked anxiously. "Mary said one of them had a rash."

Jake chuckled. "Sal had a wee diaper rash was all. She's fine now. In fact, the wee lassies are napping now. They became all tuckered out at the beach today, and have been sleeping like angels ever since Bula gave them their bath."

"I want to see them," she said. "I've missed them terribly."

They tiptoed into the house together and stood staring at the girls in their cradles. As always, the twins appeared utterly precious, and were dozing with damp, dark curls framing their cherubic pink faces. Priscilla leaned over to tuck a blanket around Nell's foot, and to pull a doll away from Sal's face.

She straightened and hugged Jake's waist. "They're so adorable. You know, everything will be just perfect, Jake, if only you'll say you'll marry me."

He scowled down at her. "Lass, you know my feelings—"

She interrupted by pressing her fingers to his lips. "But you don't know mine. Not really. Jake, can we talk?"

He hesitated, his expression troubled.

"Please?" she beseeched.

"The last time we spoke of such matters, you hurt me, girl," he admitted with surprising humility, "when you suggested we should wed only so I'll win the custody hearing."

She squeezed his hand. "I know, and I'm very sorry. Give me a chance to make it up to you?"

He fought a smile as he pulled her into his arms and stroked her back. "And how would you make it up to me, lassie?" he asked very low.

"Any way you want," she promised rashly.

He pulled back, his blue eyes twinkling with mischief. "Now, that's what I call an irresistible offer . . . and you've no doubt just gotten yourself into deep trouble."

"The deeper the better," she teased back. "But we do need to talk first."

"Aye." He took her hand and pulled her toward the door. "Let's talk out on the gallery. We'll hear the wee ones through the window if they rouse."

They went to sit on the porch swing next to the open window. Rain was falling on the beach beyond them, and a moist, cool breeze wafted over them.

Jake glanced at her curiously. "What is on your mind, lassie?"

Suddenly uncertain, she met his gaze shyly. "Jake, I want you to know I said everything all wrong the last time. I think that ever since I met you, I've been afraid . . ."

"Afraid of what?"

"Well, just as you've told me, I've been afraid of trusting you, loving you, of believing in myself. You see, most of my life, I've put up strong barriers against the world, to protect myself from being hurt again like I was as a child. I had to hide the real person inside of me behind this confident and refined exterior. I've been looking for . . . I don't know, some sort of external affirmation of my own sense of identity ... and it just isn't there. Do you understand that?"

He shook his head in perplexity.

A wistful smile curved her lips. "Maybe it does go back to my father. Even though I really did love him, I never could seem to win his approval or love, and I think I looked for the self-esteem I lacked in all the wrong places."

"Like with Ackerly Frost?"

"Yes." She clenched her hands into fists in her lap. "You see, my mother and I suffered so horribly in the community because of what my father did ... and thus I grew up convinced that I had to be accepted into the highest circles, that I had to marry a socially prominent man like Ackerly Frost, in order to be happy, to become a whole person. Most important of all, Ackerly represented emotional safety—I didn't have to reveal my true self to him, as I do with you. But now I know that men like Ackerly are as shallow as layers of frost on a windowpane. Now I realize how empty some of my values were ... when what I really wanted and needed was to be loved by a fine, genuine man like you."

He gazed at her in awe. "Do you truly mean that, lass?"

"Oh, yes." She blinked at tears. "You're the first person I've ever known who has been able to get through to me, Jake, to make me face my real feelings. I think that's why I fought you so long and hard, because you had this uncanny ability to see past my facade. It's been frightening to have to look at myself as I truly am, to face my own hurts and vulnerabilities."

"But I understand those hurts and needs of yours, girl," he said solemnly. "And you can trust me with them."

She hugged him tightly, her voice breaking with emotion. "I know I can, Jake. You never gave up on me, and that means the world to me. I love you, Jake, with all my heart—and I'll be proud to become Priscilla Blarney, if you'll have me."

"Oh, lass." He nestled her closer and they kissed fervently. Intensely he whispered, "Darling, I've hungered for you so, waited so long for this moment . . ."

"I know you have." She pulled back and smiled tremulously. "But you must be patient with me. I'm not as certain of myself as you are—and there's still a lot of hurt in me."

He smiled tenderly, brushing away her tears with his thumb. "You'll need a lot of loving, lassie—which I'm eager to provide."

"I'm sure you will, Jake. But you'll have to understand that at times I may yet be confused, unsure. I'm still in some ways feeling my way. Even now, I don't understand why sometimes the opinions of others matter to me so much more than they should."

"And they matter to me not at all," he confessed ruefully. "I can see why you might feel threatened, lassie. I'm a bit of a loose cannon, eh?"

She fondly rumpled his hair. "You're unpredictable, but fun—even when you discharge your artillery."

"Especially then—eh, lassie?" he teased wickedly, his lips making a dive for her throat.

"Now, let's stay on the subject," she scolded in quavering tones.

"Which is, lass?" he murmured thickly against her neck.

"Um . . . there will have to be compromises."

He gazed up at her. "Ah . . . Meaning, prepare for me next lecture on walking the straight and narrow path?"

She shook a finger at him. "Even though my values have changed, I will always want to have a place in this community. We need to find a place together—maybe not listening to chamber music, but within a circle of friends where we'll both be comfortable. I want your promise, Jake, that you'll give the citizens of Galveston another chance ... and that you'll try to be less of a stubborn Irishman."

He glared. "I ain't stubborn."

"Oh, you're not?" she inquired with an air of amazement. "Then I take it you'll gladly escort me to the Waverlys' Saint Patrick's Day *ceilidh?*"

He made a growling sound.

"Well, Jake?"

"You're forgetting that's the day of the hearing," he replied darkly. "I'm already missing me traditional Irish parade because of it."

"I realize that, but the party isn't until that evening."

"You're just trying to compromise me principles!" he accused.

"Oh, Jake, come on!" she chided. "You're being absurd."

"I am not!"

"America is the melting pot, for heaven's sake! You've been in this country for ten years and it's high time to put aside your vitriolic nationalism and become a part of this nation and this community."

His attempt to look forbidding became lost in a sudden smile. "And a part of *this* woman?" he teased.

"Why, Mr. Blarney, I quite forgot," she simpered back. "And that's the best part of all, isn't it?"

He roared with mirth. "Always, darling."

"Well, Jake? Will you escort me to the soirée?"

His frown returned.

She stared him in the eye. "Can you honestly tell me principles are the sole reason you behaved so obnoxiously at the Waverlys' last gathering?"

Breathing a heavy sigh, Jake got up and went over to stand at the porch railing. Rain poured down as he stared abstractedly out at the Gulf. Watching him, Priscilla thought of how much she loved him, and how complex he was—how he could delight her with his laughter one minute, have her shaking in her boots from his temper the next, and then make her quake with desire ... He made her feel truly alive, he gave her the courage to *feel* everything ... and she adored him so much for that! She knew she would always remember him this way, gazing out at the sea, with the wind whipping about his hair and clothing.

At last he turned to her. With his heart in his eyes, he softly admitted, "I know there are things I can't give you, darlin'—needs I can't satisfy. And that makes me wild, because I love you so much that I'm jealous of every second you share with others, and afraid they'll steal you away from me."

"Oh, Jake." Priscilla rose and embraced him, and they clung to each other for a poignant moment. "Darling, you should never be jealous. You are the one who gives me what I truly need! Everything else is just icing on the cake, but I want us to share that icing together, to find our place in this community, for our sake and the sake of the girls."

"You're sure, lassie?"

She nodded.

"Very well, lass. I'll take you to the soirée." He pulled back and grinned at her. "You can be a hard bargainer, you know ..."

"I know," she admitted primly, then wrinkled her nose at him. "But you can be even harder."

"Aye," he concurred with a devilish chuckle. "And I'm going to make you pay for twisting me arm."

"I'm counting on it."

Jake threw back his head and laughed. "And while we're on the subject of paying, lassie ..."

"Yes?"

He drew himself up importantly. "I've a condition I must have met."

"Oh, dear. A condition."

"If you're marrying me, I'm giving you half me treasure."

"What?" She regarded him in astonishment. "You mean the gold doubloons?"

"Aye," he said soberly.

"No! All of that should go to the twins!"

He shook his head. "Nay, half will be for you, love, to build us a grand mansion on Broadway, or whatever your little heart desires. The rest will be saved for the girls when they're grown . . . as well as for the others we'll surely have, for their education and such."

She mulled over Jake's words. "Well, I suppose it would be good for the girls to have a more substantial home as they grow up. But if we live in town . . . what about the farm?"

He stroked his jaw. "I've been thinking I might sell it, and try me hand at a lumber business near the Strand."

"Really?" she asked. "Jake Blarney, entrepreneur?"

He glowered magnificently. "Well, with all the building going on hereabouts, there's plenty of need for lumber and such. As the lassies grow, 'twill be better if we live in the city, with their schooling to consider and all."

"I suppose you're right. And you're sure about the disposition of your treasure?"

He nodded. "I want it for me loved ones."

"And not for yourself?"

He tweaked her chin. "Darlin', I'd only squander it or gamble it away. You and the children will put it to good use."

"Very well. But if you're adding more conditions, then so must I."

"What now?" he demanded, groaning.

She took a deep breath, then blurted, "I want us to marry immediately . . . before the hearing."

Angry realization flared in his eyes. "Aha! Lass, I told you I'll not have you marrying me just to help me win me battle with Octavia—"

"That's not the reason and you know it!" she cut in passionately. "I'm marrying you because I love you. But this is no time for false pride, Jake. Indeed, I just learned that Ackerly Frost will be testifying against you. This could be very serious. I'm a part of this family now—and by God, I'm fighting for the man and the children I love."

He still hesitated, but a smile tugged at his lips.

She stamped her foot in exasperation. "You're going to marry me *at once*, you pigheaded Irishman, or I'm going to force you to the altar."

"Oh, you will, will you?" He grinned his delight.

"In a New York minute! I—I'll tell Father O'Dooley you've ruined me, and then he'll prod you to the altar with a shotgun, by damn!"

Jake shouted with laughter, then grabbed Priscilla around the waist. "Feisty, aren't you, love?" He playfully spun her about. "Well, I've a way with feisty wenches . . ."

"Do I get *my* way?" she demanded stubbornly.

"Aye, lass, you will," he whispered back. "But only after I've had mine."

Priscilla moaned with sheer happiness as he kissed her, then she tensed as she again remembered the hearing. "Damn, Jake, I'd better go . . ."

"Why?"

"We must still be careful for the sake of the twins, until we marry. Octavia might drop by again—"

He gestured toward the yard. "Not in this storm, love."

She stared out at the downpour. "I suppose you're right."

"I'm always right."

She playfully punched his arm. "Oh! The instant we agree to marry, you turn into a sanctimonious know-it-all."

Laughing, Jake scooped Priscilla up into his arms and carried her inside. He set her down near the babies, and they took another moment to check on the sleeping twins. Priscilla's heart melted at the sight of them, at the realization that they were truly *hers* now, along with Jake! Her joy was overwhelming, and she couldn't wait to tell the girls. They might not understand all the words just yet, but she was certain they would share her bliss.

Jake tucked in the covers Nell had kicked off, while Priscilla kissed Sal's sweet little cheek. Jake then caught Priscilla's hand and pulled her into the bedroom, his gaze burning with passion for her. Priscilla mused that the sound of the rain pounding the roof seemed a very sexy accompaniment to the fierce beating of her heart.

He stared down at her for a moment, then tilted her chin upward with his fingertips. "Why the tears, lass?"

She hugged him close. "I'm just so happy—happy that you, and those precious girls, are mine now. And I want to make up for all the hurt I've caused you."

A low, husky chuckle escaped him. "I intend to be very demanding . . . in bed, that is."

She laughed. "You're very demanding everywhere. That's one of the things I love about you."

Priscilla began unbuttoning his shirt, and lovingly ran her lips over his hair-roughened chest. He groaned as she tongued his nipples. Meanwhile, her fingers were at his belt buckle, freeing the object of her pleasure. Unbuttoning his trousers, she slipped her fingers inside to stroke his hot hardness. His breathing grew tortured. He undid her bodice, his impatient fingers ripping the cloth. He leaned over, sucking her breasts ravenously.

Abruptly she slipped to her knees and kissed his arousal lovingly. He caught a tortured breath.

"By Saint Brigit, you should not do this to a man," he rasped. "It tempts me mightily to hike your skirts and have you this instant."

"Please," she begged. "Have me. Now."

"My God, woman."

But he did her bidding, trembling with desire all the while. He caught her beneath the arms and lifted her onto the bed, tossing up her skirts and pulling down her drawers. His eyes blazed down into hers, and her mouth went dry at the raw need she saw reflected there.

He pulled her hips to the edge of the bed and she eagerly wrapped her legs around his waist. Standing between her spread thighs, he thrust into her with incredible power. She gasped, tossed her head, clawed the coverlet.

"Oh, Jake, yes, yes . . ." Priscilla was so full of him, she could not bear it, and still she rose to take him deeper, arching provocatively against him.

Jake's eyes clenched shut in agony. Priscilla was giving herself to him so completely, so lovingly, and 'twas unbearable. Her legs were clenched tight about his waist, her feminine sheath squeezing about him exquisitely, so velvety and hot. Tears filled his eyes at the realization that she was all his, at last. They'd said the words before, but now he *felt* that rightness, that joining, to his soul. His hunger for her knew no bounds. He slid his hands beneath her and lifted her high into his relentless possession. At the sound of her soft sobs, he lost control and the coupling grew wild, shattering.

Priscilla had to bite her lip to keep from crying out. Never had their lovemaking felt so right, so full of consuming need. She was truly a part of him now. She moved with him feverishly, demanding his all even as she gave her own. At the moment of their climax, she would have shouted, except that Jake fell on her, smothering her mouth with his.

"Oh, Jake." She clutched him close and shook with emotion. "I love you so . . ."

"I love you, lassie." He pulled her bodice lower and lovingly kissed her breasts.

For endless moments Priscilla and Jake drifted together in heavenly torment, still joined. Then the torture for both became immediate again . . .

"I can feel you swelling inside me again," she panted. "So hard and so hot."

"For you, love," he murmured against her breast. "We'll savor it this time."

Running his lips and tongue over her breasts, Jake began teasing her, moving slowly in and out, until she could no longer stand it and begged him for release. Still he thrust deep and slow, tormenting her endlessly, until she pushed him over on his back and eagerly straddled him. She laced her fingers through his and pinned his hands to the mattress.

He grinned up at her. "Now who's demanding? Take everything you want from me, lassie."

Her gaze burned with love. "I'll take all that ... and more. You're mine, Jake Blarney. *Mine.*"

"Aye, lassie. Always."

She began to ride him deeply, voraciously, until Jake could bear no more and locked his forearms at her waist, pinning her against his pounding loins. A frantic cry escaped her. Her lips sought his, her tongue plundering him even as he plundered her. Jake groaned with delicious torment as both of them were again carried away on the tides of passion ...

Chapter 31

L ater, while Jake dozed, Priscilla dressed, checked the babies, then strolled out to the beach alone. The rain had stopped and the air smelled incredibly sweet. She knew she must head back to town soon, but first she took a moment to enjoy the mild March evening. She watched the waves pound the shoreline, feeling the crisp wind and the salty spray on her face.

She thought of how much her life had changed since Jake's note had brought her across that vast ocean of time to him. More and more, she sensed that she would never go back again, that this was the place where she was meant to be, the time in which she was meant to live. Yet on occasion she felt slightly melancholy, wondering what her mother, and others she had left behind, might think. Sometimes she still wished she could get a message through. Of course, she'd tried to send messages to Ackerly V, first to come get her, then to get lost. But there had never been a response. Had the missives even been received? Jake's note had worked—why hadn't hers?

Abruptly Priscilla's thoughts fragmented as she heard a distant roar. She glanced toward the horizon and observed a large wave moving toward shore—like the very wall of water that had taken her away from twentieth-century Galveston in the first place. Oh, good Lord, was the storm not over, after all? Or had her thoughts summoned another tidal wave? Was she about to be swept off in time again?

Panic seized her. No, no, she couldn't return to the present, not now that she had finally found her new life—and her only love—in another time! She couldn't lose Jake and the babies! Frantic, she began backing away from the approaching wall of water.

At last the avalanche pounded the beach, as Priscilla hovered just beyond it, terrified, wringing her hands. Then she blinked, certain her eyes must be deceiving her as she watched the waters part—as if the Gulf were indeed the Red Sea—and then a man stepped out of the waves!

Priscilla gaped in disbelief. Had she lost her mind? No, it was Ackerly Frost striding toward her, dressed in a drenched trench coat and carrying an opened umbrella! Would wonders never cease! The modern coat seemed to indicate that this man was not Ackerly I but her old flame from the present! But how could that be, and what on earth was he doing here?

He spotted her and stopped in his tracks, shaking off water as the wave receded. He lowered his umbrella, snapped it shut, and gawked at her.

"My God, Priscilla, is that you?" he cried.

"Ackerly?" she called.

"What is going on here?" he demanded.

She stepped closer to him, studying him intently, and at last fully recognized not the Ackerly she knew here in Galveston but the one she had left behind—. Ackerly Frost V. Yes, this man was definitely her ex-fiancé from the 1990s—complete with London Fog raincoat, and minus the long sideburns and goatee that so distinguished his great-great-grandfather. This Ackerly's hair was short, his face clean-shaven. All of him was dripping wet, and his features were clenched in annoyance and disbelief.

"My kingdom, Ackerly, is it really you?" she whispered.

He laughed dryly. "Of course it's me. Furthermore, I'm the one who should be asking the questions. For the love of heaven, Priscilla, what are you doing here, and why are you wearing that bizarre Victorian costume? We all assumed you had drowned." All at once he spotted Jake's house and the dairy beyond them. "What in God's name is *that?*"

"Don't ask," she advised. "Even if I told you, you'd never believe me. Just tell me how you got here."

He gazed about them in bewilderment. "Well, I was walking along the beach, examining a waterfront property for one of our customers, when I watched this bottle wash up. I picked it up, uncorked it, and out slipped this note, in your handwriting." He pulled a scrap of paper from his pocket and read, " 'Ackerly, Please rescue me.' "

"You're kidding!" she cried, flinging a hand to her mouth.

"You know I never jest, Priscilla," he replied haughtily. He scowled at the scrap again. "The truly bizarre thing is, the message is written on a Frost National Bank deposit slip dated from the year 1880."

Priscilla chortled as she remembered ripping off that very scrap months ago. "So you're here sort of on a demand note, are you?" she quipped.

Frowning at her humor, Ackerly replaced the scrap in his pocket. "At any rate, I read your message, and the next thing I knew, this huge wave came along— why, I barely had time to raise my umbrella—and it swept me away. Now, I should very much like an explanation, Priscilla!"

She clapped her hands and laughed in glee. "Oh, I love it! I can't believe my note actually brought you here through time! This is too delicious—such marvelous poetic justice! And only J. Ackerly Frost the Fifth would step out of the tide, fully clothed, with his umbrella opened."

Ackerly glared. "Priscilla, will you kindly stop ranting and tell me what's going on here? What has happened to you, and why have you dispatched this note to me?"

She laughed giddily. "A long story, Ackerly dear,

and like I said, you wouldn't believe it in a million years. How's your latest flame?"

He drew himself up with dignity. "Well, after you disappeared, after it became clear that you were likely ... er ... deceased, Ms. Sweet and I decided to marry."

"Oh!" She made a sound of outrage. "You didn't even wait until I was cold, did you?"

He appeared perplexed. "Well, I, er ... apparently you aren't cold, are you?"

She ground her jaw. "So, like your namesake, you've sold out for the empty head and the big boobs?"

Hot color shot up his face. "I beg your pardon. My fiancée is quite intelligent—"

"Oh, come off it, Ackerly," she snapped. "She couldn't carry on an intelligent conversation with a dust mop! Why don't you just admit that you dumped me and ran off to your little London love nest because I'm not beautiful?"

He smugly brushed water from his sleeves. "Your physical attributes had nothing to do with my decision, Priscilla. I 'dumped' you, as you so aptly put it, because you are a cold, heartless woman without an ounce of true passion in your body."

"Oh!" she cried. "And this insult from 'Jack Frost' himself. As for my being passionless, I know a certain Irishman who would heartily dispute that!"

He blinked at her in confusion. "Priscilla, I have no idea what you're ranting about. But I should have realized long ago that you were never good enough for me."

"Not good enough for you?" she retorted. "How dare you say such a thing, when you're clearly not worthy to wipe the sand from my slippers!"

He clenched his jaw in consternation. "Look, Priscilla, I've had quite enough of your insults and this outlandish conversation. I'm dripping wet and miserably cold. Besides, it's not as if you ever *really* cared for me, did you?"

His direct question pierced her billowing outrage and affronted pride. She considered his points more calmly. Why was she acting so hostile, when she *had* never really loved this man? Was it because she still felt vulnerable when others tried to tear her down?

"Well, Priscilla?" he pressed. "I think I'm entitled to at least some explanation."

"You know, you're right," she admitted with unaccustomed humility. "I suppose I never did care enough for you, and I had no right to expect you to care for me."

"Well, at least that's more honest."

She sighed. "How's Mother?"

He slowly shook his head. "Beatrice is all right now, though she took your disappearance very hard. Believe it or not, Priscilla, it was a difficult time for all of us."

"Yes, I suppose it was," she murmured.

"Now, if you will kindly explain what is going on here—and where in God's name I've washed up—I'll no longer impose my unwelcome presence on you."

Even as he waited, both of them became distracted as another bottle washed up a few feet away from them. "What is that?" he asked.

"Oh, my God!" Priscilla gasped, a hand flying to her mouth as the true irony of the situation began to dawn on her. "I don't think there will be much time for explanations, Ackerly."

"What do you mean?"

Priscilla glanced out to sea and went wide-eyed as she spotted a new wave forming on the horizon and rapidly rolling toward them. Realizing time was running out, she rushed over to retrieve the second bottle, dashed back, and stuffed it in Ackerly's hand.

As he glanced flabbergasted from the bottle to her, she spoke quickly and urgently. "Go back to your own time, J. Ackerly, and find your happiness with your adored Ms. Sweet. Please tell Mother that I'm alive and very happy here—"

"But where is here?" he demanded in exasperation.

Watching the wave rapidly surge toward them, she implored, "Please, just promise me you'll relay my message!"

"Of course I'll promise," he replied. "You know I've always been fond of Beatrice."

"Good. Tell my mother I'm fine and I love her. Tell her I'll meet her in heaven someday."

"*What?*" he cried, more agitated than ever as he, too, noted the advancing swell.

Priscilla was backing away and shouting, her hand cupped around her mouth. "Otherwise, I think I'd best get the hell out of here, because there's a note in that bottle with your name on it, Ackerly!"

His expression mystified, Ackerly quickly uncorked the bottle, pulled out the note, and read, " 'Jack Frost, get lost.' " He stared at her in horror. "Priscilla, what does this mean?"

His last words were almost drowned out in the roar of the surf. Priscilla had no time to reply, but could only frantically leap back as the new wave landed, rolling over Ackerly and then sweeping him away. She heard his frantic cry, watched the swell retreat, then nothing. Within a split second, the ocean had swallowed him up. Soon the Gulf was peaceful again, as if the wave had never existed and Ackerly Frost V had never appeared.

But he *had* appeared—appeared to rub salt in wounds that had barely healed. Appeared to give her a sense of closure, painful though it was to look even further into herself.

As her shock over Ackerly's bizarre appearance began to recede, Priscilla drew a heavy breath. Why was it, after all she'd been through, that the words "You're not good enough" still had the power to hurt her? She shook her head as the truth began to dawn on her. Perhaps it was because, in a truly ironic sense, both Ackerlys were really like her father, judgmental and ungiving, and the very man she had doubted all along—her darling Jake—was the truly loving one who had accepted and believed in her totally. Just as she'd earlier admitted to Jake, perhaps she had been trying to find in the Ackerlys the love and approval she'd never gotten from her father—and looking in exactly the wrong places, through pursuing men who in fact shared Whitey's emotional remoteness.

She shook her head in awe at this realization, brought to her from a most unexpected source! At least now all her ties with the present were cut. She was confident Ackerly would deliver her message to Beatrice—even if he didn't fully understand her missive—and that her mother would at last find peace regarding her disappearance.

Momentarily she heard Jake's voice calling her name. She turned to watch him coming down the steps of the cottage. He rushed over to her, pulling her into his arms and regarding her turbulent face with concern.

"Darling, what are you doing out here alone? Aren't you cold?"

She smiled. "I really must head back to town now."

He raised an eyebrow at her. "I thought I heard voices, lass. Were you talking to someone?"

"Only to an old acquaintance who just made a mini trip through time," she muttered.

Jake rolled his eyes. "You know, Priscilla Pemberton, you're a barmy lassie. But I love you, anyway. Now, let's get back inside so you can kiss me babies before you leave."

"By all means," she agreed.

They joined hands and raced across the beach to the house.

They were married four days later, on March 16. Only the twins, the Braunhursts, Sarah O'Shanahan, Mary O'Brien, and a few other scattered friends of the bride and groom attended the small service at St. Patrick's Church. Priscilla wore a high-necked, lace-trimmed, white silk gown that Sarah O'Shanahan had hastily sewn for her; Jake wore his black suit with ruffled white shirt. A beaming Father O'Dooley performed the wedding mass, and the twins behaved like angels, watching the service in fascination from the front row, where they sat on the laps of the Braunhursts. Jake slipped a plain, wide gold band on Priscilla's finger, and lovingly kissed her lips at the end of the service. Then the Braunhursts rushed forward with the happy twins.

Bula hosted a small reception for the bride and groom at her house; after cake and punch, the newly formed family went out to dinner together at the Tremont Hotel. Jake apologized to Priscilla that they could not leave at once on their wedding trip; she clutched his hand, stared into his eyes, and lovingly told him that she already had everything she needed.

Later, at home, with the twins blissfully asleep, Jake and Priscilla celebrated in private, their passion breathlessly distracting them from unsettling thoughts of tomorrow's custody hearing . . .

Chapter 32

"**W**ill the witness please state her full name
for the record?"

"Octavia Louise Overstreet."

On St. Patrick's Day, after attending an early morning mass with her new family, Priscilla Blarney found herself in the second-story main courtroom of the Galveston County Courthouse. Next to her at the defense table were her bridegroom and his attorney, Mike Mulligan. Directly behind them sat Father O'Dooley, along with Bula Braunhurst and her husband, Walter, who were holding the girls. The courtroom itself was half-filled; aside from subpoenaed witnesses, the audience consisted mostly of spectators Priscilla had never seen before, a diverse group of individuals whom she assumed were the usual courtroom hangers-on. Presiding was Judge Thurstan Briggs, an elegant old gentleman with a shock of snow white hair. Mike Mulligan had told Priscilla that Briggs was a true southern gentleman, and he'd be unlikely to allow Octavia's lawyer to malign her reputation without substantial proof. She sincerely hoped Mike's prediction would prove correct!

Priscilla mused that the members of her and Jake's team did appear a highly respectable group: Jake and Mike wore conservative dark suits, along with handsome green neck sashes bearing their badges and insignia from the Order of the Hibernians; Priscilla was attired in a tailored lilac silk frock and coordinating wide-brimmed hat lavishly trimmed with silk roses the Braunhursts were garbed in their best Sunday black; and the girls were adorably arrayed in flower-printed spring frocks with lacy white pinafores and matching bonnets. Priscilla was most proud of the fact that so far, the girls had been angelic both in appearance and behavior; but, of course, she'd brought along their bottles and favorite toys to ensure that they didn't grow restless.

Priscilla could not believe all that had transpired in the last few days, how quickly she and Jake had married and become a family. Even as they had prepared for their wedding yesterday, they had laid the groundwork for today's hearing—meeting with Jake's attorney and lining up witnesses. Those witnesses—Mary O'Brien, Father O'Dooley, Jake's friend Kirby Cassidy and his father, Morton, as well as the twins themselves and Bula Braunhurst—were all in court today. But Octavia's witnesses were also present—Delia Snodgrass, Ackerly Frost, and his new flame, Winnie. Priscilla and Jake had passed Ackerly and Winnie as they came in, and Priscilla had met Ackerly's condescending smile with a glare of contempt.

Now opening statements had been completed by attorneys of both plaintiff and defense, and Judge Briggs had ordered Stanton Smead to call his first witness, who was, of course, Octavia.

With his client duly sworn, Smead, looking much like a sly lawyer with his pomaded hair and obsequious smile, stepped forward to question her. As before, Octavia was dressed in austere black silk; she faced the court with an air of superiority.

"Mrs. Overstreet, can you tell us why you have instituted these proceedings to gain custody of your two nieces?"

"Yes," Octavia answered imperiously, casting a look of distaste toward Jake Blarney. "Ever since I met Mr. Blarney, back when my sister Lucinda was contemplating matrimony with him, I was disturbed by his obvious lack of character."

Mike Mulligan, a short, stocky man with pronounced freckles and carroty red hair, shot to his feet. "Objection, Your Honor, the witness is speculating."

Judge Briggs pounded his gavel. "Sustained." He frowned at Octavia. "Mrs. Overstreet, you will confine your remarks to the facts."

"But, Your Honor, I was stating a fact," rejoined Octavia smugly.

"Objection!" cried Mike.

"Sustained," snapped the judge. "The witness will confine her remarks to specifics she actually observed."

"Yes, Your Honor," said Octavia grudgingly. To her attorney she said, "I observed Mr. Blarney displaying drunken and abusive behavior on more than one occasion."

"Objection!" cried Mike.

Impatiently the judge drew off his glasses and leaned toward the witness. "Mrs. Overstreet, what *specifically* did you observe?"

She regarded His Honor piously. "Well, I observed Mr. Blarney drinking and losing his temper with Lucinda—"

Jake bolted up angrily. "Aye, because the house was a pigsty, and the lazy wench wanted to spend half the day in bed!"

As shocked murmurs rippled over the crowd, the judge swung his angry gaze toward Mike Mulligan. "Mr. Mulligan, please inform your client that he is out of order and will get his chance to testify later on."

"Yes, Your Honor," said Mike, taking his seat and hauling the still irate Jake down beside him.

The judge turned to Smead. "Proceed."

"What other observations did you make about Mr. Blarney's character?"

"Well, he was frequently short-tempered with my sister and at times even brought her to tears—while she was pregnant, I might add."

"And after the twins were born?"

Octavia coughed, appearing ill at ease. "I did not get much chance to see them prior to Lucinda's . . . er . . . unfortunate demise."

Jake was on his feet again. "Aye, because your faithless strumpet of a sister run off with a tonic salesman, deserting her husband and newborn babes."

"Objection!" blazed Stanton Smead.

"Sustained," shouted Briggs. He waved his gavel at Jake. "One more outburst, Mr. Blarney, and I'll hold you in contempt."

"Sorry, Your Grace," he muttered, sitting down.

As Smead continued questioning Octavia, Priscilla leaned toward her livid spouse and whispered behind her hand. "Jake, you must cease these outbursts or the judge will decide you're a madman!"

"I know," he whispered back through gritted teeth. "It just makes me so furious to hear Octavia lying."

"I realize that. But like the judge said, we'll get our chance." She patted his clenched fist and slanted him a pleading look, then breathed a sigh of relief when he remained in his seat as Smead finished his questioning.

Mike Mulligan got up to cross-examine Octavia. "Mrs. Overstreet, do you have any direct proof that Jake Blarney is an unfit father?"

"Why, yes. My friend Delia Snodgrass wrote me—"

Mike turned to the judge. "Your Honor, please instruct the witness that she is not allowed to testify to hearsay—"

"Mrs. Overstreet, you may testify only to that which you personally witnessed," scolded the judge.

"Yes, Judge," said Octavia sullenly.

"Mrs. Overstreet, you are married?" asked Mike.

"Yes. My husband, Milton, and I can provide a stable home for the twins."

"You can?" inquired Mike with an air of amazement. "Well, if your husband is so interested in providing a home for another man's children, why isn't he here with you today to bear witness to this . . . er . . . touching devotion?"

Octavia grew decidedly uncomfortable, squirming in her chair and twisting her gloved fingers together. "Milton is minding our business. We own a dry goods store in Houston."

"Ah, I see. And he couldn't get away for even one day to testify to his fitness as a potential guardian for these children?"

"Er . . . no," stammered Octavia.

"What a shame," lamented Mike. "Now, to get back to my original question. Tell me, Mrs. Overstreet, do you have any actual proof that Jake Blarney is an unfit father?"

"I've seen him drink," she replied.

"Have you seen him drunk?" demanded Mike. "And may I remind you that you're under oath."

Octavia hesitated, glaring at the attorney.

Mike turned to the judge. "Your Honor, will you please instruct the witness to answer the question?"

"The witness is so instructed."

Octavia heaved an exasperated sigh. "No, I've not seen him drunk."

"So your claims that he is unfit are largely flights of fancy, aren't they?"

Octavia's features contorted in anger. "The man is a beast!"

Mike Mulligan chuckled. "You hate Jake Blarney, don't you, Mrs. Overstreet?"

In great agitation, Octavia turned to the judge. "Your Honor, do I have to answer that?"

"Indeed, ma'am, you do."

Octavia leveled her fulminating gaze on Mike. "Yes, I hate him."

"And you love the twins?"

"Of course I do. They're my deceased sister's children, aren't they?"

"And you'd do or say anything to get custody of them, wouldn't you?" Mike pressed.

"I wouldn't lie!" Octavia retorted, panic clearly in her voice and expression.

Mike grinned. "No further questions."

At the defense table, Jake squeezed Priscilla's hand, and the two exchanged a smile.

Next, Ackerly was called. He strode forward with a pompous air, and was sworn in.

Smead popped up to question him. "Mr. Frost, please tell the court your line of employment."

"I am president of the Frost National Bank of Galveston."

Smead nodded to the judge. "A model citizen, Your Honor."

Mike burst up. "Your Honor, counsel for the plaintiff is making speeches."

"Sustained." The judge pounded his gavel. "Get to the point, Mr. Smead."

"Yes, Your Honor." He turned back to Ackerly. "Did you have occasion to run across Jake Blarney at the Cotton Exchange Ball last October?"

"Indeed I did."

Smead pivoted slightly, directing a shrewd smile toward the defense table and jamming his thumbs in the pockets of his silk brocade vest. "Explain what transpired, if you will, sir."

Ackerly directed a disdainful glance at Priscilla. "At the time, I was seeing Miss Priscilla Pemberton— who has since had the misfortune to become Mrs. Jake Blarney."

"Objection!" cried Mike.

"Sustained." Judge Briggs glowered at Ackerly. "Mr. Frost, you will refrain from editorializing."

"Yes, Your Honor. Anyway, on the night of the ball, Blarney asked Priscilla to dance, and she consented, against my better judgment, of course. Afterward, Blarney and I exchanged words, and he assaulted me."

"Explain that."

Contemptuously Ackerly related, "The brute punched me in the face and knocked me to the floor."

Ackerly's sanctimonious statement provided much less than the desired effect. Instantly the courtroom erupted in chuckles. Ackerly was left red-faced, and the judge pounded his gavel to restore order. At the defense table, Jake winked at Priscilla and she smirked back.

With an air of disgust, Smead turned to Mulligan. "Your witness."

Barely able to contain his own glee, Mike Mulligan strutted forward. "Is it true that you hate Jake Blarney, Mr. Frost?"

"I would characterize 'hate' as a very strong word," Ackerly snapped back.

"Then use your own word to describe your feelings toward Mr. Blarney."

"I hold him in contempt."

"Ah, in contempt. Is it true Jake Blarney stole away the woman you wanted to marry?"

"Objection!" yelled Smead.

"Overruled," said the judge. He nodded toward Ackerly. "The witness will answer the question."

"It's true I was seeing Miss Pemberton for a time," Ackerly hedged.

"That's not what I asked, sir. Did you propose marriage to her?"

"Yes."

"And didn't she decline your suit?"

Ackerly directed a fuming glance at Priscilla. "Well, she said she needed more time."

"And she is now married to Jake Blarney?"

"Yes."

Like a fisherman who had just hooked the big one, Mike Mulligan grinned broadly. "So it appears she left you high and dry, didn't she, Mr. Frost?"

Ackerly regarded Mulligan in blazing indignation as everyone in the courtroom again heaved with mirth.

Waiting a moment for the titters to die down, Mulligan continued. "On the night of the ball, did you provoke Mr. Blarney?"

"He struck me, sir," came the clipped reply.

"Isn't it true that right before he did so, you called him a hooligan and threatened to call him out?"

Ackerly colored and did not reply.

"Answer the question, Mr. Frost," ordered the fascinated judge.

Miserably Ackerly confessed, "Yes, I said those things . . . but only because Mr. Blarney was dancing too closely with Miss Pemberton . . . and then the brute kissed her, in front of everyone."

That comment practically brought down the house. As spectators held their sides and wiped tears from their eyes, Ackerly's face darkened by shades, and the judge pounded his gavel and barked out orders for silence.

"No further questions," said Mike.

Stanton Smead then called a seedy-looking character named Finas O'Kelly. The large, craggy-faced, shabbily dressed man tossed Jake a lame glance as he ambled toward the witness stand with worn cap in hand. "Sorry about this, Jake," he muttered.

Priscilla leaned toward Jake as the man was being sworn in. "Who is he?"

Jake flashed her a sheepish grin. "One of my drinking buddies, I'm afraid. A stevedore at the docks."

Priscilla restrained a groan.

Smead was addressing the judge. "Your Honor, since Mr. O'Kelly is a friend of Mr. Blarney's, I'm asking for permission to question him as a hostile witness."

"Permission granted."

"Mr. O'Kelly, do you know Jake Blarney?"

O'Kelly guffawed, revealing his crooked, tobacco stained teeth. "Didn't you just tell His Honor I did?"

The spectators tittered, and O'Kelly grinned at Jake.

"Order," said the judge, pounding his gavel.

"Mr. O'Kelly, please describe to the court the nature of your relationship with Mr. Blarney," pressed Smead.

O'Kelly shrugged. "Him and me have shared a few beers and a few hands of poker along Smokey Row."

"Have you ever seen him drunk?"

O'Kelly hesitated.

"Your Honor, please instruct the witness to answer the question."

"Sir, you will answer the question," said the judge.

"Hell, I seen Jake in his cups a few times," muttered O'Kelly.

"Have you ever seen Mr. Blarney involved in a barroom brawl?"

"Not one he started," came the forthright reply. He turned to the judge. "Any man worth his grog will defend himself when attacked, my lord."

"Jake Blarney has a violent temper, doesn't he?" asked Smead.

The witness scowled at the attorney, then pounded his fist on the railing in front of him. "Nay, that's a bloody lie. Jake's a good-natured bloke. And I ain't never seen him neglecting those youngsters of his—"

"That will be all," snapped Smead.

"Always leaves them with Bula Braunhurst," shouted O'Kelly.

Smead implored the judge.

"Sir, you are not being asked a question," said the judge.

"Yeah, but that don't mean I got nothin' else to say, Your Worship," added O'Kelly, much to the delight of the spectators.

"Your witness," groaned Smead.

Mike walked up. "Mr. Mulligan, what is Jake Blarney's attitude toward his children?"

"Objection!" cried Smead.

Mike turned to the judge. "Sir, this testimony goes directly to Mr. Blarney's state of mind and suitability as a parent."

"I'll permit it," said the judge.

"Jake loves the wee ones," said O'Kelly eagerly.

"He talks of 'em all the time. Most times I see him, he's the first to leave Smokey Row to get home to his little darlins'."

"Do you have any idea why Mr. Blarney might drink on occasion?"

"Your Honor!" protested Smead.

"Overruled," snapped the judge. "I'd like to hear this."

O'Kelly turned to the judge. "I think Jake went on a bender or two after his wife left him. But I ain't seen him in his cups in some time, Your Grace—ever since he found the right woman." O'Kelly grinned at Priscilla.

"No further questions," said Mike.

"Mr. Smead, call your next witness," said the judge.

"The plaintiff calls Rose Gatling."

Jake and Priscilla exchanged a bemused glance as Rose was sworn in.

"Miss Gatling, do you know Mrs. Jake Blarney, formerly Miss Priscilla Pemberton?"

Rose directed a condescending glance toward Priscilla. "I most certainly do. Up until yesterday, she was a boarder at my rooming house."

"And what are your perceptions of her character?"

"I think she may well be of loose moral character," said Rose with vindictive pleasure. "At times I've even seen Miss Pemberton sneaking in and out at odd hours, and I've also heard ... well, strange noises coming from her room."

"Your Honor, please!" exclaimed Mike. "This is no better than unfounded character assassination!"

The judge turned to Miss Gatling. "Do you have any actual proof that Mrs. Blarney is of unsound moral character?"

"No, Your Honor, but I have seen her coming and going at inappropriate times for a lady—such as at the crack of dawn."

Briggs scowled. "Very well, that part of the testimony may stand." He pounded his gavel and glowered at Smead. "Next witness."

"But, Your Honor—"

The judge pounded his gavel again and barked, "Next witness!"

A chagrined Smead then called Delia Snodgrass, who also tried to pass on gossip she had heard about Priscilla. Her testimony was quickly ruled inadmissible by the judge. Jake and Priscilla exchanged looks of confident optimism, while noting Octavia and Smead's increasingly dour, irritable expressions.

"The plaintiff rests," said the beleaguered Smead.

"Mr. Mulligan, call your first witness," directed the judge.

"The defense calls Bula Braunhurst."

At this point, although concerned that part of Rose Gatling's testimony had been allowed to stand, Priscilla had a feeling the worst was over. She turned, took the sleeping Nell from the housekeeper's arms, and offered Bula an encouraging smile. Bula heaved herself to her feet, came forward, and was sworn in. She proceeded to sing Jake's praises to the judge: Mr. Blarney was a marvelous father; he attended mass every Sunday and adored the twins; Bula had never seen him neglectful or abusive toward his children.

Mike Mulligan smilingly turned over the witness to Smead, who tried to undermine Bula's testimony, without avail: Yes, Mr. Blarney went out on occasion, Bula admitted; but he always saw to the needs of the children. When Smead repeatedly tried to insinuate that Jake was a bad father, Bula shut him up by saying stoutly, "How many men do you know who would walk the floor all night with a teething baby, or order their daughters' christening gowns all the way from Belfast? Well, I know of very few, sir!"

At that point, the dismayed Smead could only retreat with as much grace as possible.

Mike Mulligan then called Kirby Cassidy and his father, both of whom attested to Jake's character, informing the court that Jake was never late with a milk delivery at the pasteurizing plant, that he was responsible and honest in his business dealings. Smead had no luck in impeaching the testimony of father or son. Afterward Father O'Dooley testified that Jake was both a wonderful father and a faithful Catholic.

Priscilla was called next. She handed the dozing Nell over to her father, swept confidently to the stand, and was sworn in.

Mike Mulligan stepped forward. "Mrs. Blarney, kindly tell the court a little about your background."

"I'd be happy to," responded Priscilla, slanting a smile at Judge Briggs. "I was raised in Oxford, Mississippi, where my father was a university professor. Just last year, I won a master's degree from Vanderbilt."

Murmurs of approval flitted over the courtroom, and even Judge Briggs appeared highly impressed.

Appearing somewhat amused, Mike scratched his jaw. "Mrs. Blarney, just to put the court at ease, do you consider yourself to be a woman of loose moral character?"

Even as laughter sounded out, Smead bolted to his feet. "Objection! Most of Mrs. Gatling's testimony in that regard has already been stricken, so there's no need to impeach her."

"Overruled," said Briggs. He smiled at Priscilla. "I'd like to hear this."

"Do I consider myself to be a woman of loose moral character?" Priscilla repeated, preening at the judge. "Absolutely not, Your Honor! I've established myself as an elocution teacher, tutoring children from some of the finest families in Galveston—and I'm sure they and their parents would attest to my character."

"Why did you marry Mr. Blarney?"

With utter devotion, Priscilla smiled at Jake and the girls. "I married Mr. Blarney because he is a wonderful man, an extraordinary human being, a great father . . . and, of course, because I love him! I love his daughters, Nell and Sal, too, and will do my best to be a good mother to them." To the judge she finished vehemently, "And I believe irreparable harm would be done to the twins by snatching them away from such a loving environment at this critical stage of their development."

"Objection, Your Honor!" said Smead.

"Overruled," growled the judge.

"Your witness," said a beaming Mike Mulligan.

His lips set in a tight line, Smead stood to question Priscilla. "Mrs. Blarney, isn't it true that you married Mr. Blarney strictly to keep him from losing his twins?"

Raising her chin, she replied, "No, that is absolutely not the case."

"Then the timing of your wedding—just yesterday —is a mere coincidence?" he inquired with an air of amazement.

Priscilla winked at Jake. "It took me that long to convince Mr. Blarney to marry me."

Again frivolity reigned in the courtroom; even the judge was fighting to maintain a sober mien.

Through gritted teeth, Smead demanded, "Mrs. Blarney, isn't it true that prior to your nuptials yesterday, you've been carrying on an illicit love affair with Jake Blarney?"

While horrified gasps rippled over the assemblage, Mike Mulligan bolted to his feet. "Objection! Your Honor, this is a custody hearing, and Mr. Smead is totally out of line! The witness is not on trial here, nor has there been any foundation established for maligning the honor of a fine, upstanding lady who is now in fact Mrs. Jake Blarney."

As a tension-filled hush gripped the crowd, the judge stared assessingly at Priscilla, while she smiled back demurely.

Finally he spoke to Priscilla. "Mrs. Blarney, although I will not allow Mr. Smead to ask an obvious lady such as yourself such a shocking and demeaning question, the court is curious about something . . ."

"Yes, Your Honor?" she inquired eagerly.

"Is it true that you've returned to Mrs. Gatling's boardinghouse at the crack of dawn?"

Priscilla, who had already anticipated this question, was prepared. "Yes, Your Honor, I'm afraid it is true."

As ominous murmurs sounded from the spectators, Briggs cleared his throat. "Er ... may I ask why you were out and about at such an ungodly hour?"

She sighed dramatically. "Well, I suppose my guilty secret is out, Your Honor."

"Yes, Mrs. Blarney?" the judge pursued.

Regarding him earnestly, she confessed, "I go bird-watching."

That comment rocked the assemblage. Women erupted in hysterical laughter, and men slapped their knees. Even the judge broke out in an admiring grin.

Stanton Smead, however, appeared anything but amused as he bolted up. "Your Honor, this is absurd! Mrs. Blarney is obviously pulling your leg!"

"Are you pulling my leg, Mrs. Blarney?" the judge asked, attempting to appear stern.

"Absolutely not, Your Honor," Priscilla assured him in her most sincere tones. "You see, bird watching has been a passion of mine for ages now. Over the years, I've spotted some three hundred different species. And you must realize how it is for us purists, Your Honor. Why, one must arise so early to spot the great crested flycatcher, the yellow-shafted flicker, or the rare Eskimo curlew."

Admiring looks and discreet titters took the place of the boisterous laughter. The judge studied Priscilla carefully for another long moment, then nodded decisively. "I believe Mrs. Blarney," he informed Smead.

"But, Your Honor—"

Glaring at Smead, the judge barked, "It's patently obvious that such a refined lady as Mrs. Blarney would never be out at such an hour unless she were indeed bird-watching. Proceed!"

Smead threw up his hands. "No further questions."

"You may step down," said the smiling judge to Priscilla.

"Thank you, Your Honor," she responded primly.

Mike said, "I call Jake Blarney."

Priscilla and Jake passed each other as he started toward the witness stand. Amid a collective sigh from the spectators, she carefully took the sleeping Nell from his arms, and he flashed her a proud grin.

"Mr. Blarney, do you have any idea why this action is being brought against you?" Mike Mulligan asked after Jake was sworn in.

"Yes," he replied. "For some reason unbeknownst to me, Octavia blames me for Lucinda's death."

"Could you explain to the court how your wife died, Mr. Blarney?"

"Aye." Jake heaved a sigh. "Lucinda up and walked out on me and the babes when they were only three months old. Run off with a tonic salesman, she did. The two of them drowned on their way to the mainland."

Mike stared sternly at a grimly frowning Octavia. "And Mrs. Overstreet blamed you for your wife's own failing?"

"Aye. Octavia's been nosing around ever since, trying to get her hands on the twins."

"Are you a good father, Mr. Blarney?"

Jake glanced proudly at the twins and Priscilla. "Absolutely. Just as Bula said, I never neglect me wee ones. They—along with me new bride—are the light of me life."

"Is it true that recently you went through something of a personal crisis?"

"Aye." Apologetically Jake turned to the judge. "You see, Your Grace, I fell in love with Miss Pemberton. You must know how 'tis—"

The judge coughed. "Please proceed, Mr. Blarney."

Jake stared at Priscilla. "Only, Miss Pemberton wouldn't have me at first. The girl broke me heart, so

I did spend more time in the grogshops for a while. But I never let the babes be neglected. Bula told you that, didn't she?"

"Indeed she did," said Mike. "And what about now, Mr. Blarney?"

Jake solemnly crossed himself. "I swear to you by Saint Brendan that I've learned me lesson and I'm more devoted to me family than ever. Now that Miss Pemberton is Mrs. Blarney, I've never been happier." He glanced imploringly at the judge. "Just give us a chance, Your Grace. I swear we'll make the best parents ever."

"Your witness," said Mulligan to Smead.

Even as the latter stood, the judge said, "I think I've heard enough."

"But, Your Honor—"

Judge Briggs leveled a reproachful scowl at Smead and Octavia. "It's obvious to me that this is a frivolous, malicious action and that these two people are perfectly capable of raising these children." He glanced at the twins—Nell asleep in Priscilla's arms, Sal quietly playing with a doll in Bula's lap. "Why, just look at them—I've never seen two more content babies, and I'm not about to rip them away from an obviously loving home." He pounded his gavel. "Case dismissed."

A cheer went up, and Sal emitted a well-timed chortle of glee. Jake rushed to his bride's side, and the two kissed blissfully over Nell.

"Happy, darling?" he asked tenderly.

She smiled back through tears. "Never happier."

Their exultant moment was curtailed as Octavia stormed over to confront Jake. "Well, I hope you're satisfied, Jake Blarney!"

With his hand on his bride's shoulder, he laughed heartily. "Aye, I'm a well-satisfied man, Octavia. Good-bye and good riddance."

With a cry of outrage, Octavia spun about and stalked off, trailed by her shamefaced attorney. As

Jake helped his wife to her feet, their friends rushed forward to congratulate them.

"Oh, love, I'm so happy for you and Jake," cried Mary, embracing Priscilla and kissing Nell's cheek.

Priscilla glanced at Jake, who was proudly holding Sal while chatting with a beaming Father O'Dooley, along with Kirby Cassidy and his father. "Me too. I was so worried."

Mary patted Priscilla's arm. "I never doubted the two of you would win. You're wonderful parents."

Mary swept off to congratulate Jake. Priscilla was hunting for a quiet place to sit down with the sleeping Nell when she all but collided with Winnie and Ackerly as they were emerging into the aisle.

Priscilla stepped back to glare at the traitor Ackerly—and at Winnie, who clung to his arm, smirking with superiority.

He tipped his hat and smiled cynically. "Well, Priscilla, it seems congratulations are in order for you . . . and on more than one score."

Priscilla was in no mood to appreciate his sarcasm. "I can't believe you actually stooped to testifying against us, Ackerly. Of course, I realized you have very few scruples, but this is a new low, even for you."

He laughed derisively. "And I can't believe you're such a romantic fool that you would spend the rest of your life with that Irish hooligan and his two whining brats."

If Priscilla hadn't had the baby in her arms, she would have slapped Ackerly, so overwhelming was her outrage. How dare he insult her precious new family!

In a deadly calm tone she replied, "*You* are the one who has just made a very big mistake."

"No, you have made a bigger one," contradicted Ackerly coldly. "You're such an idiot, Priscilla. You've thrown away your one chance of success in this community by aligning yourself with that low-class boor." He nodded with distaste toward the child in her arms. "You and your new *family* will never be more than outcasts in this community. I'm certain of it."

"Is that a threat, Ackerly?" she asked softly.

He drew himself up haughtily. "I rather consider it my civic duty to inform the community of the hazards of associating with your kind."

"Try it and I'll bury you!" she retorted.

He ignored her outburst, turning to Winnie. "My dear, I think you've been subjected to this tawdry climate quite long enough."

"I agree, Ackerly," she said with a pout, flashing Priscilla a poisonous smile. "And didn't you promise we'd go look at *rings* today?"

"Of course I did, my pet."

Without another word to Priscilla, the two rudely turned and walked off together. Priscilla stood protectively hugging the baby and trembling with rage, glaring at the couple's retreating figures.

Chapter 33

⎯⎯⎯⎯⎯⎯⎯⎯⎯⎯⎯⎯⎯⎯

Late that day, after dropping off the twins at Bula Braunhurst's cottage, Jake and Priscilla started out in his buggy for the Waverly's party. St. Patrick's Day eve was clear, crisp, and gorgeous; along elegant Broadway, trees were budding, grass springing back to life, and tulips blooming. Newly washed windowpanes gleamed in the late-afternoon light, and the air was spiced with nectar and greenery.

Jake glanced at his bride, frowning at her preoccupied expression. "Darling, you look so down in the mouth. We won the hearing, didn't we?"

She braved a smile. "Yes, of course we did."

"Then why do you appear so tense? Are you still upset because that blackguard Smead tried to cast aspersions on your character?"

"No, I rather expected that—and thank goodness the judge believed my bird-watching story."

"Ah, yes, what have I done to you, love?" Jake asked ruefully. "Now you've committed perjury for me."

She laughed. "Perhaps not technically. You see, I did spot a lot of birds, every time I drove back from our little love nest."

Jake roared with mirth. "Lass, you do make a good impression on people."

She frowned, recalling Ackerly's ugly, menacing remarks. "Well, I should hope so."

"Then why are you so dour? Truth to tell, you look

as bemused as you did that night when I caught you on the beach talking to yourself."

Priscilla laughed at the irony of his analogy. "Actually, it's that cad Ackerly ..."

"What did he do now?" Jake asked with alarm.

Priscilla hesitated. If she told Jake the truth about what Ackerly had said to her after the hearing—how he'd threatened to besmirch the reputation of their entire family—her bridegroom would surely kill the man at the Waverly's party. That was all Priscilla needed at the moment—a new social catastrophe! It was disheartening enough to know that Ackerly would likely be present at the gathering—with his equally annoying soon-to-become child-bride, Winnie.

"Lass?" Jake pressed.

"Oh, it's nothing really," she replied. "I simply remain appalled that Ackerly had the temerity to testify against you."

Jake waved her off. "Oh, don't give that whey-face another thought, darlin'."

"But he deserves to be punished for his unforgivable behavior," she insisted.

Jake glanced at her suspiciously, eyeing her mutinous expression and clenched fists. "Lass, I'm beginning to fear there's still something between the two of you."

"There is not!"

"Then you need to forget Jack Frost and start believing in yourself, in our love," he replied. "We're married now, angel, and that milksop is not worth wasting our time on. Besides, I'm to the point where I agree with you. Let's ignore the man and find our own place in this community."

"Oh, Jake, do you really mean it?" she asked with a stirring of joy.

"Aye. You were right that we need to begin thinking of the future of the wee ones"—he paused to wink at her solemnly—"and those yet to come. So if I must suffer through chamber music, or watch the

Waverlys desecrate a sacred Irish holiday, in order to see Sal and Nell accepted, then so be it."

Charmed, she squeezed his hand. "Jake, I really will try not to make you suffer through chamber music again. And I just want you to know I'm so proud of you."

His gaze slid fervently over her. "No prouder than I am to have you as Mrs. Blarney. I promise you, girl, I'm on my best behavior from this moment on."

Priscilla tried to maintain a more pleasant expression. Although she was thrilled by her husband's continuing efforts at reform, she remained fraught with turmoil, fixated on her unsettling conversation with Ackerly—complete with a smirking Winnie on his arm. Of course, she no longer felt any jealousy toward the couple ... The two of them deserved each other, as far as she was concerned. But Ackerly's scathing insults and veiled threats rankled badly, making Priscilla feel both daunted and fiercely protective of her new family. Every time she recalled Ackerly's outrageous characterization of Jake and the girls—calling them "that Irish hooligan and his two whining brats"—she felt her blood pressure surging, along with her instincts to strangle him! It was bad enough to think the cad would malign Jake, but to target their adorable, precious babies! Had she and Jake found their happiness at last only to lose it? She would do anything to see that no harm came to those innocent angels. Thus, if Ackerly was indeed prepared to play the snake in the grass, Priscilla would be ready with her rake!

They soon arrived at the Waverlys', where Jason, the butler, admitted them and took their hats and outer garments. Jake even smiled as they proceeded inside the central hallway, to the sounds of revelry and jaunty Irish music spilling from the parlor. Along one wall of the vestibule was hung a watercolor mural picturing a rainbow, a leprechaun, and a pot of gold. Merry green streamers cascaded from the ceiling, with felt shamrocks and leprechauns attached.

Jake glanced overhead approvingly. "Well, at least they got the shamrocks right."

Maude Waverly, dressed in an emerald green velvet frock, swept forward to greet them. "Well, Mr. and Mrs. Blarney, welcome to our traditional *ceilidh*. Congratulations on your marriage, and Kirby Cassidy has already informed us of your victory in court today. By the way, where are the little ones?"

"With Bula and Walter Braunhurst," Jake replied. "And I'm sure Octavia Overstreet is halfway back to Houston by now."

"Hopefully never to bother us again," added Priscilla feelingly.

"Amen," said Maude. "If you ask me, her friend Delia Snodgrass is a real busybody to stir up such an unfounded tempest in a teapot. You'll never see that meddler invited to this home."

"Good for you," said Jake.

"I did have to invite Ackerly Frost, however," Maude added apologetically to Priscilla. "He is one of the major investors in Horace's shipping business."

"We understand," said Priscilla, biting her lip as she noted her husband's suddenly brooding expression.

Maude brightened. "Well, come along, you two. We'll get you some punch and introduce you to the newlyweds."

The threesome stopped off at the dining room, where a maid served Priscilla and Jake cups of green punch heavily laced with crème de menthe. They filled dessert plates with shamrock-shaped cookies, trifle, apple tarts, soda bread, and miniature potato pies. Then Maude led the couple into the parlor, where at least twenty guests were gaily visiting amid more streamers, leprechauns, and shamrocks, while young Charlotte Waverly was plunking out "Kathleen Mavourneen" on the piano. Several of the guests wore traditional Irish clothing such as kilts for the men and Galway shawls for the women. Kirby Cassidy appeared particularly charming in his green Irish country suit, complete with brass-buttoned tail-coat and knee breeches.

Maude introduced the couple to her daughter and new son-in-law, Sophie and Michael O'Connor. Sophie appeared the radiant bride, gowned in burgundy silk; Michael was dressed in a traditional saffron-colored kilt, with a matching sash pinned to the shoulder of his jacket with a Tara brooch. Michael and Jake hit it off at once and became involved in an animated discussion about recent developments regarding the Home Rule issue in Great Britain. Priscilla strolled off to compliment Charlotte on her music.

Priscilla was wending her way back toward Jake when she felt the hairs on the back of her neck prickle. She glanced across the room and spotted Ackerly and Winnie. Winnie was visiting with Rebecca Brown, while Ackerly stood nearby staring at Priscilla—and smirking.

Her anger flaring as she remembered Ackerly's earlier threats, Priscilla downed the punch, then went to get a refill, hoping the alcohol would soothe her surging temper. She rejoined her husband just as Horace Waverly was proposing a toast to Michael and Sophie. After the newlyweds basked in their extensive accolades, Kirby Cassidy proposed a toast to Priscilla and Jake. Priscilla enjoyed all the cheers and congratulations that followed, and she mused that Jake had never looked prouder as he stood accepting the honors with his arm around her waist. Then she spotted Ackerly across the room, ruefully shaking his head, and her fury spiked once more.

She went into the dining room to fetch more punch. Seconds later, Winnie swept in, looking as gorgeous and buxom as ever in a lime green silk organza dress.

"Well, hello, Miss Pemberton—that is, Mrs. Blarney." She extended her left hand. "Look what darling Ackerly just bought for me."

Priscilla gasped, stunned to find herself staring at the very diamond engagement ring Ackerly V had given her back in the present, the ring she had pawned shortly after she arrived in Galveston! Glancing at Winnie, she asked, "Where did you get that ring?"

"Why, at a jeweler's on the Strand," she replied defensively. "Ackerly and I went to Mr. MacDougal's to select our wedding bands, and I fell in love with this diamond. So dear Ackerly bought me this second ring as an engagement present. He's *so* generous, isn't he?"

"That's my ring!" Priscilla cried.

Winnie blanched. "I beg your pardon?"

Suddenly Priscilla laughed aloud as the full irony of the situation dawned on her. She realized she was staring straight at a genuine paradox. When Ackerly V had given her the ring back in the present, never in her wildest dreams would she have guessed that she would travel back in time, pawn the ring, and thereby engineer the circumstances that had made the ring a Frost family heirloom in the first place!

It was mind-boggling! But where had the ring actually come from? she wondered. It seemed caught up in some sort of eternal time loop.

One thing Priscilla now knew for a certainty: Ackerly Frost and Winnie Haggarty were meant for each other, just as she and Jake were meant for each other. Yes, she was definitely looking at the great-great-grandmother of Jack Frost V; indeed, Winnie Haggarty was the perfect addition to this cold, self-serving, and sanctimonious family. The realization made Priscilla chortle.

Winnie, however, appeared anything but amused. "Mrs. Blarney?" she demanded shrilly. "What do you mean, I'm wearing *your* ring?"

Priscilla laughed. "Oh, never mind, dear. Simply enjoy your ring—and Ackerly. Consider the diamond a gift to both of you from your cherished posterity."

The girl appeared irritated and confused. "Are you trying to provoke me, Mrs. Blarney?"

"Heavens, no," replied Priscilla pleasantly.

Winnie appeared unconvinced. "Ackerly tells me he had to break up with you because you proved to be a woman of questionable morals and no class."

Priscilla cackled in disbelief. "Actually, I broke up with him—but believe what you will."

Winnie's expression smoldered. "Too bad about what happened in court today," she went on poisonously.

"What do you mean, too bad?" asked Priscilla.

Winnie looked Priscilla over condescendingly. "Considering all the aspersions that were cast on your character, your reputation is surely in shreds by now."

"It is nothing of the kind!"

Winnie laughed disdainfully and played with a bit of lace on her dress. "You can't fool me, Mrs. Blarney. Indeed, I'm shocked that Maude Waverly invited you here tonight, although, of course, everyone has tried their best to be charitable toward you. But once the community is fully aware of the details of the hearing—and that you've married that blackguard Jake Blarney—I'm sure you'll find all your coveted invitations drying up. Ackerly has said as much."

Her patience exhausted, Priscilla grabbed Winnie by the sleeve. "Look, you little troublemaker, you are spouting bald-faced lies! Jake Blarney is one of the finest men I've ever known—much better than the wimp you're panting after! And if you or Ackerly *ever* again say anything disparaging about me, Jake Blarney, or our children, I'll slap you both silly!"

"Well!" Red-faced and wide-eyed, Winnie stalked off, while Priscilla stormed back to the punch table.

Priscilla drank another cup of punch and tried to calm down. She feared she was imbibing too much, but was too outraged to care. Several more times when she ventured inside the parlor, she caught Ackerly sneering at her, and it was all she could do not to charge across the room and fling her punch in his face. He and Winnie were obviously still determined to do whatever they could to assassinate Jake's character and wreck the girls' prospects in this community, and Priscilla had reached her limit. She would do almost anything to teach that viper a lesson . . .

All at once her thoughts scattered as Kirby yelled from across the room, "Here's to the wearing of the green."

As all the guests cheered and toasted with Kirby, a light bulb clicked on inside Priscilla's brain. Of course! The wearing of the green! St. Patrick's Day! Why hadn't she thought of it before now?

For tonight was *the* night J. Ackerly would presumably become a great hero in the eyes of Galvestonians, when he prevented his bank from being robbed by two notorious desperadoes—Flat Face and the Salado Kid—after Ackerly's clerk went off and left the door of the bank open, the cash drawers full.

An expression of fiendish delight gripped Priscilla's features. She *could* teach Ackerly a much-deserved lesson, after all! If she somehow detained him here, perhaps even got him drunk, then the desperadoes would rob the bank. Ackerly would be disgraced for being off carousing while his institution was being rifled, and the entire course of Frost family history would be changed. Her mind thrilled to the image of Ackerly V in the 1990s as a derelict on Post-office Street.

Yes, she would do it! She would detain him here and make him pay for *ever* maligning Jake or her adorable babies!

Then, even as Priscilla's mind raced out of control with her grandiose scheme and the buzz of the alcohol, her conscience smartly tugged on the reins. What of the depositors at the bank? After all, they were living in the days before the FDIC—was it fair to make them suffer, too?

She frowned, searching her mind for more details

of the legend, trying her best to recall the text of the
News article that had hung on Ackerly V's wall, de-
tailing the famous incident. If memory served, only
the bank's cash drawers had been left vulnerable—
she doubted the thieves would be able to crack that
"impregnable vault" Ackerly had ordered all the way
from Chicago. So the institution would not be bank-
rupted. However, Ackerly was certain to end up
looking like a fool, losing the confidence of his depositors . . . and he'd likely be compelled to cover the
losses himself.

It was perfect! He'd surely face disgrace and
ruin—and it couldn't happen to a more deserving
fellow! And besides, even if there were additional re-
percussions, she always had her share of Jake's treasure to fall back on, to reimburse any depositors who
might suffer—and to help poor Mr. Fitzgerald, who
might well be dismissed by Ackerly in any event.

Yes, yes, yes, it would work! Priscilla was all but
jumping up and down in glee over her fiendishly
clever plot. Her plan would bring the arrogant
Ackerly to his knees once and for all . . . if only she
could detain him here!

And if she wanted to succeed, she had best not
drink much more, she admonished herself. She must
try to hang on to whatever wits she still retained.
Her legs were already too wobbly!

Priscilla returned to the parlor, scanning the crowd
for Jake. She spotting him chatting with Claude and
Helen Durant. Good. Evidently he *was* on his best behavior tonight, and she was so proud of him! Best to
make her play for Ackerly while her husband was
distracted.

Priscilla half floated across the room to where
Ackerly stood, his elbow resting on the fireplace
mantel. "Mr. Frost," she greeted sweetly.

He eyed her with a combination of contempt and
confusion. "Mrs. Blarney?"

"May I have a word with you in private?"

"Well, I'm not sure." Appearing highly uncomfortable, he glanced at Winnie, who was gossiping on a fainting couch with Sophie O'Connor, and evidently hadn't noticed Priscilla's presence.

"I'll make it worth your while," Priscilla simpered.

He drew himself up and imperiously straightened his lapels. "Mrs. Blarney, I find your overtures highly improper, to say the least."

She stepped closer and spoke with determination. "We have something to discuss, Ackerly. Are you going to come willingly, or am I going to embarrass the starch out of your shirtfront?"

He glanced about helplessly. "Well, I suppose ..."

Priscilla rashly grabbed his arm and tugged him out of the room and down the hallway into a deserted study. She led him over to a leather settee, gestured eloquently for him to park himself, then collapsed onto the small sofa.

He joined her, scowling. "What is the meaning of this, Priscilla?"

Spotting a decanter and glasses on the tea table, she set down her punch cup, poured them both snifters of brandy, and handed him his. "Ackerly, I think I may have behaved precipitously after the hearing today."

"Oh?" He crossed his legs, sipped his brandy, and regarded her curiously.

Pretending to sip at her own drink, she forced a conciliatory expression. "Yes, I feel great regret that you and I have become so estranged and acrimonious. I think we should let bygones be bygones and become friends again."

He raised an eyebrow. "That sounds rather odd—and self-serving—especially coming from you, Priscilla."

"Why self-serving?" she inquired innocently.

"Perhaps because you're a woman determined to protect her new family?"

"And you aren't a man determined to ruin them?"

"Touché," he murmured. "What are you suggesting?"

She reached for the decanter. "First, have some more brandy, Ackerly."

"If you insist."

She poured him a shot and set down the decanter. "What I'm proposing is a little game of 'you scratch my back, I'll scratch yours.' "

He choked on his brandy. "I beg your pardon?"

She waved an arm. "Oh, come off it, Ackerly—I'm speaking metaphorically!"

"And you are saying . . . ?" he asked in confusion.

She smiled brilliantly. "Stop slandering my husband and our children and maybe I'll help you out."

He laughed. "That is absurd! How could you possibly help *me* out?"

"Well . . ." Barely able to contain her glee, she said, "I've been appointed the new chairwoman of Trinity Episcopal Ladies Guild."

"The Guild?" He regarded her with new reverence. "That's a prominent institution at Trinity Episcopal."

"You bet your silk top hat."

"Why, I had no idea."

Priscilla was already sensing victory within her grasp. "And we were thinking of asking you to become our spokesman to the community."

"You were?" He appeared both surprised and pleased.

"Yes. You see, Ackerly, we intend to sponsor several needy children at private schools. We would like to have you speak to some local enterprises and social groups on our behalf—you know, the Galveston Wharf Company, the Chamber of Commerce, the Artillery Club. Perhaps you can persuade each group to sponsor an indigent child."

"I see." He sipped his brandy and frowned thoughtfully.

"Of course, you would be perfect for the position, Ackerly."

"Would I?"

"Certainly. You have so much sophistication, so

much grace and charm." She grabbed the brandy decanter and refilled his snifter again.

He grinned and took a long sip. "Do I?"

She nodded. "And think of all the free PR for the bank."

"PR?" he echoed.

"Positive public relations, Ackerly."

"Ah, yes."

Concentrating intently, Priscilla summed up, "It could be a true watershed event as far as giving the bank more prestige and civic importance."

"Well, I suppose you have a point there . . ."

"Of course I do." She watched in perverse pleasure as he imbibed more brandy. "And we must discuss our plans at length, don't you think?"

"Well, I suppose . . ."

They did talk, Priscilla encouraging Ackerly to keep drinking, and refilling his snifter at every opportunity. Soon they were discussing the project almost jovially, deciding which groups would be best to approach and making preliminary scheduling plans.

Before long others took note of their tête a tête. Half an hour into their discussion, Winnie stalked in, her mouth dropping open. "Ackerly, what on earth do you think you're doing—with *her?*"

"I'm having a discussion on civic responsibility with Miss Pemberton," he slurred back.

"But you can't!" she cried, crestfallen. "And you're drinking, Ackerly!"

He waved his snifter at her. "Oh, quit being such a bothersome child and leave us alone."

"Oh!" She stormed off.

Ten minutes later, Jake strode in and stared at the couple on the couch as if he had just seen two ghosts. "Priscilla Pemberton Blarney, what in God's name do you think you're doing?"

Determined not to allow Jake to thwart her now that she was so close to winning, Priscilla answered,

"I'm having a little chat with Mr. Frost regarding Trinity Ladies Guild."

"You're what?"

She twirled a hand at him. "Run along, darling. It's for a good cause, and I won't be long."

"I'll do nothing of the kind!" he retorted, glaring at them both.

Priscilla slanted her husband an admonishing glance. "Jake Blarney, have you forgotten what you promised me right before we arrived here? You know, I'm really very disappointed with you—after you gave your word and all."

Jake made a growling sound. With his face turning red, his teeth fiercely gritted, and his hands balled into fists, he spun about on his heel and stalked from the room.

Jake paced the hallway in a terrible state. What on earth had possessed Priscilla? Why was she talking alone with Ackerly, especially after she'd told him she was so furious with Jack Frost? Had he misjudged his bride? Was she a shameless flirt, after all? He had half a mind to charge back in there, knock the cad to his heels, then drag his wife away for the sound spanking she very much deserved . . .

But then he *had* promised Priscilla that he would be on his best behavior tonight, dash it all! And a man's word was his bond!

Well, he should have exacted a similar promise from her! he thought savagely. He continued to pace, swearing and thrusting his fingers through his hair.

All at once he stopped in his tracks, snapping his fingers as he recalled Priscilla saying Ackerly deserved to be punished for his perfidy today. Did his bride have some ulterior motive in mind in playing up to the banker? But what? Whatever her true designs, Priscilla was up to no good and had seemed tipsy, to boot. Perhaps he should try again, more strenuously, to pry her away from Ackerly's clutches . . .

"Oh, Mr. Blarney?" called a feminine voice.

Jake watched Maude Waverly emerge from the parlor with Kirby Cassidy. "Yes, ma'am?" he called with forced courtesy.

The two moved closer. "Kirby was just telling us what a beautiful rendition you do of 'Danny Boy,' " said Maude. "And Helen Durant mentioned you have a wonderful voice. Won't you please come sing for us? Charlotte will be happy to accompany you on the piano."

Jake groaned. "I don't think so, ma'am."

"Jake, old man, have a heart!" beseeched Kirby. " 'Tis not Saint Pat's Day without 'Danny Boy,' eh?"

Jake stared at their expectant faces, then nodded grudgingly. "Very well."

In the study, Priscilla was amazed and thrilled to hear her husband's deep voice singing "Danny Boy" in the front room. She was dying to go into the parlor to hear him better, but dared not leave Ackerly just yet, not now that she had him firmly hooked. On the two talked, as the level of brandy grew lower and lower in the decanter. After a while she heard "The Washer Woman" spilling out from the parlor, along with stomping, shouting and laughter, and she wondered if Jake was dancing a jig. Oh, she would give her eyeteeth to go watch him!

Finally Ackerly took out his pocket watch and slurred, "Really, Priscilla, I must be going. I left my clerk, Mr. Fitzgerald, to lock up the bank, and it's his last day."

"His last day?" queried Priscilla, astonished.

"Yes, I had to discharge him because he's so absent ..." He paused to shake his head. "Absent something or other—"

"Absentminded?" she provided.

"Yes, that."

"Did you really have to fire him, Ackerly?" she reproved.

"Absolutely. The man must be jinxed or something, always forgetting everything. I must check to make

sure he didn't walk off and leave the building unlocked."

"Walk off and leave the bank unlocked?" Priscilla
repeated with a nervous laugh. She patted his hand.
"Why, Ackerly, that's the most absurd possibility I've
ever heard of! I'm sure you've no cause for worry."

"Well, I'm not so sure," he muttered, shaking his
head in befuddlement. "One time he even forgot . . .
I'll be dashed! *What* did he forget?"

"To empty the cash drawers?" she suggested.

Ackerly snapped his fingers. "Aha! No. He forgot
to shut the vault."

"He forgot to shut the vault?"

Priscilla's words came in a hoarse whisper, and she
felt a sudden sick feeling wash over her. For a
wrenching moment she feared she might become ill.
Oh, Lord, had she gambled too much? Was the vault
possibly vulnerable to the thieves, as well? How
many depositors *could* she repay with her share of
Jake's fortune? Oh, she didn't know!

Hearing footsteps approach, she jerked her head
toward the portal and watched her husband storm
in. "Jake!" she cried. "We heard you sing 'Danny
Boy.' It was wonderful."

"Good," he snapped, striding toward her. "Lassie,
go fetch the rest of your duds. It's time to head
home. We are newlyweds, after all."

"But, Jake, just a little while longer," Priscilla
pleaded, her mind still spinning with Ackerly's revelation.

Cursing, Jake leaned over, snatched Priscilla's
brandy snifter from her fingers and set it aside, then
grabbed her wrists and hauled her to her feet. "A little while longer, me rosy behind! You're coming
home with me *now*, Mrs. Blarney, and we're having
us a little chat—mayhap in the woodshed." He nodded curtly to Ackerly. "As for your precious Mr.
Frost, we'll be seeing him, but for business only, lassie, and don't you dare forget it. After all, our gold is
in his bank now."

"What?" Priscilla cried, ashen-faced and flinging a hand to her mouth.

Jake rolled his eyes. "I put the gold in J. Ackerly's bank weeks ago."

"No!" she cried.

"Yes, lassie."

"But why?" she demanded.

"Because you told me to."

Priscilla was reeling. "Oh, my God! I never said *his* bank! Why would you put the gold in *his* bank?"

Jake glanced sourly at Ackerly, who was blinking at them in perplexity, obviously trying to follow the strange conversation. "Because J. Ackerly offered me the best return on me investment, lass. I may hate his guts, but business is business."

"Oh, no, what have I done?" Priscilla wailed, pressing her palms to her spinning head.

"What is wrong now?" Jake asked in exasperation.

"My God, the twins' gold!"

"That's right, lassie. How much have you had to drink, anyway? I already told you *the gold is safe in the bank.*"

"In a pig's eye it's safe!" Her panicked gaze beseeched Jake. "Grab J. Ackerly! I'll tell Maude good-bye! We're out of here!"

Jake and Ackerly stared at each other in consternation as Priscilla stumbled from the room.

Chapter 34

❧❧

"**L**ass, would you kindly remove Ackerly's head from your shoulder?" Jake asked angrily as he snapped the reins.

"Oh, sorry. He's drunk."

"As you are, lass."

"Not any longer. Indeed, I can't recall my head *ever* clearing this fast."

"Why did you insist we tear off for Ackerly's bank at this ungodly hour of the night, anyway?"

"You'll find out soon enough."

Sitting between Jake and Ackerly in Jake's buggy as they clipped briskly toward the central part of town, Priscilla found her mind still spinning. She remained half-nauseous, sick with fear and self-recrimination. She simply couldn't believe what she had done! Had she gone totally nuts? How could she *ever* have come up with such a hare-brained scheme, even if Ackerly deserved to suffer, even if she had been half-plastered at the time? Now she could only pray that they weren't too late!

Priscilla remained appalled by her own recklessness in endangering the fortunes of many Galvestonians—including, as it turned out, her own family!—out of her determination to punish Ackerly! How could she have been so misguided as to place her wounded pride above the welfare of others?

Besides, trying to ruin the Frost family in such a despicable manner would only reduce her to their shabby level, she realized belatedly. It struck her that she was behaving just like the wounded twelve-year-old child who had once smashed all her father's bowling trophies. She was still reacting in hurt and anger, perhaps even trying to punish her father through Ackerly. It was time for her to heal completely, to let go of that scarred, uncertain child inside her.

The answer was not to get her revenge, but to give up her anger, to let go of her obsession with cold, critical men who had no idea what love really meant. Just as Jake had told her, it was time for her to believe in herself, and in his love. She had avoided and feared love, trying to shield herself from the pain, but now she knew that love had been the solution for her all along. With Jake's love, she could risk everything, even losing her esteem and social standing. And if she was ever to become truly happy, she must make a leap of faith, trust Jake, and gain her emotional sustenance from their love and their family. As for Ackerly's implied threats of social ruin for herself, Jake and the twins, she would simply have to believe that together, she and Jake would overcome all obstacles.

In the meantime, she fervently hoped they could still forestall the robbery. As they crossed Postoffice Street, she asked her husband, "Jake, do you have any kind of weapon with you?"

He raised an eyebrow. "Weapon? Whyever would we need a weapon?"

"We're going to foil a robbery and it could be dangerous."

"A robbery? Woman, have you lost your mind?"

"No, I'm just now coming completely to my senses."

He glowered. "Well, I've still got me shot gun in the boot from the last time I went turkey hunting. But 'tis not loaded."

"It'll do," she muttered.

Jake shook his head and clucked to the horse.

Priscilla tensed in her seat as they pulled up to the

bank. She could spot dim light in the lobby wafting through the closed shades. She turned to shake Ackerly. "Ackerly, wake up!"

He flinched, blinking at her in bewilderment. "What's going on?" he mumbled.

"Snap to, Ackerly," ordered Priscilla crisply. "Your bank is being robbed, and we must stop it."

"My bank is *what*?"

"Being pillaged."

He went wild-eyed. "You must be jesting!"

"No. Trust me. Flat Face and the Salado Kid are about to clean out the cash drawers—and the damned vault, too, if what you said is true and it has been left open."

Ackerly and Jake exchanged a glance of mystification.

His expression exasperated, Jake hopped down. As he assisted his bride out of the buggy, she ordered hoarsely, "Get your shotgun."

He threw up his hands. "Priscilla, this is becoming ridiculous—"

"Do it, or all of our lives could be in danger."

Jake strode off for the shotgun. Spotting Ackerly trying to clamber out of the conveyance, Priscilla rushed around the horse to assist him. Not that she wouldn't love to see him fall on his face, but they still needed his help.

Tottering on his feet, Ackerly peered at the bank's front window. "There *are* still lights on," he muttered worriedly. "Fitzgerald should have gone home by now."

"He has," Priscilla informed him. "But the robbers must still be in there."

"How do you know there are robbers inside?" Ackerly demanded.

"How do you know you have your shoes on the right feet?" she snapped back. "Do you want to stand here and argue while the desperadoes clean out your vault?"

"Yes, Ackerly, let's go foil your imaginary robbery

with me unloaded shotgun," put in Jake disgustedly as he strode up to join them.

"Very well—follow me," said Ackerly wearily.

He led off, and the threesome trooped single file toward the building. At the door, Ackerly held up a hand to halt the other two, then gingerly tried the knob. "It's unlocked," he whispered anxiously. "Just as I feared, Fitzgerald must have forgotten to secure the premises."

Jake stepped forward with his shotgun pointing toward the door. "I'd best go in first, Ackerly, in case there's some truth to what Priscilla's saying."

"You mean you finally believe me?" she inquired sarcastically.

"Maybe." He nodded to her sternly. "Just in case there's any danger, lass, you'd best stay out here where it's safe."

"Are you kidding? I wouldn't miss this for all the tea in China."

Jake groaned to Ackerly. "It's murder trying to convince this stubborn woman to do anything."

"I know," he echoed.

"Very well, lass. I'll go first, then Ackerly, then you. And mind you, stay behind us."

"Aye, aye, captain," she replied, saluting him.

Tossing his bride a forbearing glance, Jake creaked open the door, and the three crept inside, only to stop in their tracks as they viewed an amazing sight—

Across the bank near the tellers' cages stood Fitzgerald, along with two seedy, elderly characters who looked like vagabonds. Both men were heavily whiskered and wore tattered coats and hats; one was blunt-featured and gaunt, while the other had a very flat face with a bashed in, crooked nose. The duo stood with arms raised as Fitzgerald threatened them with a raised broom! Nearby on the floor was a spilled cash drawer, money and coins scattered over a wide area.

"Move an inch, you miserable scoundrels, and I swear I'll knock you cold!" Fitzgerald was ranting to the terrified men as he wielded his broom. "The nerve of you two, coming in here and trying to rob Mr. Frost's bank."

"Oh, nosir, nosir!" cried one of the derelicts. "We ain't pullin' no holdup!"

"We ain't no thieves, mister, we swear!" protested the second.

"What is going on here?" demanded Ackerly.

The three startled men turned to view the newcomers. Lowering his broom and heaving a huge sigh, Fitzgerald spoke first. "Mr. Frost, I'm so relieved you're here! I was working late, securing the vault, when these two men sneaked in here and tried to rifle the cash drawers—"

"Is this true?" Ackerly demanded of the men.

"On, no sir," insisted the first man. "We just got in town on the Houston and Henderson. We was cold, you see, and we found the bank unlocked. So we come in here to get warm, that's all."

"Yeah," added the second man. "We just wanted to rest awhile. We ain't meant no harm."

Ackerly soberly eyed the scattered contents of the cash drawer. "That's not how it appears."

The two vagabonds exchanged glances of sheepish guilt.

Wearing an expression of amazement, Priscilla stepped toward the derelicts. "You can't mean you two are Flat Face and the Salado Kid?"

The two regarded Priscilla in bewilderment. "How did you know our names, ma'am?" the first one asked.

"And the two of you ride the rails?" she inquired.

"Yes, ma'am," answered the second.

Priscilla burst out laughing. "So Ackerly is going to save the community of Galveston from a pair of elderly hobos? Oh, this is too rich!"

Now everyone, except Priscilla, appeared confused.

Ackerly drew himself up with dignity. "I think we've heard enough." He snapped his fingers at the hobos. "You two vandals are not worth troubling the sheriff with. Get out of here and never return!"

"Yes, sir!" Exclaiming their agreement in unison, the derelicts dashed for the door.

Ackerly glowered at his clerk. "As for you, Fitzgerald, if I hadn't already dismissed you, I'd discharge you on the spot. I can't believe you stayed here alone and left the front door unlocked. If you wish to receive any sort of recommendation from me, you won't say a word to anyone concerning this disgraceful incident. Is that clear?"

"Yes, sir," said Fitzgerald wretchedly.

"Ackerly, don't you think you're being a bit hard on him?" asked a frowning Priscilla.

"Yes, Ackerly," echoed Jake. "Why not give the man his due credit for apprehending the thieves?"

"Mr. and Mrs. Blarney, I'll thank you to let me handle my *former* employee myself!" Ackerly responded coldly. To Fitzgerald he said, "Now, leave us, and I will lock up."

"Yes, Mr. Frost." Dour-faced, he quickly exited.

At last appearing quite sober, Ackerly turned back to Priscilla and Jake. "Mr. and Mrs. Blarney, I must thank you for your assistance in this matter, although I remain mystified as to how you knew about the robbery, Mrs. Blarney. Nevertheless, if you'll excuse me, I must secure the premises."

All at once, staring at Ackerly, Priscilla gasped as she again remembered the *News* article. "Now I get it! And I can't believe it!"

"Believe what, lass?" asked Jake.

She regarded Ackerly with horror and disgust. "Tomorrow you're going to go to the *News*, aren't you, and take all the credit for saving the community from two desperadoes."

He actually flinched. "Why, that's absurd."

"Oh, no, it's not! It's the truth. You will go to the newspaper, play yourself up as a local hero, and for five generations thereafter, your family will take credit for poor Mr. Fitzgerald's heroism."

"Priscilla, that's the silliest notion I've ever heard!" Ackerly declared, but with a telltale falter in his voice.

"You louse!" she raved. "That kind of infamy is so typical of your shallow, phony family! Well, you can have your wealth and status, Ackerly—and you are welcome to it, all five of you!" She proudly caught Jake's arm and thrust her head high. "As for me, I've discovered what truly matters in life—and I've found a real hero to love."

Ackerly regarded Jake in bewilderment. "Do you have any idea what she's babbling about?"

Grinning, he shook his head. "Nay. Priscilla's a lunatic, but I love her." He caught her hand. "Come along now, lassie. If you'll excuse us, Ackerly?"

"Wait a minute," Priscilla said.

Jake spoke through gritted teeth. "What now, lass?"

She faced Ackerly forbiddingly. "You'll be giving Mr. Fitzgerald a most generous pension, won't you, Ackerly?"

He snorted a laugh. "Why, of course I won't! I discharged the man for gross incompetence . . . to which both of you were just witnesses."

"We just watched that poor man defend your establishment with a broom, if that's what you're referring to," said Jake heatedly.

"And tomorrow you *are* going to take full credit for Fitzgerald's courage, aren't you?" Priscilla pursued.

Hot, guilty color shot up Ackerly's face.

Priscilla stepped forward. "Listen well, you cad. You *will* give Mr. Fitzgerald his pension . . ."

"Or?"

"Or I'll be at the *News* office first thing tomorrow morning to inform Colonel Belo himself of how you were off getting drunk while the elderly clerk you had just fired held two bank robbers at bay."

He went pale. "You wouldn't!"

"Try me."

He threw up his hands. "Very well, Fitzgerald will get his pension. Is there anything else?"

"Yes. Fitzgerald is to receive equal credit with you in the *News* article."

"You are unbelievable!"

"I am deadly serious."

"All right, then! Are you finished?"

"Not quite." She smiled lovingly at Jake. "Spread one word of gossip about me or my new family and the same consequences will be in effect. Is that clear?"

"Eminently," he retorted.

"Let's go, lassie," urged Jake, taking her arm.

As he led her off, she smirked at Ackerly over her shoulder. "By the way, that's quite a nice ring you picked out for darling Winnie. I'm kind of glad I brought it here to Galveston."

"*You* brought it here?"

Priscilla exited the building with her husband, leaving Ackerly to stare after them in consternation.

Outside, Priscilla could barely contain her glee and stood clapping her hands beside Jake's buggy. "Well, wasn't I right about the robbery? Wasn't I?"

Jake stashed his shotgun in the boot. "If you say so, lass." He escorted her to the front of the convey-ance and hoisted her onto the seat.

"Ouch!" she cried.

"What's wrong?" he asked innocently, climbing in beside her.

She reached beneath her and pulled out a gorgeous diamond bracelet. At its center was a glistening me-dallion with a shamrock outlined in tiny emeralds. "My God, what is this?"

He winked at her and clucked to the horse. "Ap-pears like a wedding gift from your darling hus-band."

"It's exquisite!" she cried, placing the dazzling bracelet on her wrist and watching the moonlight glint off the gorgeous stones. "But where—and how—did you get it?"

He grinned. "Mayhap I captured another leprechaun."

Priscilla roared with laugher. "Jake Blarney, have you told me the truth about *all* the gold doubloons you've found?"

He winked. " 'Tis Saint Pat's Day, love. I captured one of those wily little elves and he led me to the pot of gold at the end of the rainbow—and to you."

Although the image entranced her, she cast him a scolding glance. "Now, wait a minute. You believe in leprechauns, but you won't believe I traveled through time?"

He chuckled.

"Well, Jake? You know I really did travel through time. It's how I knew about the robbery."

"I know, lassie," he admitted with surprising humility. "It took me a while to accept it, but now I believe me note drew you across time to me. I think I suspected for some time that you were different—brought to me from so far away."

"Now, *that's* an understatement!"

"I just didn't want to lose you, girl."

She leaned over to kiss him. "You never will. And boy, do I have one helluva story to tell you."

"Good. I can't wait to hear it. And now that our fortunes are secure, you can spend your share on a grand house on Broadway, trips to Europe, whatever your heart desires, my love."

She linked her arm through his and smiled dreamily. "Right now I just want to get the babies, go home and rock them to sleep, then help you milk the cows."

"And how will we be passing the hours in between?" he inquired.

She wrinkled her nose at him. "We'll think of something."

"You mean you're no longer determined to become the toast of Galveston?"

"After all that has transpired, we may be laughing-stocks by now," she confessed.

"Oh, nay, darling. We're going to turn this town on its ear. I've got a plan, you see."

"What plan?"

"'Tis my secret," he said smugly. "I want to surprise you."

"Jake!"

His only reply was to snap the reins and begin singing "Poor Wandering One" at the top of his lungs. Yet Priscilla Pemberton Blarney knew she wandered no more—she'd found her place in time, with the man she loved.

Epilogue

"**L**ook, Sal, it's Papa!" whispered Priscilla.

"See Papa!" Sal whispered back, pointing toward the stage.

Six weeks later, Priscilla sat next to her friend Mary in orchestra box seats at the Tremont Opera House. Since the opening night of the latest opus had been designated "family night," a number of children were in attendance, and both Priscilla and Mary held babies on their laps. The twins were dressed in lacy white eyelet frocks interlaced with lilac satin ribbons, with matching bows in their curly dark hair. All four females—as well as every other woman in the audience—were raptly watching the stage as Jake Blarney performed as the Pirate King in *Pirates of Penzance*. Dressed in plumed *chapeau bras*, false mustache, long brass-buttoned coat, dungarees, and boots, he was keeping the audience enthralled while having a melodramatic conversation with one of his men who had just been freed from indentureship but was now "a slave to duty." In the background, the rest of the Pirate King's crew were at tables drinking and gambling. A painted backdrop of a ship on the ocean added a nautical feel.

This was the surprise Jake had mentioned to Priscilla six weeks ago—and he had refused to divulge what he was doing until last week, when she had grown frustrated and jealous because of his nightly absences. She had accused her new husband of seeing another woman, and at last he had laughingly admitted, "Aye, lassie, I have a new mistress now—the opera." It was then that he'd finally revealed he had been secretly rehearsing with the Tremont Opera House Company for the early May premiere of the Gilbert and Sullivan melodrama. Priscilla had been as shocked to hear this news as she had been deeply thrilled. When she had asked Jake why he'd joined the opera company, he had replied, "Why, to make you proud, darlin'." Hugging him tightly, she had said, "I couldn't possibly be any prouder of you, Jake Blarney."

Now she wasn't so sure. Since the curtain had risen a few minutes ago, she had discovered that Helen Durant had been right—Jake was perfect as the Pirate King, performing his lines with delightful campy touches. She chuckled as he twirled his mustache, pressed a hand to his heart, and prepared to vocalize. The orchestra launched into a refrain, and he sang in his deep, beautiful voice:

> *"Oh, better far to live and die,*
> *Under the brave black flag I fly,*
> *Than play a sanctimonious part,*
> *With a pirate head and a pirate heart."*

Priscilla thought of how true those lines were. Jake Blarney was definitely the genuine article; Ackerly had been the self-righteous one "with a pirate head and a pirate heart." She was so proud of her husband, so thrilled to know he was doing this for her. She knew he was singing from the heart, singing straight to her—and never had she felt more touched, more filled with love for him.

She thought of their joyous life together. They had left the babies with Bula and taken a honeymoon trip to Houston, where they had dined at elegant hotels and gone to plays and concerts. They had shared their lives endlessly. Jake now knew all about Priscilla's life in the future, and he believed her completely. She had told him about the devastating hurricane that would strike Galveston Island in less than twenty years, and he had agreed that they must move elsewhere before the turn of the century. They had also agreed that they would try to warn the citizens of Galveston about the coming calamity—and would pray their warning would be heeded.

Now Priscilla had another wonderful secret to share with her husband—for she knew she carried his child, perhaps a little brother for Nell and Sal. She was certain she had conceived while they were on their wedding trip. She couldn't wait to tell Jake her marvelous news, and planned to as soon as they were alone tonight.

Throughout the remainder of the lively performance, Priscilla and the rest of the crowd remained captivated, delighting to the histrionics, the fight scenes, the bombastic songs. Jake was met by a standing ovation at curtain call—and he brought his bride to tears when he sang as an encore the poignantly thrilling "My Heart at Thy Sweet Voice" from *Samson and Delilah*.

Afterward, when Priscilla and Mary emerged into the lobby with the girls, they found a grinning Jake surrounded by adoring ladies begging him to autograph their programs. Priscilla was tickled to spot Mrs. Moody, Mrs. Sealy, and Mrs. Brown among the females clamoring for his attention, while their husbands stood along the sidelines observing the proceedings with amusement or indulgence.

Moving closer, Priscilla overheard the accolades with a combination of pride and jealousy:

"Mr. Blarney, you were superb! You must come sing for the Ladies Auxiliary of Saint Ursuline's."

"Mr. Blarney, I never cried so much in my entire life as I did when I thought the Pirate King would be captured."

"If only Sir William Gilbert and Sir Arthur Sullivan

could have been here tonight to hear your rendition of their work. I know they must have had you in mind for their Pirate King."

"Mr. Blarney, you are a credit to this island!"

With more praise spilling forth, Priscilla glanced at Mary, who smirked back. Priscilla stood waiting with Sal as Jake affably signed at least a dozen programs. At last she grew tired of waiting while so many others claimed her husband's attention, and she slipped through his throng of admirers to join him.

"Ladies, I think it's time for this pirate king to go home," she announced.

"Papa home!" agreed Sal, clapping her hands.

Laughing, the ladies graciously dispersed.

Priscilla beamed at Jake. "Darling, you were wonderful."

He grinned and tweaked Sal beneath the chin. "Do you agree, daughter?"

"Papa hat!" she cried, reaching for Jake's plumed headgear. Priscilla laughed as Jake plopped the oversize *chapeau bras* on the child's head.

Mary stepped up and smilingly handed Nell over to her father. "Jake, you were magnificent."

"Thanks, Mary." Jake settled Nell in his arms. As the child happily began playing with the buttons on his coat, he winked at his wife. "I'm getting us a slew of invitations, love—to the Sealys' for Sunday luncheon, to the Moodys' for a Memorial Day picnic. Looks like we're the toast of the town."

"Forget the invitations," she said. "I want you to myself tonight."

"You mean you don't want to attend the premiere party at the Durants'?"

She shook her head. "I've big news to share with you."

He wiggled his eyebrows and whispered back, "And I've always something big to share with you, lassie."

Mary coughed. "I think this is my exit line." She quickly kissed Sal and Nell. "Good night, folks."

"And good night to you," called Jake. He smiled tenderly at his wife. "Shall we, my dear?"

Priscilla proudly left the theater with her new family and her pirate king.

Avon Romantic Treasures

Unforgettable, enthralling love stories,
sparkling with passion and adventure
from Romance's bestselling authors

CAPTIVES OF THE NIGHT *by Loretta Chase*
76648-5/$4.99 US/$5.99 Can

CHEYENNE'S SHADOW *by Deborah Camp*
76739-2/$4.99 US/$5.99 Can

FORTUNE'S BRIDE *by Judith E. French*
76866-6/$4.99 US/$5.99 Can

GABRIEL'S BRIDE *by Samantha James*
77547-6/$4.99 US/$5.99 Can

COMANCHE FLAME *by Genell Dellin*
77524-7/ $4.99 US/ $5.99 Can

WITH ONE LOOK *by Jennifer Horsman*
77596-4/ $4.99 US/ $5.99 Can

LORD OF THUNDER *by Emma Merritt*
77290-6/ $4.99 US/ $5.99 Can

RUNAWAY BRIDE *by Deborah Gordon*
77758-4/$4.99 US/$5.99 Can